DEATH TO THE AXIS!

The S.S. officer stepped carelessly into the room looking down to return his Luger to its holster. The Italian officer was at his heels. The German stiffened when he saw Ryan's legs but before he could raise his pistol, Tenbrink's left arm wound around his neck and the knife drove beneath his ribs. At the same time, as the startled Italian officer fumbled at his holster, Ryan sprang at him. He pulled the Italian to him by the coat front and smashed him in the face with the elbow of the hand holding the .45 automatic...

The two officers, German and Italian, hit the floor almost together.

Von Ryan's Return

DAVID WESTHEIMER

SPHERE BOOKS LIMITED
30/32 Gray's Inn Road, London WC1X 8JL

First published in Great Britain by
Michael Joseph Ltd 1980
Copyright © David Westheimer 1980
Published by Sphere Books Ltd 1982
Reprinted 1982

For Steven, Randi,
Erica, Erin and Cody

TRADE
MARK

Printed and bound in Great Britain by
Cox & Wyman Ltd, Reading

1

Colonel Joseph Ryan, United States Army Air Forces, stood looking out of a window of his fourth-floor room in the Grand Hotel Vereina in Klosters, Switzerland. He was in the position known as parade rest, hands clasped behind him, feet spread, back straight, head erect. He was a tall man of thirty-six, hard-faced and hard-muscled. His uniform was immaculate, his dark-blond hair neatly and closely cropped. There were faint crow's-feet at the corners of the steely, unblinking eyes squinting against the bright sunshine which lit the white peaks and glinted on the waters of the Landquart River.

Though it was November 1943, and with the rest of Europe at war there were no tourists in Switzerland, the landscape he contemplated was a busy one. Young men in U.S. uniforms or British battle-dress with U.S.A. shoulder-patches were playing a noisy game of soft-ball, cheered on by a large audience of other young men in uniform. A dozen more, with their own audience, were playing basket-ball, attacking and defending a single netless hoop on an improvised backboard fastened to a telephone pole. Farther away, on the slopes where there was early snow, tiny figures skied, mostly inexpertly, tumbled off sleds and makeshift toboggans or pelted each other with snow-balls.

All of them were escaped prisoners of war. Ryan, a P-38 pilot and group commander, had been shot down and captured in Italy the previous summer. Several weeks before hand, he had brought them to Switzerland by commandeering the train carrying them to Germany from their Italian prisoner of war camp after the Italian capitulation. Three hundred American and six hundred British officers had been jammed into boxcars guarded by German soldiers. Ryan, their senior officer, had organised and carried out the killing of the guards and the diversion of the train.

Now the sounds of the Americans' game rang faintly in the high, crisp air, mingling with the closer sounds of a Glen Miller record in a nearby room, a radio tuned to a German language station, the jokes and arguments of a poker game, someone being pursued in horseplay down a corridor.

There was a knock on the door.

'Cuhnel? Padre Costanzo. You there?'

'It's open,' Ryan said without turning.

Costanzo joined him at the window. Captain Gregory Costanzo, an Army chaplain from Georgia, still retained the accent of his origins. He had been on the train, a reluctant but, because of his fluent German and Italian, often vital participant in the take-over. He was a small man, dark and thin. He wore a clerical collar and black suit which had seen years of earnest wear by someone fleshier than he. It enveloped him, and the elbows, knees, seat and coat-tails had a metallic sheen. Nevertheless, he preferred it to a uniform and, as he was a noncombatant, he dressed as he pleased.

For a while he stood at Ryan's elbow in silence, watching the scene that held the colonel's attention.

'Grand to see, isn't it, suh?' he said at last. 'But for the grace of God...' He paused and smiled. 'With a little help from you, naturally ... they'd all be stuck away in some German prison camp right now.'

'Be doing more good if they were,' Ryan said, leaving the window to sit in the only straight chair in the room, and looking with faint distaste at the heavy Swiss comfort of his room.

'Why would you say a thing like that?' Costanzo demanded.

'You're supposed to know all the answers, Padre. You're a Jesuit.'

'Ah reckon Ah missed the Von Ryan theology course at the seminary.'

In the Italian prison camp, the prisoners had nicknamed the

6

colonel 'Von Ryan' because of the rigid discipline he imposed from the day of his arrival and his insistence on unquestioning obedience of his orders. Costanzo was one of the very few who had not disliked and feared him.

'If we were in Germany, we'd be tying down enemy troops and transport and eating rations they can't spare.Instead, we're like a bunch of tourists in a winter resort while there's a war on.'

'But they're out of danger and living well. You got it for them. You ought to be pleased about that.'

'Damn it, Padre, I've got three hundred American combat officers here whose experience is going to waste.'

'They're only yours technically. They're interned in a neutral country. So there's not a whole lot you can do about it, is there?'

Costanzo looked sharply at Ryan.

'But you think there is, don't you, Cuhnel? Ah know that look. You always think there's something you can do. Ah don't suppose you'd tell me what.'

Ryan got up and looked out the window again, standing as always at parade rest. Costanzo, knowing he had been dismissed, left. Outside, the young men played and shouted as if, having escaped from enemy captivity, they were out of the war.

For the past few weeks there had been reason to feel so, beginning with their warm, though occasionally somewhat guarded reception from the Swiss, ever conscious in public of their neutrality. Less than an hour after the boxcars plunged across the border from Italy, a detail of troops and representatives of the civilian border police, the border health service and the customs service arrived under command of a captain to search for weapons and war matériel. They found none. Ryan had sent everything back into Italy — the weapons, uniforms and equipment taken from the Germans as well as the bodies of their guards — in a boxcar drawn by the unmanned locomotive.

The escapees had then been moved in their boxcars by a Swiss engine to nearby Campocologno. There they had been fed and given medical examinations, with the few requiring attention being sent immediately to Poschiavo, a larger town a few miles further into Switzerland. The Americans and British were separated and sent by different trains to their places of internment, the Americans to the hastily reopened Vereina in Klosters and the British to Davos.

At Klosters, under the purely nominal supervision of a Swiss army captain and a small staff, Ryan was permitted to take over again and organise his men into a military company-type unit, with responsibility for their discipline. They had arrived in Klosters underweight and exhausted. Well aware of this, Ryan had let them enjoy their improved circumstances unhindered, except for a strictly enforced morning roll-call and regular personal and room inspections. They were allowed to roam the Klosters area freely. Every day girls and women converged on the village from throughout the canton. Life was so pleasant that a Lieutenant Orde, who had lost an eye in combat, refused repatriation, saying he had died and gone to heaven.

But now they were all thoroughly rested and fit.

In the hotel dining-room that night, Ryan shared his usual table with Costanzo and Doc Stein, Captain Henry Stein, who had stitched up a scalp wound for him on his first day in P.G. 202, the Italian prison camp. Among the prisoners, only Costanzo and Stein had never been uncomfortable in Ryan's presence, and only they, both non-combatants and secure in their calling, had come to understand that while Ryan always had an excellent reason for anything he did, however harsh or unreasonable it might appear at the time, he was sometimes deliberately intractable just to preserve the image that made him such an effective leader. Only Stein and Costanzo realised that within the rigid disciplinarian there lurked a carefully concealed sense of humour.

The table, like the others in the crowded room, was amply provided with bread, butter, cheeses and fruit preserves. Waiters scurried bearing great trays of hearty Swiss food. Captain Haas, the commander of the small Swiss detachment seeing to the needs of the AIP — Army Interned Persons —

stopped one of them and sampled each dish. He nodded approval. Though it was the responsibility of a commanding officer to see that his men were properly fed, Ryan, who did not care what he ate, had gladly deferred to the captain, a man who did.

Haas, a well-read career officer who spoke fluent English, detested German and Italian Fascists and privately chafed at the restraints of neutrality. He played chess regularly with Doc Stein but otherwise had little contact with the internees except through Ryan. He never interfered and was, in fact, impressed by Ryan's effectiveness as a commanding officer.

He came over to make a courtesy stop at Ryan's table. Stein looked at him and complained, 'We never get pumpkin soup, Captain. We should have brought the recipe with us from P.G. 202.'

Pumpkin soup had been the much despised staple in the Italian camp.

'I'll try to arrange it,' Haas said.

'Don't bother,' said Ryan.

When the captain had left, Ryan turned to Stein and said, 'You look like you've managed to keep body and soul together without pumpkin soup. You've let your belt out at least two inches since we got here.'

'We've all put on weight here. Except you and Padre Costanzo.'

'I've noticed. They're back up to fighting weight. Work up some less fattening menus and I'll give 'em to Haas. I don't want any fatties.'

'Eating's one of the pleasures of being in Switzerland,' Stein protested.

'We're not here for pleasure, Captain.'

As always, Costanzo said grace before the meal. Ryan and Stein waited politely until he crossed himself. Stein and Costanzo shared half a litre of wine with their meal. Ryan took milk. The Swiss provided rations and quarters. The internees paid for wine and other extras.

'You don't drink much, do you, Colonel?' Stein said.

'Only when I can do it seriously.'

'From a health standpoint, that's all wrong. "Use a little wine for thy stomach's sake." Shakespeare.'

'No,' said Costanzo. 'The Bible.'

'First Epistle of Paul to Timothy,' Ryan said without looking up from his veal cutlet. 'Chapter Five, Verse Twenty-three.'

Costanzo and Stein exchanged startled glances.

'So it's not Shakespeare,' Stein said. 'But as far as I'm concerned, it's not the Bible either. Not the version I was brought up on.'

'You're a more religious man than you let on, Cuhnel,' said Costanzo.

'Negative. Back when I was taking flying training at Randolph, the chaplain was always harping on not looking at the wine while it was red and quoting chapter and verse. So I hunted until I found something to hit him with.'

Dinner over, Costanzo rubbed his hands together in anticipation and said, 'Well, a little pool, gentlemen?'

He was, surprisingly and without ever volunteering an explanation, remarkably adept with a cue. Better even than Ryan, who was skilled or quickly became so in anything he undertook.

'I already owe you two hundred Hail Marys and a hundred and seventy Our Fathers,' Stein said. 'How many before I'm converted?'

'I wouldn't mind an hour of instruction from you, Padre,' Ryan said. 'In pool, that is.'

Ryan was a Protestant, a fact he had made clear to the priest at their first encounter in P.G. 202, before he learned what manner of man Costanzo was, and how unparochial.

There were already players at the table in the day-room that Ryan had had furnished using funds contributed by the internees. They had received their back pay, some of it considerable, through the American Legation at Bern. Ryan's base pay was allotted to his wife in Santa Monica but his flying pay — prisoners of war were considered still to have flying status — for five months, converted into Swiss francs at a highly favourable rate of exchange, was a respectable sum.

Lower ranking officers who had been prisoners longer than he and who had not allotted their pay had even more.

Despite Ryan's request to carry on, they stopped at once to make way for the three newcomers. Though Ryan had made it clear that rank had no privileges in non-military activities, none of his subordinates could forget who and what he was. Without exception, they enjoyed the spectacle of Von Ryan being human enough to play a game, Padre Costanzo's incongruous wizardry and the wry comments of Doc Stein, the invariable loser.

The day-room was furnished with comfortable chairs and sofas, a record player, a short-wave radio receiver, an abundance of magazines and newspapers in several languages including English and a large bulletin board. On the board were tacked notices, company regulations and a situation map for the fighting in southern Italy. The map was kept up to date by a staff selected by Ryan to monitor radio broadcasts and screen newspapers in German, Italian and English.

The internees, when prisoners of war, had devoured, studied, discussed and argued every scrap of war news and rumour. But now they were in the main only mildly interested in the progress of the war in southern Italy except for the sector on the extreme eastern flank, along the Adriatic, where Domira, the site of their prison camp, was located. They had a betting pool going on the date and hour the British would reach it. A few days earlier, the 8th Indian Division of the British 5th Corps had taken a town less than twenty miles from Domira and the betting had heated up.

The officers left their magazines and newspapers and the record player to watch Von Ryan get beaten by Padre Costanzo. Among the spectators was Major Wimberly, a vain young man whom Ryan had once reprimanded for combing his wavy chestnut hair while being addressed by his commanding officer. He had been Senior American Officer at P.G. 202 before Ryan's arrival and never quite lost his resentment at being displaced.

Ryan called him aside while Costanzo was enjoying a long run.

'I suppose you'll be at the C.G. tonight as usual, Major,' he said.

The C.G. was the Chesa Grischuna, a small chalet hotel a few yards below the Vereina. Unlike the Vereina, it had remained open after the hostilities ended tourism. A handful of American evaders and escapees who had crossed into Switzerland in civilian clothes and were therefore not regarded as military personnel lived there. The Chesa Grischuna was the most popular spot in Klosters with the Vereina internees because of its genial young proprietor, its snug bar and the girls who came there to meet Americans.

Wimberly was startled that Ryan knew his habits.

'Yes, sir,' he said stiffly. 'You never said it was off limits.'

'Don't stay too long. Report to my quarters at twenty-one hundred.'

'If I'm in trouble I'd like to know why, sir.'

'You're not in trouble, Major. Yet.'

Wimberly left immediately, no longer interested in pool and wanting to make the most of his shortened evening.

After an hour, Ryan handed his cue to a waiting junior officer and said, 'I know when I'm whipped, Padre.'

Costanzo surrendered his cue as well. When Ryan went up to his room, the priest was not far behind.

'You following me, Padre?' Ryan asked, his hand on the doorknob.

'You intend to get everybody back into combat, don't you, Cuhnel?' Costanzo said.

Ryan did not answer.

'Can't you wait a while? They've only had a few weeks of living like human beings.'

'They're soldiers, Padre.'

'Soldiers are human beings, you know.'

'I'll keep that in mind. Padre, I'll be gone a day or two. If anyone should ask, I'm doing some sightseeing.'

'Are you telling Captain Haas?'

'I never bother him with petty details.'

Costanzo grinned.

'You're going AWOL, then. Ah'd like to see more of the

12

country mahself, long's Ah'm here, anyhow. How are you going where you're going?'

'Train.'

'Ah have the use of a car. The same benefactor gave me mah suit. He's a Jebbie, too.'

'I've been meaning to talk to you about that suit. It's inappropriate for a man of your rank and calling. If you don't get one that fits I'll have you in uniform again.'

'Vanity, all is vanity. Why don't Ah drive you where you're going, Cuhnel?'

'It's not close.'

'The farther the better. Ah like scenery with lots of mountains in it.'

In his room, Ryan stood at the window. There were lights on down at the Chesa Grischuna. Though Ryan liked the owner, he never went there at night. His presence inhibited the other officers. Mountains, visible in the strong moonlight, blocked the horizon with snow-covered buttresses, peaks and ridges. The same moonlight picked out the course of the Landquart River between dark banks, still waiting for their mantle of winter snow. When all this was over, Klosters would not be a bad place to bring his wife. The children would be old enough to enjoy it by then, too. He had three. He had not seen them or his wife for more than a year. Though his family was important to him, given the choice he would rather have been with his fighter group in Italy than sitting out the war in Switzerland — even if they could have joined him.

When Joe Ryan graduated from the Military Academy, he had more demerits than any other two cadets combined, though he was second in his class academically. A legend to subsequent classes, he was said to have collected more gigs than any Academy graduate except Ulysses S. Grant and never to have lost a fight, in or out of the ring. He had been in the boxing team, growing from a middle-weight to a light heavy-weight, fighting at eleven pounds under his normal one hundred and eighty-six. He had, in fact, lost two decisions in his career and had the worst of it occasionally in street fights,

13

where the size and number of his opponents were not limited by Marquess of Queensberry rules.

Six months after graduation he volunteered for pilot training. A gifted, natural, though reckless flyer, he might have been washed out for that recklessness early in his training had he not been a regular officer training in grade. At advanced, his squadron commander took a special interest in him, became his friend, and warned him that if he did not learn to be a more responsible pilot he would one day surely kill himself. But Ryan had killed his friend instead. In a celebratory rat-race after getting his wings, he had attempted a difficult manoeuvre and his prop had chewed off a wing of the squadron commander's trainer, which crashed in flames below. Without a propeller, Ryan had made a dead-stick landing and walked away from the scene weeping.

He had considered resigning his commission in atonement but instead had asked for assignment to a flying school. He came to be the most feared and hated, and competent, flying instructor in Training Command. His unit, after he became a squadron commander, had the lowest percentage of washouts for flying deficiencies and the best safety record in the Air Corps.

Legends grew about him, as they had done at the Military Academy — he had scraped through the Academy by courting the Commandant's daughter; he had been captain of its boxing team and won every bout by knock-out; his wife was obliged to lie at attention with her eyes fixed on a point when they made love; his children were not allowed to go to the bathroom nor his German shepherd to lift leg without his express permission.

Ryan was aware of the stories, as he was of everything that went on his squadron, but did nothing to discourage the practice. Being a living legend helped him to do his job. Other officers might threaten or ridicule — Ryan had only to direct a withering glance at a culprit. Even when he smiled, his cadets read into the expression a kind of cold ferocity. Though it secretly amused him to see cadets tremble without cause when the circumstances of training brought them to his personal

14

attention, he kept his sense of humour well hidden except with his family.

He was a captain with three young children and commandant of cadets at an advanced flying school when the Japanese attacked Pearl Harbor. He immediately requested combat duty and soon, as a major, commanded a P-40 squadron in the Middle East theatre. His squadron had the most kills in the group, the fewest aircraft shot down and the best maintenance record, which did little to endear him to subordinates or superiors. No one in the group inspired more confidence in the air or had fewer friends on the ground. From P-40s he went to P-38s. Three months after the group went into combat in North Africa, he was a full colonel and its commander. After the invasion of Sicily he had been shot down by ground fire while strafing enemy transport in southern Italy.

Learning upon his arrival at a prisoner of war camp in the Abruzzi that he was the senior officer, he had immediately assumed command. The prisoners had been dirty, ill-fed, ill-clad and undisciplined. Riding roughshod over all who resisted, and employing tact and firmness with the camp commandant, he had changed all that and forged the prisoners into a disciplined group, making no more friends in the process than he had done earlier in his career.

Now, all this comfort and activity was more galling to Ryan than the privations of P.G. 202. Outside, just behind the jutting Silvrettas, beautiful and imposing in the moonlight, lay Austria. The enemy. Far to the south, more of them, fighting desperately to prevent the Allies from driving through the mountains on Rome. While he sat here idle.

He went to his desk and began writing in the small leather-bound notebook he always carried in his pocket. He was still at it when Major Wimberly knocked on his door.

'It's open,' Ryan called.

Wimberly came in and stood at nervous attention, still wondering what he had done wrong.

'At ease,' said Ryan. 'Major, you'll be taking roll-call formation the next two mornings. I'll be away.'

'What do I tell Captain Haas, sir?'

'If he asks, which he won't, tell him you don't know where I am. Which will be true.'

It was well before dawn when Ryan rose and put on the civilian clothes he had had one of the quasi-civilians living in the Chesa Grischuna buy for him in Chur. The trousers were six inches too large at the waist but, with suspenders and the jacket buttoned up, it was not noticeable. He had a civilian overcoat as well.

It was still dark, with no one stirring, when he and Costanzo left. Costanzo drove. He said he had promised the owner of the car that no one else would be allowed to take the wheel. The car was a pampered old Fiat, black and shiny, with a heater that worked and bud vases on both sides of the rear seat.

Fog lay heavily along the winding road, smothering the headlights. Costanzo drove timidly, his face as close to the windshield as he could get it. They were almost an hour reaching Landquart, only twenty miles or so away.

'I'd better drive,' said Ryan. 'We'll be on the road all day.'

'Ah promised,' Costanzo said.

Beyond Landquart the terrain opened and, as the fog and darkness lessened, Constanzo drove with increasing confidence. Ryan kept the road map open on his lap. He had not yet told Costanzo their destination. They would be driving almost the breadth of Switzerland and, because of the mountainous nature of the land, their route was circuitous.

They left the valley and were again among mountains, snow-capped, piled range upon range. Costanzo continued to drive with the confidence he had gained in easier terrain, and they bowled along narrow roads that twisted, climbed and plunged, sometimes among tucked-away meadows that still showed traces of green and sometimes among vast snowfields.

'Have you ever seen such gorgeous scenery?' Costanzo exclaimed, looking away from the long, soaring vista of snow-covered peaks just in time to confront a sharp curve.

The rear end swung out, tyres squealing. Ryan clutched the

16

dashboard with both hands, his knuckles whitening.

'Watch where you're driving!' he cried.

'Why, Cuhnel,' Costanzo said, unperturbed. 'Ah do believe that's the first time Ah ever saw you scared.'

'I've been scared plenty of times, but not that bad.'

'Don't worry. Ah've never had an accident in mah life.'

'Have you ever done any mountain driving before?'

'No.'

'How much driving of any kind have you done?'

Costanzo looked at him out of the corner of his eye and said, 'Not a whole lot.'

'That's what I thought. This is no place for beginners. I'm taking over.'

'Sorry, Cuhnel. Ah promised Father Wetzel.'

'Render unto Caesar, *Captain*. That's a direct order.'

Costanzo pulled over.

'Since you put it that way, Cuhnel. It's not as if this were the first time you've made me bend mah vows.'

They stopped for an early lunch at a mountain inn, eating on a sun-drenched plank deck overlooked by serried peaks. They were the only guests, with the entire staff for an audience. Even the cook came out to watch them. The Swiss whispered among themselves, glancing surreptitiously at the priest and the hard-faced man who talked together in English. The waiter, little more than a boy, brought a bottle of wine they had not ordered. Costanzo asked him about it in fluent German. The waiter said it was a gift from the proprietor. Costanzo poured wine for himself and Ryan.

'I'm not calling on the Military Attaché breathing wine fumes,' Ryan said.

'So that's where we're going.'

'That's where I'm going. You can visit churches. Bern's full of 'em.'

Skirting Lake Vierwald, beyond the mountains edging its northern shore, they approached Lucerne.

'Ah hear Lucerne's one of the prettiest towns in Switzerland,' Costanzo said. 'Why don't we take a look around?'

'You'll like Bern better. Bigger churches.'

'Cuhnel, for a man who never goes near one, you're sure obsessed with churches.'

Past Lucerne, they plunged into more mountains, emerging into hilly ground beyond Konolfingen.

'Getting close,' Ryan said.

'May Ah drive now? The road looks easy.'

'Why not. Then you can tell Father Wetzel we shared the driving.'

They stopped on the outskirts of Bern to ask directions. Ryan had an address on Thunstrasse for the Military Attaché but no city map.

'Ah'm surprised you didn't already know exactly how to find it,' Costanzo said after getting the information in German from a pedestrian. 'But Ah expect you figured if you asked around in Klosters everybody would know where you were going.'

'Watch your driving,' said Ryan.

Costanzo had a few near misses on the way in the early afternoon traffic. He was blissfully unaware of how close he came to other vehicles, despite honking horns and skidding rubber.

The Military Attaché's offices were in a leafy residential neighbourhood in a building indistinguishable from its neighbours.

'Let me out in front,' Ryan said.

'You want me to come in or wait or what?'

'Have a look around the city. And buy yourself a decent suit. You got any money?'

Costanzo nodded.

'So much for your vow of poverty. I don't know how long I'll be. If you're not back by the time I'm through, I'll wait.'

Ryan rang the bell and went in. A young man sitting at a desk in the foyer looked up casually when he entered, then sprang to his feet.

'You're Colonel Ryan!' he exclaimed. 'Sir, I've got to shake your hand.'

He hurried to Ryan and pumped his hand vigorously.

'Do I know you from somewhere?' Ryan asked.

'No, sir.'

'Then how did you know me?'

'Everybody knows you, sir. Over at the Legation, too. The minister has your picture on his desk.'

'I want to see the Military Attaché.'

'Yes, sir. Right away. General Sperling's been expecting you.'

'The hell he has,' Ryan said thoughtfully.

2

The young man fetched another young man, who also asked the privilege of shaking Ryan's hand. The second young man escorted him to the Military Attaché's office. On the way they encountered other members of the Attaché's staff. They stopped whatever they were doing when they saw Ryan. Some said his name aloud or rushed to shake his hand.

'I suppose by tomorrow it'll be all over Bern I was here,' Ryan said.

'Be hard to keep a visit by someone like you quiet, sir,' the escort said.

He was a young, healthy-looking man who Ryan thought should be off fighting the war somewhere.

'Why?' Ryan said. 'Don't you have tight security here?'

'Yes, sir. For anything classified.'

'How do I get classified?'

The young man laughed. He knocked on a door. A hearty voice called out immediately.

'Come in, come in.'

The escort opened the door for Ryan and shut it behind him without entering himself. General Sperling was coming around his desk with a hand extended. He was a spare, greying man in his fifties, wearing a grey flannel suit and back brogues. He exuded a conviviality that could not entirely mask his shrewdness.

'Colonel Ryan!' he cried. He had a carrying, public speaker's voice. 'What a pleasure to meet you in the flesh at last.'

He waved Ryan to a leather-upholstered armchair bordered in brass tack-heads and sat down behind his desk. On the desk were a desk set, a humidor, a tiny American flag set in an onyx base, framed photographs and a wooden bar of triangular cross-section, the sort that normally bears the occupant's name. Instead of a name, this one said, 'I Don't Know Why We Do It This Way. It's Just Our Policy.'

Ryan smiled, confident that he could do business with this sort of man. General Sperling smiled back at him.

'It's the God's truth around here,' he said. 'Now if they'll just explain to me what our policy is.'

'Why don't we make a little policy of our own, General?'

'Call me Herman. That's a Kraut name for you, isn't it, Herman Sperling? I understand they called you Von Ryan in Italy. We're both in the wrong army. Did you stop by at the Legation?'

'No, sir.'

'The minister will be disappointed, but it's better that way. What they don't know over there won't hurt them.'

'General, I'm aware you can't do anything officially, but...'

'Excuse me,' General Sperling interrupted, picking up his phone and pushing a button. 'You can send them in now.' Turning his attention back to Ryan, 'Sorry. I expected you sooner, Colonel.'

'I stopped for lunch,' Ryan said, his face revealing no curiosity about the call or the fact that Sperling knew he was coming to Bern.

'I meant days sooner. We were wondering how long you'd stay content living the life of Riley in Klosters. I was on the point of sending for you.'

'Good. Then you know why I'm here. I need...'

General Sperling held up an arresting hand.

'Officially, I don't want to hear it.'

'Unofficially, then.'

'We'll get to that.'

The general opened a desk drawer and took out a bottle of Johnny Walker Black Label and put that and a glass beside the humidor.

'Have a blast and a cigar,' he said.

He helped himself to a cigar, leaving the humidor open.

'I never drink before battle, General,' Ryan said, taking a cigar.

The general's eyebrows lifted.

'You must want more than you think you can get,' he said.

He clipped the end of his cigar and offered Ryan the cutter. Ryan shook his head and cracked the end between thumb and forefinger. It was a long, fat Laranaga. It had been a while since Ryan had seen a good Havana. The general lit his cigar with the kind of Zippo that most GIs carried and leaned across the desk extending it towards Ryan. Ryan took it and lit his cigar carefully. When the cigar was going well he leaned back in his chair and blew a smoke ring at the ceiling, waiting.

'Have you been comfortable in Klosters?' the general asked, obviously killing time.

'It beats P.G. 202.'

Someone knocked on the door. The general looked relieved.

'Come in,' he said.

The door opened and three men filed in, followed by the man who had escorted Ryan. The three men looked superficially similar, tall, trim, light-eyed. All wore hats, like characters in a gangster film. They looked at Ryan but did not speak.

'Would you mind standing up, Colonel?' the general said.

Ryan did so. The three men ranged themselves beside him. General Sperling studied the four in thoughtful silence.

'Which do you think, Simms,' Sperling said at last.

'Dixon, sir,' the escort replied.

'I think you're right.'

'You can get back to work, fellows,' Simms said.

Two of the men left. The other stepped back. Sperling looked at Ryan as if expecting questions. Ryan said nothing.

'Colonel Ryan,' said the man named Dixon. 'I'd like to shake your hand. That was a hell of a stunt you pulled off in Italy.'

While they were shaking hands, General Sperling said, 'Colonel, will you please change clothes with him.'

Ryan took off his coat.

'No questions?'

'I suppose sooner or later somebody'll be telling me what this is all about.'

'I expect they will,' the general said, chuckling. 'Want us to leave while you change?'

'I've got nothing to hide,' said Ryan. 'Have you, Dixon?'

Dixon grinned and shook his head.

Simms went to a window, drew the curtains and looked out.

'He's still parked across the street, as usual,' he said. 'Probably got a good look at the colonel when he came in.'

'Our German friends are curious about who comes and goes,' Sperling explained.

'It's starting to rain, General,' Simms said.

'That's a break. Dixon, take an umbrella when you leave and hold it low.'

After they had exchanged clothes, Sperling studied them again. The suits fitted reasonably well. Dixon's coat was a bit tight across Ryan's chest and Ryan's a bit loose across Dixon's. Dixon's former trousers were large in the waist, but not as large as those that Ryan had removed.

'Good,' said the general. 'Very good. Dixon, as soon as you're certain nobody's on your tail take the rest of the day off.'

'What about my suit?' Ryan said.

'Oh. Dixon, I'm afraid you'll have to come back after all.'

'I'm not gonna spoil your day,' Ryan said to Dixon. 'I'll keep yours, if you don't care.'

'Your suit'll be a hell of a souvenir, sir.'

After Dixon had left them, the general held out his hand and said, 'It's been an honour and a pleasure, Colonel. Simms will take you where you're going.'

'I'm not coming back here?'

The general shook his head.

'I've got business to do with you.'

'You'll be seeing someone who can give you a better deal than I can. Hold on a minute.''

The general took a fistful of cigars out of the humidor and

stuffed them in Ryan's breast pocket. He started to give him the bottle of Scotch as well but thought better of it.

'There'll be a full one in your room at the Bellevue Palace. If there's anything else you want there, just charge it to the room. The tab will be taken care of.'

'How about twenty-five each French-English grammars and French-English dictionaries? And seventy-five maps of southern France?'

'Simms, you think you can manage that without connecting us?'

Simms nodded.

'They'll be in your room, Colonel.'

'Someone was supposed to pick me up here. Captain Costanzo. An Army chaplain.'

'You don't have to tell me who *he* is. Padre Costanzo's as famous as you are. I'll have someone tell him to meet you at the Bellevue Palace. We'll get him a room there, too.'

Simms led Ryan to a rear exit after getting trench-coats for both of them. He opened the door, looked swiftly in both directions and motioned for Ryan to follow. He hurried to a Fiat sedan similar to the one Costanzo had borrowed, except that it looked as if it had never had a single day of tender loving care. He flung open the rear door.

'Please keep on the floor, out of sight,' he said.

Ryan folded himself between the rear seat and the back of the front seat. Simms slammed the door and got behind the wheel. As they drove through the city Ryan, lying on the floor smoking his cigar, could see only the tops of trees — there were trees everywhere — and the upper floors of buildings heavy with years.

'Sir,' Simms said without looking back, 'did you really kill all those Germans with your bare hands?'

'You're supposed to be alone in this car. How do you suppose you look to people who think you're talking to yourself?'

'Yes, sir,' said Simms, chastened.

After a while, the number of treetops increased and the buildings all looked residential. The car stopped. Simms said,

'Just sit tight, sir,' and got out. His upper torso appeared at the rear door window.

'Now, sir!' Simms said, opening the door.

They were in the driveway of a three-storey house, shielded on one side by a stone wall and on the other by the house itself. There was an open door a few feet from the car. Simms nodded towards it. As Ryan was passing through it, Simms called after him, 'It was an honour meeting you, sir.'

Ryan paused briefly and looked back at him.

'I only killed half of 'em,' Ryan said. 'A limey named Fincham took care of the other half.'

A youngish man in a brown turtleneck sweater shut the door behind Ryan.

'If you'll just follow me,' he said.

He did not request the privilege of shaking Ryan's hand.

He conducted Ryan through several resolutely Swiss rooms, with lots of clocks, pictures in heavy frames and an eight-inch metal replica of the Bern bear. Ryan held his hat in one hand and the cigar in the other, looking for an ashtray. The ash was dangerously long. Just as he dumped the ash in the hat, the man in the sweater opened a door and ushered him into what was obviously the library.

A man at a spindly leather-topped desk rose immediately and came to greet him. About Ryan's age, though less used-looking, he wore a tweed jacket with leather elbow patches over a sleeveless tan pullover and was smoking a curved pipe. An ashtray was on the desk among neatly arranged file folders.

'Excuse me a minute,' Ryan said.

He stubbed out his cigar in the ashtray and emptied his hat into it. He inspected the hat, saw that some ash remained, blew into it and inspected it again. The man in the tweed jacket waited patiently.

'I've heard a lot about you, Colonel Ryan,' he said.

'That puts you one up on me.'

'Spargo. Ed Spargo.'

'What's your connection with General Sperling?'

'It's...it's ambiguous.'

'Sure as hell is. Who do you work for, then?'

'The Office of Strategic Services.'

'Now we're getting somewhere. You're just the man I want to see.'

'Then the general told you what we had in mind?' Spargo said, pleased.

'He told me doodledy-squat. You tell me what you have in mind and I'll tell you what I have in mind.'

'I think you'll approve, Colonel. Knowing your reputation.'

Ryan sat down on a rump-polished leather couch, his hat on his knees. He watched Spargo go to a rack of battleship-grey metal filing cabinets against one wall. The other walls were all floor to ceiling shelves crowded with books and equipped with sliding ladders. The books were of all shapes and sizes, mostly leatherbound and showing signs of age. The filing cabinets had lockrods running down through the drawer pulls; the top drawers had combination locks set into the faces. Spargo spun the dial of the combination padlock securing the rod on a cabinet.

'What is my reputation?' Ryan asked.

Spargo removed the rod and pulled out a file drawer.

'A man who likes action and doesn't mind danger. A man who gets things done if they can be done. Or even if they can't.'

'Also unreasonable, rigid, rather chew a butt than a steak.'

'I wouldn't say that,' said Spargo, selecting a folder.

'You'd better do more research on my reputation.'

Spargo sat down beside Ryan and handed him four pencil sketches. They were all of clean-cut young men from the shoulder up, and all in American uniform, a first lieutenant and three captains. They were like the sketches police made from the composite descriptions by witnesses. Though they were all of different individuals, they were vaguely similar.

'Recognise any of them?' Spargo asked hopefully.

Ryan studied each in turn, then a second time. He shook his head.

'Should I?' he asked.

Spargo looked disappointed.

'One of them is a German agent,' he said. 'And can pass for as American as you or me. On at least one occasion he called himself Dudley L. Hampton and claimed to be a major in the OSS. I believe you recall the occasion. You saw him face to face.'

Ryan looked at Spargo for some sign of malice or amusement. There was none.

Major Dudley L. Hampton was the man who had awoken Ryan in the middle of the night in his quarters at P.G. 202 after the Italian capitulation. He had convinced Ryan he had been dropped by parachute to relay an important message: British intelligence had learned that German troops would evacuate the area within three days and planned no action against the prisoners if they stayed put and made no trouble. All prisoners were to remain within the camp during the three-day period lest the Germans consider them a threat to their orderly withdrawal. If any of the prisoners attempted to leave, the Germans would take everyone with them. As soon as Allied surveillance showed that the German evacuation was completed, paratroopers would be dropped with food and medical supplies preparatory to returning the prisoners to Allied control. Two nights later, German paratroopers silently occupied the abandoned sentry-boxes on the walls and in the morning, Ryan and his men found themselves prisoners again. They were crowded into boxcars for the long journey to captivity in Germany. All blamed Ryan for their plight.

'He was one clever son of a bitch,' Ryan said with more admiration than rancour.

He looked more closely at the sketches. Now that he knew what he was looking for, they all bore superficial resemblance to Hampton, but there was nothing close enough for positive identification.

'Wish I could help you,' he said regretfully.

'Would you know him if you saw him?'

'I'd know him. Is he in Bern?'

'Italy.'

'Too bad.'

'We may be able to put you in a position to identify him there.'

'Say on.'

'Groups of Italians are organising themselves into bands to harass the Germans behind their lines.'

'I know. Some of them helped us when our train was stalled on the way to Tirano. And fought off the Germans when we made our final run for the border.'

'They aren't particularly effective yet, but with help from us we expect that to change if the Nazis hang on in Italy for any considerable period.'

'You expect them to?'

'Looks that way. We still haven't reached their main line of resistance well south of Rome. The point is, several of these partisan bands have been joined by American evaders and escapees. Or enemy agents pretending to be Americans. We have good reason to believe one of them is Hans Dieter Grunow. The man you knew as Hampton.'

He waited. When Ryan did not comment, he continued.

'It would be extremely detrimental to our plans if there were an enemy agent with one of the major bands. We intend eventually to co-ordinate their operations and there may be a certain amount of liaison between them. A clever agent might find himself in a position to feed them to the Germans. As he did the prisoners in your camp.'

'You've got yourself a problem, haven't you, Eddie?'

'That's why we need your help.'

'I drive an aircraft. I'm not one of your cloak-and-dagger boys.'

'We've narrowed down the possibilities to those four. Unfortunately, these are the best descriptions we've been able to get. We've compared the sketches with photographs of the Americans they claim to be and they're so close that we can't be sure they're not them. We know roughly where they're operating, though. Or can find out.'

'So you know their names?'

'We know who they say they are. They're all names of escapees or MIAs. Easy enough to substitute for if the enemy knew they were dead or captured.'

'I don't see how I can help you.'

'We want you to go to Italy and identify him. You're the only one who can.'

'Duff gen, as the limeys say. Nine hundred prisoners of war stood in line at P.G. 202 to thank their saviour in person.'

'You're the only one we think could hack it.'

'Thanks, but like I told you, my job's driving an aircraft.'

Spargo leapt to his feet, face flushed.

'Good God, man, we've giving you an opportunity to get revenge!'

'Revenge? I don't give a damn about revenge. I was slickered by a man doing his job. And a damn good job he did, the slick son of a bitch. If I was to run into him after the war, I'd buy him a drink.'

Spargo paced until he composed himself.

'I thought a man like you would jump at the chance to get back into action,' he said bitterly.

'I intend to. My own way. With all my men. That's why I'm in Bern.'

'You mean to tell me you think you can get three hundred American officers out of Switzerland and back to Allied control?'

Ryan nodded. Spargo sat down behind the leather-topped desk and looked at him incredulously.

'How?' he demanded.

'Put 'em in civilian clothes and slip 'em into France at intervals in groups of four or five. Then over the Pyrenees into Spain. I understand you can get home from Spain. That right?'

'Maybe. But getting there isn't that easy.'

Ryan took a cigar out of his pocket, cracked the end and found he did not have a match.

'Got a light?' he said. 'Like a cigar?'

'I smoke a pipe,' Spargo said stiffly, tossing Ryan his lighter. It was solid silver with an embossed bear on it.

Ryan lit up and leaned back. 'So you can see why I can't go to Italy for you,' he said conversationally. 'My first responsibility is to those poor American boys in that hellhole they call Klosters.'

'Some hellhole. And they're not your responsibility any more. You got them out of Italy.'

'But they are. If I hadn't fallen for Hampton's line...'

'Grunow's line,' Spargo interrupted.

'...but instead had led them out of the camp after the Italians took off, they'd all be home now.'

'Or dead or recaptured.'

'There's always that possibility. Comes with the uniform. Anyhow, I intend staying in Switzerland until I know they're guaranteed a shot at getting out too. You can see I couldn't go anywhere with a clear conscience, knowing I was leaving even one of my men to rot in Switzerland.'

'Some of the air-crews and evaders who made it seem to like it here,' Spargo said sarcastically.

'Not my men,' Ryan said gravely. 'They'd go through fire to get back into combat.'

Spargo gave a snort of disbelief. He leaned forward, his eyes smoky with anger.

'Are you trying to bargain with me, Ryan?'

'Colonel Ryan to you.'

'Just what's your proposition, *Colonel*?'

'No proposition. I'm just asking you to do your duty and help me get my men back into the war.'

'They're interned in a neutral country. You know what that would do to our position with the Swiss if they simply picked up and left?'

'Nothing, unless it was shoved in their faces that we were getting organised help. They'll be glad to be rid of us. Seems to me you'd be able to handle a little thing like that discreetly. That's the way you fellows do things, isn't it? Discreetly.'

'Let me get this straight,' Spargo said carefully. 'You'll go to Italy if we help your men get to Spain?'

Ryan nodded and watched a smoke ring. Spargo watched it too, as if looking for a message.

'Exactly how much help are you demanding?' he said at last.

'I'm not demanding anything. Just asking for a little co-operation. An address where they can get civilian clothes. Chur would be nice. Easy for 'em to reach on their own but not too close to Klosters. Another address near the French border where they can change their Swiss money for French francs — they won't need any financial assistance — and get the names of some Frenchmen they can count on to hide 'em when necessary and pass 'em along. They'll hire their own guides to get them across the Pyrenees.'

'That's what you call "a little co-operation?" '

'If you can't hack it, say so, Eddie. I'll just have to do the best I can on my own. As much as I'd like to help you out down in Italy...'

Spargo got up and paced some more. He stopped abruptly, said, 'Wait here', and left the library. Ryan waited until the sound of his footsteps died, walked silently to the door and eased it open a crack.

The OSS man was calling someone from a room close enough for Ryan to catch snatches of his conversation. Anger and frustration made Spargo raise his voice.

'Yes sir, Mr Dulles. I told him that...refused...said he had to get his men...three hundred...yes, I know that's a helluva ...maybe if we spread...Yes, sir. Adamant...why they call him Von Ryan...Yes, sir.'

Sensing the conversation was over, Ryan went back to his place. When Spargo returned, Ryan was calmly watching one smoke ring chase another. Spargo was fully composed, even relaxed.

'You drive a hard bargain, Colonel,' he said.

'I wasn't bargaining. Just stating the facts.'

'It'll take a while to get them all out. The Swiss would have to react to a mass exodus even if they'd rather not. And we can't have too many in the pipeline at once.'

'Understood.'

'We'll stockpile civilian clothing in Chur. Set up a pass point near the border where they can change their money, get false papers and names of reliable French contacts.'

Ryan nodded and said, 'Sounds fine. One other little thing.

31

After I've identified Grunow, can you get me through the lines?'

'No sweat.' Spargo held out his hand and said, 'Deal?'

'Deal,' said Ryan, shaking it.

They worked out the details together. Ryan was to have a week to organise his end of the operation before meeting his contact in Chur. He would leave Klosters with only the uniform on his back, as if going for a walk. Spargo gave him a two-by-three photograph.

'His name's Perry Tenbrink,' he said. 'You'll meet him in the cathedral in Chur at fourteen hundred hours a week from today. He's a captain but he'll be in command. You do whatever he says. Any questions?'

Ryan shook his head.

'Good. I'll have you taken to your hotel now. You'll like the Bellevue Palace. Hell of a location and terrific food.'

He led Ryan to the door by which he had arrived.

'Keep down until the driver tells you it's O.K. to sit up,'' he said. He paused and added, 'You were dying to get back to Italy, weren't you, you son of a bitch?'

'No,' Ryan said, straight-faced. 'You slickered me into it. Brilliantly. You can tell Mr Dulles I said so.'

3

On the drive back to Klosters Padre Costanzo appeared troubled. He had been that way since Ryan found him waiting at the Bellevue Palace, wearing a new black suit that hung on his wiry frame but did not engulf him as the other had done. The drink Ryan poured for him from General Sperling's bottle had done nothing to lighten his mood. He had been too preoccupied to comment on the view of the Kirschenfeld-brücke from the window or to ask with any real interest what they were toasting. He was only mildly curious about the cartons of books and stack of maps in Ryan's room. The bottle of wine they shared with dinner in the formidable but pleasant dining-room had only increased his melancholy. Ryan had not seen the priest look so troubled since he had been obliged to witness acts of great violence in the take-over of the train, and to stand guard with a loaded weapon over the German train commandant.

'You look like you need to see the chaplain, Padre,' Ryan said.

Costanzo smiled for the first time, wanly.

'I don't exactly qualify, but what's eating you, Padre?'

'Ah had a talk with a Jebbie in Bern. Ah can go back home any time Ah want to.'

'Great. So what's your problem?'

'If Ah do, the Orduh intends to see the Army keeps me there. Ah want to serve in Italy again.' He sighed. 'Ah could serve the Army better and those poor people, too. When we were coming up here, Ah saw their suffering.'

'Priests and soldiers go where they're ordered. You're both.'

'Do tell,' Costanzo said, looking at Ryan with something of his customary mischief. 'Seems like you always manage to do things your own way. Take last night. You looked like the cat ate the cream. You put *something* over on *somebody*.'

'Always within regs, Padre. Whenever possible.'

'Ah've been thinking about slipping back into Italy. Before Ah'm ordered otherwise.'

Ryan studied Costanzo's face. Costanzo meant it.

'You'd get yourself killed trying it on your own.'

'Priests and soldiers accept that risk,' Costanzo said, mimicking Ryan's brisk tone. 'And like you said, Ah'm both.'

'You wouldn't last a day on your own. Can you wait a week?'

'Ah expect so. You're going back yourself, aren't you?'

'You don't seem too surprised.'

'You don't surprise me any more, Cuhnel. You amaze me some times, but you don't surprise me.'

'I could use a good man who can pass for Italian if he has to.'

'Ah won't bear arms. Ah did it on the train but Ah won't do it again.'

'You won't have to.'

Costanzo was his cheerful self again. When Ryan let him take the wheel of Father Wetzel's Fiat on a relatively easy stretch of road he whistled unmusically through his teeth, paying more attention to the scenery than his driving.

'What hymn is that?' Ryan asked.

' "Dixie", ' said Costanzo indignantly.

Ryan's absence caused considerable discussion among the internees but none dared question him. Nor did Captain Haas refer to it. The mystery deepened when, on his first full day back, Ryan emerged from his quarters only for meals and morning roll-call. He remained there completing the training schedule and company reorganisation he had begun the day before he left.

At roll-call the second morning, instead of ordering Wimberly to dismiss the troops as was his custom, Ryan had the major call them to attention. He stood regarding them from the Vereina steps. They shuffled their feet in the early morning cold, their muttered protests growing in volume.

'You are at attention, gentlemen,' Ryan snapped.

It had been a while since they heard that tone. The movement and protests subsided.

'I understand there are some among us of the opinion that we've died and gone to heaven,' Ryan said.

Laughter rippled through the company. Someone shoved Lieutenant Orde out of ranks. He scrambled back into place. Ryan ignored the disturbance, which was quickly over.

'Gentlemen,' he said, 'beginning tomorrow we come back down to earth.'

All laughter stopped.

'Tomorrow morning we will begin a programme of physical training, including hiking and calisthenics.'

'Not this time, Von Ryan,' a burly captain shouted. 'This is Switzerland, not Italy.'

The captain was Emil 'Goon' Bostick. As check pilot at advanced flying school, Ryan had goaded him into a passing performance in the air, earning enmity instead of gratitude. In the prison camp in Italy, Bostick had been one of the very few who dared risk Ryan's displeasure and later, after Ryan took over the train, disobeyed orders and attempted to escape, endangering the others. Ryan had tracked him down, subdued him in a brutal fight and brought him back. For a while after that Bostick was tractable, but during the easy weeks in Klosters he had regained his bluster.

'Damn right!' someone cried. There were other scattered cries of agreement. Ryan's expression did not change.

'Captain Bostick,' he said, 'one step forward.'

Bostick shambled out of ranks.

'All you men who agree with Captain Bostick form on him,' Ryan said.

No one moved.

'In that case, I'll need volunteers.'

Unerringly he picked out every man who had protested and called him out of ranks to join Bostick.

'Thank you for volunteering, gentlemen,' he said. 'After chow, you will report to the day-room and assist Captain Bostick in copying training schedules and new platoon rosters. May I remind you that we are all part of a military unit subject to the same rules and regulations as any other U.S. military unit with the same penalties for infractions, including insubordination, up to and including general courts martial upon return to Allied control, whenever that may be.'

There were no further dissenting murmurs from the ranks. Even Bostick maintained a glowering silence.

'Now that we understand each other...' Ryan said pleasantly. 'Major Wimberly, dismiss the troops,'

That night Ryan called a meeting of his platoon leaders and Wimberly in his quarters. He had reorganised his company into ten platoons of thirty men each. He had Wimberly report to him fifteen minutes before the others. He briefed the major confidentially of the plan for getting the men out of Switzerland, giving him the address in Chur where they were to change into civilian clothing and be told their next destination. Wimberly, Ryan said, would shortly be in command of the company. Ryan did not tell him where or when he was going.

'But I can promise you this,' he said. 'I'll eventually know what kind of job you did and make my recommendations accordingly.'

The platoon leaders were told only that they were to organise their commands into five-man squads which would train together. Ryan did not want any leaks that might force the Swiss, however reluctantly, to take action. In addition to the physical training, he told them, there would be a concentrated study of conversational French. Captain Haas and his staff were not to know.

'Why French?' one of the platoon leaders demanded. 'They speak German here.'

The others watched closely, waiting to see if the Ryan who answered was the almost mellow one of the past few weeks or the Von Ryan who had resurfaced that morning.

'Captain,' Ryan said, 'you're an officer and a gentleman and a college graduate. I assume you're familiar with that classic piece of doggerel, "The Charge of the Light Brigade".'

'Yes, sir.'

'Suppose you recite it for us, as much as you can recall. We could use some entertainment.'

The captain began, embarrassed.

'Louder. And stand at attention.'

Ryan stopped him when he reached, 'Theirs not to reason why.'

'Excellent,' he said. 'Does anyone else have any questions or know any inspiring poetry?'

Silence.

'You will be informed what you need to know when you need to know it. I promise you this, I do not intend sending you charging into massed artillery.'

'You can count on us, sir,' Wimberly said with a firmness he had rarely displayed in the past.

Keeping just enough of his back pay to cover a bit more than his bill for extras at the Vereina, Ryan sent Costanzo to Chur to buy civilian outdoor clothing for the two of them and convert his Swiss francs into Italian lire.

'Be Italian at the bank,' he said. 'And if anybody asks you any questions, tell 'em you're sending it back to your dear old mother in Italy.'

'Ah won't lie,' Costanzo said.

'Then think of something convincing that's not actually a lie. Should be easy for you. You're a Jesuit.'

On his third day back at Klosters, Ryan took a run up the road toward Davos, testing himself against the incline and looking for suitably taxing hiking trails for his men. A bicyclist in a jaunty hat, approaching from the direction of Davos, stopped in his path. It was Lieutenant-Colonel Eric Fincham, dressed like a mountaineer. Fincham had been Senior British Officer at P.G. 202, the camp's senior officer until Ryan arrived and took command. He and Ryan had worked as an efficient, murderous team in the capture of the train. He and his six hundred-odd British officers and other ranks were quartered in Davos, ten miles south of Klosters beyond the seven thousand-foot Weissfluchjoch.

He was a broad-shouldered man, a few inches shorter than Ryan and even thicker through the chest. His sweeping black moustache was more luxuriant than it had been in Italy, his complexion ruddier and he had put on weight. His blue eyes were no friendlier than before. Though they had performed smoothly together in taking the train from the Germans, the association had not led to personal friendship. He and Ryan had not seen each other since the separation of the British from the Americans at Campocologno.

'What luck,' Fincham said. 'I was just on my way to see you.' He got off his bike and they shook hands without great enthusiasm.

'You've put on weight,' Ryan said. 'You must like it here.'

'It's a bloody bore and no mistake. I don't intend lying about in Switzerland much longer. I'm surprised you're still around. I came looking for you the other day. Where were you?'

'I'm very comfortable at the Vereina, Colonel.'

'Shouldn't doubt it. Your whole lot is comfortable, from the look of it. That's why I've been wanting a word with you.'

'They'll be glad to know you're taking an interest in them.'

'You and your overpaid Yanks. You've run up the price of everything all over Grisons. Paying the first price asked, spoiling the natives with tips if they so much as give you a smile. My lot have to get by on honest British pay and you're mucking things up for us. Subalterns can't even afford a decent booze-up and the other ranks, poor sods...'

'We'll send some comforts parcels for your second looies. Wine, beer, a little schnapps. And get up a fund for the O.R.s.'

'Don't bother. Just stop throwing your money around.'

Fincham tugged at his moustache.

'Where were you for two days?' he said more pleasantly. 'You're up to something, aren't you? I expect to be included, of course. I took the train with you and put up with your bloody ways, and if you have a scheme I expect you to make room for me in it. What's the drill?'

Ryan studied his costume.

'You're out of uniform,' Ryan said. 'Good climbing at Davos? I didn't know you went in for it.'

'Haven't changed, have you, Von Ryan? From now on I'm keeping my eye on you. You're not leaving without me.'

Fincham climbed on his bike and pedalled toward Davos, bent low over the handlebars. After that he was in Klosters every day, watching Ryan's comings and goings and the tightly disciplined activities of his men.

At one o'clock on the appointed day, Ryan stowed tooth-brush, razor and toilet-paper in his pockets and gave Doc Stein money to pay his and Costanzo's extras bill.

'But wait a couple of days,' he said.

'I've had a feeling this beautiful friendship was ending,' Stein said ruefully. 'I suppose if I was invited to the dance I'd have an invitation.'

'Sorry, Doc. You can leave here any time you want. You're medical personnel. If anybody asks, you don't know when I took off.'

'Good luck,' Stein said, shaking his hand.

Ryan walked up the road without apparent purpose. Costanzo would be waiting for him in the Fiat just up the road beyond Klosters Dorf, with their winter civilian clothing in the trunk. The plan was for Father Wetzel to pick up his car in Chur later in the afternoon. Ryan had gone scarcely a hundred yards when he was aware he was being followed. It was Fincham, sauntering along whistling 'Cats on the Rooftops'. Ryan halted. So did Fincham. Ryan began walking again. Fincham did too, keeping the same interval. Ryan started sprinting when he saw the Fiat.

'Open the door, Padre!' he shouted as he neared it.

Fincham's heavy boots crunched behind him. Just as he flung himself into the seat beside Costanzo, Fincham leapt on to the running board and thrust his head and shoulders inside.

'Just going for a little drive,' Ryan said.

'I could do with a bit of a spin,' said Fincham.

'You wouldn't say that if you knew how Padre drives,'

Ryan said, putting his palm against Fincham's chest and shoving.

Fincham hooked an elbow around the window-post and did not budge, saying, 'Decent of you to be concerned.'

'I'm not running the show, Fincham. If I were, I'd take you along.'

'Bloody likely,' Fincham said, crowding in beside Ryan and slamming the door behind him. 'Let's be off, then.'

Costanzo looked at Ryan.

'You heard him, Padre,' Ryan said, resigned.

Chur was twenty-five miles or so from Klosters. The first miles, toward Landquart, wound alongside the mountains by the river, among woods and sloping fields already pinched by winter. After they had driven in total silence for ten minutes, Fincham said, 'Can't you drive a bit slower, Padre?'

'I warned you,' Ryan said.

'Where are we going?' Fincham asked.

'Chur.'

'And from there?'

'You're going back.'

'If you do.'

Ryan crawled into the back and changed into civilian clothing. Fincham watched with interest.

They turned back south around the shoulder of mountains after Landquart, where the valley broadened, still touched with green where the snow-capped peaks did not block the sun for the greater part of the shortening days.

The cathedral was in the south-east part of Chur. Costanzo knew where. He had been there before. He parked the car in the Postplatz, where he had promised to leave it for Father Wetzel, and gave Ryan directions.

'I'll go with you,' said Fincham.

'I've got to meet a man,' Ryan said.

'Not without me.'

'I'll be back.'

'I don't trust you.'

'I've got to come back for Padre Costanzo.'

Fincham looked at Costanzo. Costanzo nodded. Fincham

opened the door and got out. He stretched and said, 'Now I know how the poor sods in the boxcars felt.'

Ryan headed for a narrow way between solid old buildings. 'Don't be long,' Fincham called after him. 'I haven't had lunch.'

Across Reichgasse the street widened and became Planaterrstrasse. The cobbled street curved, rising. To the left of it was a long, pointed tongue of open land planted with rows of dormant vines. The cathedral towered up ahead to the right, a hulking medieval building at the back of a courtyard enclosed by less massive buildings. It was precisely two o'clock. Ryan went in through one of the big metal double doors. The interior was dim, ornate and empty. Ryan pretended to study a sarcophagus bearing the carved effigy of the reclining Bishop Ortlieb von Brandis while keeping an eye on the doors. Farther back in the cathedral, the sun striking through stained glass painted a pool of mixed colours on the stone floor.

Tenbrink was five minutes late. He was as tall as Ryan and as powerfully built. The photograph had not revealed that. With his colouring and his cheap suit of European cut he could have been Swiss or northern Italian. The only incongruity was his bearing. He did not look like a man accustomed to wearing cheap suits.

'Hello, Ottavio,' he said in a low voice, looking not at Ryan but at the tomb. 'I'm Carlo.'

'You're late,' said Ryan. 'What joker picked my name?'

'Who are the two men who came with you?' Tenbrink demanded, still not looking at him. 'Why are they waiting?'

'We've got a problem.'

'What do you mean, *we've* got a problem? Who are they and why are they waiting?'

Sunlight spilled inside as the door opened. Tenbrink walked away as a middle-aged man in a tight brown suit came towards the sarcophagus with a guide-book in his hand.

'Guten Tag,' he said to Ryan.

Ryan nodded. The man said something else in German, motioning with the guide-book. Ryan nodded again and moved off. When he glanced back, the man was bent over the stone effigy, examining it closely. Tenbrink was in a pew, kneeling with his forehead on his folded hands as if in prayer. Ryan went to the row in front of him and did the same.

'Now,' Tenbrink demanded quietly, 'what's this all about?'

'They're coming with us.'

'What! Superman didn't say anything about that!'

Ryan assumed Superman was Ed Spargo.

'He didn't know it at the time. Neither did I.'

'They can't come. My instructions only cover you.'

'Negative. If they don't come, I'll have to abort the mission.'

'You can't abort the mission. I'm in charge.'

'Good talking with you, Captain,' Ryan said, getting up and crossing himself as he had seen Costanzo do so many times.

He walked briskly toward the exit. He could hear Tenbrink hurrying after him. Tenbrink caught up with him at the door.

'You can't back out now!'

'Watch me, Carlo.'

Ryan crossed the courtyard, Tenbrink pursuing him and trying to appear not to, and stopped under an archway on the far side. He waited for Tenbrink to catch up.

'I'll have to check with Superman,' Tenbrink said. 'I expected you to be more professional.'

'Put me in an aircraft and I'm very professional. But I'm new at this cloak-and-dagger business.'

Tenbrink scribbled something on a scrap of paper and gave it to him. It was an address.

'Meet me there in half an hour,' he ordered. 'The man's name is Gustav. Tell him you're Ottavio and it's warm in Chur for this time of year. Who are the others? Why do you want them along? I've got to tell Superman.'

'Captain Gregory Costanzo and Lieutenant-Colonel Eric Fincham. They were in on the capture of the train. I invited Costanzo. He's a priest and can pass for Italian. Fincham invited himself. But you won't find a better man in a pinch.'

'Half an hour,' Tenbrink said, and was gone.

Fincham and Costanzo were huddled in a doorway when

Ryan got back. It had been pleasant when they arrived but now the sun had dipped below the mountains and the cold was deepening.

'What's the gen?' Fincham asked.

Ryan handed Costanzo the slip of paper.

'You know how to get there?'

Costanzo said, 'I think it's somewhere near here.'

Ryan looked at his watch and said, 'I want to be there twenty minutes from now.'

They drove around the city with the heater on, Costanzo making a circuit of the major thoroughfares to avoid getting lost in the narrow streets of the older section. Ryan got one of General Sperling's Laranagas out of a coat pocket and poked it at Fincham, in the rear seat.

Fincham fondled it, sniffed it, pierced the end tenderly with the awl blade of a large Swiss Army knife, lit up and drew in reverently.

'Lovely,' he sighed. 'I presume this means I'm a member of the club.'

Costanzo drove back to the Postplatz, found his street and stopped at the number given to Ryan. The sign said 'Schönheitssalon'.

'There must be some mistake,' Costanzo said. 'It's a beauty parlour.'

Ryan rechecked the address and went in. The shop was empty except for a scowling, heavy-jowled man in a smock. Except for his hands he did not look like a hairdresser. His long, delicate fingers were manicured and dye-stained.

'Gustav?' Ryan asked.

The man nodded, expressionless.

'I'm Ottavio. It's warm in Chur for this time of year.'

Gustav nodded towards a door at the back of the shop. Ryan went through it into a large store-room, windowless, with bottles of dye and shampoo, cartons, wig-stands and an electric plate on which a coffee-pot made bubbling noises. Tenbrink was sitting in a straight chair, not looking too happy. He had changed into rougher, warmer clothing.

'Superman said only if you absolutely insisted,' he said. 'I don't mind telling you he was damn teed off.'

'Don't blame him. But I absolutely insist.'

'Amateurs can get you killed.'

'So can professionals.'

'Where are the others?'

'Outside. In the car.'

'Tell them to come in.'

'We're supposed to leave it in the Postplatz.'

'Gustav can drop it off later.'

When they were all inside, Gustav went out and closed the shutters over the shop windows.

Tenbrink eyed Costanzo and Fincham with distaste.

'Get rid of that cigar,' he said. 'It's close enough in here as it is.'

'Get stuffed,' Fincham said pleasantly.

'Do what he says,' Ryan ordered. 'He's in charge.'

Fincham put out the cigar. Gustav came in and shut the door behind him. It was hot in the room. Costanzo struggled out of his heavy coat. He looked frail in his wool shirt, heavy sweater and bulky trousers.

'He'll never be able to keep up,' Tenbrink said.

'He's stronger than he looks,' Ryan said. 'And he's got God on his side.'

'Who's for coffee?' Fincham asked, heading for the electric plate.

'Later,' said Tenbrink.

'You may have yours later if you like,' Fincham replied, rummaging around until he found three mugs. 'Nothing to eat, I suppose. I'm famished.'

He poured coffee for everyone except Tenbrink. Tenbrink got up from the chair.

'Setzen Sie sich,' Gustav said to Ryan, motioning toward the chair.

Ryan sat down. Gustav circled him slowly, studying him. He pursed his lips, nodded, and took two boxes from a shelf. He took a wig from each, studied Ryan again and put one back. He approached Ryan with the other, light brown, wavy and of a length favoured by Italian civilians. Ryan looked at Tenbrink.

'We're trying to disguise you,' Tenbrink explained. 'Every German in Italy knows what you look like.'

Gustav adjusted the wig on Ryan's head and stood back to inspect it.

'It's an improvement,' Fincham said. 'As anything would be. But there's no hiding that face.'

Gustav apparently agreed. He took some moustaches from another box, found one that matched the wig and fastened it on with spirit-gum. He gave Ryan the tube to keep. Fincham laughed. Gustav looked at Tenbrink, who nodded approval.

'How long do I wear these?' Ryan demanded.

'I'll let you know,' Tenbrink replied.

He spoke to Gustav in German. Costanzo gave the hair-dresser the keys to the car.

'He'll drop off the car and come back for us in a truck,' Costanzo said.

'So you know German, too,' Tenbrink said, looking at him with new interest.

'He talks German to Germans and Italian to Italians,' Ryan said. 'And talks to God in Latin.'

'Your cover name is Mario,' Tenbrink said to Costanzo. And to Fincham, 'You're Enrico.'

'Enrico is hungry,' said Fincham.

'You may as well get used to it,' Tenbrink said.

'I've had more practice at it than I fancy.'

Twenty minutes after Gustav left, a horn sounded twice outside.

'Gustav,' Tenbrink announced. 'When he honks again it means it's clear to load up. Mario first, then Enrico, then Ottavio. Out of the door on the double and into the truck.'

Three short horn blasts sounded.

'Get going,' said Tenbrink, opening the store-room door.

He tapped each man's shoulder as he went out of the front door, like a jumpmaster sending off paratroopers.

The truck had a canvas cover with a flap hanging down over the rear. Costanzo held the flap up while Fincham and Ryan climbed in. Tenbrink looked quickly in both directions, locked the shop door and joined them. He rapped on the back of the cab and the truck drove away.

It was empty except for two large, bulging packs and a pair of canteens.

'Anything to eat in there?' Fincham asked.

'We'll eat in Lugano,' Tenbrink said.

'When will that be?'

'Two hours or so.'

'Time for a nap, then.'

Fincham stretched out on the bare truck-bed and, with a pack for a pillow, went promptly to sleep.

'What's the drill at Lugano?' Ryan asked.

'I'll tell you when we get there.'

'Tell me now. We've got two hours to kill.'

'Let's get something settled right now. I'll tell you what you need to know when I think it's time for you to know it.'

Tenbrink spoke with casual authority, but less like an officer to a subordinate than a civilian accustomed to dealing with his social inferiors.

'I don't go into anything blind,' Ryan said.

'You'll have to trust me.'

'Last stranger I trusted was a Major Hampton.'

'But you know who *I* am.'

'I need to know you better. It'll help if you tell me how we get into Italy and where we go from there.'

'You'd better tell him, Carlo,' Costanzo said, amused. 'When the Cuhnel's like this it's best to do what he says. And he's always like this.'

'I'd have thought with a Jesuit education you'd have got rid of that irritating accent,' Tenbrink said, resenting the interference. 'Very well Ottavio, but don't think Superman won't hear about this.'

After dark they were to cross Lake Lugano to the Italian side by boat. They would walk through the mountains to a place near the village of Argegno, where another truck would be waiting. They would be hidden under a load of furniture and driven past the German checkpoint at Como, and after that by back roads to a mountainous area east of Florence. From there they would continue on foot to the hiding place of

46

the partisan band with which the first American on Tenbrink's list was operating.

'Thanks,' said Ryan.

In Lugano, the truck stopped in a dark cul-de-sac. The cab door opened and shut. Tenbrink climbed out and returned in a few minutes to lead them into an adjacent house. Gustav had left them. Tenbrink carried one pack, Ryan the other. Heavy as they were, Tenbrink had picked his up with casual ease.

The house was of two storeys and simply furnished. Tenbrink led them to the kitchen, warm and redolent of spices. A lean old man was busy with pots and pans over a wood-burning stove. He turned to look at them, scowled, and returned to his cooking.

'He doesn't seem to fancy us,' Fincham said.

'He'd only expected two,' Tenbrink said. 'He's got to locate a larger boat.'

Wordlessly, the old man set four places at the kitchen table, banging down dishes and cutlery. There was an enormous loaf of bread on the table and a wicker-covered two-litre bottle of wine. When Tenbrink spoke to the old man in Italian he took away the wine and brought water. He put the pots from the stove on the table for them to help themselves. They dined on thick, steaming minestrone, broad, flat pasta in a rich sauce and greens boiled with bacon.

Tenbrink and Fincham began eating at once. Ryan waited for Costanzo's customary prayer. When Costanzo finished and crossed himself, the old man smiled for the first time. He spoke to Tenbrink in Italian. Ryan understood enough of the language to know the old man had asked if Costanzo were Catholic, and that Tenbrink had said he was without mentioning he was also a priest. The old man left the kitchen while they were still eating.

After dinner Tenbrink looked at his watch and said, 'If he hadn't had to find a larger boat we'd be leaving now.'

The old man returned at last, still scowling, and they all went out to the truck. Tenbrink got into the cab with him. They drove through town slowly, picking up speed along the lake in the outskirts. After a while the truck stopped.

'Everybody out,' Tenbrink said. 'And bring the packs and canteens.'

The lights of Lugano were visible behind them. There were other lights up ahead. Gandria, Tenbrink said, the last Swiss town before the Italian side of the north shore. Across the lake to the south, in total darkness, lay Italy. The truck, headlights extinguished, began turning round in low gear as they left the road and climbed down a steep wooded slope towards the shore.

'Anyone with a luminous watch, take it off and put it in his pocket,' Tenbrink ordered. Ryan had already done so.

They crunched through fallen leaves, holding on to saplings to slow down their descent. Though steep, the way was short.

'There it is,' said Tenbrink, leading them towards a patch of darker shadow.

'You'd make a hell of a night fighter pilot,' said Ryan.

Their craft was a large, clumsy rowing-boat, lying low beside the water. In it were a pair of heavy oars, a tarpaulin and fishing gear. Tenbrink opened a pack and took out a U.S. Army .45 automatic in a holster, which he gave to Ryan. He took another for himself.

'Where's mine?' Fincham asked.

'You weren't expected,' Tenbrink said curtly, thrusting a wide-bladed knife in a sheath into his belt and a length of wire with a handle at each end into a coat pocket. 'Ottavio and I will row. You two keep a sharp look-out. This lake is patrolled. If we're approached, Ottavio and Enrico get under the tarp. Mario and I'll be fishing. We speak only Italian.'

They shoved the heavy boat into the water. Tenbrink, the last man, gave it a final push before he sprang from shore. He baited two lines and dropped them in the water. He and Ryan rowed clumsily until they caught each other's rhythm and the boat moved along steadily. In the middle of the lake they turned to parallel the southern shore.

The sound of an engine rolled across the water.

'Ottavio, Enrico, under the tarp!' Tenbrink whispered.

The boat drifted. Tenbrink and Costanzo hunched over fishing lines. A searchlight swept the surface of the lake. Its

48

beam fell just short of the low-riding craft. The engine sound receded. Ryan and Tenbrink began rowing again, towards the Italian shore. The moonless sky flickered with stars whose reflection shimmered dimly on the surface. After an hour of steady rowing, blackness without shimmer rimmed the lesser darkness. Italy. Ryan was drenched with sweat, his hair sopping under the wig, and the moustache tickled. He suppressed a sneeze with an effort of will.

'Easy now,' said Tenbrink. 'This side's heavily patrolled.'

They nursed the boat into the shore. As it touched, Tenbrink leaped out with the painter in his hand and held the boat there while the others climbed out with the packs and canteens. He took hold of the gunwale and swung the boat until it parallelled the shore.

'Everybody lend a hand,' he said in a low voice.

They tipped the boat until it began filling with water. As it was sinking, Tenbrink said, 'Shove', and the water-logged craft moved away sluggishly to disappear into the darkness. Tenbrink handed a pack to Ryan and slipped the other on his back. As before, the OSS man seemed not to notice the weight. The wooded hillside where they had landed sloped less sharply at first than the shore from which they had departed, but soon tilted at a steeper angle. Tenbrink climbed steadily without looking back to see if the others were keeping up.

Boots crunched and equipment rattled in the darkness. Everyone stopped without being told and remained perfectly still, scarcely breathing, until the sounds died away. The night chill permeated Ryan's sweat-drenched clothing.

Their route took them along the shoulder of a road for a while. They made wide detours to avoid habitations. Then they were climbing again, or moving along slopes where the footing was awkward. They walked among deep-piled leaves, crunched over grasses stiff with rime, crossed cold, fallow fields and waded through snow drifted in hollows or blanketing exposed hillsides. The others sometimes stumbled or fell — even Ryan lost his footing once — but Tenbrink never put a foot wrong. Costanzo was the first to begin panting, though he said nothing and kept up. Then Fincham began to struggle.

Ryan, under the heavy pack, felt the pace but controlled his breathing deliberately.

'Break,' said Tenbrink.

He played the shielded beam of a penlight briefly on his wrist compass, flicked it off, then on a hand-drawn map. He remained standing. Ryan, Fincham and Costanzo sat down.

'He's showing off to us,' Fincham said. 'I hope he lasts the route.'

'He will,' said Ryan. 'You O.K., Padre?'

'Ah am now. Just had to catch mah breath.'

'Everybody listen,' Tenbrink said, looking down at them. 'If we keep up the pace we'll just make our rendezvous. If we're not there by first light, the truck won't wait. Let's move out.'

The tortuous march continued. Tenbrink seemed immune to cold and fatigue and unhampered by darkness. He led them as if on a clearly marked path, though to Ryan there was often no indication that anyone had ever passed this way before. They stopped once more at the base of a long, steep ridge.

'This is the worst stretch,' Tenbrink said. 'It gets easier on the other side.'

There was the merest vestige of a path leading up to the crest, just wide enough for them to walk in single file. Scrubby, leafless vegetation slick with frost offered an occasional handhold, of which Tenbrink never took advantage. They were nearing the top when someone's foot dislodged a stone. It went clattering down the face of the ridge, dislodging others. They showered down into the valley below.

Voices shouted in German in the valley. Flashlights flicked on and probed the darkness.

'Freeze!' Tenbrink hissed.

4

One voice, louder than the others, bawled out orders. The flashlights began fanning out all along the foot of the ridge. One of them, bobbing with the rapid stride of its holder, made towards the beginning of the trail.

Tenbrink lowered his pack silently to the ground.

'Ottavio,' he said, 'you take Mario and Enrico and hightail it to the other side and keep going. The trail gets easier then. I'll catch up.'

'You may need help,' Ryan said.

'You'll just be in the way. Get going. You're wasting time.'

Tenbrink started back down the trail towards the approaching beam, moving silently as smoke.

'Go on,' Ryan said to Fincham and Costanzo, giving his pack to Fincham. 'We'll both catch up.'

'Damned if I like it,' Fincham said, but he went.

Ryan started down, treading carefully on the loose stones. The flashlight beam was moving up the ridge. Below, the patrol had fanned out along the entire foot, calling back and forth. The broken face of the ridge was dimly visible against the sky.

'Here,' a low voice said from beside the trail.

It was Tenbrink, crouched behind a spur of rock. Ryan joined him. Tenbrink put his lips close to Ryan's ear and said, 'We'll have this out later. Meanwhile, don't you move another goddamn inch.' The 'goddamn' sounded as if he did not use it often.

The beam moved along the trail. The German was panting

with effort, his boots sending rocks bouncing down the ridge. The beam played over the spur and went on. Tenbrink was on the German from behind, swift and noiseless as a lizard. The flashlight leapt into the air, flung there by the soldier as Tenbrink's broad knife slid across his throat. Tenbrink's forearm across his mouth stifled his last cry. Ryan uncoiled and sprang forward, catching the light before it hit the ground.

'Come on,' Ryan said, playing the beam along the trail ahead of them as the soldier had done on the way up. 'They'll think he's still looking.'

He went on at the soldier's leisurely pace, making no effort not to dislodge rocks. Tenbrink followed with the dead man's rifle, disturbing nothing in his passage, stopping only to retrieve his pack. Ryan reached the top of the ridge and started down the other side, tilting the flashlight upward so its beam would be visible for a while to the patrol in the valley. After a minute or two he flicked it off and began whistling 'Sixpence' very low.

'What the hell!' Tenbrink demanded.

'You want Fincham to break my neck?'

As if in answer, Fincham stepped out of the shadows below them.

'It's us,' said Ryan.

'I know. Or you bloody well wouldn't have seen me until too late.'

'Cut the small talk and move,' Tenbrink said, still angry with Ryan even though he had caught the flashlight. 'It won't be long before they smell a rat.' He thrust the rifle at Fincham. 'You wanted a weapon,' he said.

They plunged down the trail to where Costanzo was waiting. The four of them, Tenbrink in the lead, jolted down the reverse slope with giant strides. The trail forked at the bottom, among evergreens. Tenbrink stopped. A match flared, illuminating his face, and the once-familiar reek of Italian tobacco filled the air.

'What the bloody hell!' Fincham cried.

The match went out and the glowing end of the cigarette arched off to the left.

'If they're sharp enough to spot it they'll think we went that way,' Tenbrink said curtly. 'We go this way.' He set off to the right.

'Sorry, old cock,' Fincham said to his back.

The trail, as Tenbrink had promised, was less difficult now, mostly downhill across terrain lightly wooded with leafless trees and patches of evergreens. Tenbrink, however, went so swiftly that the pace was as demanding as in more difficult country. Costanzo's laboured breathing rasped in his throat.

For the next thirty minutes the only sounds were scraping boots and heavy breathing. The trail became a well-trodden path. Tenbrink led them away from it, across an unploughed field and into a grove of trees. He stopped and called out in a low but carrying voice, 'Volpe?'

'Va bene,' a voice in the darkness answered.

Tenbrink struck off towards the sound. The owner of the voice was waiting at the truck, just inside the far edge of the grove. He was a short man, huddled in a blanket, his features masked by darkness. When he saw how many men Tenbrink had with him he launched a tirade, no less hysterical because it was delivered in a high-pitched whisper instead of a shout. It took a while for Tenbrink to shut him up.

'Can't say I blame him,' Tenbrink said bitterly. 'He agreed to take two and I show up with four.'

'It's a big truck,' said Ryan.

'There's only room for two under the load. We'll have to enlarge the hole and it's almost daylight.'

The blackness was turning grey. There was enough light now to see that Volpe was not alone. A woman sat on the running board, also huddled in a blanket. A child's head emerged from the blanket, sleepy eyed.

'Bollocks!' Fincham said. 'He brought his whole bloody family.'

'You do that when you move,' Tenbrink said as if explaining to a child. 'It explains the furniture. Everybody. Lend a hand. We'll reload and make a bigger hole. Except you, Mario. You backtrack a quarter of a mile and wait to see if the patrol is on our tail. If you see Germans, call out and take off on the double. Lead them away from here. If you don't, wait ten minutes and come back.'

Before Costanzo could comply, Fincham went loping back the way they had come, carrying the rifle at high port.

'Ottavio,' Tenbrink said grimly, 'you'd better make it clear to your people I'm in charge here.'

He and Volpe climbed on to the truck and began handing down the load, battered and rickety old house furniture, a mattress and a big, iron-strapped wooden trunk. Volpe handled only the lighter items and kept up a stream of complaints. His family got into the cab and watched from the window.

The sky was grey now, edged in cream along the mountains, and lightening rapidly as they started reloading. They put the mattress at the bottom and built around it, leaving a hollow under the furniture. Everything was on except the trunk when Fincham came loping back.

'No sign of Jerry,' he said.

In the brightening dawn, the truck was not a reassuring sight. The tyres were almost bald, with fabric showing through the sidewalls, a front fender was crumpled and a crack ran almost the width of the windbreak.

'All aboard,' said Tenbrink.

He followed them after a final conference with Volpe. They lay flat, side by side, with a foot of headroom in cavelike gloom pierced by rays of new light filtering through the load.

'If I'd known you weren't booking us first class you'd never have persuaded me to come along, Ryan,' said Fincham.

'I told Mario to cover our rear, not you,' Tenbrink said. 'Ottavio, tell him who's in charge of this operation.'

'You heard the captain,' Ryan said. 'We do what he says. He knows what he's doing.'

'Von Tenbrink and Von Ryan,' Fincham said. 'Lovely pair.'

Outside, Volpe had called the woman from the cab and with her help slid the trunk into the opening they had left at the back. It just fitted.

The motor coughed into life. The truck lurched across open ground, its swaying load creaking. It picked up speed on the road, limping along at twenty miles an hour. Chill air poured through the crannies in the load. Costanzo sneezed.

'Watch that!' Tenbrink said. 'You do that in Como, we're in trouble.'

In Como, Volpe had to stop at a roadblock and show his papers. The men under the load lay tense silent while voices argued in Italian and German. The argument stopped and someone laughed. The truck started up again. When it was moving freely again, Ryan said, 'What was that all about?'

'They wanted money not to make him unload everything and put it back on,' Costanzo said. 'He had to pay them.'

'We'll bypass Milan,' Tenbrink said, 'then get out and grab some chow.'

When Tenbrink spoke G.I. talk it sounded affected.

'When will that be?' Fincham asked.

'Sticking to back roads, maybe two hours.'

It was closer to three. Volpe had to stop to change a flat tyre. At last the truck made a sharp, creaking right turn and for several minutes scraped along deep ruts. The sunlight piercing the load vanished abruptly and the truck stopped. The cab doors opened, footsteps approached the rear from both sides and the trunk was pulled out to fall to the earth with a thump. Everyone crawled out and stretched. They were in a wooden building smelling of manure. Volpe and the woman who had helped him with the trunk stood watching while the child shut the barn door. Fincham stamped his right foot on the ground.

'Leg's gone to sleep,' he said, sniffing the air. 'Smells like a stable in here.'

'It is a stable,' said Costanzo.

Volpe brought out bread, cheese, olives, and a bottle of wine. After a short conversation, Tenbrink produced a packet of lire and counted off several bills into his hand.

'What's that for?' Ryan asked.

'The bribe at Como and our lunch.'

'Mercenary rascal, isn't he?'

'You think he's risking his neck because he loves us? But he's one of my most reliable bennies.'

'Bennies?'

'That's what we call Italian agents. Always saying "Va bene". '

They ate sitting down with their backs against the age-ribbed planks of a wall in a space clear of cow droppings. Volpe, the woman and the child ate in the cab. Tenbrink got up and brushed breadcrumbs from his trousers. Volpe was filling the fuel tank from five gallon cans.

'Time to saddle up,' Tenbrink said. 'We've got a long way to go.'

'Exactly where?' Ryan asked, raising a hand to still the retort ready on Tenbrink's lips. 'You're in charge of this operation. No argument there. I've watched you operate and I have every confidence in you. But if something happens to you and we're on our own I've got to know where I'm going and who my contact is.'

Mollified, Tenbrink scratched a crude map in the dirt with a stick. They would go first to Novellara, a village near the centre of northern Italy. They would leave the woman and child there and keep going, with Tenbrink sharing the driving with Volpe.

They would continue driving most of the night, avoiding Bologna as they had Milan, to Poppi, a village east of Florence. Volpe would leave them there at a house where they would hole up for the day. After dark a benny named Gianni would lead them into the Pratomagno Mountains to a rendez-vous with a partisan called Lupo, *Wolf*. Lupo was leader of the band which numbered among its members the first of the American officers who might be Grunow.

'If he's our man, your job's over,' Tenbrink said. 'I'll get you to the coast, call in a sub and you'll be back to Allied control in twenty-four hours.'

'And if he's not?'

'We move south, after the next man on the list.'

Tenbrink scratched more map lines in the dirt. The second band, under the leadership of a man who called himself Tigre, *Tiger,* operated from the Mount Terminillo area, near the village of Leonessa. Leonessa was north-east of Rome, west of

L'Aquila and some eighty miles from the battle lines.

'If our man's with Tigre, I'll still get you to the coast and a sub, but it'll take longer. If he's not, and I'm not still around, Tigre will pass you along to the next possible. From then on, you'll be close enough to the lines for a benny to guide you through them on foot when you've done your job. Satisfied?'

Ryan nodded.

They crawled back into their hole, Volpe and the woman replaced the trunk and they were off again. Another flat tyre held them up for a while and they had a scare when a German motorcylist stopped the truck. They could tell from the voices that there were two Germans, one in the sidecar. Ryan and Tenbrink unholstered their pistols and made ready to surprise them when they searched the truck. However, the Germans, who spoke wretched Italian, were merely lost and asking directions. When the truck resumed its journey, Tenbrink laughed.

'That scoundrel Volpe sent them off in the wrong direction,' he said.

'Be better if he wasn't such a comedian,' Ryan said. 'They might get sore and come back looking for us.'

'You surprise me, Ottavio. I thought you believed in living dangerously.'

'Never just for the hell of it.'

They reached Novellara before dark. The woman and child got out and Volpe continued south-east until night fell. He could not get the trunk free when he stopped to let Tenbrink out and the OSS man had to help him, shoving with his feet with his shoulders braced against Ryan. The trunk popped out and fell to earth with a crash magnified by the night and the stillness.

'If there's a Jerry within miles that should fetch him running,' Fincham said.

'Nothing to be afraid of,' Tenbrink said lightly. 'This is a quiet area.'

He let them stretch and ease their cramped limbs for five minutes, then sent them back under the load with bread, cheese and a canteen of water.

'I don't like his attitude,' Fincham said. 'I heard what he

said about living dangerously. He thinks this is a bloody lark.'

'You've made a few jokes yourself,' said Costanzo.

'He wasn't joking.'

It was much colder than it had been during the day.

'I hope he doesn't have a heater up there,' Fincham said. 'I wouldn't mind it as much if he's as cold as I am.'

After two hours of steady driving, Costanzo said, 'Mah bladder feels like it's about to burst.'

'Mine, too,' Fincham said. 'Von Ryan here, he doesn't even listen when nature calls.'

Ryan squirmed around on the mattress and kicked the back of the cab. When nothing happened he did it again. The truck stopped, the cab door opened, footsteps sounded and Tenbrink's voice demanded, 'What is it now?'

'We need to take a leak,' Ryan said.

'You just went a couple hours ago. You fellows are as bad as children.'

'Move the bloody trunk before we kick it out,' Fincham said.

'Not so loud,' said Tenbrink.

He removed the trunk and they scrambled out. The three of them lined up beside the road in impenetrable darkness. There was not the faintest gleam of light anywhere in the surrounding countryside. The only light, intensified by the blackness everywhere else, was in the sky, where clusters of stars glittered among expanses of pitch in a broken overcast.

'Carlo,' Fincham said. 'You chaps have a heater up there?'

'No. What's the matter, the cold too much for you?'

'Not now,' Fincham said, pleased.

From the road ahead came the sound of a labouring engine.

'Quick!' Tenbrink said. 'Back inside!'

Two weak blue gleams broke the darkness, like the eyes of a purblind monster.

'Too late,' Tenbrink whispered. 'Volpe, accendi i fánali!'
Turn on the lights.

The truck's blackout lights went on. Tenbrink walked to the front, unbuttoning his trousers. The others crouched behind the truck, away from the passing side, Ryan with his pistol

58

ready. Tenbrink stood in the faint glow of the truck's painted headlights, eerily blue, his back in plain view of the approaching vehicle, urinating nonchalantly.

The vehicle was a small sedan, oddly misshapen. When it picked up speed, protesting, to pass by with a rush, the reason was clear. A load half as large as the car itself was lashed on top.

'No problem there,' Tenbrink said. 'He's not looking for trouble any more than we are. Let's saddle up.'

It was still completely dark when they stopped again. Tenbrink paid off Volpe, who shook hands all round before driving away. Tenbrink led them to a house set back from the road. Metal sounded faintly on metal as his key probed for the hole in a padlock on the door. Hinges creaked and he told them to enter. It seemed even darker inside that out.

'No lights,' Tenbrink cautioned. 'I don't know how well this place is blacked out and it's supposed to be unoccupied.'

Tenbrink opened shutters covering the front window and crawled out to replace the padlock. The house was as cold as the open road. The stone floor was like a sheet of ice and gritty underfoot. Tenbrink crawled back through the window and closed the shutters.

'Make yourself comfortable,' he said. 'There's some mattresses on the floor in the back room. Should be blankets, too.'

They groped their way to the back and felt for the blankets in the darkness. The blankets were warm and thick. It seemed they had slept only minutes when Tenbrink woke them at first light.

'Breakfast,' he said.

They followed him to the front room, where he opened a cupboard and brought out salami, cheese, bread and tinned German corned beef. He cut the salami, cheese and bread on a long plank table with the sheath knife that had slit the German soldier's throat.

'It's not breakfast without a nice cup of tea,' Fincham said.

'You'll have to settle for Italian coffee substitute,' Tenbrink said. 'There was supposed to be the real stuff but it looks like

Gianni couldn't find any. Or kept it for himself. It's worth a mint on the black market.'

There was a charcoal stove in the room but Tenbrink brewed the coffee substitute on a spirit stove. He punched two holes in a can of evaporated milk and put it on the table.

'No sugar,' he said, the gracious host. 'That's asking too much even of Gianni. Plenty of saccharin, though, if you like it sweet.'

Fincham took a sip, rolled it on his tongue and said, 'Same slops we refused to drink in P.G. 202.'

'I didn't ask you to come along,' Tenbrink said.

'I fancy you'll find me useful before we're done,' Fincham replied, taking a full swallow. 'It's hot. I'll say that for it.'

There was an outhouse at the back but Tenbrink said no one was to go outside. They used a bucket which Gianni had thoughtfully provided.

'Everybody go back to sleep,' Tenbrink said. 'There's nothing to do all day but wait. One man stays awake at all times. I'll take the first shift.'

He began doing strenuous calisthenics and stretching exercises. Fincham watched, grinning.

'Reminds me of when you put us all through that nonsense at P.G. 202 and almost had a mutiny on your hands.'

'It's not a bad idea', Ryan said, 'after being cramped up in the truck twenty-four hours. We'll all do it.'

'You're forgetting you're not in command here, Ryan. Carlo is.'

'Everybody exercise,' Tenbrink ordered. 'We want to be loose tonight.'

'Next time I'll keep my mouth shut,' Fincham said.

After they had finished, Tenbrink opened the shutter a crack and took a seat by the window with the German rifle across his lap. The others went to the back room. It had a single shuttered window and bare stone walls. The four mattresses were straw-filled. The blankets were Royal Italian Air Force, with the 'RA' symbol woven into the centre. Ryan and Fincham crawled under them. Costanzo draped one around his narrow shoulders and read his daily office.

'Our glorious leader out there's going to wear himself out showing us he's made of steel,' Fincham said. 'What do you make of him, anyhow?'

'Damn good at his job,' said Ryan.

'But you don't fancy his sort, right?' Fincham said with a grin. 'Exactly my sentiments about you.'

Tenbrink woke Ryan with a touch on the shoulder. Ryan was instantly alert. Tenbrink pointed at his wrist-watch to indicate it was time to stand watch.

The OSS man had reheated the coffee substitute and left a mug of it for Ryan on the table. Ryan took it to the chair by the window. The German rifle was leaning against the wall. Ryan made sure there was a cartridge in the chamber and it was on safety. Through the crack in the shutters he had a passable view of misty ploughed fields, a few bare trees, skimpy rows of dead-looking vines and the Arno River, from which the mist rose. Across the river, on a hill and shrouded in white, the rooftops of Poppi were just visible, dominated by the single turret of a fortress-like castle.

Traffic on the road between the house and the river was sparse and civilian, just an occasional truck as decrepit as the one that had brought them here, or an old model automobile. Ryan had been sitting at the window for almost an hour when a truck came grinding down the hill from the village in low gear, shifting into higher gear when it crossed the stone bridge. It was a German army truck, crammed with helmeted troops, their rifles slung. Past the bridge, at the intersection, the truck turned north, towards the house. As it passed, Ryan saw two skinny Italian civilians among the soldiers, standing and clinging to the cab to keep from falling. They were middle-aged, in shapeless drab suit-coats. One of them had a white bandage around his head.

Ryan went to the back room and woke Tenbrink, motioning for him to come. Tenbrink followed him, looking at his watch.

'What is this?' he demanded. 'It's not time for your relief. I'm not your relief, anyhow.'

'What does this Gianni look like? How old is he?'

'You got me up to ask me that?'

He cooled off when Ryan told him about the Germans and their two Italian prisoners. Neither was Gianni. Gianni was in his early thirties and of athletic build. Tenbrink thought the Germans had probably been combing the area for signs of Lupo and his band and had swept up the two Italians in a routine check of Poppi.

'They like to bring someone back for their trouble,' he said. 'And they know some of the people in Poppi must be helping Lupo. Arresting a couple gives the rest of them something to think about.'

'Does anyone in Poppi besides Gianni know about us? If one of those two...'

'No,' Tenbrink said, insulted. 'What kind of operation do you think I run? And Gianni doesn't live in Poppi. Man his age, if the Fascist Republican Army doesn't get him, the Germans would for forced labour.'

He yawned and stretched with feline delicacy.

'Since I'm up, I'll stay up and finish off your watch,' he said. 'You look tired.' It was a taunt.

'I'm fine,' Ryan said pleasantly.

He brewed a fresh pot of coffee substitute and made four enormous salami and cheese sandwiches.

'Want one?' he asked. 'I'll take the window while you eat.'

'Not hungry. And if you expect to keep up with me, you'd better get accustomed to short rations.'

'A wise old sergeant once told me never miss a chance to fill my belly or empty my bowels.'

Ryan was eating his sandwich when from outside came the sound of a vehicle passing the little stone house, sliding to a stop and backing up. Tenbrink stood up and glued his eye to the crack as Ryan hurried to join him. It was an open Italian touring car driven by an Italian non-com. Two officers were in the back seat, one Italian, one German S.S. The non-com got out and walked toward the house. Tenbrink quickly and quietly pushed the shutters closed.

The padlock rattled and the soldier called out in Italian. An order came back in Italian from the car and he began kicking the door. It was made of heavy planks and did not budge. Tenbrink had his knife out and Ryan his pistol when Fincham came running lightly from the back room with Costanzo close behind. Ryan put his fingers to his lips. Fincham snatched up the rifle as more footsteps sounded outside. The two officers had joined the soldier. Conversation in German, then an order in Italian. Fincham positioned himself in front of the door, his rifle poised to fire when a target presented itself. Costanzo pulled him aside and put his mouth close to Fincham's ear.

'They're going to shoot the lock off,' he whispered.

Tenbrink stood to one side of the door and motioned to Ryan to stand on the other. He pointed to the door, to himself and to Ryan, indicating they were to take whoever entered. Ryan waved Fincham to the window and pointed outside. He did not have to tell Fincham that if their visitors got the door open Fincham was to fling open the shutters and cover whoever remained outside.

Two shots echoed through the room in quick succession. The second one tore through the planks and ricochetted off the stone floor with a whine to smash against the back wall. The padlock rattled as someone tried it, then another shot. They could hear the lock being pulled from the hasp. Ryan stood clear as a boot kicked the door and it flew open.

5

The S.S. officer stepped carelessly into the room looking down to return his Luger to its holster. The Italian officer was at his heels. The German stiffened when he saw Ryan's legs but before he could raise his pistol, Tenbrink's left arm wound around his neck and the knife drove beneath his ribs. At the same time, as the startled Italian officer fumbled at his holster, Ryan sprang at him. He pulled the Italian to him by the coat front and smashed him in the face with the elbow of the hand holding the .45 automatic. Simultaneously, Fincham flung the shutters open and covered the non-com with his rifle.

The two officers, German and Italian, hit the floor almost together. The non-com stared from outside, transfixed with surprise and horror, and did not seem to hear Fincham's command to raise his hands. Ryan stepped outside quickly and led him, unresisting, inside and shut the door behind him. Fincham closed the shutters.

The German lay on his side with his knees drawn up, eyes closed, each laboured breath a grunt. The Italian lay flat on his back, groaning and holding his face with both hands. Blood oozed through his fingers. The non-com stood perfectly still, his back pressed against the wall. He stared with glazed eyes from the men on the floor to Ryan's group. Tenbrink dropped to his knees beside the German. He wiped his knife on the German's trousers and put it in its sheath without looking at it; [the way officers sometimes did their ceremonial swords on parade to show off]. He lifted the German's eyelids with his thumbs and looked into his eyes a moment. The

German's only response was to keep grunting with each breath. Tenbrink felt the pulse in his neck.

'Goner,' he said, getting up.

Costanzo pushed him aside, turned the German on his back, straightened his legs and opened his coat, tunic and shirt. Each layer revealed more blood. Every time the German grunted it welled from his side.

The non-com did not move when Fincham patted him down for weapons. He was unarmed.

Costanzo looked up at Tenbrink and asked, 'Do we have any bandages?'

'Not for Krauts.'

'He's bleeding to death.'

'It's internal. You can't stop it with a bandage. I wouldn't let you if you could.'

The Italian officer sat up and mopped his smashed nose and lips with a white handkerchief that was rapidly turning red. Looking from Costanzo to Tenbrink with more curiosity than fear, and obviously not understanding English, he reached into his mouth with thumb and forefinger. He took something out and looked at it in distaste. It was a tooth.

Costanzo went to the packs standing against a wall and began opening one of them.

'What do you think you're doing?' Tenbrink demanded.

'Looking for bandages.'

'I told you we didn't have any for Krauts.'

Ignoring him, Costanzo kept unfastening straps. Tenbrink started toward him. Ryan stepped quickly between them, then knelt by Costanzo and held the pack open while the priest searched inside it.

'Leave that pack alone!' Tenbrink said. 'That's an order.'

Costanzo continued rummaging around in the pack. Tenbrink unholstered his pistol and took it off safety.

'I'm telling you for the last time,' he said grimly.

The Italian officer stopped mopping his torn face to watch them quizzically. The non-com had still not moved. He appeared nailed to the wall. Fincham raised his rifle lazily and pointed it at Tenbrink's back.

'I wouldn't do anything rash if I were you, old cock,' he said conversationally.

'You haven't heard the last of this,' Tenbrink said, putting the pistol on safety and returning it to its holster.

During the exchange the Italian officer started crawling stealthily towards the door. The non-com followed him with his eyes, the only part of him that was moving. The officer had almost reached it when Fincham was at his side, poking the end of the rifle in his ear. The officer shrugged and went to the middle of the room to sit on a chair.

Costanzo found a sterile pad, a roll of adhesive tape and a tube of antiseptic ointment. He went to the German, who was not grunting any more. He put his ear to the man's chest. He sat up and folded the German's arms across his chest. He turned to the other officer and asked if the dead man were Catholic.

'All that trouble for nothing.' Tenbrink said with a smile that bore no warmth.

'Protestante,' the Italian said.

Costanzo said the Lord's Prayer in German and crossed himself. The Italian officer did not take his eyes off Costanzo until he finished. Then he crossed himself, too.

'È un prete Lei?' he said. 'Tedesco? Italiano?' *You are a priest? German? Italian?*

'Don't answer,' Tenbrink ordered.

'Si,' said Costanzo. 'Sono un prete.' *Yes. I am a priest.*

'Dovrebbe vergognarsi di frequentare questi deliquenti,' the Italian officer said. *You should be ashamed of yourself, associating with these criminals.*

Tenbrink, who had been looking grim, laughed.

'Lei è quello che dovrebbe vergognarsi,' Costanzo snapped. 'Per indossare quella divisa fascista. Per aiutare Tedeschi.' *It is you who should be ashamed. Wearing that Fascist uniform. Helping the Germans.*

He wiped the Italian's nose and lips with the sterile pad and smeared the wounds with antiseptic ointment. The non-com said something, his voice a croak.

'He wants to know if he can sit down,' Costanzo said.

'Why not?' said Ryan.

Costanzo spoke reassuringly to the non-com, who sidled fearfully to a chair and sat down on the edge, his palms pressed to his chest, one on top of the other. Tenbrink had turned a chair round and was sitting in it looking pensive, his arms folded across the back.

'This may change things,' he said. 'I'll have to find out what they wanted here. Cut strips from a blanket and tie them to their chairs while I move the car.'

He opened the door a crack and looked in both directions before going out. Fincham went to the back room to cut up a blanket. Costanzo went with him and returned with a whole blanket. He covered the German's body with it. Outside, the car started up. Tyres crunched through dried grass, went around and stopped behind the house. Tenbrink's feet shuffled as he kicked dirt and grass to hide the tracks.

The Italians were tied securely to their chairs when he returned. He stood in front of the Italian officer and stared down at him. The officer stared back. The non-com watched them, hardly breathing.

'I'm going to interrogate these men,' Tenbrink said. 'In my own way. No one is to interfere. If anybody's squeamish he can go in the back.'

Costanzo looked at Ryan. Ryan shrugged. The priest sat down on a bench with his back to Tenbrink. Tenbrink went to the table for a sandwich, took a bite out of it and returned to the officer with the sandwich in his hand. He chewed the bite thoroughly and swallowed. He asked the officer a question in Italian. The officer clenched his jaw and said nothing. Tenbrink took another bite of the sandwich. He lashed out suddenly with the back of his hand, striking the officer across his blook-caked nose and mouth. Fresh blood flowed. The non-com gasped and looked imploringly at Costanzo, who had turned round at the sound of the blow and the officer's gasp of surprise and pain. The officer stared defiantly at Tenbrink.

'Stubborn type, isn't he?' Tenbrink said with a smile. 'I like stubborn types. It's no fun when they're co-operative.'

He repeated the question. The officer continued to glare at

him, blood dripping down his chin and on to his tunic. Before Tenbrink could hit him again, Costanzo was between them.

'That's enough,' he said.

'Ottavio, tell your bantam rooster to stop interfering before he gets himself hurt,' Tenbrink said, amused.

'You're wasting time,' Ryan said. 'The other man'll talk and you know it. All you have to do is ask him.'

'To hell with that. I want this snotty son of a bitch to tell me.'

'Sit down and finish your sandwich,' Ryan said, his voice hard-edged.

'You don't give the orders here!'

Fincham came over to stand beside Ryan, grinning in anticipation of a fight.

'So that's how it is?' Tenbrink demanded.

Ryan nodded and said, 'It would be kind of stupid to fight among ourselves, wouldn't it?'

'When this mission's over I'll settle with you,' Tenbrink said. 'That's a promise.' He sat down on the bench and took a savage bite out of his sandwich.

'Padre,' said Ryan, 'ask the sergeant why they kicked in the door. Did they suspect something in this house. Are they expected somewhere where someone might get worried and come looking for them.'

Costanzo spoke to the non-com. The non-com glanced fearfully at the officer, who was staring at him grimly. The non-com looked apologetically at Costanzo.

'Take him to the back,' Ryan said.

He cut the non-com's bonds with his pocket knife. The man got up, rubbing his arms and thighs. Costanzo said something to him and he followed the priest to the back room. They were gone only a few minutes. When they returned, the non-com would not meet the officer's eye. He went straight to his chair and sat down, ready to be tied up again.

'They stopped here because they were curious,' Costanzo said. 'They didn't suspect anything in particular. And they're not expected anywhere. The Italian officer was giving the German a lift to Perugia and they'd been talking about sneaking down to Rome for the night instead.'

'You believe that?' Tenbrink demanded.

'He wouldn't lie to a priest,' Costanzo said.

Ryan put the prisoners in the back room, bound hand and foot. He and Fincham took turns loosening the strips of blanket for a few minutes at a time to permit them to move around. Every time one of them went into the room, the non-com spoke to them in pleading tones. Ryan sent Costanzo in to see what he wanted.

'He wants to join us, whoever we are,' Costanzo said when he returned. 'The officer's been telling him if they get out of this he's going to have him shot.'

Tenbrink paid no attention to any of this, not sulking but simply ignoring the others, as if he had more important things on his mind. When they ate again just before dark he sat at the table with them but as far away as he could get.

Gianni came shortly after dark. He announced himself by scratching on the shutters with his fingernails and whispering, 'Carlo?'

Tenbrink let him in at the front door. They had blocked it with a chair because the padlock was broken. It was too dark to see what Gianni looked like. Tenbrink did not introduce him. He led him to a corner, where they conversed in low voices, then Tenbrink groped his way back to the table and said, 'Listen to me, everybody.'

The others gathered round.

'Gianni'll go across the road and wait,' Tenbrink said. 'We leave one at a time when the road's clear. Mario first, then Enrico and then Ottavio.'

'What about them and the car?' Ryan asked.

'Gianni'll come back and get rid of the body. The car too. Lupo's people will come down tomorrow night for the Italians. They may be able to trade them for the civilians the Germans took this morning.'

There was no traffic on the road. They all crossed in rapid succession except for Tenbrink. They squatted around Gianni and waited for him. After a while he came out of the darkness and said, 'Let's go.' Gianni led them across a level field to the river. They went along the river to the bridge, where Tenbrink stopped them and sent them skulking across one at a time, crouching behind its stone parapet.

On the other side, they set off once again along the river, Gianni leading, Tenbrink in the rear. Ryan fell back beside Tenbrink.

'You killed them, didn't you?' he said.

'You really didn't expect me to compromise a perfectly good hideout, did you, Ottavio?'

A road and train tracks ran along the other side of the river. A locomotive chuffed in the distance and laboured by going southward, blacked out.

'There's a fair-sized junction down at Arezzo,' Tenbrink said. 'Lupo'll hit it some dark night. We're taking him explosives.'

Fincham slid down the sharply sloping bank of the river and up to his knee in the chilly water. He scrambled back up swearing quietly.

'Clumsy ox,' Tenbrink said.

Ryan reached down to help Fincham back to level ground. His pack made him top heavy and he would have fallen when Fincham grasped his outstretched hand, had not Tenbrink grabbed him by the coat.

'Thanks,' said Ryan.

'Keep moving,' Tenbrink replied curtly. 'We haven't got all night.'

They turned away from the river to a dirt road leading uphill. There were scattered houses on one side of it. They kept to the other, slogging through thick, low vegetation. After half an hour they were in hilly, open country among fields and woods. The air grew colder. Rime was forming on the tall, thick grasses. The hills became low mountains and the going more difficult. Gianni slowed his pace. After a while he stopped and Tenbrink moved up to confer with him. Gianni went on alone. Fincham stamped his foot on the ground.

'Gone to sleep again?' Costanzo asked.

'If I don't get this bloody boot off soon I'll be solid chilblains,' Fincham said.

70

'Quiet!' Tenbrink ordered. 'We're in Lupo's territory.'

'Bugger Lupo.'

Up ahead, someone whistled.

'Come on,' said Tenbrink.

Gianni was waiting with another man. The man shook hands with Tenbrink and stood aside while they passed. They went single file through a brush-choked ravine. After a few minutes a metallic click on both sides brought them to a halt. Gianni said something and they were permitted to pass. The ravine opened out and they were on open ground again, climbing. The earth levelled off and they came to the ruins of a house, just visible in the darkness. A chimney rose spectrally among broken stone walls.

'Hold it,' said Tenbrink.

Gianni entered the ruins and vanished.

'Lupo's down there with the American officer,' Tenbrink told Ryan. 'A captain. Says he's Willard Ross.'

'Did you say Willard Ross?'

'Yes. He's a MIA Air Forces officer. We checked it out. There is a missing-in-action pilot by that name. You come with me, Mario and Enrico wait outside.' As they went into the ruins he said, 'If he's Grunow, just nod. I don't think he'll recognise you in that wig and moustache, but if he does let me handle it. O.K.?'

'It's your party.'

'Watch your step,' Tenbrink said, and vanished as abruptly as Gianni had.

Ryan felt his way to where Tenbrink had disappeared, the entrance to the ramp leading down into total darkness. Ryan reached out and trailed his hand along bare earth as he descended. After three cautious steps, he bumped into Tenbrink.

'Stand clear,' Tenbrink said.

Ryan stepped back. Hinges squeaked as Tenbrink lifted a wooden door set in the ground and a rectangle of feeble light sprang out of the darkness at his feet. The smell of Italian tobacco rose from the opening. Steps led downward between rough stone walls. Tenbrink went down them, saying, 'Let the door down behind you.'

Ryan descended backwards, easing the door down as he went. When it was back in place he turned around and continued to the bottom. He was in a cellar.

The cellar was dimly lit by candles stuck in wine bottles laden with drippings. Not counting Tenbrink, there were eight men in the room, all dressed in rough peasant clothes except one, who wore a German officer's leather coat and German paratrooper boots. He had heavy brows and cheek muscles and an air of authority. It was difficult to make out the shadowed faces of the others in the wavering light. Ryan moved a little closer to one who looked American, easing the pack from his shoulders as he did so. He looked at the man only casually and let his glance rove around the room. The man looked at Ryan, eyes narrowing, mouth slightly open. No one said anything. They were all watching Ryan.

There were three double-decker bunks knocked together from unpainted wood. Part of the floor was taken up by straw mattresses heaped with tangled German and Italian army blankets. Two German machine pistols and a Thompson lay on a plank table with benches on two sides. Boxes of ammunition were stacked under the table. In a corner were open sacks of meal, half a huge wheel of cheese, three one-gallon cans of olive oil and a broken wheelbarrow with loaves of bread in it. Some salamis and several strings of garlic hung from nails driven between the rectangular stones of a wall. The dank air reeked of tobacco smoke and old sweat.

Ryan finished his leisurely survey and deposited his pack on the grimy floor. Straightening, he worked his shoulders to ease them. The others continued to watch him, Tenbrink with mounting impatience, the American-looking one with a perplexed expression on his face.

Ryan removed his wig and tossed it on the table among the weapons. He peeled off his moustache and put it in his pocket, startling the silent partisans.

'What the hell!' Tenbrink demanded.

6

The American-looking one snapped to attention.

'Colonel Ryan!' he cried. 'I thought it was you, sir, but I couldn't believe it. Last I heard, you were in Switzerland.'

'Shut up, you moron!' Tenbrink grated. 'You want to advertise who he is?'

His warning came too late. Five of the partisans reacted as if a grenade had just come bounding down the steps. One of the other two did not change his expression. Ryan assumed he was Gianni, whose face he had not seen clearly before. His identity would come as no surprise to their guide. The other man, the one in the leather coat, was more interested in the reaction of his companions than in Ryan.

'As you were, Ross,' Ryan said. 'Glad to see you're alive. I knew someone who flew the kind of formation you did would get himself shot down.'

'It was flak, sir. Not fighters.'

'Welcome to the club.'

After momentary confusion, the five partisans surrounded Ryan, shouldering one another aside to be the first to pound his back.

'Colonnello!' they cried. 'Colonnello Ry-an.'

'Knock it off!' Ryan ordered, pulling free.

'I thought you enjoyed being a celebrity,' Tenbrink said sourly. The man in the leather coat was not enjoying the display, either.

'Carlo,' Ryan said, 'don't you think it's a good idea to send somebody up for our friends so Enrico can get his shoe off?'

73

Tenbrink spoke in Italian to the man in the leather coat, calling him Lupo. Lupo gave an order and one of his men trotted up the steps.

'Our friend is very jealous of his authority,' Tenbrink said to Ryan. '*He* tells his men what to do. Keep that in mind.'

Fincham came pounding down the steps, followed more cautiously by Costanzo. Without a word to anyone, Fincham flung himself on a bench and began tearing at his shoe-laces, swearing. By the time he had the shoe off and was massaging his foot, he had a sympathetic audience.

'Dentista,' said one of the partisans, kneeling and gently removing Fincham's damp sock.

'What does a bloody dentist know about feet?' Fincham demanded as the man began deftly manipulating his toes. 'Oh,' he said, leaning back and closing his eyes, 'that's lovely.'

Another partisan brought him grappa in a tin cup. He drank it down without taking a breath, though his eyes watered. The partisans were impressed. The dentist stopped massaging Fincham's foot long enough to fetch a jar of vile smelling, tarry salve. He smeared Fincham's toes with it and spoke to him in Italian.

'He said to keep your foot warm and stay off it as much as possible' Costanzo translated, his eyes mischievous.

'Are you listening, Carlo?' Fincham said.

Costanzo thanked the dentist. The partisans turned their attention to him for the first time. Before that, they had been preoccupied first with Ryan and then with Fincham. Costanzo's fluency in Italian intrigued them. They asked if he were American or Italian.

'Americano,' Costanzo said.

'That's enough,' Tenbrink ordered before he could say more. 'They already know more than they need to.'

'I take it our chap wasn't here,' Fincham said to Ryan.

'What I told Mario goes for you, too,' Tenbrink snapped.

'Righty ho, glorious leader.'

'Knock it off, Enrico,' said Ryan.

Lupo watched, missing nothing, not understanding the words but aware of the shadings. He gave an order. The table was quickly cleared of weapons and an iron pot brought steaming from a stove in the corner. The dentist passed wooden spoons to Tenbrink's group. Lupo indicated that they were to help themselves. Ryan, Costanzo and Fincham shared a bench, and Tenbrink sat on the other with Gianni. Lupo joined them, taking a place directly opposite Ryan. There were some socks on a string by the stove. The dentist hung Fincham's among them.

'Reminds me of my old batman,' Fincham said. 'Wonder if he can do as decent a cup of tea.'

'Dig in,' said Tenbrink, dipping into the pot.

Ryan and Fincham waited while Costanzo said grace in Latin. A buzz of comment rose from the partisans. Tenbrink swallowed his mouthful and wiped his lips with a handkerchief.

'Why don't you tell them your life story while you're at it?' he muttered. He took another spoonful and said in a louder voice, 'Delizioso,' adding in lower tones, 'Act as if you like it. Lupo loves flattery.'

It was pumpkin soup with a few stringy morsels of meat.

'Lovely,' Fincham said to Lupo enthusiastically. 'I'm sure it would do wonders for my foot if I could just dip it in the pot.'

Lupo smiled and nodded.

The soup needed salt and the meat was gristly but Ryan ate with a hearty appetite. He looked up to find Lupo studying him. He waved his spoon at the pot and said, 'Buono. Molto buono.' Lupo smiled again, tightly, and spoke to Tenbrink. Ryan heard his own name and 'Tedeschi.'

'What did he say?' he asked.

'Nothing important.'

'Mario?'

'He said the great Colonel Ryan was very successful with drowsy, unsuspecting German guards on a train. He wonders if you would be as successful with first-line troops trained against surprise attacks. Perhaps you would like to join him tomorrow night when he blows up the junction at Arezzo.'

Tenbrink glared at Costanzo.

'Tell him thanks, but I'd just be in his way,' Ryan said. 'And I'm sure he's much better at that kind of thing than I am. And tell him he ought to oil those hinges on the trap-door. One of these days the wrong person might hear 'em.'

'Don't you dare tell him that,' Tenbrink ordered. 'The part about the hinges. Lay off him, Ottavio. Understand?'

'Just being helpful. And he ought to police this place up. It's a mare's nest.'

Lupo's expression grew a shade less belligerent when Costanzo told him Ryan's reply to his invitation and he began speaking directly to Ryan. This time Tenbrink translated. The partisan leader was sorry Ryan was unwilling to join him in the attack on Arezzo. It was the most promising target in weeks. Lately there had been increased traffic through the town.

'Are the Germans pulling back?' Ryan asked.

Lupo said no, just the opposite. Everything had been heading south.

'Going where?' Ryan asked, greatly interested. 'Rome, does he think?'

Lupo shrugged. He did not know or seem to care.

After they had eaten, Tenbrink took Gianni aside. Ryan indicated with a nod that Costanzo was to listen in. Costanzo got out his breviary and, reading silently, drifted towards the corner where they were deep in conversation. The breviary caused another buzz among the partisans. Something Tenbrink said made Costanzo stiffen and look grimly at Ryan. The conversation over, Tenbrink and Gianni returned to the table. Gianni shook hands all round.

'He's got to get back to Poppi,' Tenbrink said. 'Let's all turn in. We've got a long way to go tomorrow.'

Tenbrink went up the steps with Gianni. The hinges squeaked twice as the door was raised and lowered. Lupo took off his leather coat and dragged an ammunition crate from under the table. He picked it up and pumped it up and down rapidly ten times. The partisans counted as he hoisted the crate and applauded when he put it down, breathing normally though with an obvious effort to do so. He gestured for Ryan to try lifting the crate as Tenbrink returned. Ryan picked it up and lifted it nine times. He sat down, wiping his brow and pretending to pant.

'Tell him he's too much for me,' Ryan told Tenbrink.

Lupo clapped Ryan on the back and felt his arm muscles, talking volubly. Tenbrink did not translate.

'He says you're the first man he's found as strong as he is,' Costanzo said, looking tight-lipped at Tenbrink. 'If you go out with him tomorrow night, he'll show you how to kill real German soldiers.'

There was an undercurrent of anger in his tone.

Lupo gave Ryan a cigarette and lit it for him with a German lighter. In return, Ryan gave him one of the last of General Sperling's cigars. Tenbrink watched, unsmiling.

'If the love feast is over, maybe we can get some sleep,' he said.

Ryan went up to relieve himself. Captain Ross, who had hovered near him all evening, followed. He kept a respectful distance until Ryan was ready to go back down.

'Sir,' he asked, 'are you hooking up with us?'

'Negative.'

'Can I go with you when you leave?'

'Captain, I'm damn proud of you for fighting Krauts instead of shacking up somewhere. But you'll do more good flying a P-38 again. You speak Italian?'

'I'm getting better every day, sir.'

'Maybe with help you can get to Switzerland. I'll talk to Carlo.'

'I'd appreciate that, sir.'

'If you make it, go to the Military Attaché in Bern. General Sperling. Tell him I sent you.'

Ryan separated a sheaf of lire notes from the thick packet in his coat and pressed them into Ross's hand.

'What's that, sir?'

'Lire.'

'I couldn't do that, sir.'

'Don't tell me what you can't do, Captain. You've got a better chance of making it if you've got lire. Use it for bribes and food.'

Back in the cellar, four mattresses had been placed side by side. Tenbrink and Fincham were already stretched out, sleeping. Costanzo was still up. He was waiting for Ryan and sat down beside him when Ryan sat on a bench to pull off his shoes.

'Cuhnel,' he said in a low voice, 'Tenbrink killed those Italians back at the house.'

'I'm not surprised,' said Ryan.

'He told Gianni to get rid of the three bodies and the car.' A faint smile touched Costanzo's lips. 'He also told him to get a message back to Superman that he was having problems with Ottavio but he could handle them and intended to complete the mission in spite of your attitude.'

'Fine. Nothing like having a confident leader.'

'He's not my leader. Not any more. Ah may stay here with Lupo.'

'I don't think you'd be happy with this crowd, Padre. Stick with us a little longer.'

Ryan was the first one awake in the morning. There was daylight in the cellar. The candles had been extinguished and the trap-door left open. There were still the same number of partisans but there were three new faces among them. The sentries had been changed while he slept. Captain Ross was among the three who had gone out. Despite the open trap-door the air was fetid, much like the barracks at P.G. 202 before Ryan ordered a thorough housecleaning after taking command.

Ryan got a can of olive oil and went quietly up the steps. He dribbled oil on the rusty hinges until the trap-door moved noiselessly. He went up the ramp and, after looking about carefully, out into the open. There was no visible sign of life, not even the sentries.

It was full light but the sun was still below the mountains through which they had come. He stood in the high meadow taking deep lungfuls of cold, pure air. Beyond the blackened ruins of the farmhouse, the meadow fell away precipitously into a valley through which flowed a stream, a trickle of silver in the distance.

'Sir?'

Ryan turned quickly. It was Ross.

'Sir, I just wanted to thank you again for last...'

'Captain, aren't you supposed to be standing guard?' Ryan demanded, cutting him off.

'Yes, sir.'

'Then get on with it.'

As Ross was heading back to the ravine, Ryan heard the far drone of an aircraft. Ross broke into a run and Ryan went quickly to the concealment of the ruins. He met Tenbrink coming up the ramp.

'What do you mean going outside in the daylight?' Tenbrink demanded.

'There's enough level ground out there to land gliders. Lupo know that?'

'You could have been seen. Hear that plane? It's probably Kraut, taking pictures.'

'Negative. It's one of ours.'

'Who says so? You can't tell from this distance.'

'Twin engine. Synchronised. The Germans don't synchronise theirs. Makes a different sound.'

Tenbrink closed his eyes and listened.

'I'll remember that,' he said. 'About gliders, we can't supply Lupo that way.'

'Not ours. Theirs. The Germans ever locate Lupo's hideout, they won't have to fight their way through the ravine. They can land troops by glider. Wouldn't need many men. And they're damn good at it. He ought to put in some stakes.'

'He doesn't like anything that's not his own idea.'

'Make him think it's his idea.'

'Damn it, Ottavio, you're not running this show!'

'You know something, Carlo? You're a hell of a lot like Lupo in some ways.'

Tenbrink reddened.

'Does Bern know about the heavy traffic moving south?' Ryan asked in a less challenging tone.

'Not that I know of. I intend letting them know. Tigre has a radio.'

'Another thing. Captain Ross isn't the world's greatest pilot, but he could do more good driving an aircraft than playing cowboys and Indians with Lupo. Can your people help him get to Switzerland?'

'Why should I do anything for you?'

'It's not for me,' Ryan said coldly. 'I just work here. Like you.'

He started down the steps.

'I'll ask Lupo to mention it to Gianni,' Tenbrink said, following.

In the cellar, Fincham was soaking his foot in a pan of hot water. Costanzo was reading his daily office. Lupo was watching the priest, his expression contemptuous.

'Lupo's a communist,' Tenbrink told Ryan. 'He hasn't got much use for priests. How did I ever let myself get saddled with one? Not that I've got any love for communists, either.'

'I wouldn't want my sister to marry one but when they're fighting Germans, I love 'em,' said Ryan.

Fincham dried his foot and applied some of the black salve. He put his sock and shoe on and tried his weight on the foot. The dentist watched anxiously.

'Buono, dentista,' Fincham said. 'Now, what's for breakfast?'

A partisan brought bread and cheese; another poured dried figs from a wicker basket. Lupo shouted for someone to bring a salami, saying men required meat, and cut five large rounds from it. Putting three on one side of the table and two on the other, he summoned Ryan to sit beside him. The partisan leader ate whole cloves of garlic with his meal. He slid some in front of Ryan, speaking earnestly.

'He says it prevents colds, purifies the blood and gives strength,' Costanzo translated. 'If you eat garlic, maybe you'll get as strong as he is.'

'I shouldn't doubt it,' said Fincham.

'It wouldn't be polite not to, suh,' Costanzo said with a grin.

Ryan ate a clove while Lupo beamed.

'Tell him I smell stronger already,' Ryan said.

Lupo laughed and pounded Ryan's back when Costanzo translated.

'He says the smell of garlic becomes a true man,' Costanzo said. 'As perfume becomes a beautiful woman.'

Lupo said something to Tenbrink, who forced a smile. Tenbrink was the only one at the table not enjoying himself.

'He wants me to leave you here to fight Germans with him,' he said. 'You are his brother.'

'You smell like brothers,' said Fincham.

'Then it shouldn't be a problem telling him what I said about gliders,' Ryan said.

'One would think an intelligent man would have learned Italian after five months,' Tenbrink said.

'He had nine hundred prisoners to look after,' Costanzo said curtly. 'Which he did without killing any helpless men.'

After breakfast, Tenbrink sat with Lupo and spoke with him for several minutes. Lupo listened carelessly at first, then with growing interest. Soon he was doing all the talking while Tenbrink nodded vigorously. Lupo summoned Ryan to join them. He said Carlo had raised the question of tactics if the Tedeschi dropped gliders. An interesting thought. Perhaps they should drive stakes in the meadow. Carlo had agree it was an excellent idea and informed him that Ottavio was an expert on the subject. Ottavio should feel free to make suggestions, and if Lupo found them worthwhile he might consider adapting them to his own requirements.

While Ryan was telling Lupo how to arrange the stakes in a pattern best suited to obstructing gliders, Tenbrink opened the packs and gave Lupo some of the explosives in each. Lupo protested. He wanted it all, and to hell with the other bands.

'Tell him he can capture explosives from the Germans,' Ryan suggested. 'The other bands may not have that capability. They don't have Lupo to lead them.'

'When I want your advice I'll ask for it,' Tenbrink replied, but he said something to Lupo that pleased the stocky leader and stopped his protests.

Lupo brought out some Italian uniforms. Tenbrink tried on an officer's. The tunic was short in the sleeves and would not button across the chest. A partisan, sitting cross-legged on a bench, ripped the seams and altered the tunic. Tenbrink folded it carefully and put it in a pack. He called Ryan, Fincham and Costanzo to him.

'We're pulling out,' he said. 'There's a rendezvous to keep outside Loro. It's only a couple of hours if we make good time. Enrico, if you can't keep up with that foot you'll have to stay here with Lupo.'

'I'll come along,' said Fincham. 'I don't fancy the accommodation.'

They walked single file, taking advantage of what cover presented itself. They only paused when they heard aircraft, crouching in bushes or in the shelter of ravines. Fincham developed a limp which grew more pronounced as they went on.

'I told you to stay with Lupo,' Tenbrink reminded him.

'Get stuffed,' Fincham said pleasantly.

Tenbrink signalled a halt at the bottom of a low hill. He dropped his pack and got binoculars out of it.

'Stay here,' he ordered, slinging the binoculars around his neck. 'Keep your voices down and no smoking.'

He went up the hill. Fincham and Costanzo sat down. Ryan removed his pack but remained standing, watching Tenbrink.

'How's the foot?' Costanzo asked.

'It's only the one bloody toe,' Fincham replied, unlacing his shoe. 'There. That's better.' He slipped the shoe off gingerly. 'If I can't get it back on, you'll have to carry me, Padre.' He pulled off the sock. The second toe was red shot with purple. He got out the black salve and rubbed some on it. 'Lovely stuff,' he said. 'When the war's over, I'll get the UK concession. I'll need a trade, with all those hungry mouths to feed.'

'You never said you had a family,' said Costanzo.

'Neither did you.'

Near the crest of the hill, Tenbrink got down on his belly and crawled the rest of the way. He lay propped on his elbows looking through the binoculars. A stone came bouncing down and struck Fincham between the shoulder blades. He looked up long and fiercely at Tenbrink.

'When we're out of this I'll have his ears,' he said. 'He's

82

harder to swallow than you are, Ryan.'

'You invited yourself along, Colonel. If you don't like his methods, there's always Lupo.'

'Correction,' said Fincham. 'He's exactly as hard to swallow as you are.'

Tenbrink came down the hill. Without a word he put down the binoculars and got into the Italian uniform from the pack.

'I won't be gone long,' he said. 'Enrico, I want that shoe on when I get back.'

He disappeared around the hill. Ryan picked up the binoculars and climbed to the top, crawling the last yards as Tenbrink had done. The hill overlooked fields, woods and a small river with shedding trees marking its course. In the distance, sunlight struck off the windows of a village. A huddle of farm buildings lay between the hill and the village, closer to the village. Ryan adjusted the binoculars. A quarter of a mile away, a covered Italian army truck was parked on a wagon road by the river. A soldier sat on the front fender, picking his nose and smoking a cigarette. Tenbrink was walking towards him.

The Italian slid off the fender when he saw Tenbrink. He dropped the cigarette and, when Tenbrink drew near, knocked his heels together and raised his arm in a Fascist salute. Instead of returning the salute, Tenbrink sprang at him and bore him to the ground. After a moment Tenbrink got up and carefully brushed dirt from his trousers. The soldier lay flat on his back, motionless, his limbs outflung.

7

Tenbrink went through the soldier's pockets as Ryan watched. He put one item in his own pocket and replaced the others. He stripped the corpse of uniform and shoes and carried it to the river, head lolling, limbs dangling. He tied a rock the size of a basket-ball to the torso and, swinging the body back and forth for momentum, threw it out into the river. He watched the widening circle of ripples for a moment and returned to the truck for the uniform and shoes. When he began walking towards the hill, Ryan climbed down and replaced the binoculars.

'See anything?' Fincham asked.

'Put your shoe on,' said Ryan. 'He's on his way back.'

Tenbrink came around the hill and dropped the uniform and shoes on the ground. He took out the booklet he had taken from the soldier and looked from that to Costanzo, nodding his head in approval.

'Close enough,' he said. 'Mario, get into the uniform.'

'No,' said Costanzo.

'I'm ordering you to.'

'Ryan put him in an enemy uniform on the train,' Fincham said. 'He did some things that went against his calling. I don't think he'd do it again even for Ryan.'

'I'm not Ryan,' Tenbrink said. 'And I say he'll put on that uniform.'

'What was that business back at the truck?' Ryan demanded. 'Why would you knock off one of your own agents?'

Fincham and Costanzo stared from Ryan to Tenbrink, Costanzo grim, Fincham merely quizzical.

'What big eyes you have, Ottavio,' Tenbrink said. 'I've said it before and I'll say it again, I'll tell you what I think you need to know.'

'What has our glorious leader been up to now?' Fincham asked.

'I'll decide what I need to know,' Ryan said.

Tenbrink threw up his hands in an exaggerated gesture of resignation.

'He was not one of my agents. He was what he seemed to be, an Italian soldier. He thought he was picking up an Italian officer with some black market goods. Gianni set it up.'

'Why do you want Mario to put on the uniform?'

'Looks better with an enlisted man driving if we're stopped. I'll be in the cab, though.'

'I supposed Gianni arranged that, too, getting a soldier that looked like Costanzo.'

'No. That was serendipity. In my business you learn to take advantage of luck.'

'Padre,' said Ryan. 'Put on the uniform. I promise you won't have to do anything against your vows.'

'Ah don't intend to,' Costanzo said with finality.

'Understand, Tenbrink?' Ryan demanded.

Tenbrink nodded with poor grace. Costanzo put on the uniform. If fitted him better than it had done its owner.

Tenbrink briefed them before they left the shelter of the hill. They were going to Leonessa, a drive of more than two hundred kilometres, where they would meet the guide who would lead them to Tigre.

'You do drive, don't you, Mario?' Tenbrink said.

'Yes,' Costanzo replied with a glance at Ryan.

'Are there mountains on the way?' Ryan asked.

'Yes.'

'How's the scenery?'

Costanzo looked embarrassed, Tenbrink incredulous.

'Scenery?' Tenbrink said. 'You won't be seeing any. I want that back flap closed at all times.'

Tenbrink had the papers of an officer in the Fascist Republican Army. If they were stopped, Costanzo was to keep his mouth shut and not present the soldier's papers unless they were requested. One knock from the cab meant that Ryan and Fincham were to get under the tarpaulin intended to cover black market goods. Two was the all clear signal. Three meant they were to come out of the truck ready for trouble.

There was nothing in the back of the truck but the tarpaulin and no place to sit but the hard floor. Ryan folded the oily tarp and they sat on it. It was not soft but it was less cold than the truck-bed. Patched canvas on a pipe framework covered the cargo space. It smelled musty. There was another odour, faint and tantalising.

'Coffee,' Fincham said, sniffing. 'What I wouldn't give for a proper cup.'

'Must be used for black market operations all the time,' Ryan said.

The motor responded immediately to the starter, ran smoothly in the warm-up and lurched forward in a series of jerks.

'I thought Padre could drive,' Fincham said, bracing himself.

'Not trucks.'

'I hope he improves before we get into the mountains.'

'Don't count on it.'

Fincham took off his shoe and tucked his sore foot in the crook of the opposite knee.

'How did Carlo kill the poor sod?' he asked. 'The one who brought the truck?'

'Broke his neck.'

'Enjoyed it, I dare say.'

'Seemed to.'

Ryan dragged the packs close and opened one of them. Fincham opened the other. They laid the contents out on the floor — a first-aid kit, explosives, detonator caps, coils of fuse, bars of chocolate, maps in an oilskin pouch, a leather bag containing a hundred gold British sovereigns, a German camera and film, an assortment of ID papers, extra clips for the pistols, coffee, tea, a carton of saccharin tablets, bars of soap, three pairs of heavy wool stockings, a dozen pairs of

86

women's silk hose and a well-cut man's suit, chalk-striped dark flannel with a Rome label.

'And what do you suppose he intends doing with these?' Fincham said, picking up the silk stockings. 'Enlist some lady agents?'

Fincham kept out a package of tea and a pair of wool stockings when they repacked. He took off his shoe and sock and smeared his toe with salve.

'When you go into business, what will you call it?' Ryan asked. 'Essence de Skunk?'

Fincham discarded his old sock and pulled on both new ones.

They wound along a mountain road, toiling up and down grades. Costanzo had trouble shifting gears but seemed to improve a little with experience. The truck climbed at an angle that sent a pack sliding towards the rear. It levelled off then started down. Costanzo had it in neutral, on the way to another gear. The truck picked up speed, still in neutral, as Costanzo fought to get it in low, gears clashing. It plummeted down, whipping and skidding through turns. Ryan grabbed a pipe supporting the top.

'Have the wind up, have we?' Fincham said.

'If you had any sense, you would, too,' Ryan said through clenched teeth.

The truck yawed but did not slow down as the brakes were applied. Fincham reached for a pipe. There was a thud and metal scraped against stone with a hideous clamour. A sudden long rent in the canvas top let in a gush of chill mountain air.

The truck slowed gradually, still grinding against stone. They came to a complete halt in a silence broken only by the steady ticking of the engine. There was no sound from the cab. Ryan lifted the back flap. The road rose behind them, deserted. The truck was jammed against a stone wall gouged and streaked with paint for yards at fender height. He jumped down and went forward, Fincham hopping behind him with one shoe off.

The driver's door opened slowly and Costanzo came out looking sheepish. He stumbled, pushed from behind by

Tenbrink. He whirled, fists clenched, then turned round again, lips compressed, and crossed himself as if in penance for his brief flash of anger. Tenbrink was right behind, his face flushed.

'You could have killed us all!' he raged. 'You said you could drive. If I hadn't grabbed the wheel...'

'Let's check the damage,' Ryan said calmly.

'If you've wrecked us, you blithering idiot...' Tenbrink stormed at Costanzo.

'You're talking to an officer in the U.S. Army, Captain!' Ryan snapped. 'And there's no need to get hysterical. Not before we know there's a reason to be.'

Fincham chuckled.

'You've been in my pack!' Tenbrink cried, noticing the wool stockings.

They went around the truck to check the damage. The right front fender was crumpled, bright metal gleaming where the paint was gone. The tyre was still inflated and the radiator appeared intact. Ryan squatted and looked underneath to see if anything was leaking. Nothing was. Tenbrink pushed him out of the way to have a look for himself.

'Captain Tenbrink!' Ryan said, straightening. 'Don't ever try that again.'

Tenbrink looked up at him, more composed now.

'Then keep out of my way,' he said. He studied the damage and said, 'Doesn't look too serious. I'll do the driving from now on.'

'I should hope so,' said Fincham.

'Get back in,' Tenbrink said. 'Mario, in the cab. Ottavio, pull the fender away from the tyre when I give you some room.'

While Ryan was freeing the tyre, a small bus came labouring up the hill. He crouched out of sight between the truck and the wall. The bus was half filled with Fascist Italian troops, their noses pressed to the window glass, their eyes on the truck. The bus shuddered to a halt with its fender almost touching the truck's. There was not enough room for it to pass. The driver got out and ran to the cab, shouting and gesticulating. The soldiers watched, enjoying the diversion. Tenbrink swung down from the cab, hands on hips, and looked down at the driver in silence with an amused, arrogant expression on his face. Then, just as silently, he reached out and slapped him. The shouting and gesturing stopped abruptly. The soldiers cheered.

Tenbrink leaned down towards the driver, inches shorter than he, and yelled at him, waving his arms. The driver saluted and returned to the bus amid catcalls from his passengers. The bus backed down the hill and stopped. Tenbrink stood in the middle of the road and guided the driver with hand motions until it made room for the truck to pass. Ryan slipped to the back of the truck and climbed aboard. Fincham had the canvas side up a crack, watching Tenbrink and the bus.

'Interesting chap, our glorious leader,' he said. 'Nerves of steel when there's real danger but loses his head over a silly pair of stockings.'

'Padre's driving will do that,' Ryan said.

The truck edged forward. A burst of cheers announced it had squeezed past the bus. They were on their way again. Cold air rushed through the tear in the canvas top. It grew darker and colder. Ryan and Fincham sat on the packs and covered themselves with the tarp.

'I had a driver once with a way of heating water on the manifold as we went along,' Fincham said reminiscently. 'I had a proper cup of tea whenever I wanted.'

It was night when Tenbrink pulled off the road and stopped outside Leonessa. He was going in alone to pick up their guide.

'If something happens to you in Leonessa, how do we find Tigre?' Ryan asked.

'That's a good question. Ask Mario to pray for my safe return. And hope he prays better than he drives.'

Ryan had dragged the tarp out of the truck. They huddled under it in the damp, pitch-black chill. After almost an hour Costanzo said, 'Cuhnel, do you reckon he's run into trouble?'

'He's in a warm room somewhere, eating and drinking wine and laughing his head off over us freezing our bums out here waiting for him,' Fincham said.

'We'll give him another half hour,' Ryan said.

Tenbrink returned a few minutes before Ryan's dead-line, bringing the guide with him.

'I trust you've dined,' Fincham said.

'There's hot soup for you,' Tenbrink said. 'Don't knock it over when you get it. And bread.'

The guide rode in the cab with Tenbrink. Costanzo sat in the back with Fincham and Ryan. He pulled off the Italian uniform and started getting into his civilian clothes. Ryan felt through the darkness until he felt the warm side of a metal pot. There was a tight lid on it.

'Let's have a light for just a second,' he said.

Fincham struck a match. Costanzo was shivering in his long underwear, pulling on a shirt. The rent in the top had been mended. The pot held at least two litres. Beside it was a net bag with three tin mugs and half a large round loaf of bread in it. Fincham shook the match out and lit another. Ryan took the top off the pot. A rich odour of cheese and garlic rose in a cloud of vapour. Ryan dipped out three mugfuls in the darkness and tore three large chunks from the half-loaf, which he distributed in the same way. The soup was hot and tasty, thick with tough macaroni and beans.

'Lovely,' Fincham said. 'I could almost forgive Carlo for being so beastly. You chaps realise this is the first pasta we've had in Italy?'

There had never been pasta in P.G. 202.

The road to Leonessa and beyond was level, with but few turns. The village was dark and silent as the countryside. They finished the pot of soup and most of the bread.

'You must have been hungry, Padre,' Ryan said. 'You forgot to say grace.'

'Ah said it to mahself.'

The truck stopped. Both doors opened and closed and Tenbrink said, 'End of the line, everybody out', not bothering to whisper. He did not introduce them to the man who had got out of the truck with him.

While he was slipping on his pack he said, 'Giorgio says it's only two and a half hours for a strong man. I presume we're all strong men. Don't anybody lag. It's tricky in places and we'll be in snow most of the way.'

They followed their guide by the sounds of his progress, walking in single file so close together that they sometimes trod on the heels of the man ahead. When Fincham's sore toe bumped a heel he swore under his breath but did not falter.

They were climbing almost immediately, among trees and undergrowth that rustled and plucked at them. Still climbing, with only an occasional detour through a gap, they reached snow. It grew deeper as they climbed, in spots crusted and slippery, in others so loose and yielding they sank to mid-calf. Fincham began limping and Costanzo to pant. Ryan eased his pack with thumbs thrust under the straps. The trees and undergrowth thinned and came to an end. They climbed for fifteen minutes up a steep, snow-covered slope. A voice called out a challenge in Italian. Everyone stopped in their tracks at the sound. Giorgio spoke with someone, conversationally, not keeping his voice low. The name 'Carlo' was passed.

A strong light came on briefly, taking everyone by surprise. They flung their arms in front of their eyes, dazzled. For moments after the light went off, a sensation of brightness persisted, fading into blackness even deeper than before. They climbed a few more minutes, blindly at first, before Giorgio called out a warning and they stopped again.

'This is the toughest part,' Tenbrink said. 'There's a ledge we've got to cross. Nothing on one side but thin air.'

His penlight flicked on and probed ahead. A ledge, two feet wide at its narrowest and scoured clean of snow by the wind, ran along a sheer rock face rising beyond the semicircle of light. On the other side was a black void. Their guide strode along the ledge as confidently as on a woodland path.

The light flicked off.

'I'd rather not have seen it,' Fincham muttered.

He and Costanzo inched along with their backs against the rock face. Because of the pack on his back, Ryan could not. He put one foot carefully in front of the other, feeling along the rough stone of the rock face with his hand.

The ledge ran along the brink a dozen yards or so. They were challenged again on the other side before another climb through snow. Tenbrink's penlight played over a rock face as sheer as the one at the ledge. Its beam found a triangular opening three feet wide at the base and three feet high. Giorgio crawled into it. Tenbrink snapped off his light.

'We'll have to take our packs off,' he said.

Ryan was already doing so. They entered the opening and crawled on hands and knees for a yard or two. There was a thump and a curse and Fincham said, 'Mind your head. It's a sharp turn.'

There was a sudden wash of light as Giorgio pulled aside a curtain at the end of a passage eight or ten feet beyond the turn. The passage was high enough for Costanzo to stand erect and for Ryan to walk slightly crouched. Its irregular walls and roof bore no evidence that any part of it had been fashioned by tools.

Beyond the heavy oilskin curtain lay a spacious cavern with a vaulted roof almost twenty feet high at its peak. Tenbrink and Giorgio were talking with a clean-shaven man cradling a German machine pistol in the crook of his right arm. Two dozen other men lay sleeping or looking up curiously at the newcomers from rows of neatly aligned straw mattresses on two sides of the cavern. None of them was Grunow. Scores of Red Cross prisoner of war parcels were stacked against another side.

Spare clothing hung uniformly from pegs driven into the stone in a straight line behind the rows of mattresses. A variety of weapons were side by side in a long, unpainted but well-made wooden rack. There were a dozen stools, a long table, a smaller one and a chair with arms, also unpainted and well-made. The stone floor looked newly swept. A small charcoal fire glowed in a brazier set in a fireplace hewn in solid rock. Two large cast-iron pots hung over the fire from metal arms. Steam rising from one of them went up and back. The fireplace was vented to the outside.

There was a small opening high up on one wall, covered by a square of oilskin. A row of foot-long iron rods, set vertically two feet apart in stone, led up to a narrow wooden shelf below it. Powerful binoculars hung by a leather strap from a spike next to the opening. Illumination came from two oil lamps with sparkling clean chimneys set in brackets at the height of a man's head. A half-dozen other lamps were spaced at uniform height around the cavern.

'Someone knows what he's doing.' Ryan said. 'I presume this is Tigre and it's his doing,' he added, indicating the clean-shaven man.

Tenbrink shook his head.

'Tigre's out inspecting his guards,' he said. 'Captain Turner isn't here, either. He's running some sort of recce down towards Rieti. That's south-west of here.'

'When's he expected back? Captain Turner?'

'Tomorrow afternoon. There's more hot soup if you want it, and what they call coffee.'

'Why not real coffee?'

'Ah, yes, you went through the packs, didn't you?'

Fincham, who had dragged a stool to the fireplace and removed his shoe, looked up and said, 'If you can't spare anything from your private stock...' He reached in his coat and brought out the package of tea he had taken and tossed it to Ryan. 'Tea all around, waiter. And mind it's hot.'

'The coffee in my packs isn't for our personal use,' Tenbrink said bitingly. 'The partisans can get more supplies for it than for lire.'

'Ah'll make the tea,' Costanzo said, getting up from the stool where he had flopped wearily. 'If somebody'll lead me to water and something to heat it in.'

He spoke to the clean-shaven man, who brought him a jerrican and a tin kettle with a bail on it. Costanzo poured water into the pot and hung it over the brazier in place of one of the iron kettles.

Ryan had a closer look at the sleeping partisans while they waited for the water to boil. Those who had woken up on their arrival all had their heads down again. The faces he could see were mostly clean-shaven, with just the stubble that heavy-bearded men had in the evening having shaved in the morning.

Some of the men had moustaches, neatly trimmed.

Tigre came through the curtain as Tenbrink's party was drinking tea at the long table, the clean-shaven man among them. He was a man of medium height, just a stripling, with keen, brown eyes and a lustrous, neatly trimmed brown beard covering much of his face. He looked oddly familiar to Ryan. Tigre's glance went first to the clean-shaven man. He barked out something that caused the sleeping men to stir and the clean-shaven man to put down his tea mug so abruptly that its contents splashed on the table. He snatched up his machine pistol and hurried to his position at the cavern entrance. Then Tigre saw Ryan. His mouth dropped open.

'Colonnello Ry-an!' he cried.

8

'Hello, Lieutenant,' Ryan said.

Tigre was Lieutenant Roberto Falvi, a member of the P.G. 202 staff who had been a friend of the prisoners. He had been boyish, shy, and eager to please. The last time Ryan saw him, the day the Germans moved the prisoners out, Falvi had cried and vowed to kill the camp's adjutant, a Major Oriani, who had betrayed the camp to them. The confident, hard-eyed man Ryan saw now bore small resemblance to the callow youth of two months before.

'Jesus H. Christ!' Tenbrink blurted. 'Is there any place you're not known, Ryan?'

'That can't be you, Bobby!' Fincham cried.

'Colonnello Fincham! Padre!'

Falvi rushed towards Costanzo, who was hurrying to him. The two men embraced. They moved apart to hold one another at arm's length, eyes glistening. Everyone was awake now. The men scrambled from their sleeping places to gather around their leader, but there was no shoving or loud talk as there had been with Lupo's band and they kept a respectful distance, not asking questions. Tenbrink looked on, no less disgruntled than he had been at Ryan's welcome in Lupo's hideout.

'How does he know you fellows?' he demanded.

'He was on the Italian staff at P.G. 202,' Ryan said.

'That means we're off again tomorrow,' Tenbrink said, scowling.

'Why?'

'If he was at P.G. 202 he'd know if Captain Turner was your Major Hampton.'

'Negative. Falvi wasn't in camp the day Hampton was.'

Falvi told his men who the newcomers were, crisply, as if he had modelled himself on Ryan, and sent them back to bed. After Giorgio had left to take the truck away and Fincham and Costanzo had turned in, he sat with Ryan and Tenbrink at the long table. He seemed interested only in Ryan, to Tenbrink's ill-concealed resentment.

'You've been busy, haven't you?' Ryan said, sweeping the clean, orderly quarters with a glance. 'You've done a hell of a job, Lieutenant. My congratulations.'

'I learn all from you, Colonnello,' Falvi said, beaming. 'I observe-ed the changes you made at du' cento due. And I have done as you ordered.' Looking a bit guilty, he added, 'With but one exception.'

'I've brought you explosives and radio parts,' Tenbrink said. 'Funds in gold and other things I think you'll find useful.'

'Don't lose your head, Carlo,' Ryan said. 'We may have two more stops to make.'

Tenbrink's jaw tightened. Falvi looked at him, puzzled.

'Thank you,' he said in a rush, after a moment of strained silence which affected Ryan not at all. 'Most for the radio parts. Our radio does not function.'

'So I assumed,' Tenbrink said. 'We couldn't raise you.'

'Explosives we take from the Tedeschi but always we have use for more. Have you brought medicines?'

'First-aid kits?' Tenbrink said. 'One.' He looked from the sleeping Costanzo to Ryan. 'What's left of it. One way or another we'll get what you need to you. Just make me a list.'

Falvi turned to Ryan, hesitated, and said, 'Colonnello, you told me to depart Domira without delay and forget what Maggiore Oriani had done.'

'Looks like you've done just that.'

Falvi shook his head.

'I could not. I could not leave him alive. You are angry for that?'

'It was stupid. To get one man you risked your chance to accomplish all this.'

Falvi was chastened, but only for a moment.

Looking Ryan squarely in the eye he said, 'But I *have* accomplished all this, Colonnello Ry-an.'

'The Lord takes care of fools and children,' Ryan said.

Tenbrink spoke to Falvi in Italian.

'Please, English,' Falvi ordered, lifting a pre-emptory hand. 'For Colonnello Ry-an we speak only English.'

Tenbrink stood up abruptly.

'You two must be anxious to discuss old times,' he said, smiling without warmth, eyes bleak. 'Far be it from me to stand in the way.'

He stalked from the table to a vacant mattress and lay down with his back to them. Falvi looked quizzically from the supine Tenbrink to Ryan. Ryan offered no explanation.

'Do you know why I'm here, Lieutenant?' he asked.

'To lead us against the Tedeschi, I hope.'

'Tell me about Captain Turner.'

'Molto coraggioso. Very brave. One of my best men. Why do you ask?'

'What does he look like? When did he join you? Have you ever personally seen him kill Germans?'

'I do not understand, Colonnello.'

'I'm not asking you to understand, Lieutenant. I'm asking you for answers.'

'He, how do you say, looks like, looks like an American.'

'You've got to do better than that. Padre Costanzo's an American. I'm an American. You *can* tell us apart, can't you?'

'More as the colonnello,' Falvi said nervously, more like the Falvi of old than the leader of a partisan band. 'Much more as the colonnello than the padre. But younger, I think.'

'Say on.'

'He came to me in the first month. A prigioniero escaped from a campo in the north.'

'Any identification?'

'Only his uniform, Colonnello. Prigionieri have no other

identification. As you know. You were prigioniero. But he knew every information about the campo. I questioned him most closely. What is the colonnello's interest in Capitano Turner? He is your friend?'

'Have you seen him kill Germans?'

'It is dark when we attack,' Falvi said, increasingly puzzled. 'But he has taken weapons from Tedeschi he has killed.'

'Has he ever gone off solo before?'

Falvi did not understand.

'Gone off by himself?'

'Once only.'

'And?'

'He returned with informations. On his informations we surprise-ed a guarding party and destroyed thirty metres of railway tracking and a small bridge.'

'He sounds O.K. But Grunow's shrewd enough to trade a few troops and a second-rate bridge to turn in a report.'

'Grunow? A report?'

'The German who claimed to be Major Hampton.'

The part of Falvi's face not covered by the brown beard paled.

'Don't look so worried, Bobby. Two to one it's not him.'

Falvi brightened at the use of his P.G. 202 nickname.

'We'll know tomorrow,' Ryan continued. 'Tell me, do you have an alternative way out of here? Not having an escape route at P.G. was one of my blunders.'

After the Germans took over the camp, Ryan had pushed work on an uncompleted tunnel, but they had been hustled out before it got beyond the wall.

'You made no mistakes, Colonnello. You were tricked.'

'Same thing.'

'There is no need here, Colonnello. The Tedeschi cannot find this place.'

'You found it. That fireplace draws. It must lead to the out-side somewhere along the line.'

'Si, Colonnello. A small opening.'

'I'll have a look when it gets light. Tell me more about it.'

Falvi explained that the cavern was the largest chamber in

an extensive cave system. When he was first brought to it by one of his early recruits, a carabiniere born and raised in the area, he had explored the system thoroughly. There were two passages leading from the cavern in addition to the one by which they had entered. The larger of the two, which petered out in a series of dead ends, was hidden by the stacked Red Cross parcels.

'They were for prigionieri, I know,' Falvi said. 'But after the Tedeschi took you away I thought I could make better use of them than the Tedeschi.'

'Couldn't be in better hands than yours, Lieutenant.'

There were dead ends along the route from the fireplace opening, as well, but if one knew what one was doing, one would eventually arrive at a small opening in a cliff face some ten metres above the mountainside.

Ryan nodded towards the narrow wooden shelf set high above the floor.

'That's a look-out position, I take it?'

'Si, Colonnello.'

'Do you keep it manned?'

'As long as there is light for seeing, Colonnello, and when there is a moon.'

'We were challenged twice coming up. How many men at each post?'

'One, Colonnello.'

'You think that's enough?' Ryan asked casually.

'Now that you are here, no, Colonnello. I will double the guard.'

Falvi called the interior guard to him and had him wake two men and send them out.

'Back up the line. I was told there was a lot of traffic moving south, Lieutenant. Has there been any unusual southward movement through your area?'

'Si, Colonnello,' Falvi said eagerly. 'Every night, by road and railway. Also, the Tedeschi take much of our people for labour. Mending roads and tracking. And what they mend, we destroy when possible.'

'Good. What are they moving? Troops, matériel?'

'I cannot say, Colonnello. All is closed or covered.'

'Any idea where it's heading?'

'I have been unable to learn, Colonnello. I am sorry.'

'You'd have found out if anyone could, Bobby. And never say you're sorry. "Yes, sir," "No, sir," and "No excuse, sir." '

Falvi smiled with a trace of his P.G. 202 boyishness.

'So I have heard you instruct your men in the campo,' he said. 'But not so gently as now.'

'Have you passed this intelligence along?'

'I'm...No, Colonnello. The radio does not function. Perhaps with the parts Carlo has brought.'

'We'll get on to that first thing in the morning,' Ryan said, getting up. 'Have somebody wake me at first light.'

'I will do so myself,' Falvi replied, springing to his feet. He hesitated and added, 'Colonnello, I congratulate you on the escape to Svizzera. Magnifico!'

'How did you know about it?'

'All know. It was reported on the radio.'

'Too bad. Lucky they couldn't show my picture.'

Ryan found an empty mattress, took off his shoes, undid his collar and went to sleep.

'Colonnello, Colonnello Ry-an,' whispered in his ear awoke him.

'It is morning,' Falvi whispered, giving him a mug of hot, sweet tea. 'If you have need of gabinetto, it lies beyond the parcels of the Croce Rossa.'

The wall of boxes was so stacked that a tier in the bottom centre slid out easily, revealing the entrance to a chamber just high enough to stand in erect. It smelled sharply of unslaked lime. Falvi had dug a latrine trench there.

One of his men was already working on a partially disassembled radio transmitter-receiver on the small table. The spare parts they had brought were neatly arranged beside it. The other men were stirring when Falvi led Ryan to the opening in the cliff face. They went in through the fireplace with a lantern after Falvi had dragged out the charcoal brazier with a metal hook and swung aside the kettle holders. Much of the way they could not walk erect, and in places they had to crawl. Passages branched off frequently but Falvi only once took a wrong turn. They were obliged to back out when it dwindled to a dead end.

The opening, letting in light and cold, fresh air, overlooked empty space rimmed with snowy summits. It was an irregular slit just wide enough for Ryan to twist his shoulders and thrust his head through to look down. There was a thirty-foot drop to a steep snow-field. Below the snow-field, the mountainside was clad with trees thrusting up from more snow. Ryan had lost all sense of direction in the branching passages. He asked Falvi if the opening could be seen from the approaches to the cavern entrance. Falvi assured him it could not. They were on the opposite side of the peak.

'Perfect,' said Ryan. 'Get a detail back here enlarging the hole right away. Big enough for a man to climb through. But don't cut it all the way to the outside. Leave a couple of inches of rock that can be knocked out in a hurry.'

'Si, Colonnello.'

Falvi, embarrassed that he had not thought of this himself, asked no questions.

Tenbrink was waiting when they returned to the cavern.

'What have you been up to, Ottavio?' he demanded. 'Why didn't you check with me?'

Ryan told him. Tenbrink thought it was an excellent idea but resented not having been included in the exploration party.

'Do you think we should mine the front entrance?' Ryan asked. 'You'll have to take care of it if we do. I don't know that much about explosives.'

'I'm surprised you admit there's something you don't know,' Tenbrink said, somewhat mollified.

Fincham had opened some Scottish Red Cross parcels and was cooking up a kettle of porridge. Tenbrink had laid out the contents of one of the packs on the floor and there was an aroma of coffee, real coffee, in the air. Costanzo was kneeling in a corner with half a dozen partisans. Twice that number of their comrades were looking on, some covertly, several with open contempt.

'You've got a lot of Communists,' Ryan said.

'They fight well,' Falvi replied. 'That is all that is important.'

'Agreed.'

Falvi went to the table where the partisan was still working on the radio. The man shook his head and went back to work. Falvi returned and gave an order. The men arranged themselves in open ranks. He led them in the same sort of calisthenics that Ryan had forced on the complaining prisoners of P.G. 202.

Fincham groaned.

'He's acquired all your bad habits, Ryan,' he said.

After breakfast, a steaming kettle of water was put on the large table and everyone dipped tin cupfuls from it for shaving. Fincham viewed this with irony, as well. He did not shave, as he had not done so since the journey began. He was starting to acquire a beard to match his moustache.

Ryan shaved and after being informed the radio still was not functioning, took a lantern and went through the fireplace to see how the work detail was going. There was room for only two men, kneeling. One had a short-handled sledge and a spike, the other a climber's axe. As Ryan looked on, the man with the sledge tossed broken rock out of the opening.

'No,' Ryan said.

He scooped up a handful of broken rock from the floor and showed them that it was to be taken back into a side passage. The two men, sweating despite the cold, nodded.

'Bene,' Ryan said. 'Molto bene.'

They grinned and wiped their sweaty faces. Ryan passed out cigarettes and said, 'Take five.'

They understood the gesture, if not the words, and sat back gratefully on their heels to smoke. Ryan went back to the cavern and told Falvi to relieve the diggers at half-hour intervals and send a third man to clear away the broken rock. Tenbrink was tinkering with the transmitter. The partisan who had been working on it stood behind him, looking over his shoulder.

'Anything?' Ryan asked.

'We can't get it operational,' Tenbrink said, shaking his head. 'It needs more than some new parts.'

'Lupo said the Germans were moving stuff south. Falvi confirmed it. How do we get word back?'

'It'll be done, Ottavio. It's not your concern, anyhow. The only thing you need to worry about is identifying Grunow.'

Leaving him to work on the radio, Ryan motioned for the look-out to come down from his perch and climbed up the iron rods to take his place. He scanned the terrain they had traversed in the dark through the binoculars. The ledge they had crossed was even more forbidding by daylight, dropping away hundreds of feet into a rocky gorge. Fresh snow had fallen during the night and lay unbroken from the summit down to distant woods. The evergreens were mantled in white and offered cover for anyone approaching the hideout. Among them, stands of leafless hardwoods were etched sharply against the snow. Snowy peaks formed an uneven horizon. Beyond the ledge, a partisan emerged from concealment and surveyed the woods stretching below him. Ryan climbed down and sent the look-out back to his post. He told Falvi about the sentry.

'Anybody down in the woods could see him.'

Falvi sent a man out to instruct the sentry to stay down.

Ryan checked the progress of the diggers regularly. Using fresh teams every half hour, the work was going rapidly. Fincham occupied himself tending his chilblain. He washed his foot, dried it gingerly and rubbed in salve. He fashioned a pad from gauze in the first-aid kit and folded it around the offending toe. Putting on his wool socks and shoe, he walked the cavern floor without limping.

Early in the afternoon Tenbrink took explosives, caps and fuse and began mining the cavern entrance. Falvi sent two of his men to observe how it was done. Tenbrink worked quickly, pausing only to explain to them exactly what he was doing. He concealed the charge in a fissure and wedged the fuse leading back into the cavern against the side of the passage, where it would not be disturbed by anyone going in and out.

While he was setting the charge, Falvi engaged Costanzo in

103

earnest conversation apart from the others. After some minutes of this, Costanzo approached Ryan and took him aside.

'Cuhnel,' he said, 'Bobby has asked me to stay on with him.'

'You think what he's doing is compatible with your vows?'

'It never seemed to bother you before,' Costanzo said dryly. 'He promised Ah won't be involved in any of that. Ah think Ah can trust Bobby better about that than some folks Ah've been involved with in the past, don't you, Cuhnel?'

'When did I ever ask you to do anything that wasn't absolutely necessary, Padre?'

'You could say Ah'll be a chaplain again,' Costanzo continued enthusiastically, 'and Ah'll be able to work among the people. Bobby says there's need of a priest. The Germans shot the one who used to visit the local villages and help escaped prisoners. And he's letting me have some of the Red Cross parcels to use for the needy.'

'You did some bargaining with young Bobby, didn't you?'

'Just a touch,' Costanzo said, grinning. 'Ah'm going to stay, Cuhnel.'

'That's why you came along, isn't it? I'll miss you, Padre.'

The look-out called from the observation platform.

'Someone's coming,' Costanzo said.

Falvi and the look-out exchanged a few quick sentences as Ryan hurried to Falvi's side.

'Two men,' Falvi said.

The look-out had been unable to see their faces but he was sure one of them was Captain Turner. Ryan had Falvi summon him down and took his place on the platform. It took him a moment to locate the men through the glasses. They dodged among trees and disappeared in hollows, one guiding the other. The one in front wore peasant clothing, the one following had a blanket draped around his shoulders with olive drab trousers showing beneath it. Ryan could not see their faces. They kept their heads down, watching where they placed their feet. They inched across the ledge, their backs to the cliff face. The second man let go of the blanket to steady himself with both palms against the rock face. The blanket slipped from his shoulders. He reached for it instinctively and would have fallen, had not the other man caught his arm and pulled him back from the edge as the blanket sailed down into the void like a kite that had broken its string. They rested for a moment while the second man regained his nerve before continuing their slow progress along the ledge.

A sentry stepped out of concealment and halted them. Ryan could see from their attitudes that the sentry knew the first man. The pair drew closer. The first man raised his head and looked directly at the observation port. Ryan adjusted the focus of the binoculars and brought his face in clear and sharp. Ryan looked down from his perch. Tenbrink, Fincham, Costanzo, and Falvi were all looking up at him, waiting.

'It's Grunow,' Ryan said.

Falvi struck his forehead with the heel of his hand.

'Imbecille!' he cried.

A feral, anticipatory smile touched Tenbrink's lips. He did not appear at all troubled by the knowledge that the Germans now knew all about Tigre and his band. Fincham looked grim. Costanzo sighed audibly. Falvi's men paused in their various activities, understanding that something important was happening but not knowing what. Falvi ordered them back to their duties with a harshness that surprised them.

Ryan climbed down and cut off Falvi's anguished self-recriminations saying, 'He fooled me, too, and I'm an American.'

Falvi sent the look-out back to his post with orders to keep his glasses on Turner's back-trail and see if he had led anyone to the hideout other than the American escapee.

'If he really is one,' Ryan said. 'He could be another plant.'

They sat at the long table discussing what should be done. Falvi wanted to shoot him, personally, the moment he stepped through the curtain. Fincham considered that a reasonable proposal though he would have preferred to do the honours himself if Ryan did not want to.

'Fair's fair,' he said. 'You're the one he made the fool of.'

Tenbrink and Ryan agreed that killing Grunow was out of the question, a position Costanzo endorsed with enthusiasm.

'We've got to find out what he has in mind for Falvi and his people,' Ryan said. 'If we can. I'm not sure we'll get much out of a cool customer like Grunow.'

'Leave it to me,' Tenbrink said with the same cruel smile he had displayed when told of Grunow's approach. 'If anybody can get it out of him, I can.'

'You didn't do very well at Poppi,' Costanzo said. 'Cuhnel, are you going to let him...?'

'You don't have to watch, *Father*,' Tenbrink said.

The look-out called down from his post.

'He comes,' Falvi said.

He got a machine pistol from the weapons rack and took up a position to the side of the entrance.

'Don't do anything stupid the way you did with Oriani, Lieutenant,' Ryan warned. 'Fincham, you and Padre stand over there where he won't see you when he comes in.'

He slid around on the bench so that his back was to the entrance. The partisans all watched the oilcloth curtain, knowing something dramatic was in the offing. The escaped American prisoner came through first. His face was sallow and pinched with fatigue under an olive drab cap and fuzzed by a dirty, wispy caricature of a beard. He wore no insignia in his grimy OD shirt. He stopped under the gaze of so many men, his mild brown eyes frightened, then took a hesitant step forward, unsure of his welcome, his smile furtively ingratiating.

Grunow was right behind him.

'Here's a new recruit for you, Tigre,' he said.

Ryan swivelled to face him.

'Good to see you again, Major,' Ryan said calmly.

Grunow stiffened and took a step back, his hand reaching instinctively for the pistol in his waistband. Falvi raised the machine pistol to cover him. The partisans exchanged startled glances. The American shrank back, looking apprehensively from face to face. Grunow smiled.

'Colonel Ryan,' Grunow said, just as calmly. 'So the rumours are true.'

'What rumours, Major?'

'That you'd been spotted in Italy. I should have listened.'

Tenbrink spoke to Grunow in German. A murmur rose among the partisans. Falvi silenced them with a word. The frightened young American stared open-mouthed at the OSS man.

'I don't believe we've met,' Grunow said.

'I'm Carlo.'

'Oh. Then I know you by reputation.'

'Good. Then you'll probably want to save yourself a lot of trouble by co-operating.'

'I think not. Colonel Ryan, I can't say much for the company you keep.'

'You're a cheeky bastard, I must say,' Fincham said, stepping away from the wall where he had been standing with Costanzo.

Grunow showed no sign of recognition but he did look thoughtfully at Costanzo.

'Stop me if I'm wrong, but aren't you the priest?'

'Yes,' said Costanzo. 'You may not care what Carlo does to you but Ah do. Ah'd appreciate it if you just tell him what he wants to know.'

'Really?' Grunow said mockingly. 'You did some terribly unpriestly things on the train, Major Klement said.' Klement had been commander of the train that Ryan took over. Ryan had booted him out of a boxcar on the run to the Swiss border. 'Still, I'm surprised to find you with a brute like Carlo. Or should I say Tenbrink.'

Tenbrink's eyes narrowed.

'You may have more to tell me than I expected,' he said.

The American looked uncomprehendingly from one to the other, thoroughly confused.

'It's all right,' Costanzo said soothingly. 'Come over and sit down.'

'Keep out of this, Padre,' said Ryan. 'Lieutenant Falvi, pat 'em both down.'

Falvi looked puzzled.

'Check them out for weapons,' Ryan said.

Falvi gestured and two partisans stepped forward to search

the two men. Grunow had only the pistol. The American was unarmed.

'Sit down, Major,' Ryan said, nodding towards the table. 'You too, soldier. On the other side.'

Grunow sat down on one side of the table, the American on the other. Ryan sat down opposite Grunow. After a moment's hesitation, Tenbrink sat down on the same side as Ryan with the American between them. Fincham sat near Grunow. Costanzo and Falvi remained standing, Falvi clutching the machine pistol.

'What's your name, soldier?' Ryan asked paternally.

'Maguire, sir,' he stammered, grateful for the reassuring tone. 'First Lieutenant James M. Serial number...'

'Where were you held?' Ryan interrupted.

'Poggio Mirteto, sir. When Italy quit...'

'Later. He's O.K., Falvi. Have you eaten today, Lieutenant?'

'No, sir. Sir, would you mind telling me what's going on?'

'Falvi, have someone get Lieutenant Maguire something to eat.'

Falvi rapped out an order.

'I could stand a bite myself,' Grunow said. 'And is that honest to God coffee I smell?'

'Quit trying to sound like an American,' Tenbrink said. 'You'll be lucky to have any teeth to eat with.'

'Make that dinner for two, Lieutenant,' said Ryan.

'Si, Colonnello.'

'You're a colonel, sir?' Maguire said, starting up.

'As you were,' Ryan ordered, waving him back down.

'I've had enough of your meddling, Ryan!' Tenbrink grated, half-rising, fists clenched.

Grunow looked amused. Tenbrink reached across the table and hit him in the mouth, knocking him backward off the bench. Maguire gasped.

'I'm afraid you've come at an awkward time, lad,' Fincham said.

'You pull something like that again and I'll have you tied up,' Ryan said coldly to Tenbrink.

Costanzo reached down to help Grunow to his feet. The German pushed him away and sat down on the bench again as if nothing had happened, not bothering to feel his mouth. Ryan gave him a handkerchief wordlessly. Grunow acknowledged the courtesy with a nod, pressed the handkerchief to his bleeding lip and took it away without looking at it to see how badly he was bleeding.

Tenbrink spoke savagely to Falvi in Italian. Falvi heard him out in angry silence.

'I take orders only from Colonnello Ry-an,' he said when the OSS man paused for breath.

'I'll cut you off, you fumbling idiot!' Tenbrink raged. 'You'll get nothing more from us, absolutely nothing!'

'He won't in any case,' Grunow said.

'Why do you say that, Major?' Ryan asked conversationally.

'We've decided to close Tigre down.'

'I can't believe this,' Tenbrink muttered.

'I have half a company blocking your escape. They'll be closing in before dark.'

'Poppycock,' said Tenbrink.

'Too late to save your tail, Major,' Ryan said. 'And we can stand off an army from here.'

'They have patience, Colonel. And I'm expendable. As we all are.'

'We'll see how philosophical you are when I get my crack at you,' Tenbrink said jovially.

'Lieutenant Maguire,' Ryan called to the young American, who was now eating ravenously at the small table, his eyes fixed on the large one. 'Any German troops follow you on the way here?'

Maguire choked down his mouthful and said in a strangled voice, 'No, sir. We did see a whole slew of Krauts off in the distance but they didn't see us.'

'My men,' Grunow said.

'Bull!' Tenbrink snorted. 'Granted they know about this place, but you're too smart to try to take it head on. You'd wait for Tigre to come out and then ambush him.'

'You do not give Tigre enough credit,' Grunow replied with a courteous dip of his head towards Falvi.

Falvi did not acknowledge the compliment.

A partisan slammed a bowl of food on the table in front of Grunow.

'No coffee?' the German asked.

'Bring coffee,' Ryan ordered.

Tenbrink looked disgusted.

'So,' said Grunow, 'we appear to have a stand-off.'

'Hardly,' Tenbrink said. 'The whole Wehrmacht can't save your skin now.'

'You're a man of intelligence and honour,' Grunow said to Ryan, ignoring Tenbrink. 'I'm sure I can convince my superiors that you and your friends are military personnel and subject to treatment under the articles of the Geneva Convention.'

'What's your proposition?' Ryan asked.

'You intend bargaining with the bastard?' Tenbrink demanded incredulously.

'Surrender to me and I promise you will all be treated as prisoners of war. Even Tigre and his men.'

Not only Tenbrink but also Fincham, Costanzo and Falvi all stared at Ryan as if they could not believe he was actually considering this. His impassive face offered no hint of indignation or rejection.

'I don't believe I'd go for that,' Ryan said thoughtfully. 'I tried being a P.O.W. and didn't like it much.' He looked at Fincham. 'Not the kind of company I'd pick.'

Fincham smiled and twirled his moustache. Everyone relaxed.

Grunow shrugged and said, 'I'd hoped you were a practical man. Well, it's your funeral.'

'Yours first,' Tenbrink said.

Grunow took a mouthful of coffee, sighed blissfully and began eating, gingerly, because of his torn lip.

'Lieutenant Falvi,' Ryan said, getting up, 'let's you and me sortie out and run a little recce.'

'Colonnello?'

'Let's go out and see if anyone's out there. The major's been known to stretch the truth.'

'I'm only a captain,' Grunow said. 'Politics. You know how it is.'

'I'm going with you,' Tenbrink said.

'Who'll mind the store?'

'I'll look after Jerry,' Fincham said eagerly.

'I want him in one piece when I get back. He hasn't outlived his usefulness. Yet.'

Ryan got the binoculars from Tenbrink's pack. He, Falvi and Tenbrink armed themselves with machine pistols and German grenades and left the cavern. It was bitingly cold after the relative warmth of the cave. The sky was overcast, with low clouds enveloping the heights in a fine mist. Falvi stopped at both sentry posts to explain the situation and caution his men to be especially alert. They did not bother with concealment until after they crossed the narrow ledge below the crest shielding the hideout from observation.

They went down crouching, slipping from cover to cover in hollows and behind hummocks. Ryan halted them frequently to pause for a careful scrutiny of the woods below them through the glasses. There was no sun to reveal telltale reflections from the lenses. They crawled across smooth snow to a patch of low, snow-laden vegetation at the brim of a rise overlooking a shallow, wooded valley. Ryan swept the trees below him with the glasses. There was a tremble of movement among them. He fixed on it and saw a uniform blending in with tree trunks and undergrowth. Then the pale blur of a face, featureless at this distance, beneath a whitened helmet. He quartered the area methodically, finding more troops, as difficult to make out as the first soldier.

'They're down there, all right,' he said.

'I don't believe it,' said Tenbrink, snatching the binoculars from him.

He adjusted the focus.

'I don't see anything.'

'Over there,' Ryan said, guiding the binoculars.

111

'You're seeing things,' said Tenbrink, standing up for a better look.

'Down!' Ryan cried, reaching for him.

There was a meaty thud. Tenbrink grunted, staggered back a half-step and dropped the binoculars. A sharp crack sounded in the woods.

'I'm hit,' Tenbrink said incredulously.

His knees buckled. Ryan grabbed him and lowered him to the ground.

9

Ryan picked up the binoculars from the snow and tossed them to Falvi, saying, 'Tell me if anybody heads this way,' and stretched Tenbrink full length on his back. 'Where are you hit?'

'In the chest, I think,' Tenbrink said calmly. 'Fool stunt, standing up that way. Sorry about that, Ottavio.'

There was a small greasy hole in the right breast of Tenbrink's coat. Ryan pulled the coat open. Underneath, Tenbrink's sweater was wet with a circular reddish-black blotch.

'A patrol comes,' Falvi said quietly, not taking his eyes from the glasses. 'Is it severe?'

'How many?' Ryan asked, pushing up the sweater and opening Tenbrink's heavy shirt. It was wet with blood. He unbuttoned the woollen underwear and spread it open. Where it was not bloody and bruised, Tenbrink's muscular chest was stark white and almost hairless.

'Three,' said Falvi.

'They must think he's alone,'

Tenbrink lifted his head to look at his wound.

'Lie still,' Ryan ordered, pushing his head down.

He wiped blood away with his hand. More welled out of a little hole with each breath. Tenbrink coughed. His lips were touched with glistening pink froth, as if he had been eating cotton candy.

'Lung shot, isn't it?' he said without emotion, wiping his mouth with the back of his hand. Ryan buttoned him up again and took the binoculars from Falvi. The three soldiers were

113

bunched, armed only with rifles and in no hurry, like hunters coming to pick up a rabbit.

'Let 'em get close, Lieutenant,' Ryan said. 'Wait for a cinch shot.'

'Such instructions are not necessary,' Falvi said.

'Don't stick around any longer than you have to.'

'I will be close behind you, Colonnello.'

Ryan slung his machine pistol and Tenbrink's over one shoulder, and Tenbrink over the other in a fireman's lift and started down the rise.

'Leave me,' Tenbrink said thickly. He was choking on his own blood. He cleared his throat and said more normally, 'Don't be a goddamn fool. I've had it.'

'Maybe not,' Ryan said, not breaking stride.

'Always the bloody hero, aren't you?'

He sounded much like Fincham.

Ryan went as quickly as he could with such a burden, trying to maintain a smooth stride and avoid jarring Tenbrink more than necessary. Tenbrink's breath gurgled but he did not groan or complain.

Ryan was climbing up the next slope when a burst of machine pistol-fire ripped behind them with a sound like heavy cloth tearing. The patrol had reached Falvi. Another burst, shorter. It was almost a minute before other weapons answered, all more distant. The Germans in the woods were firing. Three more spaced rifle shots rang out from a spot closer than the woods, but much too soon for any of the other Germans to have reached Falvi's hiding place.

'Falvi,' Ryan said reassuringly. 'Making the Krauts think he's got company. Hell of a soldier.'

'I'd rather he was a doctor,' Tenbrink said faintly.

'Shut up. Don't waste breath.'

Hurrying footsteps in the snow and a puzzling clatter sounded behind them as they neared the ledge. Mortar shells exploded in the distance. Ryan stopped and turned, ready to drop Tenbrink and unlimber a machine pistol. It was Falvi, festooned with weapons. He had brought the fallen Germans' rifles with him.

114

'They will not follow immediately, Colonnello,' he panted. 'They believe the hill is defended.'

'I heard,' said Ryan. 'You're a good man, Bobby. Can you manage these?'

He handed the machine pistols to Falvi who, delighted with the compliment, nodded and slung them over an arm. He followed Ryan, rattling and bristling with weapons. At the ledge, the sentries came out to assist. Falvi waved them off and sent them back to their posts as Ryan shifted Tenbrink from his shoulder to his arms. He carried him like an over-grown child as he edged along, back against the cliff face. The pink froth was building up around Tenbrink's mouth, the base coagulating and turning dark. His eyes were half-closed. He opened them and wiped his mouth.

'Are we on the ledge?' he whispered.

'No sweat,' said Ryan.

'If you lose your balance, let me go and look out for yourself.'

'Don't worry, I will.'

A rifle slid from Falvi's shoulder, clattered once when it hit the rim of the ledge and fell silently into space. Falvi swore in Italian. Ryan knew some of the words. He had never before heard Falvi use such foul language.

Safely past the ledge, Ryan shifted Tenbrink back to his shoulder and hurried up the long slope toward the hide-out. Falvi whistled and made a circular motion in the air with an arm. The two sentries came running from their positions and without a word took Tenbrink from Ryan, one under the arms, the other by the legs. It was not the first time they had carried a wounded comrade. Ryan relieved Falvi of a machine pistol and a rifle.

Padre Costanzo came out of the entrance and ran to meet them.

'Is it bad, Cuhnel?' he said.

Ryan nodded.

Costanzo walked beside Tenbrink, wiping his mouth.

'Are you in great pain?' he asked gently.

Tenbrink shook his head.

The sentries put Tenbrink down at the cave entrance and ran back to their positions. Ryan dragged the wounded man backwards through the tunnel. Everyone in the cavern was bunched near the front, waiting.

'Is he dead?' Fincham asked.

Tenbrink opened his eyes.

'Not quite,' he said. 'Give me time.'

Ryan and Fincham stretched Tenbrink on the long table. Costanzo stripped him to the waist. His torso was slick with blood and more was pulsing from the small hole. One of the partisans crowded around the table handed Costanzo a gauze pad from the first-aid kit and he began wiping Tenbrink's chest, being infinitely gentle in the area around the wound. The hole was in the centre of a bruise.

'What happened?' Fincham demanded.

'We ran into Grunow's people,' Ryan said.

'Grunow!' Fincham cried, a look of guilt crossing his face.

'You should have listened to me, Colonel,' Grunow said from across the room.

He was standing all alone, a machine pistol ready in his hands, smiling.

'He crawled under the covers to take a nap,' Fincham said. 'I forgot all about the sod in the excitement.'

Shielded by the men crowding around the table, Ryan reached stealthily for the machine pistol he had put down beside it. Grunow rapped out a command in Italian. The men spread out just as Ryan got his hand on the weapon, his thumb probing for the safety.

'I wouldn't do that,' Grunow said, his machine pistol swinging to cover Ryan. He was not smiling now. 'I'm afraid my generous offer no longer applies.' He shook his head in mock sorrow. 'Too bad. You would have been treated as military. Now...'

Ryan put the machine pistol on the table, releasing the safety as he did so.

'Don't be stupid, Grunow,' he said. 'You can't take us all.'

'No? Who'll be the first to jump me? You, Colonel Fincham? It was your blunder.'

'I'm considering it,' Fincham said grimly.

Grunow played the machine pistol back and forth across the ranks of shocked partisans. He was very sure of himself.

Tenbrink opened his eyes and propped himself up on his elbows.

'Amateurs,' he croaked.

Every head swivelled towards him, even Grunow's. They had all forgotten the dying man except Costanzo. And Ryan. The moment Grunow turned his head Ryan snatched up the machine pistol. He had never fired the German weapon before but had made himself familiar with its operation. He began firing as soon as he wheeled toward Grunow, even before the barrel was elevated. The first bullets struck the stone floor and ricochetted to the wall, from which they ricochetted again. Grunow had shifted his weapon when he shifted his gaze. He turned back towards Ryan at Ryan's first move but before he could fire, the middle of Ryan's burst skipped from the floor into his thighs. The end of the burst tore into his body as he fell and peppered the Red Cross boxes across the cavern before Ryan ceased firing.

Everyone was on the floor except Costanzo, who leaned over Tenbrink as if there were no danger. Tenbrink was supine again, eyes closed. Falvi and Fincham were the first on their feet. Fincham went to Grunow and knelt beside him.

'He's had it,' he announced. 'Nice piece of work, Ryan. For a flying type.'

'More than I can say for you,' Ryan said icily.

Everyone was on his feet now except Lieutenant Maguire, who lay in a ball with his head wrapped in his arms. The seat of his trousers was stained.

Ryan dropped to his knees beside him and said, 'Are you hit?'

Maguire turned his head toward Ryan, his face slack with shame.

'No, sir. I think I messed my pants.'

'Nothing to be ashamed of, Lieutenant,' Ryan said, patting his shoulder. 'Not when you've been running on nerve as long as you have.'

He looked up at the partisans. Those not clustered around Grunow's body were grinning at Maguire.

'Break it up!' Ryan ordered.

They knew what he meant. His tone was unmistakable. They joined the crowd around Grunow.

Falvi came over and said, 'You were superb, Colonnello.'

'Thank Carlo, not me. Bobby, can you get the lieutenant some clean drawers and pants and show him the latrine?'

'Cuhnel,' Costanzo called. 'He wants you.'

Tenbrink was pale as whey from belt to brow except for the livid bruise around his wound. Costanzo had kept him wiped free of blood. His lips moved but his words were inaudible. Ryan bent over and put his ear close to Tenbrink's mouth.

'I'm here, Carlo.'

'Get...him?' Tenbrink whispered, pink froth bubbling on his lips.

'Yes. Now we'll see what we can do for you.'

'Don't...make...me...laugh. Ryan?'

'Yes?'

'You're...O.K. Go...home...now. Contessa. Contessa... Luciana...di...Montalba. Rieti. She'll...help...you.'

'Who is she?'

Tenbrink's lips moved but no sound emerged. His lips stopped moving. Costanzo felt his neck for pulse. He sighed and crossed himself, lips moving in prayer.

He turned to Ryan and said, 'He was a Catholic, he told me. Fallen away.'

'No atheists in foxholes, eh, Padre?'

Costanzo shook his head.

'He said he wanted no Catholic mumbo-jumbo over him. But it's a dying wish Ah can't obey.'

The partisans gathered around while he performed the rites, even the Communists, though the latter did not cross themselves when he was done. As soon as the last word was said, Ryan called Fincham and Falvi to him. It was growing dark in the chamber. Two men went around lighting lamps. They cast a warm yellow glow.

'Lieutenant, your men know how to lay charges?' Ryan

118

asked. 'With trip-wires?'

Falvi nodded.

'Mine the ledge.'

'The instructions have already been given, Colonnello.'

'You know German ground operations better than I do. When do you expect 'em?'

'Tonight, Colonnello. Late.'

'Grunow said they were coming today,' Fincham said.

'He said a lot of things,' Ryan replied. 'They must know how tough this place is to approach. Falvi's right, they'll need the cover of darkness. Maybe Grunow was supposed to take care of the sentries after everybody inside went to sleep. Lieutenant, the mine'll stop 'em at the ledge for a while when they do come. By the time they get here we'll be long gone.'

Falvi cleared his throat.

'With a small force we are able to kill many Germans. And here we can withstand an army.'

'He who fights and runs away, lives to fight another day,' Ryan said. 'If we don't fool around, we can slip out the back door with everything we can carry. By the time the Krauts figure out what happened, you'll have a day's head start on 'em.'

'I do not like to run, Colonnello.'

'Call it a tactical withdrawal, then.'

Falvi went out to check on the mining operation and instruct his sentries. Ryan told Costanzo to send men back to break out the last few inches of rock at the end of the escape route.

'And tell the rest to eat a good meal and start packing.'

Lieutenant Maguire, who had cleaned himself and changed pants, was sitting alone in a corner too humiliated to face anyone.

'Maguire,' Ryan called. 'Go with the digging party and help clear away the debris. They'll show you where to put it.'

'Yes, sir!' Maguire said gratefully, scrambling to his feet.

The escape hole had been broken through and the men were finishing their meal when Falvi returned with the work party.

'I sent a man to scout the approaches, Colonnello,' he said.

'The Tedeschi had not yet left their positions.' He smiled. 'The charge is placed in the centre. We will catch many Tedeschi on the ledge.'

He gave some orders and the men began opening Red Cross parcels and stowing food and their gear in pockets, bags and rucksacks. They opened only American and Canadian parcels, ignoring the less richly-stocked British ones, taking Spam, sugar, chocolate, soluble coffee, canned fish and powdered milk.

A partisan was dismantling the radio.

'First chance you get, try to get it working again, Lieutenant,' Ryan said. 'Tell your contact Grunow and Carlo are dead.'

'He was a brave man, Carlo. I regret that I did not know him better.'

'You don't know how lucky you are,' Fincham said. 'But the sod was good at what he did.'

'And tell them about the traffic moving south,' Ryan said. He looked at the blanket covering Grunow's body. 'He knew what they were up to. Too bad we didn't have a chance to ask him.'

He and Fincham emptied the packs they had brought with them. Ryan put the civilian suit and accessories, some of the coffee and chocolate, all of the .45 clips and the silk stockings in one of them. Fincham smiled when Ryan packed the stockings.

'Think we'll have time for a bit of frippet, do you?' he asked.

Ryan took ten of the gold coins out of the leather sack and gave the rest to Falvi. He got one of the iron hooks used to hang a kettle over the charcoal brazier. When it was cool enough to handle, he fastened a rope to the end with the larger hook in it. He knotted the rope at eighteen-inch intervals and stretched it out on the floor in a series of equal loops. He paced off the length of one loop.

'It'll reach,' he said. 'Fincham, wedge the hook good and solid in a crack back there and drop the rope outside. But not so solid we can't shake it loose when we get down.'

'Right-o,' Fincham said, coiling the rope between thumb and elbow.

He looked at the table where Tenbrink lay, covered by a blanket, and to the corner where Grunow was.

'Half a mo',' he said.

He dragged Grunow's body to the foot of the table, straightened it and studied the effect with a satisfied look.

'I see you've read *Beau Geste*,' said Ryan.

'Not quite the same, old cock. A dog with a dog at his feet.'

He left. Falvi rapped out orders and the laden men followed Fincham through the fireplace, from which the brazier had been removed. Only Ryan and Falvi were left.

'I'll meet you outside,' Ryan said, picking up the end of the fuse leading to the charge Tenbrink had laid in the entrance.

'I will be the last to leave, Colonnello,' Falvi said quietly.

Ryan dragged the small table to the fireplace.

'After you light the fuse, pull the table over the hole behind you,' he said. 'We don't know what the blast might do back there.'

He took a last look at the chamber. The rack was stripped bare of weapons. All that was left in the hideout were the pillaged Red Cross parcels, the straw mattresses, the wooden furniture and the two bodies.

'See you outside, Bobby,' he said.

He crawled through the fireplace, carrying a lantern with him to light his way. He had gone only a few yards when he heard the muffled crump of an explosion. The Germans had reached the ledge. Moments later, he heard Falvi in the passage behind him. A gush of sound and warm, acrid air lashed him when the entrance charge exploded. Ryan waited to be sure Falvi was all right before continuing to the end of the passage with the lieutenant at his heels.

Fincham was waiting at the hole. As soon as he saw Ryan and Falvi he climbed out and disappeared. Falvi insisted that Ryan precede him out of the hole. Ryan did not argue. He put out the lantern and went down the knotted rope. He descended in three long drops, pushing off from the face of the cliff and letting the rope play through his hands as he fell, tightening his grip to slow his descent as he swung back towards the cliff to plant his feet and push off again.

Costanzo, Fincham and Maguire were clustered near the end of the rope. The partisans waited farther down the slope in disciplined silence. Falvi came down the rope hand over hand. Ryan told him and the others to stand clear and jerked the rope with a whipping motion until he dislodged the hook. He dragged it to the edge of the hole, then gave a hard yank to make it arch out and fall to the snow behind him. He wrapped the rope around the hook and gave it to Falvi. He told Maguire to join the men below.

'Lieutenant,' he said to Falvi. 'Does the name Luciana di Montalba mean anything to you?'

'The Contessa di Montalba,' Falvi said distastefully. 'She is a friend of the Fascisti. Why do you ask, Colonnello?'

'How far are we from Rieti?'

'Ten kilometres. Perhaps a bit more.'

'Can you spare a man to guide us there?'

'I had hoped you would join us, Colonnello.'

'It's time I got back to my regular line of work.'

'It is a pity. I will take you to Rieti myself.'

'Negative. You've got your men to look after. By tomorrow the Krauts will be over here. If you're lucky, they may think you're still holed up inside and you'll have more time.'

'As you wish, Colonnello.'

'Padre, do you still intend throwing in with the lieutenants?'

'Yes, suh.'

'I'd appreciate it if you'd go to Rieti with us. I may need an interpreter. You can come back with Falvi's man.'

'Ah'll stay with you as long as you need me, Cuhnel.'

They went down the slopes to join the partisans. Falvi got his men ready to move out and called one of them to him. After a brief conversation, Falvi said, 'He will take you to Rieti, Colonnello. His name is Bruno.'

'Thanks for everything, Bobby. And good luck.'

While Ryan and Fincham were shaking hands with Falvi, Maguire, who had been hovering nearby rushed up and said,

122

'You're not leaving us, sir?'

'I am.'

'Can I go with you, sir?'

'No. You stick with Tigre. Maybe he'll put you next to someone who'll help you get across the lines. If not, you're better off with him than on your own.'

He gave Maguire a sheaf of lire notes, saying, 'You may have to pay a guide.'

Maguire followed Falvi reluctantly. Fincham slipped the pack over his shoulders.

'I'll carry that,' Ryan said. 'What about your foot?'

'Right as rain.'

Falvi and his men set out in one direction, Ryan and his party in the other. Fincham had traded the German rifle for a machine pistol and taken Tenbrink's pistol and knife. Costanzo walked ahead with the partisan. He dropped back once to tell Ryan that Bruno said they would easily reach Rieti before dawn. Once out of the mountains, they would be on easy terrain.

'Ask him if he knows where to find the Contessa di Montalba,' Ryan said.

Bruno had never heard of the lady.

'Ask him if he knows anyone in Rieti he can ask.'

The guide did.

They had been walking almost an hour, with Fincham limping only slightly, when Ryan heard a sound behind them. He halted his party with a whispered command and sent Fincham to one side with Costanzo and the partisan while he withdrew a few steps to the other. They were being followed. Stealthy footsteps halted, then came towards them. Ryan kept low, waiting. A shape came out of the darkness, picking its way uncertainly. Ryan waited until it passed him, then sprang, his arm crooked to encircle the man's throat. The man cried out in fear just as Ryan was tightening his arm to strangle him. It was Maguire. Ryan released him.

'I thought I was a goner!' Maguire said shakily.

'I told you to go with Tigre.'

'Sir,' Maguire stammered, 'I thought...'

123

'Negative. You didn't think. I ought to leave you out here to freeze your butt off and maybe get picked up by the Krauts.'

Fincham, Constanzo and the guide had come over.

'Father...' Maguire implored, turning to Costanzo.

'Ah'm afraid Ah have more influence with the Lord than Ah do with the Cuhnel, Lieutenant.'

'Give him a boot in the bum and let him try to find his way back,' Fincham suggested.

'If he gets picked up he'll spill his guts,' Ryan said.

'Nothing for it but to cut his silly throat, then.'

Maguire gasped.

'Come on,' Ryan said. 'But keep your mouth shut and keep up. You're going back with Bruno.'

'Yes, sir,' Maguire said abjectly.

In another half hour they were out of the snow. They reached level terrain and walked across planted fields and through vegetable gardens. It was as if they had gone back a season, from dead winter to early fall. There were roads now, and dark houses. Bruno stopped and said they were near Rieti. He would slip into the town and wake his aunt who lived there. She would know where to find the contessa if anyone did. And his aunt could be trusted. The Fascists had killed her husband and the Germans had taken her sons for forced labour.

'Can we trust him?' Fincham said.

'Falvi trusts him,' Ryan replied. 'That's good enough for me.'

They settled down to wait in a grove of saplings. Maguire sat by himself a few feet from the others until Costanzo went over to join him. Bruno returned before anyone had time to speculate that he might have run into trouble. He had a long conversation with Costanzo.

'He promised to bring her coffee for helping,' Costanzo said. 'She doesn't live far from here.'

'What about the contessa?'

'She has an estate on the Turano River the other side of town. Bruno's aunt said she's a rich widow and entertains Fascist big-shots and high-ranking German officers. Cuhnel, are you sure you've got the right party?'

'That's what Tenbrink said. He's been right so far. Except about getting up when he should have stayed down.'

'We all make our little mistakes,' Fincham said. 'Except Von Ryan.'

Burno led them in a wide circle to avoid outlying dwellings and farm buildings. They took cover when a blacked-out truck convoy snaked along a road ahead of them. Ryan counted the vehicles. There were nineteen of them, grinding along as if heavily loaded. They ran across the road, came to another and turned to follow it, keeping to the fields. They crossed the road to a stone wall parallelling it. They followed the wall, keeping close to it. Their feet disturbed the gravel of a private road barred by double iron gates and disappearing into darkness between two rows of cypress trees.

'The river's at the back,' Costanzo whispered. 'Bruno says we have to get inside from there. And to be careful. She has a dog roaming the grounds.'

'I'm good with dogs,' Maguire said.

It was the first time he had opened his mouth.

They followed the wall to the end and then the one that joined it at right angles. It was a large estate and it took some minutes to reach the Turano. The wall stopped at the river bank, with enough room between the end and the water for them to feel their way around it without getting their feet wet. A dog barked. Fincham unsheathed Tenbrink's knife.

'I'm good with dogs, too,' he said.

The dog came snarling out of the night, eyes and fangs gleaming. Everyone except Maguire froze. Maguire dropped to his knees and held out his hand.

'Nice fella,' he crooned.

'He'll tear your throat out, you silly ass!' Fincham cried, advancing toward the animal with the knife ready.

But the dog had stopped snarling, fangs still bared, and was looking warily at Maguire. Ryan reached out and caught Fincham's sleeve.

'Come on, fella,' Maguire coaxed. 'Good boy.'

The dog inched forward and sniffed gingerly at the back of Maguire's hand.

125

'You keep your hand palm down so it's quicker to pull out of the way if they snap at you,' Maguire said.

He let the dog take a good long smell and very slowly stroked its muzzle.

'If they snap,' he said, 'it throws your hand off.'

He moved his hand slowly to the dog's ear and scratched where it joined the head. The dog sat down. Maguire worked his fingers under the collar and kneaded the fold of skin under it. The dog groaned in ecstasy.

'He's a Dobermann,' Maguire said. 'I like Dobermanns.'

'They seem to like you, too,' said Ryan.

Maguire, displaying confidence towards his companions for the first time, told everyone to let the dog smell them, slowly and one at a time. Everyone complied except Bruno, who refused to go near the animal despite Costanzo's reassurances. The dog sniffed each hand without acknowledging the owner, keeping its neck arched to help Maguire get at it.

'Now he knows you,' Maguire said. 'Just don't make any sudden moves at him.'

'Never fear,' said Fincham. 'What now, Ryan?'

'We can't barge in on her in the middle of the night. She'll have servants and we don't know where their sympathies lie.'

Ryan told Costanzo to ask Bruno if he could wait until daylight with them. Bruno said he could. He and Costanzo could stay with his aunt until it got dark again. They would need to sleep, anyhow, before starting out to catch up with Tigre. Tigre had told Bruno where to find him.

'And he hopes you have not forgotten his aunt's coffee,' Costanzo said.

They tramped the grounds, the Dobermann trotting along beside Maguire. Bruno kept the others between him and the dog. They blundered into a hedge and groped along it until they reached a gravelled path running through it. Leaves rustled, a twig snapped and Fincham swore.

'I'm in bloody thorns,' he said.

'We're in a garden,' Ryan said. 'We'll stay here until it's light enough to see.'

They spent four cold, uncomfortable hours behind the

hedge. When dawn came at last, it was cloaked by a mist rolling in from the river. They were in a formal garden, patterned with hedges. The thorns Fincham had caught himself in were roses with green leaves among the brown. There was a dry fountain in the centre of the garden. The garden was decorated with statues of nymphs and goddesses, almost life-size. Urns full of dry brown plants sat on the stone pillars where hedges intersected.

Ryan spread an opening in the front hedge with his hands and looked out at the villa. There were three storeys, solid yet graceful, with French windows on the lower floors opening on to a flagstoned terrace. The terrace was set with more statuary, cushionless chaise-longues, some uncomfortable-looking white wrought iron chairs and a round white wrought-iron table. Despite the season, the table was shielded by a large black and yellow umbrella on a pole thrusting up through its centre. The second-storey rooms had curtained casement windows and stone balconies. Stone flowerboxes, empty, lined the stone balustrades. There were lights on in two third-storey dormer windows, and in the left corner of the first storey, where the windows were smaller than elsewhere, a white wooden door with green trim gave entry.

Behind the villa and to the right of it, at the end of a gravelled drive, stood a squarish two-storey building of whitewashed brick with a windowless first storey. There were no lights on.

Fincham was whistling under his breath and rubbing his toes with black salve, Costanzo was reading his daily office and Bruno and Maguire slept, sitting back to back. Bruno's weapon was in his lap, the sleeping Dobermann in Maguire's.

As Ryan watched the villa, the white door opened and a balding man in shirt-sleeves, wearing a white apron over black trousers, came out, stretched and whistled. The Dobermann was instantly awake, pricking its ears. Its movements woke Maguire. He smiled sleepily, opened his eyes and looked about him, puzzled and with growing dejection.

'I dreamt I was back home,' he said.

Bruno woke at the sound of Maguire's voice and reached

instinctively for the weapon in his lap. He grinned when he saw Ryan and let go of the weapon. The man in the white apron whistled again. The Dobermann sprang to its feet and looked uncertainly from Maguire to the villa.

'Tell him to go,' Ryan said.

'Go on, boy,' said Maguire, pointing toward the villa.

The Dobermann loped through the opening in the hedge and across the damp lawn. The man in the white apron bent down carelessly and patted its head. They both went into the house.

'When you're finished, Padre,' Ryan said.

Costanzo nodded, read a moment longer and closed his breviary.

'This is what I want Bruno to do,' Ryan said.

The partisan was to slip back around the side wall to the road and then go openly to the front door and knock. He was to tell the servant who answered that he had a message for the contessa from her cousin Carlo and was to insist it was for her ears only. If the servant asked who Bruno was, he was to say he worked on one of Carlo's farms.

Bruno was gone almost half an hour.

'He's no doubt in the kitchen with his feet up, pinching cook's bum and having a smashing breakfast,' Fincham said.

Bruno did not look happy when he returned.

'The maid didn't want to wake her mistress,' Costanzo said. 'He had to put his foot in the door and threaten to go up and tell the contessa himself.'

Bruno kept nodding violently, as if he understood what Costanzo was saying and was affirming it.

'When the maid finally went, she came back in tears. The contessa was furious with her for waking her up.'

'And?' Ryan asked. 'What did the contessa say?'

'She never came down. She told the maid to send Bruno away, she didn't know anybody named Carlo.'

10

'That bloody Tenbrink!' Fincham said. 'Sending us off on a fool's errand.'

'Negative,' said Ryan, undismayed. 'He wouldn't do that. Either he wasn't her regular contact or she doesn't want the servants getting ideas.'

'What do you propose, then? I don't intend freezing my bum out here indefinitely.'

Ryan took two pairs of silk stockings from the pack and gave them to the puzzled Costanzo.

'This should get her attention once you get in to see her,' Ryan said. 'No matter how rich she is. They're scarce in Italy.'

'Me, Cuhnel?'

'You're slicker than Bruno. Too bad Tenbrink's civilian suit's too big for you. You could be Cousin Carlo. At least shave and put on the necktie. Tell whoever comes to the door you've got to see the contessa of grave importance. You're a lawyer or a doctor and you were sent by a Fascist big-shot. I don't have to tell a Jesuit how to be persuasive. When you see the contessa, give her the stockings and tell her to come out to the garden for an explanation. You can tell her you're a priest, but that's all.'

Costanzo shaved with ordinary soap and cold water from a canteen, wincing, and put on the necktie. It was brown silk with a diagonal gold stripe and a Roma label. Ryan had to tie it for him. Costanzo had not worn a necktie for so long that he had forgotten how. He slipped back through the garden and around the wall as Bruno had done.

The others breakfasted on Spam and big round Canadian biscuits. Bruno kissed his fingertips at his chunk of Spam and said, 'Delizioso! Cibo americano.'

'I'll bet he'd even like creamed chipped beef,' Maguire said.

Since his triumph with the Dobermann, Maguire had grown a little cocky.

Ryan kept one of their number constantly at the hedge, watching the villa. Fincham was there now, munching on a dry biscuit.

'I say, Ryan,' he said without turning around, 'do you remember how we soaked Canadian biscuits in water for a lovely fry-up at the cook-house? I'd fancy one now. What's this? Someone's coming out.'

Ryan crouched beside him. It was the houseman, smoking a cigarette. He had a cardigan over the apron now. He began taking down the black and yellow umbrella. The white door pushed open and the Dobermann stole out. The dog lifted its muzzle to sniff the air, then streaked for the garden. The houseman, folding the umbrella, watched it run. The dog pelted through the gravelled entrance to the garden and straight to Maguire. Maguire fed him a piece of his Spam. The house-man was staring at the garden. He laid the umbrella across the round table and walked towards it. Fincham crawled to the entrance and waited behind the hedge.

'Don't kill him,' Ryan said.

Fincham looked back over his shoulder.

'I'm not bloody Tenbrink.'

'Lieutenant,' Ryan ordered. 'Get that dog out of here.'

Maguire half rose and hooked a finger under the Dobermann's collar.

'Don't take him! Send him. Can you do that?'

'Sure. Sir. Go on, fella. Va via.'

The dog did not budge. The houseman was halfway to the hedge.

'Vattene a casa!' Maguire ordered with a severity totally uncharacteristic, giving the Dobermann's rump a shove.

The dog gave him a startled look and trotted away. He went past the houseman, who stopped to wait for him, and continued towards the house. The houseman looked uncertainly from dog to hedge and back at the dog, then turned to follow the animal.

Costanzo was gone longer than Bruno had been. When at last he came up from the river everyone went to meet him. Costanzo's expression told them nothing.

'Out with it, then,' Fincham said. 'Did you get in to see her?'

Costanzo nodded.

'What was she like?' Fincham demanded. 'One of those ripe Italian beauties? Did she admit she knew Carlo?'

'Ah never got a chance to ask. Cuhnel, she was cold enough to burn at first. She hadn't had her breakfast.'

'You told her you were a priest?' Ryan asked.

'Yes, suh.'

'Did it help?'

'Ah don't think she quite believed me,' Costanzo said with a grin. 'Ah expect she thought Ah was black market. The way her eyes lit up when Ah gave her the stockings. Ah told her there was more out back. And real coffee.'

'She's coming out?'

'Yes, suh. Wild horses couldn't stop her. Soon's she's had her breakfast. She said she'd buy anything nice Ah had.'

'But what was she like?' Fincham said. 'A real smasher?'

'Right handsome.'

'Suppose you let me deal with the lady, Ryan. You're apt to frighten her.'

Ryan did not bother to reply.

The sun slid higher in the pale, almost cloudless sky. The garden lost its chill. A french door opened and a slim woman stepped out on the terrace. She wore a broad-brimmed straw hat and loose sweater-dress in broad, merging bands of different shades of brown reaching below her knees. She walked towards the two-storey brick building without a glance towards the garden. She moved elegantly across the lawn, her back straight, not looking where she put her feet, like a model effortlessly balancing a book on her head. She disappeared from view around a corner of the building. When she reappeared

131

she was wearing heavy gloves and carrying a straw basket over her arm. She approached the garden.

Ryan sent everyone except Costanzo back to the shelter of an inside hedge. Fincham went grudgingly. Costanzo hurried to meet her when she came through the entrance. She stopped when she saw Ryan standing behind him at polite attention. Her eyes, clear, blue and alert, studied him without surprise or apprehension though it was obvious she had expected no one but Costanzo. She regarded Ryan with suspicion and faint distaste. Black hair showed beneath her hat. Her white skin was flawless and almost without wrinkles, though her slender neck showed a trace of crêpiness. She was in her late fifties at the youngest.

She spoke sharply to Costanzo in Italian.

'Tell her I am a friend,' Ryan said.

'That remains to be seen,' she said coldly in exquisite English. 'Who are you and what are you doing in my garden?'

'I am called Ottavio,' Ryan said with a small bow.

The social graces had not been overlooked in his West Point education.

'Ottavio, indeed. You are an American if ever I saw one. Leave at once or I shall have you arrested. And you,' turning on Costanzo, 'calling yourself a priest. You are also an American. I should have suspected as much from your atrocious accent. But I thought you were worse. A Sicilian.'

'You are the Contessa Luciana di Montalba?' Ryan asked politely.

'Your pronunciation is wretched.'

'I'll try to improve,' Ryan said as courteously as before. 'I was told you could help us.'

'How, and by whom?'

'Carlo.'

'That wretched name again. I know any number of Carlos, none of whom would presume to make such a statement.'

'Carlo from Switzerland, Contessa.'

Her shrewd eyes narrowed but nothing else in her face gave any clue to her thoughts.

'I know no Carlo from Switzerland.'

'I believe you serve the same cause.'

'I serve no cause but my own. I am rather notorious for that. Now leave before I have my butler telephone the authorities.'

'That would be unwise, ma'am,' Ryan said regretfully. 'They might learn things about you you would prefer they did not.'

The contessa studied him with greater interest.

'I have no secrets, Ottavio, or whoever you may be. And if I had, you do not seem to be a person who would betray them.'

'Not willingly, I assure you ma'am. But they are experts at extracting information. And I am not a strong-willed man.'

'I dare say. What is it you wish of me?'

'Only a name, and a place to wait.'

'I haven't the faintest notion what you are speaking about.'

'One of your contacts with the Resistance.'

'The Resistance? You pretend to know secrets about me, yet you are obviously unaware that my sympathies lie in another direction.'

'I know you're an agent of the Allies.'

'How utterly preposterous! But I would not wish to see you and this...this spurious priest shot. I will give you something to eat and a warm place to hide until tonight. Then you will be on your way before I change my mind.'

'If helping us interferes with your mission here, I apologise. But I'm afraid there is no other way.'

'Mission? I have no mission.'

'You have now, ma'am.'

The fine eyes narrowed again, the thin lips compressed and the patrician nostrils flared with rigidly-controlled anger. Her face quickly regained its repose though her posture remained stiff and challenging. Without warning she threw back her head and laughed, long, silvery peals of pure delight, teeth too white and even to be her own glistening in the sunshine.

'Oh! she cried wiping her eyes and catching her breath. 'But this is delicious!'

She thrust the basket, which held garden shears, at Costanzo, saying pre-emptorily, 'Fill it with flower stalks so I will appear to have been busy,' and, taking Ryan firmly by the elbow, propelled him towards a concrete bench.

'He really is a priest,' Ryan said, letting himself be thrust along.

'Forgive me, Father,' she said contritely. 'Ottavio will do it while I speak with him.'

'Ah don't mind,' Costanzo said, dropping to his knees and starting to clip brown stalks.

'Please use my gloves, in any case,' she said, taking them to him.

Ryan waited beside the bench. He spread his coat out on it for her to sit upon. She acknowledged the courtesy with a nod that indicated she had expected no less. She eyed him quietly, as if waiting for him to speak. Ryan maintained a patient silence.

'What are you doing in Rieti?' she demanded at last.

'Trying to leave it, ma'am. Where are our forces now?'

'By "our", I presume you mean yours?'

'Yes ma'am.'

'Somewhere in the south,' she said vaguely. 'I do not concern myself with such matters. When they come, they come.'

'I wouldn't have thought you were a fatalist, Contessa.'

'I am a survivor. And quite good at it.' She gave him a sly glance. 'Do you know what OSS means to an Italian?'

'Depends on the Italian, ma'am. To some it means friend. To some it means enemy.'

'How delightfully naive. It means "Opera Sistemazione Spostati". But I forget you do not speak Italian. "Welfare Organisation for the Repatriation of Refugees".'

She laughed again. Ryan joined her. Costanzo, crouched by a flowerbed, looked back at them, startled.

'You understand.' she said approvingly. 'Perhaps you are not so naive as I imagined. After the landings I found myself on the wrong side of the lines. It was most awkward, not being able to return to my home. So I did as many others. I presented myself to the Americans and said I burned with desire to free my poor country from the Fascist yoke. I must say my reception was astonishing. You democratic Americans are

134

overwhelmed by titles, are you not?'

'Yes, ma'am. Did I tell you how honoured I am to be sitting on the same bench as you?'

She looked at him shrewdly.

'It is just as well you were not one of those to whom I told my story. In any case, I was accepted with open arms and in less than one week was back in Rieti. Never dreaming, of course, that I would actually be called upon to do something. And now you appear. How tiresome. Exactly what is it you expect of me?'

'Put me in touch with someone who can guide me through the lines. And get a message through to Allied headquarters for me.'

'I would not think you required such assistance,' she said. 'You seem quite capable of anything.'

'Thank you. But if it's all the same to you, ma'am, I'd rather make the trip with somebody who knows the country and speaks Italian.'

'I know of no such person.'

She took off the wide-brimmed hat and turned her face to the sun, eyes closed. Her meticulously styled black hair showed no trace of grey, denying her age. And despite her age she was, as Costanzo had said, a handsome woman.

'They must have given you a contact.'

'No,' she said, without opening her eyes. 'Terribly inefficient of them, was it not?'

'They wouldn't have brought you back without somewhere to channel your information.'

'Do you believe a contessa would lie to you?'

'You lied to get here, ma'am.'

She opened her eyes and turned them on him, baleful but amused.

'You are no gentleman. My contact is, or was, in Roma. But I have never reported to him or replied to his inquiries. You can understand how awkward it would have been for me to do so.'

'Very awkward. But not as awkward for you as it would be if I were picked up.'

'You dare to threaten me?'

'Just advising you of the situation, ma'am.'

'Stop addressing me as ma'am. It does not suit you.' She rose and put on her hat. 'I will see what can be done.'

'I'd appreciate it, Contessa. If you make contact, tell him the Germans are building up to something down south.'

'I have no intention of attempting to make such a contact. If I help you it will be some other way.'

'We'd like to move on tonight.'

'Impossible.'

The contessa was giving a pary that night. Many important people would be there, Fascist officials and German officers of rank. She would be much too busy with arrangements to be of any assistance to Ryan. Tomorrow would be more convenient for her.

Ryan could not budge her. He asked her to keep her ears open for information about the large-scale German movement to the south. Where was the destination and what was the purpose?

'We do not speak of the war at my parties. We have more interesting things to discuss.'

She instructed Ryan and Costanzo to remain in the garage, the two-storey building, and to make themselves comfortable in the chauffeur's quarters. They were temporarily unoccupied.

'The poor man was picked up in Rieti and sent off to mend roads in the south before I got word of it. It will be a day or so before I have him back. Red tape, you call it.'

They were to remain in the garden until she signalled to them from the house by coming outside that no servants would be in a position to see them crossing the lawn.

'Enrico,' Ryan called. 'You can come out now.'

Fincham, oozing charm, his moustache twisted rakishly, came out from behind the hedge followed by Maguire and Bruno. The contessa clapped her hands to her face. Her rings sparkled in the sunlight.

'Mother of God!' she cried. 'How many of you are there?'

136

'Only two, ma'am,' Ryan said. 'The others will find their own way.'

Fincham's charming smile faded when he saw that the contessa was not a young woman. Bruno pulled his cap off and hugged it deferentially to his chest, realised what he had done, put the cap back on and scowled defiantly. Maguire looked down shyly at his broken shoes instead of at the contessa.

Ryan held out his hand as the contessa turned to leave. She ignored it. He stepped forward quickly and captured her hand. She was too startled to pull it back. He slipped off one of her rings, an emerald of some size, and dropped it into his pocket. For the first time he had truly surprised her.

'You will please return my ring,' she commanded.

'When we say good-bye. If you turn us in you'll have a hard time explaining how I happened to have it, ma'am.'

'You are unspeakable!'

'Yes, ma'am. And practical.'

She took the basket of clipped stems and the shears from Costanzo, saying, 'What is a priest of the faith doing in such company?' and left them.

'You notice how often Ah get asked that, Cuhnel?' Costanzo said.

Ryan watched through the hedge as she entered the garage and emerged without the basket. She walked to the house as regally as she had left it.

'Well, Padre,' he said. 'I guess you'll be on your way now. If you haven't changed your mind.'

'Ah haven't.'

'Maguire, you're going back with them.'

'Sir, I've been in Italy for almost a year. I want to go home. If you won't take me with you I'll just have to try it on my own.'

'That's an order, Lieutenant!'

'You'll just have to court-martial me then, sir,' Maguire said quietly, standing at attention.

'Fancy that,' said Fincham. 'Amazing what a victory over a dog will do for a man's spirit.'

Ryan's lips twitched but when he spoke his voice was brutal.

137

'I'll do just that, Lieutenant. And make sure you get back to stand it.'

Costanzo and Bruno prepared to leave.

'Just a minute,' Ryan said.

He gave Costanzo half his gold coins and lire and some chocolate from the pack. He opened a can of coffee and poured the contents into Bruno's pocket.

'Wouldn't be smart for your aunt to have an American can in her house,' he said in answer to Bruno's puzzled look. 'Padre, look me up when I get back north with my group. You may need a character witness.'

'Ah'll pray for you, Cuhnel.'

'Do you more good than me. But thanks.'

Costanzo looked back once. He waved. Fincham threw him a salute.

'Good man, that,' he said, crouching beside Ryan at the hedge, where Ryan was waiting for the contessa's signal

'Our best man,' Ryan replied. 'Present company included.'

'If you felt that way, you might have told him.'

'He didn't need it. Come on, there she is.'

They ran across the lawn, Ryan carrying the pack, Fincham limping slightly, Maguire holding himself back so he would not get ahead of the older men. The contessa, bare-headed, had changed her brown dress for a turquoise sweater. The high wooden doors of the garage were closed, as was a smaller door at the side. Ryan tried the smaller door. It opened easily on to steep wooden stairs between blank walls, one rough brick, the inner one brown-painted wood.

There was another door at the top of the stairs, also unlocked. It opened into a large, sparsely furnished room with a rich but worn carpet on the floor, apparently a cast-off from the villa, as were the tall chestnut-wood cupboard and a patched easy-chair. The other furnishings were a narrow brass bed, neatly made, metal gleaming; an ancient console radio, a plain chest of drawers and a small table piled with old magazines.

There was a crucifix on the wall above the chest of drawers and on the chest a plaster bust of the Madonna. The other walls were decorated with a profile poster of Il Duce and magazine photographs of Italian film actresses, including several of the same one, Alida Valli. Windows at the front and back were covered with blackout curtains.

Two doors in the side opposite the entrance opened to other rooms. One of them was ajar. Ryan put down the pack and looked in. It was a kitchen with a sink and one-burner stove. There was nothing in the cupboard but a single cup and spoon, an open packet of coffee substitute, a vial of saccharin and a cardboard box with almond cakes in it.

'Ryan,' Fincham called, 'have a shuftee!'

Fincham had found a bathroom behind the other door. It had a huge, white-enamelled cast-iron tub on clawed feet. A black rubber plug dangled from the spigot on a brass chain between handles marked F, for *freddo*, cold, and C, *caldo*, for hot. A dish held a sliver of dark, flinty soap. Fincham turned the C handle. Nothing happened immediately, then there was a gurgle, followed by a gush of brown water which slowly clarified and steamed.

'All the comforts,' said Fincham.

The closet bowl had a pull chain. There was a packet of slick Italian toilet-paper on the floor beside it. An open wall cabinet held shaving tackle, hair oil, and an array of partially filled cologne bottles.

Fincham began running a tub of water, adjusting the taps until the temperature pleased him.

'Shall we toss for first?' he said. 'The hot may be in short supply.'

'You go first,' said Ryan. 'You're the dirtiest.'

Maguire was going through the cupboard when Ryan went back into the bedroom.

'Sir,' he said, impressed, 'there's a regular chauffeur's uniform in here, with boots and everything. She really must be rich.'

'Colonel Fincham's taking a bath. You take one when he's done. And shave. You'll find what you need in the cabinet. You ever used a straight razor?'

'No, sir,' Maguire replied, fingering the straggle of soft

139

whiskers on his face self-consciously.

'Try not to cut your throat.'

Ryan pulled the front window blackout curtain aside just enough to peer out with one eye. The villa was visible from the window, and also the gravelled drive alongside leading from the garage to the gates between its twin rows of cypresses. A plump woman in an apron came out of the white door, shook a tablecloth and went back in.

Fincham was singing in the bath-tub. Ryan told Maguire to take his place at the window and went into the bathroom. Fincham was up to his chin, soaking.

'Knock it off,' Ryan ordered.

'Don't you fancy music?'

'I don't want anyone coming out here to find out who's being tortured.'

Ryan went out, got a bar of soap from the pack and threw it into the tub.

'Scrub up and get out,' he said. 'The lieutenant's waiting.'

'He may prove to be a problem.'

'My problem, not yours.'

'If we get through, will you actually put him on charges?'

'Certainly.'

'I wouldn't be surprised if that's why you let him come along, Von Ryan.'

Fincham came out of the bathroom in his long drawers, shivering. He had shaved his beard and slicked down his hair and smelled strongly of hair oil and cologne.

'I don't want any of that stuff on you when you leave,' Ryan said. 'They could smell you coming in the dark a mile away.'

'There's only one towel,' Fincham said. 'I'm afraid you'll find it a bit dampish by the time you have your crack at the tub.'

After he had dressed, Ryan put him at the window and went to the kitchen to make coffee from the pack. Though he was not fond of sweets, he ate one of the almond cakes while he waited for the coffee to boil. It was stale, hard and flavourless. He took cup and saucer to the bedroom and sat in the easy-chair.

'What a lovely smell,' Fincham said, turning round. 'You're drinking alone, I see.'

'Only one cup. And you had the first bath.'

'The contessa's had a visitor. In a small lorry. Cases of vino and baskets of provisions. How many live with her?'

'She's giving a party tonight.'

'Overdoing our welcome a bit, isn't she?'

'All the local Fascists and Kraut brass are coming.'

'If we had the charges we gave Falvi we could strike a blow for our side, couldn't we? I hope the contessa doesn't let anything slip about us.'

'Not accidentally, she won't. She's a cagey woman.'

Ryan took the window again while Fincham had coffee. The contessa came out in a close-fitting black lamb coat with matching hat and gloves. A large black purse swung from her shoulder. She came straight for the garage, not giving the second storey as much as a glance. She opened the garage doors and went inside. An automobile engine roared into life.

'What's that?' Fincham cried, starting up and slopping coffee into the saucer.

Maguire stood wide-eyed in the open door of the bathroom, the towel draped around his skinny hips, shaving cream on one side of his face and a bleeding nick on the other, the straight razor in his hand.

'The contessa's going out,' Ryan said.

The engine settled down to a smooth throb and a gleaming black Rolls Royce came backing out. Though not new, it looked in mint condition. The chauffeur's compartment was open, with right-hand drive. The contessa, looking tiny in the broad front seat under the huge steering-wheel, manoeuvered the car expertly until it was pointing towards the road, then drove off in a spurt of gravel.

'Do you suppose she's going to Rieti to turn us in?' Fincham asked.

Maguire gulped.

'And ruin her party?' said Ryan. 'Lieutenant, stick some paper on your face before you bleed to death.'

The hot water was gone by the time Ryan had the tub.

Maguire had left it scrupulously clean and wiped the basin dry with toilet-paper. The towel, neatly draped on the rim of the tub, was sopping. Ryan bathed cheerfully in cold water and, rummaging in the chauffeur's chest of drawers, found a flannel nightshirt to use as a towel. Maguire was at the window and Fincham was tucked under the covers of the brass bed, sleeping. Ryan told Maguire to get some rest and dragged the easy-chair to the window while the lieutenant stretched out on the floor.

There was another delivery — a bakery truck disgorging bread, rolls and pastries, the last unusual in wartime Italy — and much activity in the villa as servants scurried past the French windows. The contessa was gone an hour and forty-five minutes. Ryan timed her. After she had driven the car into the garage and closed the doors, her brisk footsteps, heavy for such a slender woman, sounded on the stairs. Fincham woke up and grabbed the machine pistol that lay beside him. Maguire slept on. Ryan shook his head at Fincham and went to the door. The contessa was standing there tapping her foot, a large, cloth-covered basket hanging from her crossed forearms.

'Are you going to take it or must I stand here all day?' she demanded.

Ryan took the basket. She followed him into the room. Fincham tucked the covers modestly under his chin and said, 'Excuse me for not getting up. I'm not dressed.'

Maguire sat up with a cry and a start. The coat with which he had covered himself fell away, revealing a pale, bony and hairless chest. He blushed deeply and covered himself again.

The contessa acknowledged neither of them.

'I agreed to two, only,' she said, fixing a stern gaze on Ryan.

'An unexpected change of plans, ma'am,' said Ryan.

'He is a mere child.'

'No, ma'am,' Maguire blurted. 'I'm twenty-two. At least I will be next month.' His voice trailed off self-consciously.

'That is still a child.'

She ordered Ryan to put the basket on the chest of drawers.

142

'I am sure you must be famished,' she said. 'I have brought you food and drink.'

'Very thoughtful of you,' Ryan said. 'Wouldn't it have been simpler to bring something from the house? Or were you in Rieti looking for our guide?'

'I am not trusted in Rieti. I dare say for good reason. It would have been too difficult for me to bring food from the house without the servants being aware of it. Now that I have demonstrated my concern, I will have my ring.'

'I'll need a better demonstration than a Christmas basket, ma'am. But we do appreciate it.'

She left without another word, not closing the door behind her. Ryan went to the window and watched her stride angrily to the house. Fincham whipped the cloth off the basket and poked around inside it.

'I say!' he cried. 'A roast hare. With rosemary.'

'Rabbit?' said Maguire. 'Ugh.'

There was also a roast chicken, polenta, crusty rolls, cheese, boiled chestnuts, tiny apples, and three bottles of wine: a lambrusco, a soave, and an asti spumante.

'She does lay on a smashing spread,' Fincham said. 'Pity we're not invited to her party.'

He carved the chicken and hare with Tenbrink's knife. The contessa had thoughtfully provided cutlery and napkins. Ryan said they could have one bottle of wine between them.

'Half the lambrusco and half the soave, then,' said Fincham. 'Red with the hare, white with the fowl.'

'I don't like wine,' Maguire said. 'Somebody else can have mine.'

'Good lad,' said Fincham.

They ate everything. Maguire refused the hare. When he timidly expressed a preference for the drumstick, Ryan gave him both legs and half the breast.

Ryan slept until the guests began arriving in chauffeured automobiles with dimmed-out headlights, the first one waking him when its tyres rolled across the gravel to within a few yards of the garage. Maguire was at the window.

'They're lining up all the way back to the road,' Maguire said. 'I can just see the headlights.'

Car doors slammed. Men and women called out greetings in German and Italian. The chauffeurs came round to the white door, which spilled light every time it opened. The German drivers, soldiers in smart uniforms, did not walk with the other chauffeurs.

No light showed anywhere else in the villa except for a vagrant gleam where blackout curtains gaped. An orchestra began playing — piano, strings, clarinets, and an accordion with a bass viol overriding all because its deep, thumping notes carried better across the lawn to the garage. As the evening progressed, laughter and loud voices floated across with the music.

Bellowed German suddenly split the night. The talk and laughter stopped and only the music continued. Then the talk and laughter resumed, in greater volume. From time to time the French windows showed rectangles of mellow light as German officers came out on the lawn to relieve themselves.

'Bloody swine,' Fincham muttered.

They had pulled aside the blackout curtain enough for all of them to look out of the window at once.

A French window opened and, instead of a German officer, framed a bare-shouldered woman in a long gown. She came out on the terrace laughing and looking back, leaving the door open. She ran towards the garage, still laughing. A German officer came reeling out. He stood there for a moment, looking into the darkness, then set out in pursuit of the laughing woman, calling to her drunkenly in Italian. She was halfway to the garage, looking back at the lumbering German and shrieking with laughter, when someone shut the door and the night enveloped them.

Ryan whirled, ran to the bedroom door on tiptoe and went silently down the steps. He put his ear to the door at the bottom. Light footsteps disturbed the gravel, then heavier ones. They emerged and stopped as the woman's voice cried out in mock terror only a few yards from where Ryan stood.

'Jetzt hab' ich Dich erwischt!' the officer cried. *I've caught you at last.*

144

'Non qui fuori,' the woman whispered. 'Fa troppo freddo.' *Not out here. It's too cold*.

There was a squeal and a grunt, and one set of faltering footsteps moved towards the door. The officer had picked her up and was carrying her. Ryan put his shoulder against the door, jammed an insteps against the second step and gripped the doorknob. He held it firmly in place against the German's twisting.

'Verdammt!' the German cried. 'Es ist verschlossen.' *It's locked*.

Heavy boots kicked the door. Ryan set his shoulder more firmly. Fincham came noiselessly down the stairs and put his back against the door next to Ryan.

'If he doesn't give up, step back when I tell you,' Ryan whispered. 'Open the door and I'll take him. You grab the woman, but don't kill her.'

'Non vale la pena.' the woman said. 'Ritorniamo.' *It's no use. Let's go back*.

'Eine kleine Tür hindert Helmut Kleber nicht,' the officer muttered. *A little door will not stop Helmut Kleber*.

There was a scuffle of gravel as he put her down. A heavy weight smashed at the door and the German grunted in pain and frustration.

'Get ready,' Ryan whispered.

He turned the doorknob.

11

'Kleber, Du ungezogener Mann,' a teasing voice called out. 'Was willst Du mit Magdalena?' *Kleber, you naughty man. What do you want of Magdalena?*

It was the contessa.

The officer muttered something blustery and sheepish and the young woman gave a small cry. Her footsteps fled across the gravel.

'Wenn Du versuchen wolltest, mich eifersüchtig zu machen, hast Du es geschafft, mein lieber Herr Oberst,' the contessa said coquettishly. 'So, jetzt musst Du wieder hereinkommen und mit mir tanzen.' *If you wanted to make me jealous, you have succeeded, my dear Colonel. Now you must come back inside and dance with me.*

When their departing footsteps had died away, Fincham said, 'Near thing, that. Bloody cool type, your contessa. Earned her ring back, I'd say.'

'Not yet.'

Maguire was waiting at the top of the stairs.

'What was that all about, sir?' he asked tremulously.

'Jerry wanted our digs for a boudoir,' Fincham said. 'The contessa sent him packing.'

The guests began leaving. When the front gates closed behind the last car, a terrace door opened and the Dobermann ran out. The contessa appeared on the terrace in a shimmering gown, a fur thrown carelessly over her shoulders, and looked towards the garage. She raised her right arm in what could have been either a gesture of victory or a mocking Fascist salute.

During the remaining hours of darkness, Ryan, Fincham and Maguire rotated between the bed, the floor and the window. They breakfasted on coffee, sharing the cup, and the tasteless almond cakes. The houseman and another male servant came outside straining under the weight of a long, gold-coloured sofa with a curving back and set it on the terrace where it could catch the full winter sun.

'A pound to a tanner someone was sick on it last night,' Fincham said. 'I wonder will she find a way to bring us breakfast.'

'You've had your breakfast,' Ryan said.

'That? It only gave me an appetite.'

The contessa did not appear until mid-morning, dressed smartly in a severely tailored glen plaid suit and matching Glengarry worn at a rakish angle and looking thoroughly feminine despite the mannish cut. A dark mink jacket was draped over her shoulders. The houseman was a deferential step behind her, balancing a wooden box on his protruding belly. They made directly for the garage.

'What's she up to now?' Fincham demanded.

Maguire ran to join them at the window.

'She sure is pretty for an old lady,' he said

The garage door opened, there were sounds below and the houseman returned to the villa. The contessa came up the stairs and rapped on the door. Maguire ran to open it. She smiled at him. It was the first time Ryan had seen her display any real warmth. She walked directly to the easy-chair and sat down. She took a cigarette from a flat gold case and held it between two fingers, American fashion. Ryan quickly struck a match for her. She accepted the light without looking at him. She inhaled deeply and held the smoke a moment before letting it trickle from her mouth.

'You,' she said to Fincham, not deigning to look at him, 'Englishman, go down and fetch the box you will find beside the motorcar. If you remain close to the wall, you will not be seen from the house. Mind you do so.'

'Mind I will, madam,' Fincham said, touching an imaginary forelock.

She looked at him as he left, the corners of her lips turning in the ghost of a smile.

'Come here,' she said to Ryan. 'I do not wish to shout.'

Ryan looked down at her, his knuckles on his hips.

'Exactly the way the little rospo postures.' she said 'Rospo means toad.'

'You surprise me, Contessa. I thought you were a good Fascist.'

'I doubt if anything surprises you. I am a good whatever it is advantageous to be. That is how one manages to reach the age of sixty-one and live well every day of it.'

'Sixty-one!' Maguire exclaimed. 'You're not that old.'

'I am, indeed, young man. But it is charming of you to think otherwise.'

'You were saying, ma'am?' Ryan prompted.

'My German friends were full of gossip last night, once they were full of wine.'

'Did they mention the matériel moving south?'

'No. They spoke of more interesting matters. It was most enlightening.'

There had been talk, she said, of an action only a few kilometres from Rieti. A locally notorious brigand who called himself Tigre had been trapped in his lair with his fellow ruffians but had somehow contrived a miraculous escape. The Germans had lost one of their best agents. An American agent had also died. Tigre and his men were now being hunted down mercilessly.

'They say it is only a matter of hours before they will be apprehended. But I do not suppose you are interested in such small talk.'

'I'm only interested in getting through the lines, ma'am. Are you doing anything about that?'

Fincham came in with the wooden box.

'Brekkers,' he said. 'Is madam joining us?'

'If you are at loose ends when this tiresome war is over, perhaps I can find a place for you on my staff. You appear trainable.'

'Thank you, madam.'

148

'That's enough, Enrico,' Ryan said. 'I'd appreciate it if you got to the point, Contessa. You've got something on your mind.'

'How kind of you to say that.'

Because of the trouble with the partisans, her guests had said, Rieti was now under tight surveillance. It would be impossible for her to find a guide there.

Ryan asked her casually if the sweep of Rieti had netted any suspects.

'If you are inquiring about the priest, put your mind at rest. No foreigners were apprehended.'

'What else?' Ryan asked.

'Such single-mindedness!'

Though Rieti was closed tight, she might be able to make inquiries in L'Aquila, forty or fifty kilometres to the south-east.

'We will drive there today and hire someone suitable,' she said.

'It's not that simple, ma'am.'

'Not for you, perhaps. But for a contessa. . .I intend getting rid of you as quickly as possible.'

She had Fincham lay out the contents of the box. An inner box held jugs of chocolate and hot milk, breakfast rolls and soft cheese. A tightly corked bottle of black liquid, rubber gloves, slender wooden sticks and cotton were in a smaller box. The carrying-box also contained a suit of clothes of the sort worn by Italian adolescents and a man's suit resembling a uniform or livery.

The contessa smoked another cigarette while they ate breakfast, showing neither interest nor impatience. When they were done, she instructed Ryan to remove his coat and shirt and go to the bathroom. She followed with the little box containing the bottle of black liquid and other paraphernalia. As she neared the open kitchen door she said, 'Is it possible that is veritable coffee I smell?'

'Yes, ma'am,' Maguire said quickly. 'Do you want a cup?'

'Bring it to the bath, like a good boy.'

In the bathroom, she sat Ryan on the toilet seat and draped

the still damp towel around his shoulders. She laid out the bottle, the cotton and, in a neat row, the wooden sticks.

'You mind telling me what this is all about, Contessa?'

'You look hopelessly American. Even more, German. I must make you as Italian as possible.'

She pulled on the rubber gloves, twisted cotton around the end of a stick, uncorked the bottle and dipped the cotton swab in it.

'Look at the ceiling,' she ordered.

The black, sopping cotton probed towards his left eye.

'What do you think you're doing?' he demanded, closing the eye but not flinching.

'I know precisely what I am doing. I am dying your eyebrows. And then your hair. You should feel flattered. It is what my maid uses for my hair, and hard to come by.'

'Your hair's dyed? It looks natural. Even with your blue eyes.'

'I sincerely hope yours will, as well. You should try flattery more often. You are better at it than one would have expected.'

Maguire brought the coffee in the cup and saucer, which he had carefully washed and dried. He would not look directly at Ryan, sitting on the toilet seat shirtless, having his hair dyed, though he was fascinated.

'Find yourself something to do in the bedroom,' Ryan ordered.

The contessa drank two more cups of coffee and smoked another cigarette while she dyed his hair. She did not apologise when hot ash fell on his nose.

'Wait a few minutes then dry your hair vigorously,' she said when she was done. 'With hair as short as yours it is nothing. Mine requires half the morning.'

She put everything back in the box and left him. Ryan looked in the mirror and grinned at his reflection. He was expressionless when he came out of the bathroom. The others were waiting. Maguire's mouth fell open and Fincham burst into laughter.

'Paesano,' he said. 'Speaka da English?'

'You will do nicely,' said the contessa, who was sitting in the easy-chair having another cup of coffee.

She finished it leisurely, put the cup down and got up.

'You will dress yourself in Guiseppe's uniform,' she said. 'And you, caro, in the suit of my great nephew. Englishman, see if you can stuff yourself into the dark suit.'

'I've got something better,' Fincham said.

He rummaged in the pack and brought out the civilian suit, scattering more of its contents on the floor. The contessa's eyes glittered at the sight of the coffee.

'I will have that,' she said.

'Certainly,' said Ryan.

The contessa said she would return in exactly half an hour. The servants would all be in the cellars conducting an air-raid drill.

'I have told them the Germans expect an air attack on Rieti at any time, and the Americans' aim being so notoriously inaccurate, bombs may fall even this distance from the town. You will be ready to depart as soon as I return.'

'I hope you know what you're doing, ma'am,' Ryan said. 'If we're caught, they'll shoot you with the rest of us.'

'I always know what I am doing.'

'Contessa,' Fincham said, 'you sound remarkably like someone else I know.'

'I don't think she ought to come with us, then,' Maguire said. 'We ought to wait till tonight and try on our own.'

'How thoughtful of you, caro. And how unlike my great nephew. But have no fear for me. Nothing will happen to anyone if you all do exactly as you are told.'

They dressed as soon as she had gone. The chauffeur was a big man and his uniform fitted Ryan tolerably except in the waist. There were braces with the trousers. He tied two back belt loops together with twine for a snug fit. The uniform was of grey gabardine, the trousers with a black stripe down the sides and the tunic with a high collar buttoning snugly at the throat. The shiny brown leather gaiters were meant for calves less muscular than Ryan's. They fitted tightly even when buckled through the first holes in the straps. The shoes were too small. Ryan found polish in the cupboard and shined his own to a gloss matching the gaiters'.

Maguire looked like a schoolboy in his suit. He kept going back to the mirror. It was the nicest suit he'd ever had, he said, except for the colour. It was brown and he liked navy-blue. His hair was long and, once coaxed into order with the chauffeur's brushes, added to his passably Italian appearance. The great nephew's shoes fitted, though they were a little narrow.

The most remarkable transformation was in Fincham. Everything fitted him perfectly. Except for his sweeping moustache, he looked like a prosperous Italian businessman of the ruddy-faced northern type. Ryan made him trim an inch from each end of his moustache, which he did with great reluctance, and brush it differently.

'You should have a hat,' Ryan said.

The contessa brought one with her when she returned, an expensive dark felt one with gold initials in the leather sweatband, and a youth's cap for Maguire. The hat was too large for Fincham. The brim sank down to his ears. Even the contessa smiled at the effect.

Fincham folded pages torn from the chauffeur's magazines into vertical strips and slipped them under the sweat-band. The hat rested properly on his head.

The contessa also brought top-coats for Maguire and Fincham. Fincham's had a fur collar and lapels, and a pair of fine black gloves in one of the pockets.

'Where did you get all this?' Ryan asked.

'I keep a wardrobe for my great nephew, on the chance that he may condescend to visit me. The other things...my guests are sometimes forgetful. The Englishman's coat is the property of an important Fascist bureaucrat; the hat belongs to a prince. He wore it rather more elegantly than the Englishman.'

A greatcoat came with the chauffeur's uniform, darker than the trousers and tunic, with frogging and a double row of buttons down the front and flaring skirts for easy sitting. Gauntlets reaching halfway up Ryan's forearms completed the uniform.

The contessa had the three of them stand in a row for her

inspection. She walked slowly down the line, chin in hand, missing nothing. She told Ryan to set his visored cap more squarely on his head. She shook her head and murmured to herself in Italian. The word 'Tedesco' was clearly audible. She straightened Fincham's tie. When she reached Maguire, she smiled fondly and touched his cheek.

'How like my own little Paolo,' she said. 'Though hardly so degenerate.'

Maguire, who was a good five inches taller than the contessa, blushed.

'Who's Paolo?' Fincham asked.

'My great nephew, of course.'

'Only a lad, then. And you say he's degenerate?'

'Italian boys mature rather early. Remarkably, their fathers never do.'

'Let's get moving before the servants come out of the cellar,' Ryan ordered.

'We will depart when I am ready to depart,' the contessa said. 'None of you speak Italian, I gather.'

'A few words here and there,' said Fincham. 'Not enough to get along.'

'I know some, ma'am,' Maguire said. 'I hid out with this Italian family for about a month after I...'

He stopped short and blushed again.

Fincham grinned and reached for a moustache tip that was not there.

'And they had a bella ragazza, right?' he said.

Maguire blushed more deeply.

'Perhaps there is a bit of Paolo in you after all,' the contessa said dryly. 'What is your name?'

'Ma...' Maguire began, stopping at Ryan's hard look. 'James, ma'am. Everybody calls me Jimmy.'

'I shall call you Paolo. It is more convenient. Listen carefully, all of you. If we are stopped, none of you is to say anything. Not one word. I will speak for all. If I address you, are to say only, "Si, Contessa." And in the Italian manner. Everyone, "Si, Contessa." '

She made a gesture like a maestro conducting an orchestra.

Only Ryan pronounced 'contessa' to her satisfaction at the first attempt. Maguire was hopeless.

'Paolo, you will answer, "Si, zia." You can say that properly, can you not?'

'I think so.'

He said it and the contessa mimed applause.

'Excellent,' she said.

'It means aunt,' Maguire said, proud of his knowledge.

'Indeed it does. You are very clever. Now, we go.'

Leaving out the coffee for the contessa, Ryan stuffed everything else except their weapons into the pack. The contessa wanted him to put away the weapons as well, but he refused. They had two .45s, the German machine pistol and Tenbrink's knife. He and Fincham tucked the pistols in their waistbands. Fincham belted the knife at his hip. Before they left, Ryan rechecked the rooms for signs of their occupancy. On the way down the steps, he asked the contessa if she spoke French.

'Of course,' she said. 'Why do you ask?'

'We'll use it in case of emergency. It's risky, but not a dead give away like English.'

The contessa was surprised he knew French.

'It is the language of diplomacy,' she said. 'German would seem more appropriate for you. A barbarian's tongue.'

In the garage, Maguire said, 'This is a thirty-seven limousine de ville, isn't it? I never saw one before, except in movies.'

'How clever of you to know, Paolo,' the contessa said.

'I'm up on cars.'

'I neglected to ask you if you drive, Ottavio. I assume you do. All Americans drive motorcars.'

'Can I drive, Contessa?' Maguire said eagerly. 'I never drove a Rolls before.'

'You will sit with me, Paolo. And you, also, Englishman.'

'Enrico's the name. I'll sit up front with Ottavio.'

'Certainly not. A gentleman riding beside the chauffeur?' she smiled wickedly at Ryan. 'And you will be much more comfortable in back. It is rather chilly today.'

Ryan put the pack and machine pistol in the sloping trunk under one of two travelling-rugs he found in it. The other rug he tucked around the contessa in the back seat. The courtesy took her by surprise but she did not comment.

There was a speaking-tube between the back and the open chauffeur's compartment. Ryan made several dry runs through the gears, the contessa giving him instructions through the tube. He started the engine and shifted smoothly at first try.

The contessa put the tube to her lips as he was backing out and said, 'Perhaps there will be a place for you as well as Enrico after the war.'

Ryan picked up the tube and said, 'Si, Contessa.'

The day was sunny but very cold. Fincham, sitting comfortably in the back seat with his overcoat unbuttoned, grinned at Ryan when Ryan got out to open the iron gates. Maguire reached for the door-handle when they stopped, as if to jump out and open them himself, but the contessa gripped his elbow firmly in a gloved hand. He looked apologetically at Ryan when Ryan got back in.

After Ryan had driven through and returned from closing the gates, the contessa instructed him to turn right. The broad, flat valley through which they drove was patterned with the green and yellow of crops and meadows and the brown of ploughed fields. Many trees still had their leaves. The mountains ranging along the west side of the valley had russet shoulders and tops, like those of southern California in summer. Those to the west, from which they had hiked two nights before, were clad in trees except along the snow-covered summits.

Rieti lay ahead, an unbroken mass of buildings in the distance from the heart of which a flat-roofed bell tower thrust upwards. A roadblock barred their way into the square outside the central part of the town, which loomed behind an ancient crenellated wall running along the intersecting road to the east. The roadblock was a wire-topped movable wooden barrier manned by two German privates and a sergeant in full battle gear. A personnel carrier, its motor running, and empty except for the driver and a soldier manning a post-mounted machine gun, was parked in the square. Ryan slowed down.

'Do not stop,' the contessa ordered, 'and left at the piazza.'

She looked straight ahead, ignoring the soldier who strolled to the middle of the road to take a stand in front of the barrier. When the Rolls continued to move slowly forward, the sergeant shouted something and the soldier got out of the way. He and the other private swung the barrier clear. The sergeant saluted as the Rolls passed. Ryan touched the brim of his cap in acknowledgment.

There were no young men among the civilians they passed, just women and a few old men and small children. There were scattered buildings on their left. On their right, the old wall blocked the view of the town. A German soldier standing by the wall gave the car a searching glance and looked away. The wall ended just before the railway station square, where there were many soldiers, both German and Italian. Across from the station, within the central part of the town, the buildings stood in unbroken blocks. There was almost no traffic in the narrow streets of the town or on the road. The wall picked up again beyond the square. Past the end of the wall the road curved around a two-storied, battlemented stone structure which had once been an entrance gate to the walled town. Beyond it was another roadblock.

It was the same sort of movable barrier they had passed earlier, but parked beside it was a motorcycle with a leather-coated German lieutenant sitting in the sidecar. He was drinking from a metal mess cup, something hot, judging from the gingerly way he sipped. Several civilian vehicles were lined up one behind the other beyond the barrier, waiting to be inspected. Ryan was obliged to stop. The officer looked curiously at the Rolls and got out of the sidecar, still holding the cup.

The vehicle at the head of the line, its inspection completed, started up. A soldier swung the barrier forward, leaving enough space for it to drive through.

'When it is through, drive on before the barrier is closed,' the contessa said quietly through the speaking-tube.

Ryan eased the Rolls into gear. The vehicle, a little Fiat Topolino, edged past the partially open barrier. As soon as it was through, Ryan angled across the road towards the opening. The officer shouted something.

156

'Ignore him,' the contessa ordered.

Ryan drove slowly, ignoring the officer. The officer dropped the cup and blocked the way. He stood with his hands on his hips, legs spread, facing the approaching car. Though his expression was challenging, he did not reach for the holstered pistol belted outside his long leather coat. Ryan stopped.

The officer walked deliberately to the car and, putting both gloved hands on the driver's side door, leaned toward Ryan and barked something in German. Ryan looked straight ahead. The contessa leaned across Maguire and let down the window. She spoke to the officer in a tone neither ingratiating nor demanding. He clicked his heels and went back to the window. The contessa smiled at him and mentioned her name and that of a General somebody, a German name, pronouncing 'general' in the German manner. The officer returned the smile, saluted and stepped back. He waved them on.

The Rolls bowled along an empty road. Eddies of cold air lapped at Ryan. Fincham's voice came through the tube.

'Bit brisk up there, old cock? Pity I can't relieve you. But you've the only proper costume.'

The valley narrowed. Beyond a loop of river the road pierced a small village, the stone buildings clamping it on both sides. There were no civilians out of doors. Beyond the village, distant mountains rose more than a mile high on either side of their route. The road climbed gently.

The engine faltered and a plume of smoke drifted from the exhaust. The Rolls bucked forward, the engine running normally for a moment, then strangling, before running normally again. The moments of normal running grew shorter and less frequent until, at last, the engine died and the Rolls spat a cloud of smoke from its rear. The car stopped. Ryan put it in neutral and set the handbrake. He tried the starter. The engine caught but died when he put the car in gear. Smoke billowed out behind them.

'Is there a fire?' the contessa asked, without panic.

'No,' said Ryan.

'Are we out of petrol?' Fincham asked.

'Impossible,' the contessa replied. 'Only yesterday it was

filled to capacity. Ottavio simply does not know how to handle a fine car.'

'It's the fuel pump, sir,' Maguire said.

He jumped out and ran round to the front of the car. Ryan joined him as he was lifting the hood.

'I think you're right, Lieutenant.'

Fincham, buttoning his overcoat, came up and peered at the engine.

'Lovely piece of work,' he said. 'We build the finest machines on the road. What seems to be the problem?'

'It won't run,' Ryan said.

The contessa let down the window.

'Do whatever must be done and let us be on our way. I must return before curfew.'

'I wouldn't think little things like curfews bothered you, ma'am,' Ryan said.

'I am not "bothered". But it would cause a tiresome delay and I have guests tonight.'

Ryan asked if there were tools. Of course, the contessa said, in the chest on the running board. Without being told, Maguire opened the tool-box and got out wrenches, pliers, and a screwdriver. Ryan held out his hand.

'Can I, sir?' Maguire asked hopefully. 'I've worked on cars a lot.'

'Just make it snappy.'

Maguire removed his overcoat and went to work. He obviously knew exactly what he was doing. A car driven by an Italian civilian came down the road. He grinned and honked his horn derisively as he passed the Rolls.

'The sod,' Fincham said.

'Better that than for him to stop,' said Ryan.

Maguire disassembled the fuel pump, putting the parts on the running board in precise order.

'Here's the trouble, sir,' he said.

The rubber membrane containing the flow of petrol had ruptured.

'Bad show,' said Fincham. 'What now?'

'I'll get the spare tyre, Lieutenant,' Ryan said.

Maguire nodded, equal to equal.

'It's not the tyre,' Fincham said, mystified. 'It's this bloody bit.'

'Paolo,' the contessa called. 'Do not soil your suit.'

'No, ma'am. Don't worry about your car. We can fix it.'

'I have every confidence in you, caro. But do it quickly.'

Maguire removed the ruptured membrane while Ryan dismounted a spare wheel. Together they got the tyre off the rim and removed the inner tube. Fincham watched, baffled. Ryan cut a section of the tube with his Swiss Army knife and, using the ruptured disc as a pattern, cut a duplicate with the scissors blade. He handed the new part to Maguire, who adjusted it over the opening where the old had been and eyed it judiciously.

'Perfect fit,' he said approvingly.

He forgot to say, 'sir'.

While Maguire was fixing the rubber disc in place, a motorcycle and sidecar bearing two Germans came up the hill behind them.

'Back in the car, Fincham,' Ryan said.

Fincham did so, unbuttoning his overcoat and suit jacket to make it easier to get to his pistol.

'Lieutenant, keep your head under the hood,' Ryan ordered.

The motorcycle drew close enough for them to see that the driver was wearing a helmet, the passenger a peaked officer's cap. The officer was the lieutenant from the roadblock at Rieti. The motorcycle wheeled to a stop by the side of the road ahead of the Rolls. The lieutenant climbed out of the sidecar and approached Ryan, tightening the pistol belt he had loosened for comfort.

12

He spoke to Ryan in Italian, condescendingly. It was a question. Ryan nodded and gestured towards the open hood, Maguire had gone rigid, his body bent under the hood at an awkward angle. The lieutenant stooped to look for himself and asked Maguire a question.

'Tenente,' the contessa called gaily from the open window.

The lieutenant straightened and went to her. Ryan looked his way once, swiftly, and bent under the hood next to Maguire.

'Keep working,' he said.

Maguire's hands were trembling too much for him to tighten the nut on which he was working.

'It's the cold, sir,' he said shakily.

'I know. It's even worse in the driver's seat. You're doing fine, Maguire.'

Maguire took a deep breath and let it out. His hands stopped their trembling. He got back to work. Ryan sat back against the front fender and studied the motorcycle driver out of the corner of his eye. The soldier's face, pinched with cold, was inscrutable under his big goggles. He held his gauntleted hands in his armpits for warmth. Ryan shifted his gaze to the lieutenant. The contessa's face was at the window, looking up at the officer. The officer's voice was insistent, hers equally so but cordial. The officer made a gesture of good-natured defeat, saluted and turned away. He spoke to Ryan as he went by. Ryan nodded and touched his cap. The officer loosened his belt and climbed back into the sidecar. The soldier kicked the starter, the motor caught and the machine continued its interrupted journey toward L'Aquila.

'Gee,' said Maguire, coming out from under the hood and brushing hair from his forehead with the back of a grimy hand, 'that was close.'

'How's it coming?'

'Just about done.'

'Lieutenant.'

Ryan's voice was hard. Maguire stiffened.

'Is that the way to address a superior officer?'

'No, sir. Just about done, *sir*.'

'Get her buttoned up. We don't want the contessa to keep her guests waiting.'

Ryan walked back to the contessa and told her they would be ready to go in a few minutes.

'What did the lieutenant want?' he asked.

'Such a charming young man.'

'He wouldn't have been if he'd known the kind of company you're in.'

'Bit of luck for him he didn't,' said Fincham.

The contessa looked at Fincham quizzically.

'He'd be dead now,' Fincham explained. 'His driver, too. Bit upsetting for you, I dare say. Damned rude killing a German officer in front of a lady who's fond of them.'

'You may have found killing him rather difficult. The Germans are excellent soldiers. And the officers have beautiful manners, I may add. You are obviously not an officer.'

'Been a piece of cake. Thanks to you, Contessa. He was so busy being charming he didn't even undo his holster.'

'What did he want, Contessa?' Ryan demanded. 'Did he ask who we were?'

The lieutenant had not. He wanted to know if he could be of any assistance, said that his driver was an excellent mechanic, and offered to take her to L'Aquila in the sidecar. His driver would follow in the car after he had mended the engine. It was not fitting for a Grafin, a countess, to sit beside a freezing mountain road when there was warmth and good cheer at L'Aquila's Grand Hotel.

'I assured him my great nephew was quite capable, and my banker excellent company.'

'Did you find out anything about the situation in L'Aquila?'

'Of course. I asked if it was safe for me there.'

The lieutenant had told her to have no fear. L'Aquila had its share of misguided dissidents, as did so many other Abruzzi towns, but they did not dare show themselves. The townspeople were, on the whole, loyal and the Wehrmacht had experienced no incidents.

'Bags of Jerry there, then,' Fincham said.

The contessa looked at her tiny jewelled watch.

'I shall never be back before curfew,' she said, annoyed.

'Paolo,' Ryan called. 'How're you coming?'

'All finished, sir.'

Maguire let down the hood and came back wiping his hands on a rag from the tool-chest.

'Oh, dear,' said the contessa. 'You've soiled your lovely jacket. Get in quickly and let us be on our way.'

The road wound through a long valley not yet fully browned by winter, between a river and a railway on which nothing was moving. Hills verged into mountains on both sides and up ahead. The area was in easy range of Allied fighter planes and there was no other traffic on the road, civilian or military. Ryan watched the road ahead for sheltered places in which to hide if strafing aircraft appeared. The chauffeur's compartment offered an unbroken view of the sky. Ryan glanced in the rear-view mirror and saw the contessa cleaning Maguire's oil-encrusted nails with an elegant manicuring implement. Maguire looked uncomfortable but pleased.

L'Aquila came into view beyond a long curve in a high valley lying at the foot of convoluted hills growing in the distance into mountains with snowy summits. Only glimpses of streets and squares broke the ranks of its thickly packed stone buildings.

'It is not visible from here but the Gran Sasso is just over there,' the contessa said. 'I do not suppose you ski, Ottavio.'

'No, Contessa.'

Ryan pulled off the road and stopped before reaching the outskirts.

'Why are you stopping?'

'We'll stay here while you go into town and find us a guide.'

'We must remain together until I am rid of you entirely.'

If they encountered Germans without her there to intervene, they would be lost, she said.

'Drive to the Grand Hotel. I will direct you to it.'

The contessa would get them rooms at the hotel where they could wait without fear of discovery, a suite for Paolo and Enrico and a servant's room, appropriate for a chauffeur, she said with a smile, for Ottavio. She would also engage a suite for herself, as if they intended remaining there for the night. She could then see to their guide at her leisure. She knew someone on the hotel staff who might be helpful.

'I don't like it,' Fincham said.

'The Grand Hotel is quite the best L'Aquila has to offer, such as it is.'

'Then the place will be swarming with Jerry officers.'

'And what do you think, Paolo?' the contessa asked.

'I'll do whatever the colonel...' He caught himself, aghast at what he had revealed.

'Ottavio a colonel? Perhaps he has qualities I have failed to detect. But then you Americans are notoriously democratic.'

'If you're sure you can bring it off,' Ryan said. 'But remember, I have your ring, ma'am.'

'I do not respond kindly to threats, *Colonnello*. And I have no intention of placing Paolo in jeopardy.'

The contessa directed him through the town to the hotel, across from a park on a street lined solidly with buildings on both sides. German staff cars and a few luxurious civilian cars were parked around it. Among the military vehicles was an American jeep with Wehrmacht markings. Two German officers came out of the flat-roofed, four-storey hotel, laughing. They looked appreciatively at the Rolls, piled into the jeep and drove away.

'What now?' Ryan asked, double-parking.

'Sound the horn,' the contessa said.

Ryan did as he was told. Nothing happened.

'Again. More insistently.'

Ryan pressed on the horn. Germans appeared at the downstairs windows and a window on the third floor was thrown open. A man in shirt-sleeves leaned out and shouted, 'Schweigen Sie!' *Be quiet.* Two German officers, one in S.S. uniform, came out on to the pavement. The contessa motioned to them to come to the car. The S.S. officer did so. The contessa spoke to him in German. He saluted and went back into the hotel.

'I instructed him to send out the director,' the contessa said. 'I shall never get back before curfew. I will have to telephone my regrets.'

A man in a frock-coat came trotting out of the hotel. He hurried to the car and greeted the contessa profusely. He looked dismayed when she told him what she required. He was volubly apologetic. The contessa was firm. He pressed both hands to his heart and looked up at the sky. The contessa insisted. He sighed, bowed and went back inside.

'There were no accommodations,' the contessa said. 'I instructed him to place some of the other guests together. German officers, if necessary. And not to hesitate to inform them it was the wish of the Contessa di Montalba.'

'You seem to carry a lot of weight around here.' said Ryan.

'Of course.'

After a while the manager came out all smiles. The contessa thanked him curtly. They followed him into the lobby, leaving the Rolls double-parked. The lobby of the Grand Hotel was more ornate and luxurious than the exterior promised. Half a dozen German officers were lounging in it. They rose quickly when the contessa appeared and bowed with much clicking of heels. A German colonel who had been waiting at the desk came to her and bent to kiss the gloved hand she offered. No one paid the least attention to her companions. The colonel spoke to her in halting Italian. She replied in French and he responded fluently in the same language. Ryan moved closer, as if waiting for instructions.

The colonel had been honoured to see that room was made for the Contessa di Montalba, such a valued friend of the

Reich, and her party. If there was anything else she required, she had only to ask. Perhaps she would have a drink with him after she had settled herself in her suite, though he was risking the eternal jealousy of his general, when his general heard of his good fortune. The contessa said she was honoured but she had errands to attend to. He suggested she send her chauffeur. She replied that they took rather more intelligence than her chauffeur possessed. The colonel left her with reassurances that he was at her command.

The contessa took off her fur coat. A boy in porter's uniform scurried up to take it from her. She waved him away and gave it to Ryan, speaking to Ryan in Italian.

'Si, Contessa,' said Ryan, draping it over his arm.

The manager conducted them to their rooms himself. The contessa refused to be shown to her suite until she had seen her great nephew and her financial adviser installed in theirs. When Fincham and Maguire were safely behind its closed door, she motioned for Ryan to accompany her and the manager to her suite. Inside, she took Ryan's key from the manager and dismissed the Italian.

'Hang up my fur,' she said, when the manager closed the door behind him. 'And do be careful. They are irreplaceable in Italy now.'

'I presume you have something to tell me, ma'am.'

'Yes. When you have hung up my coat.'

She was going down to the salon. A waiter there had once been in her employ and could be trusted to find a man who knew his way through the mountains. She would tell him she wished to send a message to a relative on the Allied side of the lines. An urgent family matter.

'The man he gets. How do I know he won't back out when he finds out he's supposed to take some fugitives through the lines instead of just a message?'

'That is your concern, Colonnello, not mine.'

'Will you do something else for me, ma'am? While you're out, have that drink with the colonel.'

'Why, may I ask?'

'See if he knows what's behind the flow of traffic south.

165

Where it's heading and for what purpose.'

'I agreed only to find a guide for you. I am not a spy.'

'But you are a survivor, ma'am. Your German friends aren't permanent fixtures around here, you know. Sooner or later my side will be here. If you co-operate now, I guarantee that when they arrive you'll be persona grata. The only change will be that you'll be entertaining British and American brass instead of German.'

The contessa looked thoughtful.

'Is that a threat?' she said at last.

'No, ma'am. An offer in good faith. I have it on the best authority the Contessa di Montalba doesn't respond kindly to threats.'

'I will see what can be done. But I make no promises.'

'I have every confidence in you, ma'am.'

'If that is true, may I have my ring?'

Ryan took it from his pocket and held it out to her. The contessa took it from him and slipped it on her finger.

'So you do trust me at last,' she said. 'How touching.'

'I'm a trusting person, ma'am. And you know which side your bread is buttered on.'

The contessa gave him his room key and accompanied him to his door so he would not be encountered alone and spoken to in Italian. A young maid came round a corner as they were parting. The maid smirked.

Ryan locked his door from the inside and left the key in the lock. He took off his top-coat, tunic and gaiters, and lay down on the bed on top of the covers. The bare, simple room was cold but not nearly as cold as the open Rolls. There was just the bed, somewhat too small for Ryan to stretch out full length, a chair and a marble-topped bureau with a china ewer and tin wash-basin on it. There was a white chamber-pot decorated with twining roses under the bed.

After a while Ryan got up, put on his tunic and went looking for the lavatory. In the hall he encountered the girl who had smirked at him and the contessa. She leered at him, waggled her finger in the universal gesture that said naughty, naughty, and said something coquettish. Ryan scowled at her.

She laughed. A German officer came out of a door buttoning his trousers. He approached them, ignoring Ryan and ogling the maid. He pinched her bottom as he passed. She gave Ryan a look that told him plainly he was not the only fish in the sea. Ryan went to the door from which the officer had emerged. It was the lavatory. The maid was lurking in the corridor when he came out, writing on a piece of paper held against the wall. She stopped long enough to say something, with a gesture indicating that he was to wait. When she had finished, she folded the paper, whispering something as she pressed it into his hand, and fled, giggling, looking back at him twice.

When he was locked in his room again he unfolded the paper. It had the name of the hotel and *Lavanderia* at the top. Below that was a crude, hastily drawn diagram showing the location of the hotel in a web of nearby streets, an address and a line of arrows leading there from the Grand Hotel. Underneath the diagram was a childishly printed note with indiscriminately mixed capital and lower case letters. The language was simple enough for Ryan to puzzle it out. It said to come after ten at night and beware of German patrols. There was reference to the contessa which he could not translate. Ryan grinned and tore the note into tiny pieces which he put in the chamber-pot.

He removed his tunic and lay on his back with his hands under his head. A faint knock on the door awoke him instantly. He picked up the automatic at his side and went silently to the door.

'Ottavio?'

It was the contessa.

'Si, Contessa?'

'In five minutes, come to my room.'

Ryan put on his tunic and gaiters and carried his cap. The maid saw him out come out of his room and followed him. She made a vulgar arm gesture when he knocked on the contessa's door. Ryan shrugged and threw her a kiss. Her frown became a smile; she nodded understandingly and left.

The contessa was waiting in the living-room of her suite. She was sitting in the centre of the sofa inspecting her emerald ring. There was a bowl of hot-house flowers on the table that had not been there earlier.

'I was wondering how you chanced to select the most valuable piece to take for ransom, Ottavio,' she said. 'I suppose it can only mean it is rather too ostentatious.'

'You could never be ostentatious, ma'am. Did you get us a guide?'

'Yes. His name is Arnaldo. He will meet us on the road to Rieti early tomorrow morning.'

'The road to Rieti?'

'I could hardly leave L'Aquila without my chauffeur.'

'Did you learn anything from the colonel?'

'Only that his wife has never understood him. I was quite flattered by the implications. A woman of my age.'

'The colonel has excellent taste.'

'Your gallantry surprises me, Ottavio. Though I suspect it is rather calculated. I have the impression everything you do is calculated.'

'Usually, Contessa. But not always.'

'Do you have a wife, Ottavio?'

'Yes. And three children.'

'They have my sympathy.'

The contessa was dining in the hotel that evening with a General Wahlberg, who talked freely when he drunk enough brandy, which she had no doubt he would. He had never left her villa completely sober on the occasions when he had been a guest there. She would see what she could learn from him.

Ryan's dinner would be brought to his room, as would Enrico's and Paolo's to theirs. She had told the manager that her great nephew was indisposed and her banker was looking after him.

'Naturally a chauffeur cannot expect to dine as well as the great nephew of a contessa,' she said. 'Even if one is a colonel and the other is a mere lieutenant.'

Because she was so anxious to be rid of them, the contessa would be rising before dawn. Ryan was expected to collect Enrico and Paolo and bring them to her suite no later than six-thirty in the morning. The three of them would be breakfasting in her suite and she would see that a little something would be waiting for Ryan in his room once he had brought them to her.

'Are you comfortable in your quarters, Ottavio?'

'Si, Contessa.'

'How disappointing.'

Ryan's dinner, brought to his room on a tray by a disgruntled waiter whom Ryan did not allow inside, was better than the contessa had promised. A large omelette filled with cheese, pasta, a small piece of boiled mutton, half a litre of red wine and a bottle of Fiuggi water. Ryan drank only one glass of the wine and put the tray and empty dishes on the floor outside his room.

Early in the evening, there was much coming and going in the hall and banging of doors accompanied by hearty German conversation. When the hall at last grew quiet, Ryan tucked his pistol in his waistband under the chauffeur's loose-fitting shirt and went to Fincham's suite. Though he took great pains not to be seen, he could not avoid an encounter with two German officers. He stood aside deferentially, looking down at his feet. The Germans were in field uniform and obviously thought he was a hall porter. They spoke only a few words of Italian, and those poorly. They shouted to make up for the deficiency. They wanted him to wait. The younger of the two went off down the hall. The other, a major with haunted eyes, kept repeating, 'Americani, Inglesi, cattivi, si? Tedeschi buoni.' *Americans, Englishmen, bad, yes? Germans good.*

Ryan nodded vigorously each time, saying, 'Si, Maggiore, Tedeschi molto buoni.' *Yes, Major, Germans very good.*

The younger officer returned with an armload of shirts and underwear and dumped them in Ryan's arms.

'Domani mattina,' he said. *Tomorrow morning.*

He pushed back Ryan's cuff and, seeing no watch — Ryan had put it in his pocket before leaving his room — pointed to a number on his own, indicating that they wanted their laundry back by eight in the morning.

'Si, Tenente. Domani mattina.'

The officers went striding down the hall. Ryan, with an

armful of dirty German laundry, continued on his way less guardedly. He heard laughter and conversation, the talk loud enough for him to make out an English word or two. He knocked politely on the door. The conversation stopped abruptly. There was the sound of a bolt sliding back; the door-knob turned and the door opened a crack. Fincham's eye appeared in the opening.

'It's only Ottavio,' he said, opening the door just enough to let Ryan slip through and closing it quickly behind him.

Fincham had Tenbrink's knife ready in his hand.

'What have we here,' he demanded, eyeing Ryan's burden, 'a change of linen?'

Maguire stood at attention beside a well-spread table with a chicken leg clamped between his teeth.

'Lieutenant,' Ryan said in a confidential but humourless tone, 'do you consider yourself at proper attention with a drumstick in your face?'

Maguire snatched the chicken-leg from his mouth and held it next to his side like a side-arm, making a grease spot on Paolo's trousers.

'As you were, Lieutenant,' Ryan said. 'Fincham. I could hear you talking English all the way out in the hall. You two keep it down in here, understood?'

'Yes, sir,' said Maguire.

'If you're doing a bit of dhobying, I've a few things for you,' Fincham said. 'Or have you been out pinching the odd vest and drawers?'

They sat down at the table and, while Fincham and Maguire finished eating, Ryan told them about the contessa's arrangements. Fincham objected to meeting their guide north of L'Aquila when the contessa might just as well have arranged their rendezvous south of town, perhaps a considerable distance south.

'Save us a bloody lot of walking,' he said.

'And the contessa would have a bloody lot of explaining to do when she came back through L'Aquila minus her chauffeur, her great nephew and her distinguished banker.'

'That's right,' said Maguire.

'Who consulted you?' Fincham demanded. 'Can we trust this Arnaldo? What does she know about him?'

'Nothing. But she trusts him.'

'Or pretends to.'

'I don't think the contessa would intentionally throw us to the wolves.'

'No, sir,' said Maguire. 'She's too nice.'

'And she likes to be on the winning side,' Ryan said. He rose and gathered up the German's laundry. 'I'll come for you at six-fifteen. Be shaved and dressed.'

'What with?' Fincham demanded. 'Our kit's out in the car. In the middle of the street.'

'No sweat,' said Ryan.

He put down the clothing and rummaged through them for the Lavanderia list with the room number. He went to the German's room with the laundry in his arms. He passed a porter on the way and got only a cursory glance and nod. The door was locked. He pushed back the latch with a long blade of his pocket-knife, sliding it between the door and jamb. He found a safety razor, a brush and a metal box containing soap in a fitted leather kit and took them to Fincham.

'Finest German steel,' he said.

Before returning to his room he left the clothing outside a room on another floor.

He was wakened around midnight by noise in the hall. German officers were coming up from the salon. Footsteps stopped outside his door and metal grated on metal as someone thrust a wavering key at the lock. Ryan padded to the door and waited. The fumbling stopped and footsteps retreated. Ryan went back to sleep.

It was five-thirty by his watch and still dark when he woke up as he had planned to, as if an alarm-clock had gone off. He washed his face in the tin basin and scrubbed his teeth with a wet forefinger. After setting-up exercises he dressed and sat in the chair until it was time to fetch Fincham and Maguire. They were waiting for him. Ryan shaved with the German razor before taking them to the contessa. When he had finished, Fincham put the toilet kit in his overcoat pocket.

'Souvenir of the big war,' he said.

'I guess my tent-mate got my souvenirs when I was captured,' Maguire said wistfully. 'I hope he saves 'em for me.'

The contessa opened her door at Ryan's first knock, as if she had been waiting for it, and shut the door quickly behind them. Her face was skilfully made up and her hair as well-styled as if she had just come from her hairdresser. There was a conspiratorial gleam in her blue eyes and she was unusually cheerful.

'Paolo,' she said. 'You appear tired. You did not sleep well?'

'Oh, yes, ma'am. Like a log. Only Enrico kind of snores.'

'Did you get anything out of the general?' Ryan demanded.

'You are hopelessly blunt, Ottavio. You should cultivate the virtue of patience.'

'Did you?' he insisted.

'I was marvellous. I had no idea I was such an accomplished spy. Had I known, perhaps I would have responded to that imbecile in Roma. But I will tell you everything on the road. Go now and have your breakfast, then wait for us in the motorcar in exactly thirty-five minutes.' She gestured toward the laden table set for three and said, 'Paolo, next to me.'

Ryan lingered long enough to hold the contessa's chair for her as she sat down.

'You are full of surprises, Colonnello,' she said dryly, 'but I suppose even an American acquires a deceptive vestige of civilisation with rank.'

'You sure talk keen English, Contessa,' Maguire said.

'Thank you, Paolo. But "zia", not "contessa".'

'Yes, ma'am.'

Ryan's breakfast was on a tray beside his door. He ate quickly, put on his top-coat and sat in the chair until five minutes before he was to meet the others at the car. In the hall, he passed the maid who had given him the note. She had a stack of neatly folded linen in her arms reaching to her chin.

'Finocchio,' she said, sticking out her tongue at him. *Faggot.*

There were no Germans in the lobby when he dropped his

172

room key on the desk, only three well-dressed Italian civilians, freshly barbered and smelling of aftershave cologne.

The German vehicles were gone. Someone had pushed the Rolls to a place by the pavement in front of the hotel, in a line with two Italian sedans. Ryan stood by the passenger door and watched the hotel entrance. The door opened and the manager came out. He held it open ceremoniously. The contessa emerged, followed by Maguire and Fincham. The manager hurried to the Rolls. Ryan snapped to attention, his hand on the door-handle. The manager pushed him aside and flung the door open, bowing. Ryan took the contessa's elbow, helped her inside, leaned in and adjusted the robe on her lap. She ignored him, speaking animatedly to the waiting Fincham and Maguire. Ryan backed out and stood at attention again while they joined her. The manager remained in the street, bowing, until the Rolls pulled away in a U-turn.

'Where do we meet Arnaldo?' Ryan asked through the speaking tube.

'Exactly five kilometres beyond the city. We are to stop beside the road and lift the bonnet. He will appear and ask if there is a problem with the carburettor. I will tell him what is required of him and continue to Rieti alone. And you, as you Americans say, will be on your own.'

'What did your general have to say?'

'The Germans will celebrate the anniversary of your Pearl Harbor with a surprise for the British.'

'7 December,' Ryan said. 'That's only five days away. Where will it be? And in what strength?'

'I could not tactfully ask. But one may assume it will be a major undertaking. General Wahlberg seemed quite pleased with himself and said if all goes as planned it will change the complexion of the war in Italy.'

Fincham whistled.

'We can't waste time getting through then, can we?' he said.

'And I have some information,' the contessa said, pleased with herself. 'The nearest British forces are below Roccaraso. Perhaps one hundred and ten kilometres to the south of L'Aquila. At a standstill, as are the Americans before Cassino.

173

Only in the east, in the direction of Pescara, are your friends making even modest gains. Tell me, Colonnello, are you not surprised at how much I discovered?'

'No more than I expected, ma'am. You have a way of rising to the occasion.'

Ryan looked in the rear-view mirror. He saw a familiar sight, a motorcycle and sidecar. The motorcycle sped up and drew alongside the Rolls. The lieutenant from the Rieti roadblock shouted at Ryan and waved him over. Ryan unbuttoned his top-coat and tunic, got the automatic from his waistband, took it off safety and slipped it under his thigh. He stopped the car at the side of the road. They were two kilometres outside L'Aquila.

The lieutenant climbed out of the sidecar and approached the window the contessa had let down. Their conversation was much like that of the previous day, when the lieutenant had proposed leaving his driver to repair the engine, the German cordial but insistent, the contessa equally cordial in demurring. The lieutenant got back in the sidecar. The motorcycle moved just ahead of the Rolls and stopped, idling.

'What's going on?' Ryan asked.

'We are to follow him to Rieti,' the contessa said calmly. 'He will see that we are not delayed going through the town. I am afraid we are back to square one. C'est la guerre.'

'Damn it, madam!' Fincham said. 'Why didn't you send him packing?'

'Do not be abusive,' the contessa said icy dignity. 'He refused to take no for an answer.'

The motorcycle horn sounded and the lieutenant waved them forward. The motorcycle started up the road. The Rolls followed. A truck loaded with German troops sped by toward L'Aquila, horn blaring. The soldiers waved at the Rolls.

'Let him get out of sight,' Fincham said. 'We'll get out and the contessa can follow him alone. By the time they reach Rieti we'll have found our man and be on our way.'

'Negative,' said Ryan.

Nevertheless, he let the Rolls fall behind the motorcycle. Up ahead, a bridge spanned a river. The Rolls slowed and fell farther back as the motorcycle disappeared around a curve. Ryan stopped the car at the bridge and said, 'Out, Enrico, on the double! Paolo, you sit there and don't make a move. Contessa, when he comes back tell him we're having the same trouble as yesterday.'

He got out of the car quickly, putting the pistol back in his waistband but leaving top-coat and tunic open, and lifted the hood of the car. He beckoned for Fincham to join him.

'When the lieutenant gets back he'll probably want to look for himself,' Ryan said. 'You taxi over towards his driver, not too fast, and when I say "Now", get him.'

'Will do.'

When Ryan heard the motorcycle returning, he stood besides the open hood and looked towards it in a waiting attitude. The motorcycle came across the bridge and stopped on the other side of the road. The contessa called to the lieutenant, her tone exasperated. The lieutenant came to her. After a brief exchange he strolled to the front of the car. Ryan shrugged helplessly and pointed under the hood. Fincham moved casually towards the motorcycle, a hand thrust under his open overcoat, scratching his side. The lieutenant stood with his hands on his hips, watching Ryan. Ryan stuck his head under the hood and, reaching back, motioned for the lieutenant to have a look for himself. The lieutenant leaned down beside Ryan.

Ryan stepped back quickly, shouted 'Now', and slammed down the hood. The lieutenant's neck was pinned between hood and fender. The motorcycle driver shouted a warning that came too late, unslinging his rifle. Fincham's broad-bladed knife flashed and whipped across the soldier's throat. The contessa cried out, only once, sharply. Ryan held the hood down until the lieutenant stopped moving.

13

Still holding down the hood, Ryan looked back at the contessa. Maguire had a protective arm around her and was trying to comfort her. She was pale but did not appear in need of comforting. There was as much anger in her face as shock.

Ryan lifted the hood. The lieutenant's body slid down the fender, balanced on its knees for a moment, then collapsed limply on its side. Ryan listened for a heartbeat. Hearing none, he felt in the lieutenant's pockets for his identification.

'Fincham,' he called, not looking up, 'get your man's ID.'

Ryan found what he was looking for and dragged the body to the motorcycle. Fincham had the soldier's ID. That and his hands were bloody. Fincham wiped the blood off on the soldier's greatcoat. Ryan stuffed the lieutenant's body in the sidecar and trundled the machine towards the bridge. Fincham followed, dragging the soldier's body under the armpits. Ryan draped the body across the seat and, with Fincham's help, guided the machine down the bank and under the bridge. Back on the road, Ryan looked towards the bridge. The machine and the bodies were not visible. There were tread marks from the road to the side of the bridge. He scuffed them away with his feet. He went to the contessa, who was no longer pale but still tight-lipped.

'Are you all right, ma'am?' he asked.

'Was it necessary to murder them?' she demanded.

'Yes.'

'You could have disarmed them and taken them prisoner.'

'And then what, ma'am?'

176

'You did it so brutally.'

'These are brutal times.'

'And you fit them perfectly.'

'I'm sorry you had to see it, Contessa. But you've been enjoying this war. Maybe it's good for you to see what it's really like to the common people.'

Maguire looked as if he wanted to defend the contessa but said nothing.

'Let's get cracking,' Fincham said, climbing into the car.

'Yes,' said the contessa. 'Let us find Arnaldo. I cannot wait to be rid of you.' She patted Maguire's hand. 'Not you, of course, dear Paolo. When this wretched war is over, I hope you will write to me.'

'Yes, ma'am. You've sure been swell to us. I'm just sorry this had to happen in front of you. We soldiers are used to it but it must really bother a civilian.'

Ryan slid under the wheel and continued towards their rendezvous. He checked the odometer and rear-view mirror regularly. A civilian car passed them going towards Reiti. Two of the Italians from the hotel were in it. Nothing went by towards L'Aquila. Exactly five kilometres from the outskirts, Ryan pulled off the road and stopped. There was no one in view. He put the car keys in his pocket and lifted the hood. The contessa got out and came to him, holding out her hand.

'The keys,' she said.

'You'll have to give Arnaldo his instructions,' Ryan said. 'If and when he comes. You said he doesn't speak English.'

'If it were not for Paolo I would leave you to your own devices. But, very well. I will wait a few more minutes.'

An old man came out of nowhere, driving a runty donkey wearing a straw hat with its ears sticking out through holes. The old man was muffled to the ears in a ragged brown sweater, with a wool hat pulled down to meet it at the neck. His hands were thrust deep into his pockets. When he came abreast of the car he said nothing but 'Piccolina'. The donkey stopped and looked back at him, switching its tail. The old man looked at the raised hood with his hands still in his pockets and, without a glance at anyone, said something about the *carburatore*.

'Arnaldo?' the contessa said.

The old man nodded, his expression surly.

The contessa spoke to him as to a servant, pointing first at Ryan, then at Fincham and Maguire. The old man began shaking his head at her first gesture. The shaking grew more emphatic with each man. The contessa's tone grew commanding.

'No,' said the old man. 'Piccolina.'

The donkey started walking. The old man followed it. Ryan reached out and grabbed a handful of his sweater. The old man turned, his eyes unafraid and deadly.

'He refuses,' said the contessa.

'Tell him it's too late for that,' Ryan said.

The old man's attitude changed abruptly. He broke into an incredulous grin, showing stained, gapped teeth.

'Americano?' he cried. 'Inglese?'

'Americani,' Ryan said, pointing to himself and Maguire. 'Inglese,' pointing to Fincham.

Arnaldo spoke volubly to Ryan, waving his arms, pausing only to shout, 'Piccolina!' at his donkey, which turned round and came back.

'He will take you through the mountains,' the contessa translated. 'And without pay. It is his pleasure to assist the liberators of his country.'

'Good show,' said Fincham. 'But do you think at his age he's up to it?'

'He is an Italian peasant,' the contessa replied. 'I dare say he is "up to it" more than any of you. Now, Colonel, the keys, if you please.'

'Colonnello!' Arnaldo cried, clutching his heart. 'Fantastico!'

'You won't be needing them, Contessa,' Ryan said regretfully. 'I'm afraid you're coming, too.'

'What!'

'You can't go back now, ma'am. You're hopelessly compromised.'

'Utter nonsense.'

178

'The lieutenant's expected in Rieti. When he doesn't show up for duty, somebody'll call L'Aquila. They'll start looking for him between L'Aquila and Rieti. It's only a matter of time before they find the bodies. We took the IDs but that's just in case somebody stumbles on them who's not looking for them.'

'What has that to do with me?'

'A truckload of German troops saw us following the motorcycle. It's common knowledge who the Rolls belongs to. You were seen by plenty of Germans in the company of three men at L'Aquila, yet you'll be coming back through Rieti alone. What happened to us?'

'I will have an acceptable explanation.'

'They'll grill your servants. The Germans are very thorough.'

'The servants know nothing of you.'

'But they know things that will make the Germans suspicious. Why did your houseman carry a heavy box to the garage? You had guests coming but you went off and were gone all night.'

They would search her grounds and the garage, Ryan continued. There had been five men milling around the garden and three had occupied the chauffeur's quarters. They had been careful but did she suppose that a meticulous search would uncover no evidence of their presence? And they would question the staff at the Grand Hotel. The waiter in the salon, the one who found Arnaldo for her, did she think he could stand up to a clever, ruthless German interrogation?

The contessa grew increasingly thoughtful as he spoke. For a moment, but only a moment, her composure crumbled. The spark went out of her eyes and her shoulders sagged.

She straightened quickly and, with a sigh of resignation, said, 'Unfortunately, there is much to what you say.'

'Ma'am,' said Maguire, 'I'll stay and show you how to hide out. You'll never make it through the mountains.'

'That's a dear boy,' she said, patting his hand. 'But I was climbing before you were born. And I am not so aged that I cannot do it again.' She looked sharply at Ryan. 'I should not be at all surprised if you planned it this way. What would you have done for an interpreter?'

'That's a terrible thing to say, ma'am. And not very logical. I'm afraid even with your languages you'll be more a liability than an asset.'

'We shall see.'

Arnaldo was impatient to be off. When he learned the contessa was coming with them he protested even more stridently than he had done when first told he was to guide three men through the mountains instead of simply delivering a message.

'He will not assist a Fascist witch,' she said wryly.

'How do you say "secret"?' Ryan asked.

'Segreto. Why do you ask?'

'Arnaldo,' Ryan said, pointing to the contessa. 'Un agente segreto Americano.'

Arnaldo looked doubtful.

'Veramente,' said Ryan.

'You actually know a few words of Italian,' the contessa said. 'How frightfully clever.'

Ryan told her to tell Arnaldo she would require different clothes for getting through the mountains, something warmer and sturdier, and boots, though her walking brogues might do at a pinch. Arnaldo said his wife was the same height as the contessa but of a more gracious figure. His little house was not far away, towards Coppito. He would lead them there. It was not a good road for such a fine machine but they would have to make the best of it. Ryan motioned for him to get in the car, up front by the driver. Arnaldo nodded and said something about Piccolina.

'His donkey knows the way home,' the contessa said. 'She will be all right.'

'I'm relieved,' said Fincham.

Arnaldo's tiny square house was some yards off a rutted track, more cowpath than road, all alone in a browning, stony field with a vegetable garden and a few stubs of leafless vines. It had a single window, tightly shuttered against the cold. A trickle of white smoke escaped from the chimney, to be quickly dispersed by the wind. The house was built of rough stones, heavily mortared, as was the outhouse just beyond it.

The house had but one dim room, with a bed in one corner and a stove, vented to the chimney, in another. There was a heap of twigs, bound together in bundles, by the stove, and a few pots and pans and strings of onions and garlic dangling from the wall beside the stove. The only furnishings other than the bed were two chairs and a table, crudely handmade, and a tin trunk. There was a crucifix over the bed.

Arnaldo's wife, awed and silent in the presence of such distinguished company, could not take her eyes off the contessa though she did not once look at her directly. She was not, as Arnaldo had said, of a size with the contessa. She was shorter and much broader, with ample bosom and bottom, thin legs and big feet. She was much younger than Arnaldo, and plain.

'Her clothing will not fit me,' the contessa said, wrinkling her nose at the fusty, smoky odour of the cramped room.

'I'm afraid we have no other line to show madam,' Fincham said.

'Arnaldo's will,' said Ryan, studying the little old man. 'And pants will be more practical than skirts.'

Arnaldo was wearing everything he owned except a pair of trousers, a collarless flannel shirt and a suit-coat that did not match the trousers. Of his wife's few bits of clothing, a hat that pulled down over the ears and a rough sheepskin coat with the wool inside both appeared suitable. Arnaldo's wife looked dismayed when he added them to the pile on the table but she held her tongue. Ryan gave her a wad of lire notes and told her, through the contessa, to buy herself replacements. She was to do so discreetly, saying nothing of where she had got the money or of her visitors. Arnaldo assured Ryan through the contessa that she would not. She was a good wife, who did as she was told. She was his second wife, he added, barren, unfortunately, unlike his late first wife, who had born him six fine sons, now grown and God only knew where. It was all due to the Fascists — let them roast in hell.

Ryan took the clothes out to the car and got the maps from the pack. He cleared the table and spread out those covering the L'Aquila-Roccaraso area and portions of the front to the east and west. They were 1:500,000 topographical maps and it took two of them to encompass the area.

He drew in from memory the Allied positions as marked on the situation map in the Hotel Vereina day-room. If the contessa's information was correct, they would not have changed much below Roccaraso. To the south-east of L'Aquila, towards Roccaraso, the spine of Italy was ridged with mountain ranges whose peaks towered up to nine thousand feet. The chains ran south-east, parallelling the most direct route to the nearest friendly positions. At Roccaraso they curved southward, like the blades of field hockey sticks, along the German main line of defence, the Gustav Line. Roccaraso lay like a plug at the end of a high, broad valley, the Piano della Cinquemiglia, the *Five Mile Plateau*.

Ryan called Arnaldo and the contessa to the table. Arnaldo said he required no maps; he knew the mountains well. Ryan asked to be shown the route they would take. Beyond Sulmona, said Arnaldo, tracing the route with a finger, seventy kilometres south-east of L'Aquila, it would not be safe to continue directly toward Roccaraso. Too many Tedeschi. They must turn west, out of the valley, cross the mountains and continue along the south-western slopes. On that side the valley was narrower and the approaches from the south so difficult for tanks and motor transport that few Tedeschi would be required to block them.

'How long will it take to get through?' Ryan asked.

If he were alone, Arnaldo said, four days. But burdened with four persons unaccustomed to the mountains, and one of them an old woman, no less than five.

'We haven't that much time,' said Fincham, who had joined them.

'Don't worry about it,' said Ryan. 'Thank you, Arnaldo. You're a ground officer, Enrico. Where would you guess the Germans are concentrating?'

'Von Ryan asking advice?' Fincham demanded, feigning disbelief.

'Ryan?' the contessa said. '*The* Colonel Ryan?'

'Cut the comedy,' Ryan said to Fincham, ignoring her

question. 'Where do you think?'

Fincham studied the overlapping maps. A donkey brayed outside. Arnaldo gestured and his wife opened the door. Piccolina trotted in and made herself at home in a corner heaped with straw. Arnaldo's wife took off the donkey's hat and hung it on a peg. Maguire knelt beside Piccolina and stroked her neck.

'Opposite the British sector, certainly,' Fincham said, 'since the contessa's general said it was the British getting the surprise. If the general said we're making modest gains over here on Jerry's left flank — I say, there's Domira, of fond memory — it must mean we're doing rather better than that. Jerry could have a counter-attack laid on there. But I doubt it. Rome's the key and Pescara's on the other side of Italy. And the terrain there doesn't lend itself to the concealment of a massive concentration of forces.'

He spoke crisply and with precision, unlike his usual flippant self.

'It's more likely here, towards the centre,' he continued. 'Among the mountains. There's ample room to concentrate here on the Piano delle Cinquemiglia. And see how the terrain opens out below Roccaraso. If they could break out in strength here they'd find room to manoeuvre and drive a wedge between the British and Americans.'

'Inflicting heavy casualties and putting us on the defensive and taking the pressure off Rome,' Ryan said.

'Precisely,' said Fincham. 'And a precious lot of good the information will do ours if we're five days getting it to them. We'll not get through at all if we're right and there's heavy fighting in progress where we hope to cross the lines.'

'We'll get there in three.'

'And how do you propose doing that? Getting a lift on a Jerry convoy?'

'Close, Enrico. We're going as far as Sulmona by limousine.'

'I was wondering why you lumbered us with the contessa, old cock. I suppose you'll abandon her with the car at Sulmona.'

'Negative. She saved our hides. The least we can do is save hers.'

Ryan called everyone together.

'We're going to Sulmona by car,' he said. 'The Germans won't be looking for us until they find the late lieutenant and that'll take a while.'

'I have something that might prove quite useful,' the contessa said.

She opened her purse and unfolded a note on Grand Hotel stationery. The note was in angular German script. Under the illegible signature, 'Wahlberg, General', was printed in block letters.

'A pass to see me through Rieti,' she said. 'But it makes no mention of Rieti. It says only that the Contessa di Montalba and party are to be shown every courtesy.'

'Maybe we can get even closer to the lines, then,' Ryan said.

'Here's a thought,' said Fincham. 'Instead of trying for Sulmona, we should take the road for Pescara. When we get so close to the fighting that Jerry turns us back, we'll abandon the car and strike towards the lines on foot. We could save a whole day. The terrain's easier towards the Adriatic coast. And with out troops on the move we might meet them coming.'

'Too risky,' said Ryan. 'And I want a look at the Piano delle Cinquemiglia.'

'Do you propose changing the course of the war single-handedly, Colonel Ryan?' the contessa asked.

'No ma'am. There are five of us to do that.'

Ryan refolded the maps, stuffed the ones they no longer needed and the two German IDs in the stove and said, 'Time to go.'

Arnaldo's wife came out and watched them get in the car, wiping away tears. Ryan had Arnaldo lie on the floor in the back and covered him with a robe from the trunk.

'I had no idea I was assisting the notorious Colonel Ryan,' the contessa said when he helped her into the car. 'The account of your adventure with the train has reached even as far as Rieti.'

'Would you have turned me in if you had known?'

'Possibly. But it is rather too late to do so now, is it not?'

'Glad you understand the situation, ma'am.'

When they were on the road again, Ryan picked up the tube and told the contessa that if they were stopped anywhere, she was to present the pass and say she was going to Sulmona with her banker to pick up some valuables in the bank there.

They entered L'Aquila unchallenged. Ryan stopped long enough for the contessa to buy bread, cheese and a bottle of brandy. They drove past the Grand Hotel and the park opposite it, a place of trees and paths with a World War I monument in the centre. Beyond L'Aquila, the mountains towards the Adriatic were streaked with snow and those to the west bare brown. Villages clung to slopes, huddled clumps of stone buildings looking more like ancient, abandoned ruins than dwellings. There were burned-out military and civilian vehicles along the roads and sometimes, in the adjacent fields, a bomb crater. Holes in the road had recently been filled, and along the route were signposts bearing the warning, 'Achtung! Tiefflieger!' *Attention. Low-flying aircraft.* The only aircraft they saw were a flight of R.A.F. fighter-bombers, too high to be prowling the stretch of road along which they were driving.

The first roadblock was outside a characteristically compact village. The contessa's pass got them through unquestioned, though the sergeant in charge warned them of enemy dive-bombing and strafing. Buildings shouldering the road were scarred and paint-streaked where wide loads had brushed them. Beyond the village the road showed heavy use, with fresh-patched holes too small to be bomb craters and marks of tank treads along the sides.

Work gangs, young Italian men in civilian clothing, were busy along the route working on the road and raking away the treadmarks. They moved aside slowly when Ryan honked and their German guards shouted. They made obscene gestures which could have been either for the Rolls or the German soldiers.

'I wonder if we will see my poor Umberto among them,' the

contessa said. 'It will shatter him to see someone else driving his precious motorcar.'

An armoured car pulled out from under camouflage netting and blocked the road. A sergeant climbed out of it and thrust a scowling face at Ryan, demanding something in a loud, angry voice. The contessa spoke through the tube in Italian.

'Si, Contessa,' Ryan said.

He nodded towards the back seat, where the contessa was motioning imperiously. She showed the sergeant her pass. He looked doubtful as he read it twice. He gave it back, said something to her, got back in the armoured car and backed it under the netting.

'He warned me we were proceeding at our own risk,' the contessa said.

'We've been doing that for quite a while now,' said Ryan.

They were stopped twice again at roadblocks, the second time outside a large village where they were detained for some minutes and collected an audience. A sergeant summoned a lieutenant, who summoned a captain, who summoned a major. The major took off his cap and scratched his head while a detail of helmeted soldiers surrounding the Rolls waited impassively for his decision. At last, after a conversation with the contessa in which she explained the necessity of her journey to Sulmona, he permitted them to continue.

They were stopped again on the other side of the village. This time the contessa was obliged to leave the car and accompany an officer to a sandbagged office beside the road. A knot of curious soldiers gathered to inspect the Rolls. A corporal spoke to Ryan in German.

'Non capisco,' Ryan said.

'Macchina,' said the corporal. 'Bella.'

'Bellissima,' Ryan said, nodding.

The contessa emerged from the office escorted by a bare-headed, weary lieutenant-colonel. Ryan got out quickly to open the door for her. The lieutenant-colonel stepped in front of him and opened the door himself. He reached down for the robe covering Arnaldo. Maguire snatched up the robe the contessa had left on the seat and handed it to the officer. The contessa seated herself deliberately, planted her feet on Arnaldo and thanked the lieutenant-colonel with a gracious smile when he placed the robe across her lap. He shut the door and saluted. The contessa gestured regally for Ryan to drive on. The soldiers parted to let them through.

Ryan turned west at the first crossroad.

'This is not the way to Sulmona,' the contessa protested.

'I know.'

'Why have you turned off, then?'

Ryan did not answer.

'Von Ryan always has a good reason for the mad things he does,' Fincham said. 'If you're unlucky enough to be around him for any length of time you'll learn that, Contessa.'

'Insufferable arrogance.'

'It is that.'

The road was barely wide enough for one car and appeared little used. The level valley through which it ran was a broad one, the mountains to the east distant and shrouded in cloud. Ryan drove swiftly until there were no habitations in view. He stopped the car and had Arnaldo join him up front. Arnaldo brought the robe with him and draped it over his shoulders. Ryan unfolded the map to show him where they were but he already knew. They used the speaking-tube to communicate with the contessa. Arnaldo asked why they had turned off the main road. Ryan told him about the increasingly stringent security along it and he agreed that it would have been too risky to continue. In any case it did not matter, he said. The road they were on intersected one coming west out of Sulmona. It would take them over the mountains to the valley on the other side, the one they would follow to reach the front lines. Once across, they would have to leave the motorcar, however. Arnaldo said it with regret. He had never before driven in such a fine machine and now he would be obliged to leave it just when he was in a position to sit up and enjoy the drive.

It would be difficult after they left the car, he said. He wondered if the woman and the boy would be up to it. The contessa spoke to him with some asperity about that before translating for Ryan.

'Paolo and I shall do very nicely, thank you,' she added in English.

They drove another kilometre or so and Arnaldo indicated that Ryan was to turn south. There was nothing resembling a road, just a hint of track, only slightly less bare and unmarked than the surrounding country. Ryan asked Arnaldo if he was sure it was passable. The contessa told him Arnaldo considered his doubts insulting. Ryan apologised, and Arnaldo said it was forgotten. The Rolls bumped along the track for another fifteen minutes, skirting foothills that were green at the base and turning an increasingly darker shade of brown towards the summits. Ryan drove with care, not fighting the wheel when the tyres glanced off ruts and stones.

They reached a narrow but honest road crossing the track at right angles. Railway tracks were visible off to the left, and beyond them the huddled rooftops of Sulmona. Ryan turned right. The road twisted and wound and turned on itself, always climbing. They passed a clump of miserable stone buildings and partially timbered outbuildings. Chimneys smoked, dirty sheep huddled together in a pen. A woman prodding a cow from a barn stared at the gleaming Rolls.

The road climbed sharply towards a crest streaked with patches of snow. Below lay a long, narrow valley, stretching further south-east than the eye could see. A road wound invitingly along its floor. Ryan asked Arnaldo if he thought it safe to take it for a while. Arnaldo said that if they did so, they would have to climb back up the mountain on foot. And no road was safe for them this near to the battle lines, not from the Tedeschi or from Allied planes. They must abandon the car now.

'It has been like a friend to me for many years,' the contessa said regretfully when she translated Arnaldo's reply. 'But, it is only a machine.'

'Ask him how long it will take to reach the lines now.'

For himself alone, said Arnaldo, three days. But, begging the colonnello's pardon, accompanied by men who did not know the mountains, not to speak of a woman and a boy, more likely four. And part of one night. The actual crossing of the lines must be accomplished after dark.

'We can't take four days,' Ryan said. 'Even three is cutting it close.'

'But the attack is not for five days,' the contessa said.

'It takes time to bring up reinforcements,' Fincham explained. 'Even if they know what Jerry is up to, it'll do precious little good if they've nothing to stop him with.'

'Tell Arnaldo we have to make it in three days,' Ryan said.

Arnaldo said that depended entirely on the others keeping up. If the woman and the boy did not delay them too much, they could reach a cabin he knew by nightfall. Since before the war it had been used from time to time by persons anxious not to be found by authorities or vengeful relatives. He had rested there himself on more than one occasion. After a good night's rest they could make an early start and perhaps accomplish the day-time part of the journey in the required time.

Ryan left the road and drove across rough ground to an outcrop of rock at the brink of deep gorge.

'Everybody out except the contessa,' he said.

He got Arnaldo's clothes and his wife's hat and coat out of the trunk and gave them to her.

'It's warmer in the car,' he explained. 'and more private.'

'You are not a complete barbarian after all,' she said.

Ryan, Fincham and Maguire changed into their own clothes, shivering in the cold. They put the Italian suits and everything of the chauffeur's except the leather gaiters and gauntlets in the trunk. The contessa did not want to give up her fur coat.

'It is nearly as warm as this wretched thing,' she said, fingering the sheepskin coat gingerly.

'It isn't,' said Ryan. 'And you'll ruin it anyhow scrambling through the mountains.'

She handed it over and he stuffed it in the trunk with the rest of her clothing. She did not like Arnaldo's old suit jacket. She dug the fine coat Maguire had discarded and exchanged it for Arnaldo's. The sleeves came down to her fingertips. She turned them up.

'There,' she said, 'I am sure it is ever so much more becoming.'

'You look swell,' said Maguire.

Ryan squatted and fastened the gaiters over the contessa's trousers. Overlapping at the sides and with the straps pulled to the last notch, they fitted snugly.

'There,' he said, straightening. 'Almost as good as boots.'

'I had decided not to keep you as my chauffeur after the war,' she said. 'I may reconsider my decision.'

The pack, the machine pistol, the travelling-rugs, and the food and brandy the contessa had bought in L'Aquila were heaped in the snow beside the Rolls. Ryan got in the car and started the engine. Keeping the clutch pedal depressed, he put it in low gear. He opened the door and, keeping the pedal down with his left foot, reached his right foot out past the running board and poised over the ground. The others gathered to watch. He leapt from the Rolls. It moved forward as deliberately as a ship. The front seemed to hang in the air for an instant, then it tilted down and the car plunged over the side in a shower of rocks. It struck the side of the gorge, bounced off, turned sideways, struck again and landed on its top at the bottom, one wheel askew, the others spinning.

'Mamma mia!' Arnaldo said, clutching his hands to his chest. The chauffeur's gauntlets that Ryan had given him hid his forearms.

Arnaldo started out slowly, looking back to see how the others were keeping up and gradually increasing his pace to a rate accommodating the slowest member of the party. That was Fincham, whose toe was still tender, not the contessa. She was nimble as a ewe, scrambling up inclines, leaping from rock to rock and seemingly enjoying herself. Maguire, though intimidated by the more hazardous stretches, kept protectively close to her. She let him assist her at passages she might have negotiated more easily alone and once, when he slipped, steadied him, to his great embarrassment. Fincham wanted to alternate with Ryan carrying the pack despite his limp, but Ryan said it would delay them too much to keep switching it from one to the other.

Despite her agility, the contessa was the first to tire. She did not complain or ask to rest but her face grew pinched and she began breathing through her mouth, puffing out white vapour as if she were smoking a cigarette. She grew less sure-footed, stumbling on rocks and touching tree trunks for support. She frequently accepted Maguire's assistance. That, and a growing familiarity with the terrain increased his confidence and he no longer hesitated when they skirted a long drop. Ryan fell behind them, where he could keep a watchful eye on her. Arnaldo, obliged to slow the pace, kept looking back at her, scowling.

They reached a rock face, only a dozen feet high but almost vertical, liberally traced with cracks providing hand and footholds. Arnaldo was halfway up to it when Ryan stopped him by calling out his name. When he looked down, Ryan motioned for him to descend.

'Why are we stopping?' the contessa demanded, panting.

'Lunch break.'

'I am quite able to continue.'

'We've got to eat sometime, ma'am.'

Ryan got two travelling-rugs, bread, cheese and the bottle of brandy from the pack. He spread one of the rugs on the cold ground and cut a slit in the middle of the other while Fincham sliced five slabs of bread and cheese with his big knife.

'Slip this on,' Ryan said, handing the contessa the rug.

'With all this exercise I am quite warm,' she said.

'You'll cool off fast. I don't want you getting too stiff to keep up.'

'I am quite capable of keeping up.'

'Humour me, ma'am.'

She slipped the rug over her head, poncho fashion. They all sat down close together on the other rug and ate their bread and cheese. Ryan passed a canteen around, giving it first to the contessa. When they had all had water, Ryan opened the brandy and passed the bottle to the contessa. She looked at it doubtfully, then put it to her lips.

'Rather inferior,' she said, 'but welcome all the same. I

191

believe this is the first time I have taken brandy directly from the bottle.'

'Next time we'll bring a snifter,' said Fincham.

The contessa passed the bottle to Maguire. He shook his head.

'I can't drink liquor,' he said. 'I get sick.'

'All the more for the rest of us,' Fincham said, reaching for the bottle.

Ryan took it out of his hand and recorked it.

'We may need it later on,' he said.

Arnaldo was impatient for them to be on their way. The contessa had her colour back. Ryan nodded. He shook the dirt and leaves from the rug they had been sitting on, folded that and the contessa's rug and stowed them in the pack with the brandy. Arnaldo scrambled up the rock face as if going upstairs. Fincham climbed halfway up and reached down for the pack Ryan held up to him. His boots wedged in a horizontal crevice, his free hand in another, Fincham slid the pack upwards along the stone. Arnaldo lay on his belly and hauled it to the top.

'How's the foot?' Ryan asked.

'Right as rain,' said Fincham. 'How's yours?'

The contessa was next. The stiff gaiters made it difficult for her to bend her knees when she raised her leg to probe for a crack. She bent to remove them, saying she could climb better without them, that she had climbed much more difficult rocks than this. Ryan said it would take too much time and gave her a boost from behind. Fincham reached down and hauled her up as unceremoniously as he had done the pack. Arnaldo reached down and offered his hand but she ignored it and climbed the remaining few feet unassisted. At the top, she adjusted the coat that hung on her like a tent, put her hands on her hips, and stared down at Ryan.

'You are rather free with your hands, Colonel,' she said.

Maguire went up easily.

'I guess I'm getting O.K. at this stuff,' he said buoyantly when they had all assembled again.

'You are doing beautifully, Paolo,' the contessa said.

'Andiamo!' Arnaldo cried impatiently, starting off. *Let's go.*

He found a dim path in the woods and urged them along it. They no longer had to place their feet as carefully but the way was still taxing. They were getting into snow now. The air grew colder and the ridges cast ever-lengthening shadows. A tear-shaped lake in the valley below changed hue from sapphire to indigo. Arnaldo accelerated the pace and said they must hurry if they expected to reach the cabin before nightfall. The contessa was labouring but disdainfully rejected assistance from anyone except Maguire. A light snow began to fall. Darkness overtook them, making the chill seem more intense. Ryan said he had a flashlight in the pack.

'Niente luce!' Arnaldo ordered. *No light.*

They had only a short distance to go, he said. They must form a chain.

The contessa held on to his coat, Maguire to hers. Fincham was next and then Ryan. Arnaldo stopped abruptly. They all ran together except Ryan, who stopped immediately when Fincham blundered into Maguire.

'E la!' Arnaldo cried. 'La cabina.'

No one else could see anything. They climbed for a few minutes more. A small, low structure was outlined against the lesser blackness of the snow-clad slope.

'Un momento,' said Arnaldo.

He left them and continued towards the building. Ryan caught up with him.

'Silenzio,' Arnaldo whispered, putting a gloved finger to his lips.

They felt their way along the wall. At the rear, a faint crack of light showed at the edge of the single window. The cabin was occupied. Ryan touched Arnaldo's shoulder. Arnaldo looked at him and shrugged. Motioning for him to follow, Ryan went back to the others and led them a dozen yards down the slope.

'Somebody's in there,' he said. 'Ask Arnaldo if he has any idea who.'

Arnaldo said it could be anyone. A German patrol, Fascisti,

partisans, someone trying to get across the lines. If they were Tedeschi he would cry out as if in surprise to warn Ryan and they were to hurry down the mountain as quickly and as silently as they could. He would tell the Tedeschi he was alone, a simple shepherd who had lost his way and was looking for shelter.

'Negative,' said Ryan. 'We need him.'

'Your humanity is overwhelming,' the contessa said 'What do you propose, then?'

Her teeth chattered with cold but there was no fear in her tone.

'Lieutenant,' Ryan said, dropping the pack, 'you stay here with the contessa and Arnaldo. Fincham.'

Ryan started towards the cabin, pistol in hand. Fincham was at his heels, unlimbering the machine pistol. Ryan stopped before reaching the cabin. 'I'll kick in the door,' he said. 'You be right behind me. If it's a fight, try not to shoot me in the back if you can help it.'

'Never accidentally, old cock.'

Ryan felt along the cabin wall until he found the entrance. With a finger he silently traced the outline of the door and centred himself in front of it. He stepped back, drew his bent right leg until the knee touched his chest and lashed forward with his heel. The door burst open and crashed against the inside wall. Ryan plunged in and stepped aside quickly to give Fincham a free field of fire.

14

An Alpine trooper in a greatcoat sat at a rough wooden table eating a hard-boiled egg. There was a tin plate of them on the table in front of him, and beside the plate a kerosene lamp and a carbine. Two other Alpini were stretched out in a bunk-bed, their carbines slung from the ends by the straps.

The soldier at the table turned in shock and grabbed for his weapon, egg yolk spilling from his open mouth. The soldiers in the bunk-bed started up, the one on top reaching for his carbine, the other bumping his head on the upper bunk. Ryan shot the one at the table as he picked up his carbine. Fincham cut down the man in the top bunk before he could fire and killed the other as he swung his legs over the side. Feet pounded outside the cabin and Maguire burst in, crouched and ready for action. He stopped in his tracks and looked at the dead men.

'I appreciate your enthusiasm, Lieutenant, but I told you to stay with the contessa,' Ryan said. 'If it had been them shooting you'd be a goner. And the contessa, too.'

'I thought you might need some help, sir. But I guess you never do.'

'We British never get mentioned in Yank dispatches, do we?' said Fincham.

'Start dragging the casualties outside,' Ryan said. 'Poor bastards.' He went to the door and called out, 'All clear. You can come up now.'

Arnaldo, carrying the pack, and the contessa arrived as Fincham was bringing the first body out. They had to stand aside to let him pass. Inside, Maguire was lifting a body from the top bunk. Arnaldo pushed in ahead of the contessa, glanced at the dead men and, pursing his lips, nodded approval.

'Fascisti,' he said contemptuously.

'Don't look, Contessa,' Maguire said, dragging a body by the armpits.

'So now it is my countrymen you are murdering, Colonnello,' she said, not flinching at the sight.

'We do what we have to, ma'am,' Ryan said quietly.

The contessa sighed and said, 'I will say you do not appear to have taken pleasure in it.'

Arnaldo took out the third body while Ryan examined the cabin for indications that it was being used as a permanent post. There were none. No fuel for the charcoal stove, no possessions other than the soldiers' packs with one day's rations and no bedding except an army blanket for each of them.

Fincham was the first one back.

'Poor sods,' he said. 'So surprised they tried to resist instead of surrendering. Not like the desert, I must say.'

When Arnaldo returned with Maguire, Ryan had the contessa ask him what he made of the soldiers' presence in the cabin and if he thought there might be others patrolling the area. Arnaldo said there was no reason for soldiers to be there. It was not an area where patrols should be active and if they had been after partisans, there would have been more than three, and with officers. He suspected they were deserters.

They had placed the bodies by the back wall. They could hide them in the morning before they left, under the snow where they would not be discovered, if at all, before spring.

Ryan went outside with the flashlight, not turning it on until he was behind the cabin and shielding the beam with his hand. He removed the boots from the smallest body. They were well worn but in good condition, oiled and supple. He took them inside and told the contessa to try them on.

'With an extra pair of socks they should fit,' he said. 'Be better than the leggings.'

'I could not,' she said.

'You'll get used to it, ma'am.'

He got a pair of wool stockings out of the pack and gave them to her.

'Fold the ends up over your feet. They'll fill up space and not rub the blisters.'

The contessa pulled the boots on gingerly and took a few tentative steps around the cabin, looking away when she passed the bloodstained straw mattresses.

'They will do nicely,' she said. 'Thank you.'

Ryan arranged with the others to stand two-hour watches fifty yards down the path. He would take the first.

'We'll eat now and turn in,' he said.

'We've a bit of problem,' said Fincham. 'Five of us and only four boiled eggs.'

'We could mash 'em up and divide 'em,' Maguire said.

'How clever,' said the contessa without irony.

Ryan said not to bother, he did not want an egg. They ate the soldiers' skimpy rations. Everyone had a nip of brandy. Afterwards, Ryan and Maguire turned the mattresses over to hide the bloodstains. Ryan assigned the bottom bunk to the contessa and the top one to Arnaldo. Arnaldo protested that he could just as easily sleep on the floor but Ryan insisted.

'Fincham,' Ryan said, 'You can sleep on the table until I come off duty. Maguire, find yourself a soft place on the floor. RHIP.' Rank has its privileges.

Ryan gave the contessa one of the travelling-rugs. The other, he said, was for whoever was on sentry duty. Those inside could have an Italian army blanket each, courtesy of the Alpini.

Outside on the trail, Ryan's boots squeaked in the snow. Thunder muttered intermittently in the south. Artillery. They were twenty miles or so from the battle lines as the crow flew, but considerably further than that through the mountains. He walked up and down to keep warm during his watch. After two hours he woke Fincham and gave him the travelling-rug. Arnaldo was to stand watch after Fincham. Ryan gave Fincham his wrist-watch for Arnaldo to have while their guide was on watch. Maguire would relieve Arnaldo. It would still be dark when Maguire came off and Ryan would stand another watch. They would leave at first light.

It was dark when Ryan came off his second watch but he did not send out a replacement. They ate the last of their bread and cheese, after which Ryan took Arnaldo out with him to bury the soldiers in the snow. When they returned he gave the soldiers' knapsacks to the three men, each with a blanket in it. There was room in the knapsacks for items from the big pack. The German camera and film went into Fincham's knapsack with Red Cross food, and more of the Red Cross food with some of the chocolate into Maguire's. Ryan kept the binoculars out and slung them around his neck.

The Alpini each had a few extra rounds of ammunition for their carbines. Ryan gave a carbine and half the ammunition to Maguire. He told the contessa to ask Arnaldo if he could shoot. Arnaldo could, having hunted for food in his day. Ryan gave him a carbine and the other half of the ammunition. By now it was growing light outside.

Ryan took the third carbine with him when they left. He took it by the barrel and started to heave it out into the snow.

'No!' the contessa cried. 'I will take it. I am quite an excellent shot.'

'It's not like shooting rabbits, ma'am,' Ryan said. 'And it's extra weight to carry.'

'It is very small,' the contessa said, 'hardly larger than a toy. And perhaps if necessary, I, too, will learn to shoot men like rabbits, as you do.'

Ryan gave her the carbine.

They walked all morning below the crest of the range, often on trails visible only to Arnaldo, passing through stands of evergreens that showered them with snow when they pushed branches aside, skirting canyons and trudging across smooth expanses of white with the ribbon of the winding road sometimes visible on the valley floor far below.

The distant rumble of artillery fire was more muffled than in the still, cold night air. Aircraft passed overhead, German going south and Allied north, fighters, fighter-bombers, medium bombers and once, at high altitude, a strung-out formation of B-24s, streaming contrails. Six Spitfires, in two

198

elements of three, streaked over from the south and dived, going into trail. The chatter of their machine-guns was faintly audible as they strafed the Sulmona-Roccaraso road deep in the valley on the other side of the range. Maguire stopped to listen and had to hurry to catch up with the rest of the party.

The contessa bore up remarkably well, as if the previous day's exertions and nine hours of exhausted sleep had somehow tapped a long-dormant well of vitality. It was only after they had been tramping steadily for three hours that she began to falter. Ryan called a halt among snow-clad pines and passed around cigarettes. Maguire refused, saying he wished he had some chewing-gum.

'Ask Arnaldo if there's any way we can reach the lines by tomorrow morning,' Ryan told the contessa.

Only by walking day and night, Arnaldo said. And they would still have to wait for the following night to cross them under cover of darkness. It was better to rest tonight and tomorrow go as close to the lines as prudence allowed, resting again before the final dash.

'Such impatience,' the contessa said. 'It will still be two days before Wahlberg's surprise.'

'The sooner we get word through, the more chance we have of stopping the Krauts,' Maguire said. 'They could blow right on through if we're stretched thin.'

'You are so wise for a lieutenant, Paolo. But please say "German". Kraut is vulgar.'

After two hours they paused again to eat a few squares of dark, grainy chocolate and have a sip from the brandy bottle. Ryan asked Arnaldo if they would have another shelter for the night. Arnaldo said they would, not a cabin but a shallow cave beneath an overhang where they could safely have a fire. They could break off their march before dark to gather wood and still have ample time next day to reach a suitable place in which to await nightfall for the final dash.

In mid-afternoon, just after they had left the shelter of the woods for an open snow-field, Arnaldo stopped them with an abrupt gesture and motioned for them to return to the trees. From the shelter of the woods he pointed up ahead to a mountain crest. Ryan raised the binoculars to his eyes and picked out a white-clad German patrol slanting down the slope on skis. There were six men in single file, angling towards their hiding place.

'Everybody down!' Ryan ordered. 'Burrow in.'

He lay flat and pushed a mound of snow up high enough to conceal his body. He plastered two handfuls of snow on his cap and tracked the patrol through the binoculars. They kept coming, stolid and careless, weapons slung.

'Be ready,' Ryan whispered. 'But don't make a move unless I give the order.'

'How many?' Fincham asked.

'Six. Single file.'

The patrol drew close. Ryan could see the leader's face clearly, framed in a white parka. He wore no insignia of rank as far as Ryan could see. His white cape was crusted with snow, as if he had taken a fall.

'Get ready,' Ryan whispered.

The leader held up his hand and the patrol halted. He looked down into the valley and then directly at Ryan. Ryan remained perfectly still, holding his breath and focusing the glasses on the patrol leader's eyes, pale blue beneath thick, straw-coloured brows. It was as if their eyes locked. The patrol leader gave no start of discovery. He motioned for his men to follow and the patrol curled back towards the crest. Ryan kept the glasses on them until they disappeared over it.

'All clear,' he said.

They scrambled to their feet and brushed away the snow.

'Tell me,' said the contessa, 'what could we have done against six Germans?'

'Not much, if they'd been expecting trouble,' Ryan replied. 'But they weren't.'

'Yes,' the contessa said. 'You seem to be at your best against unsuspecting persons.'

'That's right, ma'am. And I hope it stays like that.'

Ryan told her to ask Arnaldo why he had not warned them of the danger of German patrols. Arnaldo said there should not have been one this far behind the battle lines.

'They may have found the lieutenant by now,' Fincham said. 'They could be looking for the contessa and friends.'

'They wouldn't expect partisans·this close to the front,' Ryan said.

'Partisans, sir?' said Maguire.

'They'd assume partisans killed the lieutenant and kidnapped the contessa.'

'What?' the contessa demanded.

'They'd never suspect the Contessa di Montalba of being involved with the murderers of German soldiers,' Ryan said calmly.

'But you said...'

'I know what I said, ma'am,' Ryan said in the same calm tone. 'But we needed your car. And I couldn't leave you behind after what you'd seen. You might have had another change of loyalties.'

'You are unspeakable.'

'Tender-hearted, ma'am. It was bring you along or knock you in the head. Wouldn't want to do that to a lady.'

'I dare say you could have brought yourself to it, Colonel.'

'Never know for sure, will we, ma'am?'

They descended the slope through the woods to keep more distance between themselves and the patrolled upper reaches of the mountains. Ryan instructed everyone to walk in the foot-prints of the person ahead. If a patrol should stumble across their track it would make it difficult for the Germans to determine how many were in the party. After they had been walking for a few minutes, Maguire fell back until he was just in front of Ryan. He kept looking back at Ryan over his shoulder.

'Something on your mind, Lieutenant?'

'Sir,' Maguire said hesitantly, 'Sir, you wouldn't really have...? Not a nice old lady like her.'

'She's not a nice old lady, Lieutenant. And don't you forget it.'

They walked until late afternoon, slaking their thirst with snow scooped up on the move, taking time to pass the canteen around only once, when Ryan called a halt to let the contessa catch her breath. They went more cautiously than they had done before seeing the patrol, with Ryan making periodic sweeps of the terrain through the glasses.

When Arnaldo announced they were within a kilometre or so of the night's bivouac, they dropped their packs and weapons and foraged in the snow for firewood. Everyone except the contessa had an armload when they resumed the walk. Arnaldo led them to a narrow, brush-choked ravine. They followed it to a spur of rock beetling out five feet above its floor. There was a hollow space beneath the spur extending back eight or ten feet into solid rock. The blackened remnants of old fires lay against the back wall.

'Ask Arnaldo how sure he is that it's safe,' Ryan told the contessa. 'It looks like he's not the only one who knows about it.'

She did so without acknowledging Ryan's existence. She had been ignoring him since learning he had tricked her. Arnaldo said he was the only one who knew about the cave. The fires were his. He had been coming here since he was a boy and not once had he encountered another living soul.

Arnaldo lit a fire on the site of the old ones, building carefully from a nest of small twigs to increasingly thicker pieces of broken limbs, using only one match. Fincham sat down by the fire, took off his shoe and sock and rubbed his toe with salve. The contessa turned her head in distaste. When it was dark, Ryan went back out of the ravine to see from what distance the glow was visible. It could be seen only from well within the ravine.

They supped on Canadian biscuits and slices of Spam broiled over the fire on the rapier-shaped bayonets folded below the barrels of the Italian carbines.

'This is delicious,' the contessa said. 'What is it called?'

'Spam,' said Maguire. 'It is good. Before I got captured, I didn't like it.'

'I hope the Germans did not treat you too badly, poor boy.'

'It was the Italians had me. They were O.K., I guess.'

'I am pleased it was not the Germans. Italians are more simpatico. Congenial.'

Fincham chuckled.

'That was the word for our friend Oriani. Congenial. Right, Ryan?'

'Oriani,' the contessa said, musing. 'I am acquainted with some Orianis. Torino. Was the Oriani of whom you speak from Torino? Perhaps I know him.'

'Knew,' said Fincham. 'He's dead.'

'This tedious war,' the contessa said with a sigh. 'I am surprised he was a friend of yours. The Orianis I know are all loyal.'

'A friend? Not bloody likely. He preferred Jerry. Like you.'

'I suppose it was Colonel Ryan who killed him, then.'

'No, ma'am,' said Ryan, 'that honour belongs to an Italian. Fincham, the lady doesn't prefer Germans. She prefers whoever is in charge at the moment. Right, Contessa?'

'True,' she replied, speaking directly to Ryan for the first time in hours. 'However, as you seem to be in charge at the moment, I am finding it rather difficult to maintain that philosophy.'

Fincham stroked his moustache and grinned at her.

'Contessa, it's worth tramping the length of Italy to hear Von Ryan get a bit of his own back.'

'You are not the best of friends, are you? I find that rather puzzling.'

'Even now that you've come to know him so well?'

'I suppose not,' she said, smiling. She glanced at Maguire, who was scowling. 'What is it, caro? Why are you sulking?'

'You ought not to talk about the colonel that way,' he said stiffly. 'If it wasn't for Colonel Ryan, none of us would be here.'

'Precisely the point, caro.'

Ryan sent Maguire out with an empty knapsack to bring in snow. When he returned, Ryan packed the canteen with snow and pushed it down among live coals. He continued to melt snow until the canteen was three-quarters full of boiling water. It required most of the contents of the knapsack. He poured in a handful of coffee and let it boil a while longer.

'Anyone like their coffee sweet?' he asked.

They all did.

'I'm outvoted,' said Ryan, dropping in three saccharin tablets.

'Mark this, Contessa,' Fincham said. 'You've just seen history made. That's the first time Von Ryan ever put anything to a vote.'

Ryan lifted the canteen from the coals with a folded Italian blanket and added a shot of brandy. When the canteen cooled a bit he handed it to the contessa, still nested in the blanket. She sipped at it, savouring each swallow.

'It could be a bit sweeter,' she said. 'But marvellous.'

She held the canteen out to Maguire.

'No, thanks. It's got brandy in it.'

'Try it, Paolo,' the contessa urged. 'It's delicious. And you need something warm. It is quite chilly here.'

Maguire took a tentative sip.

'Hey,' he said. 'This is swell.'

'The first step towards corruption,' said Fincham.

Maguire drank more and passed the canteen to Ryan, who offered it to Arnaldo.

'Dopo Lei, Colonnello,' Arnaldo said politely. *After you*.

He accepted the canteen only after Ryan had taken a swallow. They passed it around until it was empty. Ryan sent Maguire out for another knapsack of snow and spread out his maps in the firelight. He summoned the contessa and Arnaldo to him. Now, a single map encompassed their position and Roccarosa. If they went as quickly as today, Arnaldo said, by the next afternoon they would have travelled as far as they safely could by daylight. He assured Ryan that it would take but a few hours to reach safety. They would be obliged to climb the range barring access to the valley beyond, descending some kilometres to the south-east of Roccaraso. The Tedeschi would have strong-points on the downslope, and across the valley the British would be just as strongly positioned and just as ready to open fire at any hint of movement towards their lines. And, of course, there would be minefields in the valley between the opposing forces.

'Will I be able to have a look at the Piano delle Cinquemiglia on the way tomorrow?' Ryan asked.

Arnaldo said there would be time but he would not advise it. It would mean climbing to the summit and risk being seen by the Tedeschi, who would be present in ever-increasing numbers as they drew closer to the battle lines.

'Tell him I appreciate the warning,' said Ryan.

Maguire returned with the snow. Ryan melted some of it to rinse out the canteen and filled the canteen with snow water. He spread the Italian blankets out side by side and covered them with the travelling-rugs.

'We'll sleep side by side,' he said. 'Head to toe. And use our coats for cover.'

'All of us together?' the contessa asked.

'Yes. Except for the man on watch.'

She laughed.

'Mark this, Enrico. Now you will see history being made. It is the first time the Contessa di Montalba has shared a bed with more than one man.'

Maguire was shocked.

'Forgive me, caro,' said the contessa. 'I quite forgot how very young you are.'

There would be two-hour watches, Ryan said, as before. It would be more comfortable for the man on duty, however. He had only to remain awake and keep the fire going. Ryan took the first watch. Maguire lay at one edge of the blankets, his head towards the fire; the contessa lay next to him with her head at his toes and her wool-stockinged feet, empty toes drooping like a hound's ears, warmed by the fire; then Fincham, with his big feet thrusting out beyond the hat pulled down over the contessa's ears, and on the outside, Arnaldo. Arnaldo snored. It did not affect the slumber of the others.

After two hours, Ryan changed places with Arnaldo after indicating with gestures that Fincham was to follow the little Italian on watch. Ryan fell asleep at once, as was his habit. A stone glancing off the spur at the front of the cave woke him. Fincham did not stir beside him. Maguire, sitting up by the fire, looked at Ryan in alarm. Ryan put a finger to his lips for silence. He woke the others in turn, cautioning each with the finger at his lips. He crawled to Maguire on hands and knees and asked in a low voice, 'Hear anything besides the rock falling?'

Maguire shook his head. Fincham crawled to them.

'What's up?' he whispered.

'Maybe nothing,' Ryan replied.

Arnaldo and the contessa were sitting up, watching them. The contessa opened her mouth to ask a question. Ryan shook his head and closed it, the question unasked but lingering on her face. The wavering firelight was kind to her. She looked like a much younger woman.

'Everybody sit tight,' Ryan whispered.

He crawled out beneath the lip of the overhang and lay flat. Someone floundered in the snow above the cave. Snow showered down and a voice swore in German. Men laughed. More snow came down. An order was given. The laughter stopped and feet squeaked in the snow, walking towards the ravine mouth. Ryan backed inside, found his shoes and Tenbrink's knife, shoved the machine pistol towards Fincham and emptied the canteen on to the fire. The cave filled with acrid smoke.

'Don't anybody cough,' Ryan said.

A light flicked on above the ravine and moved towards its entrance.

15

Ryan slipped into his shoes, not taking time to tie the laces. He paused outside, Fincham at his shoulder. He spoke into Fincham's ear.

'I'm going to the entrance,' he said. 'You drop off about halfway up. There's just one man. If he comes poking around inside I'll get him. When the others come to see what happened to him I'll let 'em pass me. When I whistle, it means they're all in. Keep it waist high. I'll be flat.'

Ryan went quietly towards the entrance, crawling through the undergrowth and hugging the steeply sloping side of the ravine. Above him, feet skirted the edge. A flashlight beam probed down. Ryan burrowed into the thick, leafless vegetation. The beam slid past him and along the opposite side of the ravine. Ryan continued his crawl, halting a few feet short of the ravine mouth. He flattened himself against the side in the undergrowth, the knife ready in his hand, his .45 still in his waistband. The flashlight reached the entrance and played inside, revealing nothing, neither Fincham nor the rock overhang deep within the ravine.

'Zu klein,' a voice called out. *Too small*.

'Wiederkommen,' another voice ordered from above the cave. 'Wir werden hier bleiben.' *Come back. We'll stay here*.

The light withdrew and went back along the edge of the ravine. Ryan slipped back to the cave, picking up Fincham along the way.

'Contessa,' Ryan said in the inky darkness. 'Did you hear?'

'Yes.'

'What did they say? The last part.'

'They are remaining above us.'

'Did they say for how long?'

'No.'

There was a flurry of activity above the cave as the Germans settled in, muffled by the solid stone between Ryan's group and the patrol, then silence broken only by the painfully muted breathing of the occupants. They huddled together under the blankets, scarcely moving. As the cold cramped their limbs it became increasingly uncomfortable to remain still. Ryan looked at the luminous dial of his watch. Dawn was still two hours away. He groped for the brandy bottle and, with a whisper, passed it around. Maguire took a swallow and choked. Ryan put a hand over his mouth until he was quiet again.

Daylight seeped into the cave. Ryan slowly flexed his stiff arms and legs, indicating that the others were to do the same. When they had eased their cramped limbs, he motioned for Arnaldo and the contessa to draw close.

'Ask him how long it'll take to reach where he planned after waiting for darkness,' Ryan said.

'At least six hours,' Arnaldo said. At this time of year there were only ten hours of daylight. If the Tedeschi did not go away soon, they could not pass through the lines until the night after tomorrow.

Fincham crawled over to join them.

'What's the drill?' he asked.

'It's up to them,' Ryan said, tilting his head towards the roof of the cave. 'Arnaldo says if we have to stay here much longer we'll lose a whole day.'

'Let's take them, then.'

Ryan shook his head.

'We don't know how many of 'em are up there.'

'Do you think they will find us?' the contessa asked.

She did not sound alarmed. The daylight was not as kind to her as the firelight had been, accenting the tired lines of her face with shadows.

'Let's hope not, ma'am.'

Someone shouted an order. Men called to one another in surly tones. Boots stamped on crusted snow, equipment rattled and snow sifted down past the overhang. The patrol was moving out.

It was almost nine in the morning. They still had more than seven hours to reach the day's destination. Before they left the cave, Ryan consulted with Arnaldo over the map about the best place along their route from which to climb to the summit for a view of the Piano delle Cinquemiglia. If they did not dawdle they would reach such a place early in the afternoon, Arnaldo said. He still advised against it, particularly now that they were aware of constant patrol activity.

They kept within the tree-line, eating Canadian biscuits and cold Spam and scooping up snow for water as they walked. Within an hour the contessa began lagging and Arnaldo had to slow the pace. He kept looking back at her, scowling and muttering to himself. After half an hour of this he stopped walking and harangued Ryan, waving his arms and shaking his fingers at her.

'Arnaldo wants to abandon me,' she said calmly. 'He does not believe I am an American agent. It would be better for the rest of you, of course. I am surprised the suggestion did not come first from you, Colonel.'

'Look here!' Maguire cried, grabbing Arnaldo by the front of his coat.

A knife materialised in Arnaldo's hand. He stared balefully at Maguire.

'You don't scare me,' Maguire said defiantly. 'Nobody's going off and leaving her, you hear?'

'Lieutenant!' Ryan snapped. 'Arnaldo!'

Maguire let go of Arnaldo immediately and the Italian put his knife away.

'We have no intention of jettisoning you, Contessa,' Ryan said. 'We'd never have got this far without your help.'

'Do I detect a note of gratitude, Colonel? I am astonished.'

'Besides which,' Ryan continued, 'if you get picked up by a patrol, I wouldn't give a nickel for our chances.'

'I find that far more reassuring than your gratitude.'

Ryan motioned for Arnaldo to move out, which he did at a vindictively increased pace, muttering, 'Stregona d'una fascista.' *Witch of a fascist.* The contessa overtook him and blocked his way. Standing very erect, face cold but composed, swallowed in her bulky coat, she spoke to him in ringing tones. Arnaldo made as if to push by. She thrust out one gloved finger and put it in his chest, her voice stinging. Arnaldo stopped.

'That's telling him, Contessa,' said Maguire.

'Scusi, Contessa,' Arnaldo apologised grudgingly.

She let him pass and fell in behind him. Arnaldo continued at a brisk but more sensible pace. Before long the contessa started lagging again. Teeth clenched, face set, she forced herself on and only with reluctance took Maguire's proffered arm and permitted him to carry her carbine. Ryan stopped long enough for her to ask Arnaldo how much longer it would take to reach the point from which he would climb for his view of the Piano delle Cinquemiglia.

'Un'altr'ora,' Arnaldo said. *Another hour.*

'You'll have to hang on a little longer, ma'am,' Ryan said. 'You can rest while I'm gone.'

She nodded, white-lipped.

They climbed among trees. The ascent grew steeper and the blanket of snow thicker. The contessa pushed through the snow, eyes half-closed, holding on to Maguire's coat. Even Ryan was breathing heavily, sucking in great lungfuls of cold air. Only Arnaldo seemed unaffected.

The contessa let go of Maguire's coat and sat down in the snow.

'I am afraid you must go on without me,' she said calmly between gasps.

'You can make it,' Maguire said, a pleading note in his voice.

They gathered around her, all except Arnaldo, who stood looking down at her in ill-concealed triumph.

'Just another few minutes,' Ryan said. 'Now get up off your behind and start walking.'

Maguire bit back a protest.

210

'I will try,' she said.

Ryan and Maguire helped her to her feet and they continued up the mountain. Fincham dropped back to walk beside Ryan.

'She's in a bad way,' he said. 'Think she's up to it?'

'She'll do her damnedest.'

'You weren't too gentle with her back there, Ryan. You're even nastier than I thought.'

'If you think sweet talk'll be more effective than nastiness, snap to it, Colonel.'

After ten minutes the contessa collapsed. Sprawling in the snow, propped up on an elbow, dignified even in her exhaustion, she looked up at Ryan and shrugged. Maguire dropped to his knees beside her.

'I thought you were a survivor,' Ryan said without sympathy.

'And so I am. But even survivors have their limits.'

Ryan squatted and uncorked the brandy bottle.

'Maybe this'll help.'

'I am beyond that.'

'Damn it, we're only minutes away from a rest stop! And after that it'll be downhill again for a while.'

'Tempting, but my limbs refuse to support me another step.'

Ryan thrust the machine pistol at the surprised Maguire. He slipped out of his pack and gave it to Fincham, then reached down and took the contessa under the arms.

'Did you hear nothing I said?' she demanded with asperity, despite her fatigue. 'I cannot continue.'

'Save your breath,' Ryan ordered, propping her up and turning so that she leaned against his back. 'Put your arms around my neck.'

'If I must.'

Ryan bent, slipped his arms behind her knees and hoisted her up piggyback. He motioned for Arnaldo to resume the march and fell in behind him. Ryan ploughed through the snow which came over his ankles. She was heavier than the pack he had been carrying.

'I should get out the camera,' Fincham said, right behind them.

'I suppose it is rather a droll spectacle,' the contessa said. 'It would be amusing if I were not so uncomfortable. Paolo, I often carried my Paolo thus when he was a child.'

'Whatever happened to him?' said Maguire.

'He is living in Roma. And quite well, so I have heard.'

'Chip off the old block,' Ryan said.

After a few minutes, Maguire offered to carry her. Ryan told him to save his strength. The contessa agreed.

'He is enormously strong, caro,' she explained, 'but so is a mule.'

At last Arnaldo called a halt in a sheltered hollow just within the tree-line. The contessa slipped from Ryan's back and tested her legs, then sat on the knapsack Maguire had placed at the foot of a tree and leaned back against the trunk. Her colour had improved greatly.

Arnaldo pointed out a crease stretching from near the hollow to the summit. If the colonnello would remain within it on the way up, it was less likely that he would be seen by the Tedeschi. But not to take too long. There was still some distance to go and they would want to rest a bit before the night-time crossing of the lines. Three hours of hard going if the *stregona* did not hold them back.

'By the time you return from your excursion I will be quite capable of walking three hours more, Colonel Ryan,' the contessa added when she translated the information, not omitting Arnaldo's reference to 'the witch'. 'I have enjoyed a most refreshing mule ride.'

'You ought not to talk about the colonel in that way,' Maguire said severely.

'You are right, caro. I apologise, Colonnello. A mule has four legs and you carried me with but two.'

'We'll take our rest break here,' Ryan said, 'and keep going after I get back.'

He and Maguire made a cosy nest in the hollow with the Italian blankets and travelling-rugs. Ryan distributed chocolate and American Red Cross parcel raisins and passed around the brandy bottle. The contessa lay down with a knapsack for a pillow. Maguire brought her her ration. Ryan ate quickly and got the camera and two rolls of film from the big pack.

'Going to snap us, are you?' Fincham asked. 'Something nice to put in the album and doze over before the fire when the war is over.'

Ryan slung the binoculars around his neck.

'I won't be gone long,' he said.

'I'll come with you,' said Fincham. 'Should be a lovely view and I'm tired of looking down at my boots.'

Maguire wanted to go with them, saying he was not tired. Ryan ordered him to stay with the contessa and gave him the machine pistol in exchange for his carbine.

'Know how to use one of these?' he asked.

'Yes, sir. I had one for a souvenir before... I'll bet they divided my stuff and somebody took it. Cost me fifty dollars, too.'

'Take good care of this one and you may have it when we're done,' Fincham promised. 'As well as a thrilling story to go with it. I shouldn't be too frightened while we're gone if I were you, Contessa. Paolo will protect you from Jerry's patrols and Arnaldo's advances.'

'He is quite capable of doing so,' the contessa said, not amused. 'Do not sulk, caro. If you do not remain with me I will find it quite tedious having no one to speak with other than this wretched old mountain goat.'

Ryan and Fincham climbed to the summit, keeping to the shelter of the crease. They crawled the final yards. The mountains fell away in a billowy sweep of snow and woods to a broad, treeless plain, snow-streaked and mottled brown, bordered to the east by another snowy range. The two ranges converged towards Roccaraso. The village itself was hidden from view by broken ridges. The intermittent rumble of artillery was louder than it had been down the western slope.

The vast plain was empty except for a single vehicle speeding along the Sulmona-Roccaraso road, a pencil line tracing the length of its level surface.

'So much for my brilliant analysis of Jerry's intentions,' Fincham said ruefully. 'There's damn-all here.'

With a startling shout of engines, four Spitfires darted from

213

the gap where the converging mountains pinched the Rocca-raso end of the Piano delle Cinquemiglia. Two of the fighters went into trail and swooped low towards the vehicle. It turned off the road desperately, a fleeing beetle, as tracers poured lazily towards it. The vehicle erupted into a tiny spurt of flame like a struck match and careered across the valley floor as all four Spitfires sped northward.

The vehicle stopped abruptly and exploded with a ringing clang, reaching Ryan and Fincham's vantage point moments later. A black patch, small and growing, bordered in flame, appeared in the brown, revealing a concealed tank into which the vehicle had crashed. Ryan trained the binoculars on the hole.

Running soldiers appeared as if out of the ground and converged on the vehicle, revealed by the glasses to be a half-track. Some of them pulled bodies from the half-track while others fought to beat out the burning edges of the black patch. Within it, Ryan saw the back of a second tank and the protruding gun of a third. Silently, he handed the glasses to Fincham.

'Good God!' Fincham whispered, awed.

'The plain must be swarming with 'em,' said Ryan. 'Seems like you were right after all, Colonel. Congratulations.'

Ryan took two pictures of the scene and then finished both rolls in long-exposure, overlapping shots of the plain from its narrow neck to as far north-west as he could see. He rewrapped the exposed rolls and put them back in their boxes.

They passed the binoculars back and forth while soldiers extinguished the fires in the half-track, the tank it had rammed and the camouflaging. Other soldiers swiftly unrolled more camouflaging and stretched it over the burned-out area. Once again the Piano delle Cinquemiglia was an unbroken expanse of mottled browns.

'Let's go,' said Ryan. 'The quicker we deliver this film the better.'

'Do you think the pictures will show anything?' Fincham asked as they hurried down the slope. 'That's the cleverest camouflage I've seen.'

214

'They should. Fine grain film and slow shutter speed. And low oblique angle. Blown up, they'll show things you can't get with aerial reconnaissance.'

'Lovely,' said Fincham. 'Ours will lay on some air and smash them before Jerry knows what's hit him.'

'If we make it through.'

The snow outside the hollow among the trees was marked with ski tracks and patterned with milling bootprints. Motioning for Fincham to take cover, Ryan dropped to his belly and crawled towards the hollow. He stopped and held his breath, listening. The only sound was the far-off crump of artillery. He inched to the edge of the hollow and lifted his head with infinite caution, the carbine in firing position.

There was no one in the hollow. The only evidence that Maguire, the contessa and Arnaldo had ever been there was a torn Italian blanket, an empty Spam tin and an Italian carbine flung against a rock, its stock shattered.

'Fincham,' Ryan called softly, standing up.

Fincham came on the run, halting when he saw that the hollow was empty. He looked at Ryan through narrowed eyes and pulled at his moustache.

'No blood,' Ryan said thoughtfully.

'And we heard no firing. They let themselves be taken by surprise, the bloody idiots.'

'Let's have a look around.'

They circled the hollow and picked up ski tracks herring-boning towards the heights in the south-west. There were three sets of bootprints among the tracks and a pair of parallel ski marks, as if something were being dragged.

'If nothing else, they're all mobile,' Fincham said. 'Do you think Jerry knows he doesn't have the whole lot?'

'Been waiting for us if they did. We'll follow for a while. We've got a better chance of getting through with Arnaldo than without him and they're going in the right direction.'

'Wouldn't go after them if they weren't, would you? What do you propose doing if we catch up?'

Instead of answering, Ryan began walking swiftly along the trail left by the patrol. The sun fell below the level of the distant peaks as they continued the pursuit. Shadows filled the hollows and blanketed the woods below the tree-line.

'It'll be dark soon,' Fincham said. 'What then?'

'We'll keep going. Have to if we expect to get across the lines before morning.'

Darkness fell abruptly. Ryan followed the ski tracks by feel, sliding his boots along and angling back when they felt unbroken snow. Their progress was slow. At intervals Ryan consulted Tenbrink's wrist compass, shielding the luminous markings with a hand. Fincham drew alongside him.

'We could find ourselves at the bottom of a long drop if we don't watch out,' he said.

'Not as long as we follow the patrol.'

'So that's it. Not a gallant rescue. For a moment I thought Von Ryan was doing something impractical. Should have known better.'

'Knock it off. Sound carries.'

The trail went on, unswerving. Fincham's boots crunched in the snow.

'Set 'em down easy,' Ryan said.

Sometimes they stumbled in the deep tracks of the parallel skis. One would silently steady the other as they continued feeling their way along in pursuit of the patrol.

Someone laughed in the darkness. A woman's laugh. A man's voice responded. Fincham clutched Ryan's arm, his fingers digging in.

'Your bloody contessa's gone over,' he whispered.

With no need to confer, they crouched and moved towards the sounds. The darkness gleamed dimly up ahead, as if a low hummock of snow was faintly phosphorescent. They crawled towards the gleam. The deliberate crunch of boots in the snow halted them. They pressed themselves flat against the snow. A form bulked dark between them and the gleam as a sentry moved past the hummock, walking towards them. He stopped thirty feet away, stamped his feet, slapped his arms against his sides and turned to retrace his steps. Ryan gripped Fincham's shoulder in a warning to remain motionless. He lay listening and watching until the sentry walked back and forth twice.

The sentry moved slowly, stopping often to stamp his feet and slap his sides. Two voices, the contessa's and a man's, carried from the faintly gleaming hummock just audible enough to tell they were speaking German.

Ryan pushed the camera and binoculars into the snow and passed his carbine to Fincham. He timed the sentry's route by counting his own breaths. It took the German a little more than a hundred and twenty of them to come and go. The moment the sentry reached the closest point to them and turned to retrace his steps, Ryan began crawling towards him. He went quickly, the sentry's movements covering the small sounds of his approach. He stopped two yards short of the end of the sentry's post and pushed up a mound of snow to hide behind. He lay face down, listening, as the footsteps returned. The sentry came towards him and stopped, his boots scuffing the snow only six feet from where Ryan lay. Elbows pressed to his sides, Ryan planted both palms flat against the snow, waiting for the moment when the sentry turned to present his back.

'Diese verdammte Kälte,' the sentry muttered. *This damned cold.*

Snow squeaked as he turned. Ryan tensed and leapt on him, digging in his toes and pushing with his hands.

A light flicked on and caught him as he started up and a voice cried out, 'Rühren Sie sich nicht!' *Don't move.*

16

Ryan stopped, frozen in a crouch, blinded by the powerful flashlight beam playing on him.

'Was zum Teufel!' the sentry cried, whirling and snatching the slung rifle from his shoulder with instinctive ease. *What the devil*!

'Hände hoch!' said a voice from behind the light. *Up with your hands*!

Ryan straightened slowly and raised his open hands to shoulder level. The sentry's rifle was pointed not at him but beyond, where he had left Fincham lying in the snow. Three German soldiers, tunics unbuttoned, crawled pell-mell out of a low white tent clutching weapons. From the hummock, revealed by the light to be a smaller white tent dimly lit inside, stepped an officer with a pistol in his hand. Between the tents, Maguire and Arnaldo stared at Ryan from a nest of Italian blankets, travelling-rugs and German greatcoats.

'Was ist los?' the contessa called from inside the officers's tent. *What is going on*?

The officer answered in German as he walked towards Ryan, the pistol dangling. The soldier with the flashlight had come closer and thrust his weapon in Ryan's ribs. Fincham came up to join Ryan, his hands clasped on top of his head. Neither of them glanced at Maguire and Arnaldo, who were now sitting up, thier hands tied behind them.

The officer, a young lieutenant with short, fair hair and a day's growth of golden whiskers, slowly circled Ryan and Fincham. The contessa thrust her head out of the tent. She was muffled in a German greatcoat with only her head and a lapel of Paolo's jacket showing. Her face betrayed no recognition, only curiosity.

The lieutenant poked the barrel of his pistol under Ryan's chin and lifted, his eyes cold and menacing. He spoke to Ryan in halting Italian. Ryan looked straight ahead, saying nothing, holding his head level though the front sight dug mercilessly into the flesh beneath his chin. The officer lifted harder and repeated the question more firmly. Ryan kept silent.

'Sehr interessant,' the lieutenant said. 'Du bist denn kein Italianer.' *Very interesting. You're not Italian, then*.

He turned toward Maguire, who was watching, blank-faced.

'You, know you these men?'

'No,' said Maguire.

The lieutenant spoke to Arnaldo in Italian. Arnaldo shrugged and shook his head. The lieutenant took the flashlight from the soldier who had surprised Ryan and held it on the new prisoners while the soldier searched them cursorily for weapons, taking only their .45s and the broad-bladed knife.

The lieutenant examined the pistol.

'Ach, so,' he said 'Amerikanisch.'

'I guess the jig's up,' said Ryan. 'Smith, William A., Sergeant, U.S. Army. Serial number 38056485. This here's Corporal Atkins. Prisoners of the Eyeties before they quit.'

'Kriegsgefangenen, say you?' the officer demanded, poking Ryan in the ribs with his own pistol. 'With G.I. pistol and killer knife?' He said 'G.I.' German fashion. 'Saboteurs!' he cried. 'Wie die anderen zwei.' *Like the other two*.

He gave a command and the two soldiers stepped forward. They bound the prisoners' hands behind them roughly. The lieutenant inspected the knots and gave another order. The soldiers shoved them toward the nest of blankets and greatcoats. The lieutenant turned towards the tent. The contessa pulled her head back inside. The lieutenant went in and closed the flap behind him. Ryan burrowed under the greatcoats next to Maguire.

'What happened?' he demanded.

'First thing we knew, they had us surrounded, sir. Yelling at us in German. I'm sorry, sir. They took us by surprise.'

'I know that. What about the contessa?'

'She talked to the Lieutenant in Italian at first. Near as I could make out, she said we were *briganti*. Bandits. We'd murdered her chauffeur and kidnapped her and she thanked 'em for saving her. And I thought she was such a nice old lady!'

'She didn't say anything about Colonel Fincham or me?'

'Not that I know of, sir. After a while they started talking in German. His Italian's not much better'n mine. So I don't know what she said. One of the Germans took off his skis and they made a kind of sled for her so she wouldn't have to walk. Sir, what will they do to us?'

'See what they can get out of us and then put us up against a wall,' Fincham said. 'I've half a mind to see your bloody contessa stands up there with us.'

'Nobody's up against a wall yet,' said Ryan. 'Everybody simmer down. Pretend to sleep.'

They lay on their sides, unable to be comfortable on their backs because of their bound wrists. The soldiers had returned to their tent and the sentry to his post. At first the sentry flashed a light on the prisoners when he passed but, seeing no movement, he began ignoring them. When the guard changed, the lieutenant came out of his tent with a light.

'Nobody move,' Ryan whispered.

The lieutenant came over and played the light on them. Ryan muttered peevishly, as if half-awake, eyes closed, and turned his face away. The lieutenant went back to the tent. Ryan watched through half-closed eyes as he came back out with a sleeping-bag and crawled into it. The light in the tent went out.

The new sentry sang softly to himself as he trudged back and forth. Ryan waited until he went by and rolled over, shoving his back against Maguire's.

'Lieutenant,' he whispered. 'See if you can reach into my trouser pocket. They missed my pocket-knife.'

Maguire's hands fumbled aside Ryan's coat, slid across his

belt and groped down to his pocket. The sentry started back from the end of his route.

'Hold it,' Ryan said.

The sentry went by.

'O.K.,' said Ryan.

A hand thrust awkwardly into his pocket.

'Got it!' Maguire whispered truimphantly. 'Jesus, I dropped it.'

Ryan rolled on his back, his wrists digging into his spine. He felt the knife pressing into his hip. He raised his buttocks a few inches and slid down until he could take the knife between his palms. On his side again, he held the knife in one hand and felt for the long blade with the curled fingers of the other. He slide his thumbnail into the niche in the side of the blade and lifted. He worked the blade fully open and slid back up until his hands were next to Maguire's. The sentry passed again and he lay still.

'Take it and hold on tight,' Ryan said, pressing the knife into Maguire's hands with the cutting edge turned towards himself.

He moved his wrists up and down along the blade. The knife slipped once and he nicked himself. He stopped each time the sentry approached. It was tedious work. Though the blade was sharp, Ryan had to saw with great caution because of the awkwardness of his position and Maguire's. His hands came free. He rubbed his wrists, feeling a slick film of blood on one of them, and flexed his arms beneath the greatcoats.

'What the devil are you up to?' Fincham whispered.

Ryan felt for Fincham's wrists and cut the cord binding them. Then he freed Maguire's. Arnaldo lay on the other side of Maguire, sleeping soundly.

'Give me the knife, sir,' Maguire whispered. 'I'll cut Arnaldo's.'

'Tell him to stay put. That goes for you, too. And you too, Fincham.'

The next time the sentry approached, Ryan gave a low moan. The sentry stopped.

'Was?' he demanded. 'Was ist los?'

Ryan moaned again. The sentry drew closer, wary, his weapon ready. Ryan struggled to a sitting position, his hands behind him.

'Sick,' Ryan said weakly. 'Krank. Water.'

The sentry leaned down for a closer look, the muzzle of his weapon drooping. Ryan's right fist shot out and hit him in the throat, hard, as his left hand seized the front of the sentry's greatcoat to pull him down. Fincham immediately pinioned the sentry's thrashing legs as Ryan clamped a hand over his mouth to stifle any outcry. It was unnecessary. The sentry's larynx was crushed. Arnaldo started up. Maguire put a hand over his mouth and whispered, 'Silenzio'.

Ryan pressed his thumbs into the sentry's throat until all movement ended. Fincham had his weapon. Ryan listened for sounds from the lieutenant's sleeping-bag and the troop tent. There were none.

'What've we got?' he whispered.

'Schmeisser,' Fincham whispered back.

'Cover the troop tent. I'll get the lieutenant.'

'Will do.'

Fincham crawled towards the troop tent cradling the machine pistol as Ryan crept towards the sleeping-bag, the open pocket-knife clenched between his teeth. While Ryan was still some feet away, the lieutenant's voice spoke quietly from the sleeping-bag, the tone casual.

'Halte wo Du bist, mein Freund, sonst bist Du ein toter Mann.' *Stop where you are, my friend, or you're a dead man.*

Ryan froze. There were no sounds behind him. Fincham had not heard. The officer's tent rustled. From it came a spurt of flame and a sharp explosion. The lieutenant gasped. The troop tent boiled with cries and movement and the machine pistol spoke in short, ripping bursts.

Knife in hand, Ryan hurled himself on the sleeping-bag and plunged it in as Maguire rushed through the darkness towards him shouting, 'Colonel? Are you all right?'

'Down!' Ryan cried, rolling away from the tent mouth.

'Ryan!' Fincham called. 'Did you get the sod?'

222

'I got the sod,' the contessa called back flatly, emerging from the tent.

A light came on and swept the scene. Fincham had found the sentry's flashlight. The troop tent, riddled, was still and silent. The contessa stood erect, her face infinitely sad, one hand shielding her eyes from the light, the other gripping an Italian carbine. Ryan, on hands and knees, looked up at her. Arnaldo watched from the blankets, his face incredulous.

'Contessa!' Maguire cried, running to her. 'I thought...'

She pushed him aside and went reluctantly to the sleeping-bag. She looked down at the lieutenant. His open eyes were fixed. A Luger lay beside his outflung hand. She sighed heavily.

'Poor boy,' she whispered.

She let the carbine fall beside his body.

'He wanted it for a souvenir,' she said to on one in particular. 'And the others, Colonel Ryan, dead also?'

'The lot,' said Fincham. 'What happened, Ryan?'

'He had me. She shot him. Lieutenant, you and Arnaldo put the lieutenant in the troop tent with the others.'

'We thought you'd gone over, ma'am,' Fincham said. 'Our apologies.'

'What a horrible thing it is to kill,' the contessa said, watching Maguire and Arnaldo dragging the sleeping-bag towards the troop tent.

'Yes, ma'am,' said Ryan. 'But it beats getting killed.' He lifted the flap of the smaller tent. 'After you, ma'am'

She looked at him thoughtfully before entering.

'Lieutenant,' Ryan said, 'when you and Arnaldo are through over there, send him in. Fincham, you come in too.'

'Sir,' Maguire said, 'could I say something to the contessa first.'

'Later.'

The tent was far too low for them to stand. The contessa switched on a flat electric lantern hanging from a folding metal tent pole. Their packs were piled against the rear of the tent. The contessa's sheepskin coat and the lieutenant's great-coat and white cape were spread out to make a pallet.

'He apologised for the rudeness of my accommodations,' the contessa said ruefully.

'Don't let it bother you, ma'am,' Ryan said. 'If he'd known whose side you were on, you'd have been out in the snow with the rest of us.'

'No. He was a gentleman.'

'And it got him killed.'

'I think I am beginning to understand you, Colonel Ryan. It makes me no fonder of you, but I understand. Perhaps we are all fortunate that you are as you are.'

Arnaldo entered the tent, sat on his heels and spoke to the contessa with respect. She nodded absently.

'Ask him if we can still get across the lines before dawn,' said Ryan.

Arnaldo said it was not possible. They had lost far too much time.

'Is there some place where we could sneak across after dawn?'

'Impossible!' Arnaldo said emphatically. They would be obliged to cross much open ground between the lines, where they would almost certainly be seen by one side or the other. It did not matter which. Either would open fire on them.

'That still leaves a full day and night to smash Jerry's concentrations with air,' Fincham said.

'Two days would be better. But it can't be helped. We can't stay here. Other patrols may use this for a base camp. Contessa, tell him to take us as close to the lines as he can where we can hide out until it is time to cross.'

They would take everything of their own with them, Ryan said, leaving nothing to betray their presence. And they would take a white cape and parka for each of them. The lieutenant's was in his tent. When Ryan and Fincham left to get the others from the troop tent, the contessa asked Ryan to send Paolo in to her.

'He wished to speak with me, I believe,' she said.

Maguire looked worried when told the contessa wanted to see him.

'Is she mad at me, sir? For thinking she'd turned traitor?'

'You'll have to ask her.'

The capes were bloodstained and holed by bullets. Ryan and Fincham wiped them as clean as they could with snow. Ryan took a flashlight and retrieved the camera and binoculars he had buried before going after the sentry. Fincham poked among the bodies in the troop tent for Tenbrink's knife and the two .45s. The Germans had eaten the last of the Spam and Canadian biscuits and taken the coffee and tea. One of the Germans had hidden the gold coins under his shirt. Fincham gave them to Ryan, who put them back in his pack. They buried the empty Spam cans and biscuit boxes in the snow. After stowing the capes, some hard German biscuits, the Italian blankets and travelling-rugs in the packs, Ryan went to the smaller tent.

'Let's go,' he said.

Maguire crawled out close behind the contessa. When he passed Ryan he whispered happily, 'She's not mad at me, sir.'

Ryan carried the big pack, Arnaldo, Maguire and Fincham the Italian knapsacks. Ryan had the machine pistol and a .45, Fincham the other .45, a carbine and Tenbrink's knife, and Maguire the other carbine. Maguire had wanted the lieutenant's Luger for a souvenir but the contessa would not permit it. She wanted no reminders of what she had done. The only German arms they took were two grenades. Each of the soldiers had had a pair.

Snow fell, whirling down softly in the darkness, frosting their caps and shoulders.

'Jolly good,' said Fincham. 'Cover our tracks.'

'You'd better hope the weather clears by the day after tomorrow,' Ryan said, 'or they'll have to bomb through an undercast.'

Sporadic artillery fire rumbled along the battle-front. A new sound overtook them from behind, a distant grinding and roaring of heavy engines.

'Listen,' said Maguire. 'Sounds like tanks. They wouldn't have tanks in these mountains.'

'Wouldn't they?' Fincham said, falling in step with Ryan. 'Jerry's bringing up more.'

Arnaldo said it was time to stop. He was not sure where they were, and if they kept on it might take them further from their destination, or worse, they might blunder into German positions in the dark. They scooped a hollow in the snow, lined it with the blankets and travelling-rugs and covered themselves with a tent improvised from the ski patrol's capes.

By morning the snow had covered them, blending their refuge in with the surrounding terrain. Ryan scooped an opening through which he could scan the mountainside. It had stopped snowing but an overcast still hung over twin peaks rising from the curving ridge of the range. Arnaldo took the binoculars and said they were now south of Roccaraso. The Allied lines, if they had not changed in the past week, were across a valley on the other side of the mountain on which they were camping. They must remain where they were all day, and if everything went satisfactorily they would be in friendly hands well before the next dawn.

When the contessa translated the information she added, 'I cannot stop thinking about Lieutenant Dietrich. Do you often think of the men you have killed, Colonel?'

'Only of the men who might kill me, ma'am.'

'Yes, I suppose that is the proper attitude. I hope it never becomes mine.'

'If you're lucky, it won't.'

They ate the German ration biscuits, the only food they had, and drank melted snow. Someone was always at the peep-hole with the binoculars. There was no evidence of battle all morning except for scattered artillery fire coming from beyond the mountain that was sheltering them; no shells exploding within view, no patrols and no aircraft to be heard flying above the overcast.

'Ours haven't an inkling what Jerry's up to,' Fincham said in frustration. 'And here we sit on our bums.'

Late in the morning, Maguire was at the peep-hole.

'Colonel!' he cried.

Ryan crawled towards him. Maguire gave him the binoculars, pointing. Two men on skis, barely discernible in their white capes and parkas were pulling a loaded sled, also covered in white. A third man was pushing from behind. They were climbing towards the twin peaks.

'What is it?' Fincham asked.

'Looks like a supply detail.'

'They'll be finding our friends of last night, then.'

'Negative. They're heading the other way.'

Fincham took the binoculars and looked for himself.

'There's damn all up there,' he said, giving them back. 'But they seem to know what they're about. Setting up another base camp, do you think?'

'Maybe,' said Ryan, continuing to watch them.

They neared the summit. And vanished. One moment there were three men and a sled, then nothing.

'There's a position up there,' Ryan said. 'Well hidden. Observation post, probably.'

He unfolded the map and studied it.

'Bird's-eye view of the entire sector from up there,' he said. 'Be nice if we could see what they can.'

'Wouldn't it,' said Fincham. 'If we had a shuftee from up there before we start down tonight it could save us some nasty surprises.'

Ryan kept watching the spot where the supply detail disappeared. It was a long time before they emerged from the summit with an empty sled. They skied down the slope and passed from view beyond a scarp.

'It's about time to do just that, Colonel,' Ryan said, putting the binoculars away.

The others watched silently while he and Fincham checked their weapons and tucked the German grenades in their pockets. They remade the shelter, removing two of the white capes. They put them on, Ryan taking off his coat before donning his.

'Lieutenant,' he said matter-of-factly, 'if we don't get back, stay here until dark. Arnaldo'll take you and the contessa across.' He gave Maguire the two packages of exposed film. 'Give these to someone in authority and tell him the Germans will be launching a major attack out of the Piano delle Cinquemiglia sometime the day after tomorrow.'

'Do I detect a note of doubt in the notorious Colonel

Ryan?' the contessa asked. 'I am shocked.'

'Von Ryan never has doubts,' said Fincham. 'Just alternatives. One of his few saving virtues.'

'Colonel Ryan, I cannot say I have enjoyed your company, but if you do not return I will be most distressed.'

'I'll do my best not to distress you, ma'am.'

'Sir,' Maguire said quietly. 'I'm coming, too.'

Ryan fixed him with his coldest stare. Maguire did not flinch.

'Why not?' Ryan said. 'We can always use another good man.'

'Paolo...' the contessa protested.

'Let's get cracking,' said Fincham.

Maguire gave the contessa the film and put on a white cape. Ryan covered her and Arnaldo with the two that remained. They were not large enough to conceal them and the packs. Ryan added a travelling-rug and the three of them piled on handfuls of snow until it was covered.

They went in single file, walking in each other's tracks. Ryan, in the rear, dragged his coat to fill in their bootprints. He looked back when they had gone a hundred yards. The mound beneath which the contessa and Arnaldo were hidden was indistinguishable from the surrounding terrain.

When they intercepted the tracks of the supply detail, Ryan shook the snow from his coat and put it on under the cape. They followed the tracks upward, Ryan now taking the lead. Near the summit, he stopped the others with a hand signal and went up alone, keeping low. The snow was banked deep, with a hard crust. Just below the crest an opening was cut through the snow. Five feet wide, with vertical walls of snow higher than a man's head, it led to a low wooden door without a handle. Ryan crept to the door and put his ear against it. There were movements inside, and the sound of voices. Ryan went back to the others.

'It's an O.P., all right,' he said. 'At least two men in it. Entrance through a cut in the snow. Door must open in. No handle. When we get up there, you cover it with the Schmeisser, Colonel. Lieutenant, you stay just inside the cut and keep a look-out to our rear.' He gave Maguire his .45. 'Just so you won't feel naked. I'll slip around and lob the grenades through the embrasure.'

Ryan took Fincham's grenade and circled the peak, moving silently on the crusted snow. He could not get directly below the embrasure. It was a long, horizontal slit, curving so that it afforded a view of more than one hundred and eighty degrees, in concrete of the same colour as the stone in which the observation post was constructed. Below the observation post, the face of an escarpment dropped sheer for several hundred feet before the mountain fell away less precipitously for almost two miles, to a valley curving south along the range. Nothing below marked the battle lines, though an occasional shell exploded in the hills on the far side of the valley, and brief spurts of flame from the hills attested to answering fire. A road traversed the valley, crossing the Sangro River to the south. Nothing moved anywhere.

Ryan took off his cape and coat and laid them on the snow. Putting one of the grenades on his coat and taking the other in his right hand, he planted his feet carefully, grasped a protruding edge of stone in his left and leaned out over the void to look up at the embrasure, some five or six feet above his head. He took two practice swings, moving his arm from the shoulder, arm straight. He pulled himself back to safer ground, armed the grenade, leaned again and lobbed it up into the embrasure. Voices cried out within the observation post as Ryan swung quickly back to get the second grenade. There was a muffled explosion behind the concrete as his hand touched the second grenade. He aimed it, leaned out again and tossed it into the smoking embrasure. Someone was groaning. A second muffled explosion, flame and smoke gushing from the embrasure, bits of metal spewing from it striking sparks on the concrete, and silence as Ryan pulled himself back from the sheer drop.

Maguire was on his stomach looking around the front of the cut, with only his eyes and parka showing, when Ryan came back around the crest. He scrambled to his feet, bouncing with excitement.

'We did it!' he cried.

Fincham looked back over his shoulder, the machine pistol

on his hip still covering the door. A shiny spike of shrapnel protruded from the splintered wood.

'Lucky for me Jerry builds well,' he said.

He tossed Ryan the machine pistol and kicked in the door. It flew open. The three of them flattened against the vertical wall of the snow as acrid smoke drifted out. There were no sounds from within. Ryan bent and entered cautiously. There was immediately room to stand erect. The observation post, burrowed into solid rock with its forward face of raw concrete, was almost circular. A partial ceiling-high wall of heavy undressed planks, now gashed by shrapnel, partitioned off the rear third. A German colonel lay slumped on a crude wooden table across a map which was thumb-tacked to it. His bleeding head was butting against a shattered radio transmitter. A dispatch case, undamaged, lay beside his twisted legs. A second officer, a captain, sprawled on a soiled but exquisite piece of Oriental carpeting covering most of the stone floor, one arm hooked around the base of a metal tripod supporting enormous binoculars. The carpet was smouldering where live coals had spilled from a gashed overturned brazier, fashioned from a five-gallon tin.

Ryan stuck an arm out of the entrance and motioned for Fincham and Maguire to enter. He went to the table and rolled the colonel off the map. The body struck the carpet with a soft thud. Fincham knelt beside the officer at the tripod.

'Colonel!' Maguire yelled.

A pistol shot reverberated in the stone chamber as Ryan flung himself to the floor and rolled. Something clattered on the stone behind him, by the partition, and then something meatier hit, followed by a second shot. Ryan, still rolling, lifted the machine pistol. Fincham had whirled, crouched, pistol in hand but unfired. Maguire stood looking down at a third German body on the floor. The snout of a machine pistol protruded from beneath it. The .45 that Ryan had given Maguire hung easily in the lieutenant's hand. Maguire looked at Ryan like a schoolboy who had brought home a good report card.

'Let that be a lesson to you, Lieutenant,' Ryan said gravely, getting to his feet. 'Never fool around in an enemy position until you've checked it out.'

Maguire's expression showed that was not what he had expected to hear.

'Thanks, Maguire,' Ryan said. 'You saved our butts.'

Maguire grinned.

'That you did,' said Fincham. 'You and your contessa have bloody well earned your keep.'

He went to the third body, a sergeant, and squatted beside it. The back of the head was a bloody mat. He turned the body over. There was a hole just under the left breast insignia.

'Bloody good shooting,' he said. 'Killed the sod twice.'

'From the looks of it, this wasn't your first Jerry.'

'First one I'm sure of. I never got this close to one in North Africa.'

'You intend stuffing him for a trophy?' Ryan asked. 'Or maybe just taking an ear? Don't gloat, Lieutenant. That was a man, not a twelve-point buck.'

'Yes, sir.'

Fincham joined Ryan at the map table. Ryan wiped a smear of blood from the map. It was a large scale, gridded topographical chart of the entire sector visible from the observation post as well as part of the immediate German rear. The symbols were similar to those on American military maps and easily understood. The Gustav Line was clearly defined, a series of strong points in depth, snaking north-east and south-west along the mountains. Across it, a German Panzer corps faced a British corps, reduced on the map to symbols denoting unit headquarters, artillery positions, troops and minefields. On the German side, a paratroop division defended the sector between Roccaraso and Castel di Sangro, a village in the valley seven miles to the south, across the Sangro. On the other side of the Gustav Line, arrows indicated thrusts by Canadian and English divisions enveloping Castel di Sangro to the south and north. The Piano delle Cinquemiglia was a thicket of tanks and motorised infantry, identified down to battalion size.

'There's more than two divisions hiding on the plateau,' Fincham said. 'Here's our Thirteen Corps and your Six Corps. If Jerry can get everything through the Roccaraso narrows before they know what he's up to, he'll have no trouble driving a wedge between them.'

'If we could catch 'em sitting there with heavy air attacks we could break up the concentrations.'

'You think air can do bloody everything, Ryan. It takes tanks and artillery, too. In any case, it doesn't look as if the weather intends co-operating.'

'The way they're jammed in there, heavies and mediums could carpet-bomb through the undercast with fair effectiveness. And fighters and attack bombers can get in under it.'

Ryan traversed the sector through the embrasure with the tripod-mounted binoculars. Both sides were well dug in and he could see little except for sandbagged openings here and there, patches of camouflaging that could be concealing tanks or artillery batteries, and desultory burst of smoke and flame from concealed guns. He thrust his head out of the embrasure and with his own binoculars searched the mountainside below. Only a few of the German positions shown on the map were visible.

According to the map, the nearest friendly troops were those of the British 5th Division north of Castel di Sangro in foothills rising no more than three thousand feet before the outer defences of the Gustav Line. Together, Ryan and Fincham charted a path to the British front lines through the German positions.

'With a bit of luck we should make it before dawn,' Fincham said.

The dispatch case at the colonel's feet was stuffed with messages and field and operation orders for an Operation Donnerschlag. Ryan knew enough military German to read the time and date it would begin.

Operation Donnerschlag, *Operation Thunderclap*, would be launched at 5.00 a.m., 6 December 1943. Not 7 December, but before dawn tomorrow.

232

17

Fincham swore.

'Let's move out,' Ryan said.

He unpinned the map, folded it and slipped it into the dispatch case. Maguire had been exploring the living quarters beyond the partition. He found machine pistol ammunition, a bottle of schnapps, tins of German corned beef and a loaf and a half of bread. Ryan and Fincham filled their pockets with the ammunition.

'You keep the forty-five,' Ryan told Maguire. 'You're better with it than I am.'

They took the sergeant's machine pistol, the schnapps, three tins of corned beef and the bread. Maguire carried the schnapps and food, tucking the bread under his arms. Ryan carried the captured machine pistol and the dispatch case. They hurried down the slope, following the ski tracks before striking off towards the contessa's hiding place along the faint trail left by Ryan's dragged coat.

'It's us, Contessa,' Maguire called as they drew near.

'Come on out,' said Ryan. 'We're moving on.'

The contessa emerged first, lifting a corner of the covering and managing to look dignified even on hands and knees.

'Paolo,' she said, getting to her feet, 'I feared for you. You were gone so long.'

'Sir,' Maguire whispered to Ryan, 'don't tell her I shot that sergeant.'

The contessa was pleased to be going. She was rested and impatient. Arnaldo wanted to wait until dark.

'Tell him we're too exposed here,' Ryan said, 'and we've got to be closer to the lines when we cross tonight.'

Ryan took the film from the contessa and buried everything except essentials under the snow. They took only what they could carry in their hands or cram into a single Italian pack — weapons, what they were wearing on their backs, the capes, binoculars, gold coins and what they had taken from the observation post. Ryan had Arnaldo take them down into the shelter of the tree-line though it led them away from the direct route to their night-time departure point.

Once in the shelter of the woods, Ryan called a halt. He gave the contessa the contents of the dispatch case to translate and unfolded the German map to show Arnaldo the route he and Fincham had marked through the German positions. Fincham and Maguire opened the tins of corned beef and divided the bread. Arnaldo approved of the route. He said that knowing the location of the German positions would prove most useful.

Ryan went over the dispatches and orders with the contessa. A message dated the previous day instructed the observation post to make half-hourly reports by radio of all unusual movements in the British sector. If there were no such movements, negative reports must be submitted. It had now been more than an hour since they attacked the post.

'That means they've already missed sending at least two reports,' Ryan said. 'It won't be long before somebody comes to find out why. We've got to put some distance between us and the O.P.'

The military phrases in the German operation plan were awkward on the contessa's lips. Some of the German terms were close enough to English for Ryan to be able to grasp their significance better than she. The plan listed a series of objectives contingent on the success of the initial assault. The immediate objective was to break out in force, inflicting maximum casualties and creating confusion along the entire front from the Mediterranean to the Adriatic, but the major aims of Operation Donnerschlag were far more ambitious than merely driving a wedge between the British and Americans attacking along the Gustav Line.

The intention was to drive past Castel di Sangro in the first surprise onslaught and wheel south-west across the lower ground behind the American divisions attacking towards Cassino, the key to Rome. If Donnerschlag succeeded in this without incurring unacceptable casualties yet inflicting significant casualties on the surprised enemy, the Germans would pour in additional forces from other sectors to exploit the break-through and press on night and day. They would race behind a British corps on the Allies' left flank to reach the coast some forty miles above Naples before the demoralised enemy could regroup and counter-attack.

'Cut off the better part of two full corps,' Fincham said grimly. He had brought over corned beef and bread and remained to listen. 'Make the débâcle at Tobruk resemble a garden party.'

'Instead of pressing towards Rome, they'd have to fight for their lives just to break out of encirclement,' Ryan said.

'I seem to have changed allegiances prematurely,' the contessa said drily.

'We've got to get this intelligence to them before the Germans can deploy out of the Piano delle Cinquemiglia,' said Ryan. 'A few hours can make a lot of difference.'

'Not enough,' Fincham said.

'And why not, pray?' the contessa asked. 'It seems quite simple to me. You warn your friends of the Germans' intentions, and the moment they come out of hiding they will be destroyed.'

'It's not like moving toy soldiers about,' Fincham said. 'You can't concentrate the forces required to stop a massive assault at a moment's notice. It's already too late to stop Jerry completely.'

'I can't argue with that, Colonel,' said Ryan. 'But if we catch 'em coming out, plaster 'em before they're fully deployed below Roccaraso, we'll knock their timetable into a cocked hat. And gain time for our forces to shut the door to the coast.'

'Right,' Fincham said with mounting enthusiasm. 'Bloody them every yard of the way and they'll lose the initiative along with the surprise. It could turn into a débâcle for Jerry. *If* we get across with the gen. before he has everything out where he can manoeuvre.'

They ate bread and cold, greasy corned beef with their fingers. Everyone except Maguire had a long pull from the schnapps bottle. The contessa found it too harsh and took hers through a mouthful of snow.

They continued through the woods, parallelling the ridges but well below them. An aircraft droned to the north.

'Multi-engine,' Ryan said, halting to listen. 'Theirs.'

He lifted the binoculars to his eyes, looking back through the trees. A lumbering Junkers skimmed just above the peaks beneath the undercast. In the distance, it appeared to be only a hand's breadth above the steep slope as it drove towards the peak concealing the observation post. Figures tumbled from it, one after the other in close succession. They jerked abruptly to a stop as puffs of parachutes exploded above them, drifted down and settled into the snow almost immediately. There were eight of them. They freed themselves of chutes and harness, buckled on skis and toiled up the mountainside towards the observation post.

'They've dropped a patrol to see why the O.P. failed to report,' Ryan said. 'Let's go. They'll be looking for us.'

They went swiftly through the woods, still parallelling the summit. Ryan stopped frequently to look back through the glasses. The others kept going and he had to run to catch up with them. The contessa was tiring and Fincham limped. Ryan called a halt and climbed up the slope to where the trees were thin enough to afford a clear view back along the mountain. The patrol was just visible through the glasses, pushing along in single file below the summit.

He hurried back down and started his party moving again. They descended deeper into the woods and pressed on. Ryan took off his belt and passed one end to the contessa, pulling her along. Maguire took over when he climbed back up the slope to check on the patrol. The patrol gained on them steadily, keeping to the open snow-field towards the summit.

'We should have crossed early on,' Fincham said when Ryan told him. 'If we try to climb over now, we're buggered.'

'They'd have seen our tracks,' Ryan said. 'That's what they're looking for. As long as they know they've got us pinned on this side they won't come down looking for us. We can't risk leaving the woods until dark.'

In mid-afternoon Arnaldo said it was time to turn towards the lines. Ryan said they could not leave the shelter of the woods. There was too great a chance of getting caught on the open snow-field. The others huddled under their white capes while he crawled up to look for the patrol. It was almost directly above them. He watched until it went by.

'We wait here,' he said when he returned. He called Fincham aside. 'They know they're making better time on skis than we can ploughing through the snow. Let's hope they don't realise they've overshot us in time to back-track and come looking for us down here while there's still light to see by.'

'And if they do?'

'You take the film and dispatch and take off with Arnaldo and the contessa while Maguire and I keep 'em as busy as we can.'

'Negative,' said Fincham, mimicking Ryan. 'I'll stay and you go. You're fitter than I am.'

'First time I've heard you complain, Colonel.'

'I'm the sort who suffers in silence, old cock.'

Ryan went up the slope again and buried himself in the snow under his cape from where he could watch the patrol's back-trail. The sun plunged below the peaks. The shadows spreading over the slopes brought a chill of their own. It would soon be dark. Ryan rose stiffly and returned to his companions.

'Looks like we've lost 'em,' he said. 'We'll move out at full dark.'

The darkness thickened. They buried their white capes, no longer an asset, and began climbing, Arnaldo leading the way, Ryan in the rear. They were on the open slope when sounds of blundering movement rose from the woods below. Snow crunched, small branches snapped. The patrol had back-tracked. Arnaldo picked up the pace without being told.

Someone shouted and a light flicked on. The patrol had stumbled on their hiding place. There were more shouts, more

237

lights and much milling around. All the lights but one went out, the voices died away. The light emerged from the woods.

'They've picked up our trail,' Ryan said.

He took the contessa's arm and hurried her forward to Arnaldo.

'Ask him about the down slope,' he said. 'Are there woods? How far down does the snow go?'

When Arnaldo stopped to answer, Ryan seized his elbow and hustled him on. The southern slope was wooded and the snow stopped at a higher point than on this side.

'Tell him we've got to get out of the snow as fast as we can.'

Arnaldo scrambled upwards. The others laboured to keep up with him.

'I'll drop off and pin them down,' Fincham whispered, breathing heavily. 'Give you time to get clear.'

'Negative. No firing if we can help it.'

They reached the summit. The light was still far below them but coming on. Muzzle blasts winked far across the valley among the British positions and shells exploded on both sides of the battle lines in quick red blossoms. Ryan halted them briefly below the crest.

'Tell Arnaldo to get us down double-quick,' he said to the contessa. 'You hang on to his coat. Maguire, you hang on to the contessa's, then Fincham and me. If anybody loses contact, we all stop until we hook up again. Other than that, no stopping until we're out of the snow.'

They plunged down the mountain in giant strides, the crunch of their boots in the snow seeming much louder than it actually was. The only other sounds were their laboured breathing and the crump of guns. They reached trees. Behind them, a light pierced the darkness at the crest and went out.

'They've stopped chasing us,' Maguire said.

'Negative. They won't show any lights on this side.'

The snow thinned, then they were out of it. The contessa stumbled. Maguire caught her before she fell and Fincham blundered into him. Arnaldo stopped at once when the contessa lost her grip on his coat. They relinked silently and continued downwards.

238

'Tell Arnaldo we'll stop now and take cover,' Ryan said.

They lay prone close together. Ryan and Fincham faced the crest, machine pistols ready. The patrol crashed through the trees towards them. Ryan thrust the dispatch case at Fincham and whispered, 'Get going. I'll catch up.'

'That wasn't the drill,' Fincham said.

'That's an order, Colonel.'

Fincham and the others moved out cautiously behind Arnaldo. The patrol kept coming. It stopped at a low command some yards above Ryan's hiding place. A light came on, swept the ground and went off. Another low command and the paratroopers spread out and came down through the trees. One of them passed within a few feet of Ryan. They reassembled down the slope and, after a whispered conference, spread out again and moved off through the woods to the east. Ryan waited until he could no longer hear them before hurrying after the others.

'Over here,' Fincham whispered in the darkness.

They linked up again and crept downwards. Off to their left there was a brief chatter of automatic weapons, stopping as quickly as it began and leaving a heavier silence in its wake. Arnaldo stopped. The contessa said he wanted to consult the map. They squatted, facing each other, and spread out their coats, tentlike, while Arnaldo studied it. He jabbed it with a forefinger. They were well within the German strong points now, within a mile of the forward positions of the Gustav Line. Beyond that lay the disputed valley where they might expect both German and British patrols, one as threatening as the other to anyone moving in the night.

The descent grew steeper. They dug in their heels and went down stiff-legged. Fincham started skidding down. Ryan, carrying the dispatch case in his free hand, hauled back on Fincham's coat, bracing himself against the weight of the four in front of him. Arrested, Fincham pulled back, pulling the others towards him. Because of the steep tilt of the incline they landed sitting, one behind the other like a toboggan crew. The barrel of Fincham's machine pistol clanked against the binoculars suspended from Ryan's neck.

Behind them a voice called out a nervous challenge. There was no sound but their breathing. Even the guns seemed to have stopped firing for the moment. The voice called out again and was answered by another off to the side. There was a soft pop, not loud enough to be a weapon firing. Ryan snatched the binoculars from his neck and flung them forward into the night as a flare bloomed in the darkness above them. The binoculars landed far down the slope, clattering on stone, bouncing and clattering again. Automatic weapons began firing towards the sound from the positions behind them and to the sides, sending up showers of sparks.

They lay bathed in the magnesium glow, not moving. The flare drifted down slowly, moving down the mountainside away from them. Other positions opened fire above and below them towards the valley. The darkness twinkled across the valley as British positions returned the fire. Flares blossomed between the opposing lines and heavier guns opened up from the British sector, probing. A shell exploded on the mountain above them, showering them with dirt and fragments of stone.

The flares drifted down and died. The firing diminished and stopped entirely except for the intermittent artillery fire that had marked the night at the beginning of the descent. Ryan sat up and prodded Fincham. Fincham nudged Maguire, who helped the contessa to her feet, and they continued their descent. Arnaldo led them with greater assurance now, having seen the German positions during the exchange of fire and the terrain in the glow of the flares. They reached less precipitous ground and went more quickly. Arnaldo stopped and sent back a whispered warning to press against the bare stone shoulder they were skirting. There was a long drop at their feet. They let go of the coats to steady themselves against the stone and edged along the invisible brink until Arnaldo reached back for the contessa's hand and resumed his steady pace.

They were among blasted trees. The earth was pitted with shell craters. Arnaldo led them around the holes, sliding his feet along until they encountered the tumbled earth that indicated the lip of a crater. They blundered into fallen tree trunks, stopping at the first contact and feeling their way around. Ryan stopped his party and drew them into a tight circle, heads close together.

'We must be getting into their forward positions,' he whispered. 'They'll be extra alert, on the look-out for our patrols. There'll be wire and beyond that, mines. So we're not in the clear even when we're through the German lines. There'll be patrols from both sides in the valley. The British will shoot at us, too.'

He pushed up his sleeve and looked at his watch, the face turned to the inside of his wrist. It was only a little after eight.

'Ask Arnaldo how much longer.'

If all went well, Arnaldo said, another four hours. Perhaps less.

'That should give them time to call in air before Jerry comes out,' Fincham said. 'And start bringing up tanks and mobile artillery.'

'Andiamo,' said Ryan.

It was no longer necessary to hold onto coat-tails. The terrain was easier and they had grown accustomed to Arnaldo's pace. If they remained close enough together they could make out the dim shape of the man immediately in front.

There was a rustle of cloth behind them, a soft tread of boots, a tiny clink of equipment. Everyone stopped without being told, no one overrunning anyone else. Three days of walking together in the mountains and Ryan's iron discipline had forged them into a team, an incongruous one but still a team. They huddled together, prone, face down. White faces were more visible in the night than dark clothing.

The sounds went past them. It was a patrol moving towards the line. Someone called out a challenge and the patrol halted. Its leader replied with a password and an obscenity.

The challenger laughed and said, 'Alles gute für Dich auch, Du Lump.' *Good luck to you too, you yokel*.

'Quick!' Ryan whispered. 'After 'em! But not too close.'

They followed the patrol, remaining just close enough behind it to hear the sounds of its movements. They were not challenged. Metal rustled up ahead and one of the soldiers cursed softly. The patrol halted in a flurry of muttered obscenities.

'He is caught in wire,' the contessa whispered as Ryan's party halted.

'Everybody down,' Ryan whispered back, 'and follow me.'

He crawled towards the stalled patrol, stopping a few yards short of the Germans and feeling behind him with a foot for Arnaldo. Arnaldo stopped when he felt the touch, and the others lay still behind him. Freed, the soldier passed through the wire with his companions. Ryan crawled after them. When the sound of quicker movements told him that the patrol was through the wire he stopped again and waited until the small noises of its advance faded in the night. He continued crawling forward for a few minutes before getting cautiously to his feet. The others joined him. He gave the dispatch case to Fincham.

'There'll be mines,' he said. 'We've got to string out. Everybody stay just close enough together to hear the man ahead of him. Colonel, you know what to do with those papers if I'm stupid enough to get my tail blown off.'

When the contessa translated Ryan's instructions to Arnaldo, the little Italian was indignant. He would continue in the lead, mines or no mines. He had undertaken to get them safely to the British and it was his right to take the position of greatest risk. It was a matter of honour. And he knew the terrain while Ryan did not.

'Tell him I defer to his sense of honour. And direction,' Ryan said.

He retrieved the dispatch case and took his accustomed place in the rear after sending Fincham to follow Arnaldo. He wanted the Englishman up front with a machine pistol if they blundered into the German patrol. The contessa was next, then Maguire. Ryan waited until Maguire moved out a few paces before following.

The ground tilted down sharply. Ryan was obliged to turn and continue backwards, feeling for purchase with his feet. All sounds ceased below him. He reached level ground.

'Colonnello,' Arnaldo whispered.

They were in the valley. Arnaldo had stopped and waited for the others to join him.

'We will soon be across the valley and among friends,' the contessa translated. 'I presume they will be my friends as well as yours, Colonel Ryan.'

'Count on it.'

Arnaldo said there were mines ahead and they spread out again. They assembled once more on the road running along the valley floor. Arnaldo said they would take the road until they were very close to the British positions. If the road was mined, it would be with anti-vehicle charges and the weight of a single body would not activate them.

Someone kicked a stone. It skipped along the road. Machine pistol fire from the German side of the road snapped at the sound out of the darkness, to be joined quickly by more small arms fire. Everyone dove for the far side of the road, Maguire dragging the contessa with him. They landed in a heap at the bottom of a ditch. The contessa stifled a groan.

'Are you hit?' Maguire said anxiously.

'My knee,' the contessa gasped. 'I am afraid it is wrenched.'

Small arms fire rattled above them. Beyond the road, the Germans had spread out and taken cover.

'Does it hurt bad?'

'Yes. How tedious.'

Ryan and Fincham crawled to the lip of the ditch. The small arms fire stopped for a moment, then resumed in greater fury.

'The sods mean to pin us down while someone crawls close with a grenade,' Fincham whispered. 'Look sharp.'

Ryan fired at a sound just across the road. He ducked back as a man cried out in pain and fire converged on the spot he had just vacated.

'Good shooting,' said Fincham, 'for a flying type.'

Figures came running out of the darkness towards them, firing as they came. Machine-gunfire ripped the night from the British positions just across the valley, pouring into the attacking Germans. Ryan and Fincham added their own fire. Men shouted and fell. What was left of the German patrol withdrew, dragging the bodies of the fallen with them. The fire from the British positions intensified and was joined by mortar shells exploding on both sides of the ditch, raining debris on Ryan's party. The forward positions of the Gustav Line returned the fire. Tracers and shells arched over the ditch from both sides.

'We seem to have stirred up a hornet's nest,' Fincham said. 'I reckon they'll be at it for a while. We may as well make ourselves comfortable.'

'It's already aften ten. We can't waste any more time.'

'It won't improve matters if we get ourselves killed, old cock.'

'All that stuff's going over high. And it'll pin down any patrols that may still be out. Can you walk, Contessa?'

'I'm afraid not.'

'I'll carry you,' Maguire said.

'Take these,' Ryan said. giving him the dispatch case and machine pistol. 'Piggyback time again, Contessa.'

He crouched before her. She put her arms around his neck. When he rose, she bit back a cry.

'Put me down at once!' she gasped.

Maguire helped Ryan put her down with her injured leg stretched out straight.

'Colonel,' Ryan said, 'you stay here with the contessa. We'll send a litter party back. Maguire and I'll go on with Arnaldo. Lieutenant, if I get hit you know what to do."

'I'm staying with her, sir.'

'I haven't got time to argue with you, Lieutenant,' Ryan said. He gave Maguire the machine pistol. 'Don't use it unless you absolutely have to. Stay right here and don't move a muscle.'

'Yes, sir. Don't worry about us, sir.'

'Fincham,' Ryan said. 'Arnaldo. Let's go.'

He led them out of the ditch. Arnaldo took the lead, trotting, bent at the waist. Tracers arched overhead as they zigzagged towards the British-held higher ground. They maintained an interval so that if one blundered into a mine it would not get them all.

The fire-fight slackened into a desultory exchange. They ran erect, panting, until the ground began rising. Ryan caught up with Arnaldo and took the lead, slowing to a cautious walk.

Feet scuffled on the hillside above them and a voice whispered, 'Here now, why'd you bloody stop like that?'

The three men threw themselves to the ground.

'Sssh. I 'eard something down there.'

'You up there,' Fincham called. 'We're friends.'

He was answered by a burst of fire that riddled the ground just behind them.

'Sodding idiots!' Fincham bawled. 'Stop that bloody nonsense!'

''E's one of ours, right enough. Come up slow and let's 'ave a look at you.'

'There's three of us.'

'Three? Watcher doing mucking about down there? Don't you know there's a flamin' war on?'

'So that's what all the noise was about.'

The three of them started up the hill.

'That's far enough! Just who the bloody hell might you be?'

'Lieutenant-Colonel Fincham, Fifth Battalion, Green Howards.'

'Green bloody Howards! There ain't no bloody Green Howards here, sir.'

'We'll do the introductions later,' Ryan said. 'We're coming up.'

Farther up the hill, five figures rose to confront them.

'Have you got a radio or field phone?' Ryan demanded.

'I'll ask the questions,' one of them said.

'What's your name and rank, soldier?'

'What's yours is more to the point, mate. Yank, ain't you? Don't tell me you're a Green Howard, too.'

'I'm Colonel Ryan, U.S. Air Forces and you're wasting valuable time,' Ryan snapped. 'I'll ask you one more time, have you got a radio or field phone?'

'No, sir,' the man said, patiently humouring him. 'You just follow me and we'll sort this out.'

He led them up the slope. The other four soldiers followed close behind them, weapons ready.

'In here,' he said, stopping and standing aside. 'Mind your head.'

They were herded into a low, cramped and intensely dark space, so close together that it was difficult to move.

'Let's get this over with!' Ryan ordered. 'I've got intelligence that can't wait.'

'All in good time, Colonel, sir.'

The tone was ironic.

A match flared and wavering candlelight revealed a rude bunker, timber-lined, its entrance shrouded by a hanging ground-sheet. The patrol leader, squat and bulky, his fatigue-etched face unshaven and streaked with dirt, was a sergeant. Sten-gun rock steady in his broad, grimy hands, he studied them, eyes hard and searching beneath untidy brows. The other four soldiers blocked the entrance, competent and wary, their rifles loosely held but ready.

Ryan's was not a reassuring group. Their clothing was stained and torn, their faces bewhiskered. Ryan's whiskers were much fairer than his dyed hair and eyebrows. Fincham had the machine pistol cradled in his arms. The sergeant stiffened when he saw it.

'What's this?' he demanded. 'Civvy dress. A flippin' Schmeisser. And one of you a bloody Eyetie by the look of it.' He held out a hand. 'I'll have that Schmeisser.'

'Get stuffed,' said Fincham. 'Mind your manners or I'll have you on charges. We've important gen. for Thirteen Corps, you bloody idiot,'

'Have you now?'

He raised the Sten-gun and nodded. The four soldiers levelled their rifles.

'The Schmeisser,' he said.

Fincham tilted the weapon until the muzzle pointed at his chest.

'It would be messy for all of us if bullets started flying about in here,' he said calmly. 'And you'd have a bit of explaining to do. If you survive.'

The sergeant's eyes flicked uncertainly from his Sten to Fincham's machine pistol. Without lowering his weapon he said, 'Let's not be foolish, sir.'

'Now we can talk sensibly,' said Ryan. 'I'm Colonel Joseph Ryan. He's a Lieutenant-Colonel Eric Fincham. We're escaped prisoners of war.'

The sergeant's jaw dropped.

'Colonel Ryan? The one who took the train?'

'And this gentleman is the guide who brought us through the German lines. We left two others in a ditch back by the road. One of them incapacitated. They'll need a litter team. We're a little pressed for time, Sergeant. I suggest you get your butt in gear and take us to the nearest field phone.'

'My relief's not due for two hours yet, sir.'

'Bugger your relief,' said Fincham.

'You'll take us now, Sergeant. That's an order.'

'Yes, sir.' He turned to the others. 'Don't stand there gaping like bloody tarts. Let the colonel pass. Watkins, you're in charge until I get back.'

The soldiers stepped aside. The sergeant pulled back the groundsheet and said, 'After you, sir.'

'We'll follow you,' Ryan replied, looking at his watch.

It was 11.45. In a little more than five hours, German tanks would began pouring out of the Piano delle Cinquemiglia.

'On the double,' he said.

They were half an hour reaching an advance command post, though the sergeant, for all his bulk and short legs, was indefatigable. They were challenged only once on the way. The sergeant responded without pausing. The command post was occupied by a major, a lieutenant and two other ranks. It was well dug in and, in a primitive way, comfortable, with bunks, a petrol-burning stove, pin-ups stuck to the walls and room to stand erect. The major was not inclined to believe Ryan's story and gave the sergeant a dressing-down for not blindfolding possible enemy agents before bringing them to his post. He had heard of Colonel Ryan, Von Ryan, of course, but doubted that Ryan was he.

'Colonel Ryan's in Switzerland,' he said. 'And fair, so I've heard.'

'My hair's dyed, Major.'

'I can't be sure of that, can I?'

'I'll tell you something you can be sure of. At least two divisions of German tanks and motorised infantry will be breaking out of the Piano delle Cinquemiglia at five this morning, and if you don't get on the phone to Corps headquarters pronto it'll be your butt. If it doesn't get shot off.'

'You can hardly expect me to believe that, old boy, can you? Jerry's been absolutely quiet up there for days.'

'You're a bloody fool and no mistake!' Fincham said.

Ryan opened the dispatch case and spread out the German map over a chart tacked to a table.

'Have a look at this,' he said. 'And if you can read German, here's the field and operation orders for the attack.'

The major studied the map, rubbing his chin. It had a small cleft in it and, like the rest of his face, was clean shaven except for a brush moustache. He was a tall, straight-standing man, thin to gauntness. He bent over the map, storklike, still rubbing his chin.

'I read German, sir,' said the lieutenant.

Ryan handed him the orders. The lieutenant scanned them rapidly.

'Sir!' he cried, excited. 'It's pukka gen.'

'How am I to know they're not forgeries?' the major said, unimpressed, straightening. 'Intended to draw off our forces from other sectors.'

Ryan took the machine pistol from Fincham.

'This says so,' he said, holding the barrel to the major's furrowed temple. 'I haven't got time to argue. Now get on the phone and get me through the Corps headquarters.'

Fincham pulled his pistol from his waistband. The other ranks made a nervous motion towards a corner where two rifles leaned against the wall. Fincham made a casual gesture with his pistol and they stopped at once. The major did not budge.

The lieutenant, who had made no move towards his sidearm, said 'Right away, sir.'

The major threw him a baleful glance.

The lieutenant cranked the hand generator, waited then

spoke to someone at the other side. After another, longer wait, he handed the phone to Ryan.

'Corps headquarters, sir. And may I say it's an honour to be of assistance.'

'You haven't heard the last of this, Hendricks,' the major said stiffly.

The line crackled but there was no one on the other end.

'Tea, anyone?' the lieutenant asked behind Ryan.

'Smashing,' said Fincham.

'No milk, I'm afraid, but bags of sugar.'

There was still silence at the other end. Ryan looked questioningly at the lieutenant, who had his back to him, busy with a kettle at the petrol stove.

A crisp voice said, 'Colonel Tribble here.'

'This is Colonel Joseph Ryan, U.S. Army Air Forces. Give me the Corps Commander. It's urgent.'

'I'm afraid he can't be disturbed, Colonel. Perhaps I can help you. I presume you've been shot down and want help getting back.'

Colonel Tribble did not sound at all concerned.

'I've just come through the German lines,' Ryan said. 'I've got solid intelligence they'll launch a major attack out of the Piano delle Cinquemiglia at five this morning.'

'The Piano delle Cinquemiglia,' Colonel Tribble said, his voice cool and amused. 'Really, now.'

'Damn it, man, I've got pictures and their operation orders!'

'Have you? Suppose you bring them along and I'll have a look. And we'll see if it warrants waking the general.'

'There isn't time!'

The line went dead. Colonel Tribble had hung up.

18

Ryan contemplated the phone.

'The son of a bitch hung up on me,' he said, bemused.

'Typical staff wallah,' said Fincham. 'What next?'

'Lieutenant!' Ryan barked.

The lieutenant was pouring tea. He put the kettle down immediately, stiffened and said, 'Sir!'

'How far to Corps headquarters?'

'Fifteen miles, sir.'

'Have you got transportation?'

'I'll take over now, Hendricks,' the major said before the lieutenant could answer. He had been poring over the German map while Ryan was on the phone. 'We've a lorry just across the way, sir. Not much of a road the first few miles, but passable if one knows the way. I'll drive you to H.Q., if I may.'

'Let's get cracking,' Ryan said, folding the map while the major shrugged into a greatcoat. 'Lieutenant, we left two of our party between the lines. One can't walk. Can you organise a litter party to bring them in? Arnaldo here'll show 'em the way.'

Arnaldo had been sitting on a crate, watching everything, his seamed brow knit in a vain effort to understand what was going on. He had said not a word since their first encounter with the British, though his face had shown his disapproval of the nature of their reception. The sound of his name brought him to his feet.

'I'll put in a call right away, sir,' the lieutenant said, tight-lipped, glancing at the major. He obviously resented reverting to a subordinate role with the major's change of attitude.

Ryan indicated with gestures that Arnaldo was to remain while he and Fincham left with the major.

'Contessa,' Ryan said. 'Paolo.'

Arnaldo nodded.

Fincham had poured a mug of tea and sugared it liberally.

'Lieutenant,' he said, 'would you mind if I took this along?'

'Not at all, sir.'

'Mind things for a bit, will you, Hendricks?' the major said. 'You were quite right and I was quite wrong, and your quick grasp of the situation will not go unreported.'

'Move it,' said Ryan, already at the door. 'My thanks, too, Lieutenant. And get that litter party started as soon as you can.'

Arnaldo insisted on shaking hands with Ryan and Fincham before they left.

They hurried out behind the major, Fincham nursing his mug of hot tea. The major led them around the command post to an open truck. They all got in the cab, Fincham in the middle. The cold engine started reluctantly and had to be run a few minutes to warm up.

The underside of the truck scraped on stony ground as they followed a pair of parallel ruts, creeping, able to see only a few feet ahead in the feeble beam of blacked-out headlights. Fincham grasped his tea mug in both hands, sipping between jolts.

'Faster,' said Ryan.

'Too tricky with damn-all visibility,' the major replied.

'Stop this thing.'

'Sir?'

'I said stop.'

The truck stopped abruptly. Hot tea splashed in Fincham's lap. He swore.

Ryan hurried to the front of the truck and kicked out the lenses of both headlights, bathing the way ahead in a sudden flood of light.

'Open lights are strictly forbidden,' the major said when Ryan climbed back into the cab.

'Step on it, Major,' Ryan said. 'You can see now.'

They bounced along the ruts. Fincham stopped trying to drink his tea, clutching the dash board with one hand and the mug with the other. Someone yelled angrily from the darkness outside the range of the headlights. Ryan looked at his watch. It was almost one.

'Four more hours,' he said.

'Precious little time, isn't it?' the major said.

They left the ruts for an only slightly less primitive track bulldozed through rocky soil. The truck picked up speed. Voices shouted from both sides.

'Bloody idiots!'

'Kill those flippin' lights!'

The road improved. The major pressed down harder on the accelerator. He seemed to be enjoying himself.

'I made rather an ass of myself back there, Colonel,' he said without taking his eyes from the road. 'My apologies.'

'We all make mistakes, Major.'

'Hear, hear,' said Fincham, sipping his tea.

'I simply found it too difficult to believe you could have come all the way from Switzerland. I was certain you and Colonel Fincham were imposters. Jerry can be deucedly clever.'

'I know. One of 'em sucked me in at P.G. 202.'

'Really?'

'Can't you drive faster?'

The major speeded up.

A red light traced the darkness with nervous arcs in front of them. The major slowed down.

'No,' said Ryan. 'Keep it floored.'

'The road may be blocked. Sorry, sir.'

He continued to slow down. The headlights picked out a military policeman waving a baton light. There was a camouflaged gun position on one side of the road and on the other a detail of bundled-up soldiers, heavily armed, huddled beside a tank.

'Keep going,' Ryan ordered. 'He'll jump out of the way.'

'No authorised transport runs without lights,' the major said apologetically. 'They'll fire on us if we make a run for it.'

He stopped short of the M.P.

'Douse them bleedin' lamps!' the M.P. shouted, running towards them. 'What the bleedin' hell you…' He stopped short when he saw that he was confronting an officer, but his furious expression remained unchanged.

'Let us through, Corporal,' the major said briskly. 'There's no time to waste.'

'Beggin' your pardon, sir,' the M.P. said with rigidly suppressed indignation, 'not with them lamps on. And I'll need your name and organisation, sir.' He leaned towards the window for a closer look. 'Here, what's this? Civilians, sir?'

'I'm a colonel,' Ryan said. 'And the Corps Commander's expecting me at headquarters, lights and all. Now get your butt out of the way and I'll try to forget you held me up.'

The M.P.'s face showed indecision.

'Sounds bloody queer to me,' one of the soldiers at the tank said.

'I'm afraid you'll have to step out and show indentification, sir,' the M.P. said.

'Enough of this bloody nonsense!' Fincham cried, throwing open the door and climbing out with the tea mug in one hand and the machine pistol in the other.

'Schmeisser!' the soldier cried.

The soldiers surrounded the truck and bleary-eyed men, half-dressed, tumbled out of the gun position to join them.

'Stand clear and let us through,' Fincham demanded.

The M.P., emboldened and self-righteous, said firmly, 'Out, if you please. The major, too, begging your pardon, sir. And get those lamps out, sir, or I'll be obliged to give 'em a taste of me boots.'

The major turned off the lights and got out. Ryan followed and thrust his face within an inch of the M.P.'s.

'I know you're just doing your duty, soldier,' he said firmly but without heat. 'But you're holding up something too big to stand on ceremony. Now either let us proceed with lights, or give us an escort to Corps.'

The M.P. wavered.

'He looks like a Jerry,' one of the soldiers said. 'It's a bloody trick!'

'Papers, if you please,' the M.P. said, playing a flashlight over their faces, showing the soldiers that he didn't intend to be cowed or tricked.

'We haven't any bloody papers!' Fincham said. 'We're escaped prisoners of war.'

'We'll see about that, won't we?' the M.P. said. 'You men, see they stay right here, while I call the O.I.C.'

'We're getting back in the truck,' Ryan said savagely. 'You try to stop us and I'll personally see your tail in a sling.'

The soldiers levelled their weapons, their dirty faces grim and belligerent.

'Come on, Major,' Ryan said curtly, turning abruptly towards the cab.

'I shouldn't try that, sir,' the major said quickly, grabbing his arm.

'We're running out of time.'

Out of the night, the distant clatter of a speeding motorcycle threaded through the darkness, growing louder as the machine approached. It was running with its headlight on. It slid to a halt near the truck, its light catching Ryan's group, the M.P. and the soldiers in a dimly-lit tableau. The M.P. shone his flashlight on the machine as an officer stood erect in the sidecar.

'Just in time, sir,' he said, snapping to attention and saluting. 'I've apprehended a sabotage party, sir.'

'Colonel Ryan?' the officer called out, ignoring him.

'Here,' said Ryan.

'Please follow me, sir,' the officer said, sitting back down. 'The general's waiting at Corps.'

The M.P. and the soldiers looked uncertainly from the officer to Ryan. The soldiers lowered their weapons.

'Carry on, you men,' the officer said as the motorcycle wheeled around.

'I was only doing my duty, sir,' the M.P. said stiffly to the major.

'We all make mistakes, Corporal,' the major said with a glance at Ryan.

They climbed back into the truck. The motorcycle driver revved his machine impatiently as the major got the truck started and switched on the headlights. The truck sped away behind the motorcycle.

Within minutes, a squat building loomed out of the darkness. It was 1.55 by Ryan's watch. The sentry posted at the entrance, only his eyes and nose showing in the balaclava that he was wearing under his helmet, did not challenge them as the motorcycle's light snapped off and the machine skidded in a swerving stop. The truck almost ran into it as the major jammed on the brakes. The officer started out of the sidecar before it was full, stopped, one foot dragging along the ground, and ran towards the sandbagged entrance, shouldering the sentry aside.

'Follow me, sir,' he shouted over his shoulder.

Ryan ran after him with the dispatch case, Fincham at his heels.

'I'll be getting back, then,' the major called after them. 'Good luck, sir.'

The officer flung open the door and hurried in behind Ryan, leaving Fincham to follow, still carrying the tea mug. Inside was a small square room with two desks pushed together and a red-eyed clerk typing furiously at one of them. An officer with the insignia and red lapel facings of a staff-colonel was waiting for them.

'Colonel Tribble,' he said quickly, opening an inside door to a muted babble of voices. 'The general's waiting. I'll do my apologies later.'

The room was large but low-ceilinged, brightly lit and heavy with tobacco smoke. Staff-officers, silent now, standing in twos and threes or sitting at desks, looked expectantly at Ryan. On one wall was a huge, large-scale map stuck with coloured pins and covered with a transparent overlay marked with symbols and drawn with solid and broken lines of various colours. A short, spare man, greying and very erect, was looking at it, one hand on his hip and the other holding a mug and a cigarette. A signals clerk was at a switchboard bristling with plugs. Another was at a radio transmitter-receiver, scribbling on a message form.

The man at the map turned to face Ryan. He was a lieutenant-general, his breast stacked with ribbons. His eyes were bright and piercing. He smiled broadly.

'Colonel Ryan!' he cried, walking to him with a hand outstretched. 'Delighted to meet you, and under such remarkable circumstances. Lieutenant...'

'Hendricks, sir,' Colonel Tribble said.

'Yes, Hendricks. Don't let me forget that name. He's been on the phone with the most extraordinary tale. Shall we just see what you've brought along, Colonel?'

He rubbed his hands in anticipation. Ryan opened the dispatch case and spread out the German map on the table. The general passed the field and operations orders to two staff-officers who took them to another table and began translating them. The general and his top staff gathered around the map. They spoke in low, excited tones as they examined it. The general asked if Ryan had any doubts about its authenticity. Ryan told him how he had obtained it, of the reports he'd had of German matériel moving up for weeks, of the tanks he had heard two nights earlier, of the great expanses of camouflage on the Piano delle Cinquemiglia and of the tanks he'd seen under it with his own eyes. He had photographs, Ryan said, bringing out the two rolls of film. The general gave them to a staffer, who rushed off to have them developed.

The general studied the hastily translated orders and dispatches, making terse comments to an aide who jotted notes on a pad. Ryan and Fincham sat side by side on a desk suddenly spectators.

'You British take your own sweet time, don't you?' Ryan said. 'All hell will be breaking loose in another two and a half hours.'

'It's a bit different from potting the odd Jerry lorry from a P-38, Ryan. Takes a bit of planning.'

'I'm aware of that. But there's no rule saying you can't

show a little hustle. I hope they moved faster getting out to the contessa and Maguire.'

'I expect they're having tea with Lieutenant Hendricks by now.'

The general began rapping out orders. Staffers made notes and scribbled on message forms. Others spoke into telephones, quickly but with no hint of panic, as the switchboard lit up. The radio operator sent and received messages at a furious pace. Other ranks hurried between the officers at the phones and the signals clerks with orders and message chits. Ryan drew closer to the centre of activity, a cluster of senior officers surrounding the general in a controlled swirl as he paced the floor, slapping his palm with a swagger stick, pausing to point something out on the big overlay where men were making coloured markings, to listen attentively to something whispered in his ear, or to give crisp orders in a calm voice that could not conceal an undertone of excitement. The room bustled and crackled but there were no wasted words or motions.

'We do things rather well once we get cracking, eh, Von Ryan?' Fincham said.

It was obvious, as Ryan was only too well aware, that sufficient forces to halt the German assault could not be assembled at such short notice. It would take many hours, perhaps days, to bring up tanks and guns to blunt the German thrust and even then the British would be outnumbered and outgunned at the point of attack.

The plan emerged as Ryan watched and listened. Corps had alerted every headquarters soon after the general had spoken to Lieutenant Hendricks. Aircraft of the U.S. Army Air Forces and the Royal Air Force had been placed on stand-by alert and were already loading ammunitions and bombs. The British units at Castel di Sangro were withdrawing quietly to prepared positions across the valley, where they would not be cut off by the initial thrust. The American forces before Cassino had been fully appraised of the situation as soon as the general had digested the information brought by Ryan. They were easing their pressure to the north and manoeuvring to block the German advance towards the coast should Operation Donnerschlag pierce the thin British defences.

Much depended upon dealing the Germans a significant, unexpected blow when they were most vulnerable, at the moment of the break-out from Roccaraso at the southern neck of the Piano delle Cinquemiglia. Every gun within range, tanks, heavy batteries and mobile artillery, was zeroing in on the narrowest point. They would hold their fire until the massed German tanks clogged the narrows in the opening assault. They would destroy as much German armour as possible there, creating confusion and slowing the assault, forcing the enemy to regroup before deploying in the broadening valley towards Castel di Sangro, where they would have greater manoeuvrability and could spread their forces to offer a less concentrated target for the withering but concentrated fire of the British guns. The tanks and mobile artillery that were already converging on the southern flank of the advance laid out in the German plans would join the barrage piecemeal as they drew within range. It would only be a trickle, but a steadily increasing one. Air attacks on the concentrations on the Piano delle Cinquemiglia would begin as quickly as the planes could bomb up and take off. The attacks would inform the enemy that his attack was expected but too late for any change in plans.

It was 3.05 a.m. Operation Donnerschlag would be launched in less than two hours.

'We'll never bring it off without air,' the general said. 'What's the gen on air? And the weather?'

An aide handed him a sheaf of message chits.

The general scowled as he leafed through them.

'That filthy overcast is still hanging over the valley,' he said, almost to himself. 'Bags of aircraft available. Minimum weather conditions everywhere but they can get off. Not much use to us if they can't find targets.'

Pathfinder planes could drop markers for medium and heavy bombers to aim on, but the tank force in the Piano delle Cinquemiglia would already be on the move by the time they could reach their targets. Ryan's photographs would already be obsolete, though the southern reaches of the plain would still be so crammed with tanks moving up that massed pattern bombing through the undercast could still be effective. U.S.A.F. and R.A.F. fighter- and attack-bombers were loaded and close enough to reach the critical area before 5 a.m. But they had the weather to contend with.

'What's the ceiling, sir?' Ryan asked.

The general looked at him as if just recalling that he was there.

'Three thousand feet and a bit,' he said. 'The mountains go six thousand and more.'

'The fighters and attack-bombers could come in underneath with a little help from the ground,' Ryan said. 'I employed the tactic once with my group.'

'Say on,' said the general, eyes narrowing.

Ryan borrowed his swagger stick and traced a route between the ranges and through the Roccaraso narrows.

'You can mark a corridor with searchlights and flak, sir,' Ryan said. 'They can be thinly-spaced, just close enough for the pilots to see from one to the next. The searchlight batteries here...' he pointed to the British positions nearest Roccaraso ... 'sweep up in a vertical arc through the overcast, hold a few seconds and lay down a heading for Roccaraso. And keep doing it. Your artillery lobs star shells into the Piano delle Cinquemiglia to light things up while the searchlights direct them in, and they let down through the undercast between the mountains and hit the tanks forming up to break out.'

'Splendid,' said the general. 'You heard the colonel. Get on with it.'

The tempo of activity increased again. After twenty-five minutes it slackened. The signals clerks remained busy, but the staff-officers had little to do except take reports, which they screened and passed to the general.

It was 3.40 a.m.

The general came over and collapsed wearily in a chair by the desk on which Ryan and Fincham were perched, motioning them to remain seated when they started to rise. He stretched his legs out straight in front of him and lit a cigarette as if he had nothing more important to do at the moment.

'Nothing for it now but to wait,' he said. 'You've done us an invaluable service, Colonel.'

'It was a team effort, sir. Lieutenant-Colonel Fincham, a Lieutenant Maguire and two Italian civilians. The Contessa Luciana di Montalba, working with the OSS, and an Italian mountain guide.'

'You all have our undying gratitude. You've had a long evening, gentlemen. Colonel Tribble, see that Colonel Ryan and his friends are well taken care of. I think we might even manage hot showers.'

'I'd like to check on the contessa and Lieutenant Maguire, sir,' Ryan said. 'We had to leave them between the lines. The contessa hurt her knee. Lieutenant Hendricks sent a litter party for them.'

'Be a good chap and see to it, Tribs,' the general said, closing his eyes and leaning back.

Tribble led them to a desk where there was a telephone. There was so much traffic that it took him several minutes to get through to the command post.

'Colonel Tribble, here,' he said. 'I have Colonel Ryan. He would like to speak with the Contessa di Montalba if she's still there.'

He listened for a moment.

'Really?' he said. 'I understand. No. I'll carry on from here.'

He hung up and turned to Ryan, his face grave.

'What with all the flap, Hendricks wasn't able to organise a stretcher party,' he said. 'They're still out there.'

'Right in the path of the German advance,' said Fincham.

19

They ran outside and tumbled into a staff sedan. Colonel Tribble rushed them to a field hospital, blowing the horn continuously. Though the hospital was gearing up to deal with the expected deluge of casualties, Tribble commandeered an ambulance and a husky medical orderly. Ryan knocked the lenses from the headlamps and they drove with lights on, Tribble at the wheel, Ryan in the seat beside him. Fincham sat in the back with the orderly.

The road was clogged with tanks and self-propelled guns moving up. The ambulance raced along the uneven shoulder, horn blowing, scraping steep banks, dodging in and out among the columns of vehicles. A knot of soldiers scattered at their approach, yelling obscenities. The ambulance continued with scarcely diminished speed on the bulldozed side-road and jolted wildly in the twin ruts leading to the command post. A front tyre blew violently. Tribble fought to control the careering ambulance and keep it in the ruts. Strips of the disintegrating tyre slapped against the fender and the bottom scraped along the higher ground between the ruts.

They reached the command post and slid to a halt. Fincham and the orderly tossed splints and a first-aid kit on the litter while Ryan ran to fetch Arnaldo. The Italian came out with the major and Hendricks before Ryan reached the entrance.

'Frightfully sorry, sir,' said Hendricks. 'I couldn't get through to anyone on the telephone and I couldn't leave my post.'

Fincham, Tribble and the orderly ran up to join them.

Fincham carried the folded litter across a shoulder. The orderly had the splints and first-aid kit.

'Arnaldo,' said Ryan. 'Andiamo!'

'I must be getting back,' Tribble said. 'Good luck, Colonel.'

Arnaldo led them at a trot. All along the heights, the white shafts of searchlight beams rose straight up into the overcast, marking the air corridor to Roccaraso. From the south, above the overcast, came the sound of aircraft engines.

'Listen,' said Fincham, limping beside Ryan. 'What time is it getting to be?'

'Four-fifteen.'

Arnaldo slowed to a walk, picking his way. The orderly fell and they had to wait until he found the splints and the medical kit in the darkness. Ryan carried the splints when they continued.

Someone called out a challenge.

'Litter party,' Ryan called, not stopping. 'Going after a casualty.'

Aircraft throbbed above them. There were no sounds other than the spaced fire of anti-aircraft guns along the heights sending flak through the overcast to augment the searchlights marking the corridor, and the muted rumble of distant guns towards Roccaraso firing star shells into the Piano delle Cinquemiglia. The base of the undercast glowed palely above the intervening ridges.

They slid and scrambled down a hillside and were on the gently sloping floor of the valley. Bombs exploded to the north-east as aircraft drummed overhead in an increasing stream. The undercast behind Roccaraso was dyed with splashes of red.

Arnaldo began running. The others pounded behind him.

'There's mines about, sir,' the orderly panted.

'We know,' said Ryan, not slackening his pace.

A machine-gun chattered behind them. Tracers streamed overhead. They dropped to the ground and crawled. The firing stopped. They got up and ran again. Ryan was just behind Arnaldo. Arnaldo disappeared with a sharp exclamation of surprise. Ryan stopped short at the sound of his tumbling body.

'Colonnello,' Arnaldo called. 'La fossa.' *The ditch.*

The others rolled down behind him.

'Contessa,' Ryan called. 'Maguire.'

There was no answer.

'Arnaldo,' said Ryan. 'Quale direzione?' *Which way.*

Arnaldo shook his head. He was not sure.

'Fincham! Take the orderly and go that way. I'll go with Arnaldo.'

A roar of tank engines starting up rolled faintly through the valley from the north-east. The heights on both sides of the valley erupted in flame, the fire from the British side converging where it narrowed at Roccaraso, that from the Gustav Line falling all along the British front, sending up gushes of crimson in a rolling din.

Operation Donnerschlag had begun.

'Contessa!' Ryan shouted, running ahead of Arnaldo. 'Maguire!'

A single-engine plane roared down out of the undercast on a collision course for the German-held heights. Warned by the flashing guns along the mountain face, it banked away sharply and streaked low towards Roccaraso, trailing thunder. Others followed. Their guns clattered as they strafed and bombed tanks far up the valley by the light of flares. The staccato beat of aircraft engines, the rumble and grind of tanks, and the crash of shells and bombs turned the Roccaraso end of the valley into a cauldron of rolling sound and fire.

Ryan kept running and calling.

'Here, sir! Over here!'

It was Maguire, his voice faint in the heavy thunder of battle.

'Arnaldo, get Enrico!'

Arnaldo ran back the other way while Ryan continued along the ditch. Maguire came running to meet him, coatless and shivering. He led him to the contessa. She lay propped against the side of the ditch, motionless, her legs swaddled in Maguire's coat.

'Is she conscious?' Ryan asked.

'Unfortunately, yes,' the contessa said, her voice thin with

263

pain. 'Promptness is not one of your virtues, is it, Colonel Ryan?'

'Help'll be here in a minute,' Ryan said, taking off his coat and covering her. 'How's the leg?'

'Such a dreadful clamour,' she said. 'The Germans are coming, are they not? You failed after all, Colonel. Paolo, you were right. One does not stop Germans on a moment's notice.'

'Don't you worry, ma'am,' Maguire said, kneeling beside her across from Ryan. 'We'll get you out of here. Sir, how does it look? We'll stop 'em, won't we?'

'Eventually. But it's not doing us a whole lot of good right now.'

Fincham and the orderly came pounding up behind Arnaldo. Fincham unfolded the litter and laid it down. The orderly dropped down next to Ryan beside the contessa.

'Let's get her on the stretcher and out of here,' Fincham said. 'Here comes Jerry.'

The orderly pulled Maguire's coat from the contessa's legs.

'Try not to be so clumsy,' she said sharply. 'That is my leg, not a stick of wood.'

'Gar!' the orderly cried. 'It's a woman.'

'She's a contessa,' Maguire said. 'And don't you forget it.'

'Stop nattering and let's be off,' Fincham said.

'In a bit, sir,' the orderly said, palping the wrenched knee. The contessa gasped.

'Sorry, ma'am,' he said. 'I'll give you something for the pain. It's a dislocated knee, sir. I'll need a light.'

The din of exploding shells and bombs and the grind and clatter of tanks grew louder. A flickering, rosy glow suffused the shadows in the ditch.

'Make it snappy,' Ryan said, playing the feeble beam of Tenbrink's penlight on the contessa.

The orderly slit open the three layers of sleeves covering the contessa's arm and got alcohol and a needle-tipped tube of morphine from the medical kit. He swabbed a spot with alcohol and squeezed part of the tube into her arm. He slit her trouser leg, waited several minutes and said, 'How is it now, ma'am?'

'It is the first time in days I have been even reasonably comfortable,' the contessa said drowsily.

'Let's be off, then,' said Fincham.

'Not yet, sir,' the orderly said. 'Colonel, will you hold fast to the lady, sir?'

Ryan held the contessa under the arms. The orderly took her foot, tugged and said, 'There. Back in place.'

He began splinting the leg.

'Have to immobilise the knee,' he said as he worked. 'Wouldn't want it popping out again, would we?'

'How very thoughtful of you, young man,' the contessa said, sounding tipsy.

'All done, sir,' the orderly said.

He and Maguire lifted the contessa on to the litter. The orderly took the front and Ryan the rear. Fincham and Maguire helped them up the steep side of the ditch. A mile or so away, a wavering line of German tanks was crawling down the valley, illuminated by their own muzzle flashes and shells and bombs exploding among them. Here and there, tanks burned or tilted crazily in the destruction raining down from diving aircraft and the British guns, but more kept coming on behind them.

The rescue party stumbled across the valley floor towards the sheltering hills, making no attempt at concealment. Arnaldo ran ahead to warn them of obstacles though their way was lit by the furious battle. Fincham and Maguire trotted along on either side of the litter.

'Is she out, sir?' Maguire panted.

'No, caro,' the contessa murmured. 'Just beautifully relaxed. Colonel Ryan?'

'Yes, ma'am?'

'When I am presented to the British commander, I trust you will bear in mind how clever I was convincing everyone I was sympathetic to the Fascisti until I was needed.'

'Of course.'

A thunderous explosion only a hundred yards away buffetted them. It showered them with debris and sent Ryan and the orderly reeling under the clumsy weight of the litter. They would have dropped it had not Maguire and Fincham steadied them. A second shell fell behind them.

'They're shooting at us!' Maguire cried indignantly. 'Can't they see we're carrying a stretcher?'

'Wave something white at them, Paolo,' Fincham said. 'They'll no doubt apologise.'

They began zigzagging. The fire of a single tank pursued them, then the tank itself wheeled out of the line towards them, spitting tracers from a thousand yards' distance. The string fell short as ricochets whined overhead. The tracers lifted and inched closer. The orderly went to his knees. A litter pole snapped and the contessa went sprawling as the stretcher jammed into his back. Maguire flung himself down beside the contessa.

'Are you all right?' he cried.

'Sleeping, sir,' the orderly said.

He had not been hit but had merely stumbled.

'Spread out!' Ryan ordered, scooping up the contessa and running towards the encroaching hills.

Machine-gunfire followed them, kicking up dirt. Arnaldo was the first to reach a protecting fold in the rising ground, with the orderly just behind him. Fincham, though limping, was well ahead of Ryan and Maguire. He stopped and ran some yards to the side, as if to draw the enemy fire. Maguire kept behind Ryan and the contessa, keeping himself between them and the tank.

The tank halted to create a steadier platform for its erratic machine-gun. A burst snapped just overhead and Ryan flung himself to the ground with the contessa before the gunner could adjust his aim. Maguire covered the contessa's body with his own. A light anti-tank gun spoke from the hills above them. A flat trajectory shell struck the tank turret with a ringing clang but did not pierce its heavy armour. The machine-gun stopped its clatter as the turret cannon traversed. Ryan shoved Maguire off the contessa, picked her up and ran for the fold. Fincham was in front of them again. Another shell bounced off the tank. It began firing into the hill, probing for the anti-tank gun. Its machine-gun resumed its chatter as Ryan reached the fold and dodged within it. Maguire dove for the opening and fell short. Fincham reached out and pulled him inside as slugs tore the ground where he had been.

The tank broke off its duel with the anti-tank gun and turned back to rejoin those grinding down the valley. The valley was crawling with tanks as far back towards Roccaraso as the eye could see in the stroboscopic flare of exploding projectiles. There was infantry among the tanks. Antlike, the troops crept up the slopes toward the British positions.

'Go on, sir,' Maguire panted, unslinging his machine pistol. 'I'll cover you.'

'They're not after us,' Ryan said. 'But they will be if you start shooting at 'em.'

He began climbing with the contessa in his arms, keeping to the shelter of the fold. The foremost wave of infantry was fanning out towards it. A British forward position higher up the slope engaged them. The Germans took cover briefly, then rose to advance again, coming on doggedly despite their casualties.

Two of them appeared on the brim of the fold, silhouetted by the lightning flashes of guns and bombs in the valley behind them. Maguire sprayed them with a burst from the machine pistol as they started down. A body rolled down into the fold and lay still.

'This way! Up 'ere!' voices shouted from above. Machine-gun and small arms fire rattled towards the advancing troops. 'We'll cover you.'

Fincham came back to help Ryan with the contessa. Maguire stepped between them and took her under the arms. Together, he and Ryan scrambled upwards to join Arnaldo and the orderly. British soldiers came boiling out of holes and ran past them, shouting and firing. Hands reached out and pulled the three of them into a sandbagged position.

The contessa was still out when they reached the command post where they had left the ambulance. Battle sounds rolled up from the valley, aircraft swarmed overhead and the red-mottled undercast was taking on a pearly hue as dawn approached. The major and Hendricks were still on duty in the command post but a colonel had taken over. The colonel was fully informed about the rescue party and had been in touch with Colonel Tribble about them by telephone despite the instrument's incessant use for battle communications.

'Will the Contessa di Montalba require hospitalisation?' the colonel asked after the introductions.

Ryan looked at the medical orderly.

'No, sir,' the orderly said. 'Rest and ice-packs should do for her nicely, sir.'

'Good. We've casualties queuing up at the hospital.'

'Colonel, your medic did a great job under fire,' Ryan said. 'I'll put that in writing if you want.'

The colonel instructed Hendricks to get the orderly's name, number and organisation.

'I'll see to it that his conduct does not go unrecognised,' he promised.

The contessa was stretched out on a bunk, covered with blankets. Maguire, red-eyed and weak-kneed with exhaustion, was keeping vigil. The colonel went over to look at her.

'Bit long in the tooth for this sort of thing, isn't she?' he said.

'If it wasn't for her, none of us would have made it,' Maguire said, nettled.

'He's right, Colonel,' Ryan said.

'She's in the way here, in any case. Do you suppose she's fit to be moved?'

'I'll ask the medic,' said Ryan.

The contessa's eyes opened.

'I am quite capable of speaking for myself,' she said.

'I know,' said Ryan.

'As for you,' the contessa said, fixing the colonel with a cold stare, 'I shall try to forget your remarks when I give my report to your general.'

Colonel Tribble had taken the command post's lorry and left the ambulance. Hendricks had seen to it that the ruined tyre was replaced. The orderly drove them to Corps headquarters, where the contessa was taken to the general's trailer and the men, including Arnaldo, were led away for a hot meal, hot showers and beds.

They slept through the day. Late in the afternoon Colonel Tribble came to brief them on the battle situation. The general sent his apologies for not coming himself but he had been summoned to 8th Army Headquarters to make a personal report to General Montgomery.

The German tanks were still advancing down the valley but the infantry had been unable to achieve significant gains in the heights commanding it. The enemy had taken enormous losses and his offensive was losing momentum. There were already indications that the Germans would soon be forced to break off Operation Donnerschlag and withdraw behind the mountains with the remnants of their attacking force. The Americans before Cassino, no longer threatened from the flank, had already shifted their attack northward again.

'Is the contessa O.K.?' Maguire asked.

'Blooming,' said Colonel Tribble. 'Extraordinary powers of recuperation for a woman that age.'

'She's not all that old,' Maguire said.

'She's been asking for you.'

Maguire beamed.

'All of you,' Tribble said.

Maguire tried to hide his disappointment.

Tribble took them to the general's trailer, an office-sleeping place, spartan but snug. The contessa, wearing the general's dressing-gown, was sitting up in his bed with an ice-pack on her knee, drinking tea, helping herself from a plate of Peek Frean biscuits and chatting with a dazzled and attentive captain. Handsome and fresh-faced, he did not appear much older than Maguire.

'Paolo!' she exclaimed. 'Caro. Chuffy, Paolo is my very dearest friend. And of course you have heard of the noted Colonel Ryan.'

The captain sprang to his feet. Maguire looked jealous.

'Sir!' the captain said. 'The contessa's been telling me what a smashing job you did helping her bring out Jerry's attack plans.'

'The contessa is too kind,' Ryan said gravely.

'I was afraid I would not see you before I left, Paolo. Chuffy will soon be escorting me to Naples. I have friends there.'

Maguire looked even more jealous.

'There, now,' the contessa said. 'This wretched war will be finished one day and you shall visit me in Rieti for as long as you wish. Now you must all leave me for a moment while I prepare to go. My dear general has somehow managed to find a dress for me.'

As they prepared to leave, Arnaldo, who had been hanging back, spoke to her.

'Arnaldo has apologised for anything unkind he may have said to me,' the contessa explained. 'And tonight he must return. He has left his wife alone too long. She will be worried. Oh, dear, I have nothing to give him for his trouble.' She glanced at her emerald ring. 'Not this, I am afraid. It has a certain sentimental value. Does it not, Colonel Ryan? And of course it is far too valuable.'

Ryan took out the gold sovereigns he had been carrying since Tenbrink's death.

'Give him these,' he said.

Arnaldo did not want to take the gold pieces but the contessa insisted. Outside, Arnaldo embraced each of them in turn.

'Arrivederci, amico,' Ryan said. 'And mille grazie.' *Goodbye, my friend. And a thousand thanks.*

Arnaldo left them waiting for the contessa to come out of the trailer. A sedan flying the general's pennant pulled up and stopped. The contessa emerged on crutches, wearing a brown silk dress that was too large for her under an even larger officer's shortcoat. The splinted leg had a bright red woollen stocking on the foot. The Alpine boot on the other was newly polished. Despite her costume she managed to look regal. The captain sprang to open the car door for her. Maguire beat him to it.

'Come, Paolo,' she said. 'I must kiss you good-bye.'

She embraced him and kissed him on both cheeks, balancing on her good leg. Maguire's expression was sheepish but blissful.

'Ma'am,' said Ryan. 'In case I don't see you again...'

He bent and kissed her on the cheek. For once, the contessa was speechless.

She gave Maguire her crutches to hold and slid into the back seat. The captain retrieved the crutches and climbed in after her.

'Driver,' he said.

'One moment,' said the contessa. 'Colonel Ryan?'

'Yes, ma'am?'

'When this tedious war is finished, there will no longer be need for men of your sort. Should you require employment, you might consider a permanent position as my chauffeur. You drive quite well.'

'I'll remember that, ma'am.'

Maguire stood in the road waving as the sedan pulled away.

'She sure was a nice lady,' he said with a sigh. 'And I'm gonna come back and see her some day. After I've had time back home. Colonel, we will be going home now, won't we, sir? I mean straight home?'

'Roger,' said Ryan. 'I'll see if I can persuade 'em to conduct your court-martial at the nearest army camp to your home town.'

'Sir?' Maguire demanded, stunned.

'You disobeyed a direct order in Rieti, Lieutenant. I promised you a court-martial. I always keep my promises.'

'And I thought you'd softened a bit, Von Ryan,' Fincham said in disbelief. 'But you're still the same bloody martinet.'

'Maybe your Silver Star'll get you off with just a reprimand, Paolo,' Ryan said.

'I don't have a Silver Star, sir,' Maguire said wretchedly.

'You will,' said Ryan.

A SELECTION OF BESTSELLERS FROM SPHERE

FICTION

LOVENOTES	Justine Valenti	£1.75 ☐
VENGEANCE 10	Joe Poyer	£1.75 ☐
MURDER IN THE WHITE HOUSE	Margaret Truman	£1.50 ☐
LOVE PLAY	Rosemary Rogers	£1.75 ☐
BRIMSTONE	Robert L. Duncan	£1.75 ☐

FILM & TV TIE-INS

FORT APACHE, THE BRONX	Heywood Gould	£1.75 ☐
SHARKY'S MACHINE	William Diehl	£1.75 ☐
THE PROFESSIONALS	Ken Blake	£1.00 ☐
THE GENTLE TOUCH	Terence Feely	£1.25 ☐
BARRIERS	William Corlett	£1.00 ☐

NON-FICTION

OPENING UP	Geoff Boycott	£1.75 ☐
SCIENCE IN EVERYDAY LIFE	William C. Vergara	£2.50 ☐
THE COUNTRY DIARY OF AN EDWARDIAN LADY	Edith Holden	£4.50 ☐
WHAT THIS KATIE DID	Katie Boyle	£1.75 ☐
MICHELLE REMEMBERS	Michelle Smith & Lawrence Pazder M.D.	£1.75 ☐

All Sphere books are available at your local bookshop or newsagent, or can be ordered direct from the publisher. Just tick the titles you want and fill in the form below.

Name _____

Address _____

_____

Write to Sphere Books, Cash Sales Department, P.O. Box 11, Falmouth, Cornwall TR10 9EN

Please enclose a cheque or postal order to the value of the cover price plus:

UK: 45p for the first book, plus 20p for the second and 14p for each additional book ordered to a maximum charge of £1.63

OVERSEAS: 75p for the first book plus 21p per copy for each additional book

BFPO & EIRE: 45p for the first book, 20p for the second book plus 14p per copy for the next 7 books, thereafter 8p per book

Sphere Books reserve the right to show new retail prices on covers which may differ from those previously advertised in the text or elsewhere, and to increase postal rates in accordance with the PO.